TINAREE - TRIAL BY INFERNO

SHADOWS OF PEACE
BOOK 1

NIC PLUME

Cover Designed by Brooke Burgess

To Marty

For your never-ending support and the amazing life you have given me. I am looking forward to many more years of adventure and exploring.

1

ATTACK

The troop bay vibrated with the steady hum of the SILC's engines. The twelve members of the 315th Special Forces Unit's 1st Squad sat in pairs, three on each side of the cabin, facing their teammates across low storage bins and tied-down equipment. The setup left just enough deck space to gear up, though the atmosphere felt heavier than the confines of the bay.

Most of the squad exuded a practiced ease born of countless missions. Some traded jokes, others checked their gear or meditated, and one even slept. Despite their different activities, the veterans had one thing in common: they seemed relaxed; used to the lull of mission insertion. Mark Taylor felt rigid and out of place in comparison. Chest tight, heart racing, he had to keep reminding himself to breathe slow and steady, to not hyperventilate.

"Your challenge will not be incorporating into your unit or being accepted by your squad mates," the Academy trainer had said a few months before. "No, your first real challenge will be striking the balance between calm preparedness and tense anxiety. Too much of either will kill you—and worse, it'll make you a liability."

At the time, Taylor had thought neither would be a problem for him. He still didn't, it would simply take a bit more work than he had expected.

"They're not as calm as they seem," Kaydeen A'Tourie said softly, her voice slicing through his thoughts. "They merely had more practice hiding it."

Taylor met her hazel eyes, steady and knowing. Of course, she'd noticed. Din always noticed.

"If this wasn't a big deal, they wouldn't have their rituals," she said, her gaze sweeping the bay.

Taylor followed it. Botch, the squad's medic, was reading a small book while fondling the medallion hanging from the chain around his neck. He had pulled both from an ornate box he kept in one of his bunk's compartments. It had been one of the most involved pre-mission rituals Taylor had seen so far. But he wasn't the only one going into combat with a good luck charm. Mitwa, the squad's designated sniper, had a plasma slug hanging around his neck. The story went that he had been shot with it on his third mission. Lucky him, it had malfunctioned and not discharged its deadly contents into his biceps, or he would have lost the arm. Dieran toyed with a piece of cloth in his pocket, and Tooley had a figurine stowed nearby. Even Hix, their team chief, passed a worn photo from hand to hand, muttering to himself.

"Luck is for people lacking skills." His mother's voice rang in his ears, as sharp and unyielding as ever.

Taylor thought back to their last goodbye. The officer at the recruiting station had called for parents to say their final farewells, offering words of reassurance. Skye Taylor had scoffed. "If my son needs luck, I've failed to prepare him properly," she'd said. When it was time to board, she hugged him, kissed his forehead, and added, "You will be the best. The top of your class. I expect nothing less." She'd walked away without a backward glance.

He'd only been sixteen, and never been without her for more than a few hours. To others, she might have seemed callous, but he knew better. For as long as he could remember, his goal had been to join the Intergalactic Freedom Defense Force, or Intergal for short, in their fight to stop the Traverse. She'd encouraged that dream, trained him for it, and supported him every step of the way. By the time he had arrived for his Academy Entrance Exams, his survival and combat skills far surpassed those of the average sixteen-year-old recruit. He had never asked where his mother had acquired them. It hadn't been his place. She had given him all her love, her time, her knowledge—and, in the end, her life. The moment he had stepped onto the Academy shuttle's ramp that day four years ago, he had known he wouldn't see her again. And as vague, or as accurate, as his hunches and feelings were at times, he had learned a long time ago they were never wrong.

"Hey." Kaydeen's touch on his forearm snapped him back to the present. "You with us?"

"I'm here."

"Now you are, but a moment ago, you were with your mother." Her voice softened, but her gaze held steady.

And they say Din needed to touch you to initiate a Reading. He knew Din required contact, more specifically bare hand-to-neck contact, to use their 'Gifts.' It was the largest misconception humans had about their ancestral cousins and one of the reasons Din usually preferred to blend in and not announce themselves.

Taylor sighed. "I lost her four years ago."

Kaydeen frowned, unconvinced. "You know what I mean."

He did. As painful as that shuttle trip to the Academy had been, he was glad he had had four years to get used to the thought. So, when the notification of her death finally came, it didn't shatter him. Though it had still been painful to hear that she had killed herself the day he graduated, the day she had considered her life's work complete.

He looked at her. "Kay, I'm fine. I had four years to get used to the thought. So, I'll be fine."

Four years. The first had been easy. The schedule at the Basic Academy, where recruits learned to be soldiers, had kept him too busy and exhausted to let his mind wander too far. After that, Kay, Sal, and Tonee had been there.

"You know a Reading could ease—"

"Did Sal put you up to this?" Taylor cut her off, glancing across the bay at Salayla K'Kaya, who was chatting with Anthony Patonee, their fourth teammate.

Kaydeen's frown deepened. "Salayla? Why would she—?"

"Because she's been trying to dig that tidbit out of me since she found out."

"Grief isn't a tidbit," Kaydeen said, her voice bristling. "She just wants to help ease your pain. The ache I know is in there." She touched her chest for emphasis.

Taylor opened his mouth to retort, but she cut him off. "Others might believe the hard shell you put around you, but I know better. So does she."

"Do you now?" He could almost see her every hair stand on end at his words.

"Of course. Three years of living, eating, and training together tends to bring people closer."

Especially if two are Din, he thought but did not say.

"Not that I needed three years to figure you out." She smiled, shaking her head. "And who says I would share your *tidbits* with Salayla?"

"Because you two have been sharing each other's secrets since you were little."

"You've been listening to our conversations?"

"As you said, three years of living, eating, and training together doesn't afford much privacy."

She shook her head. "That's not what I said."

"Close enough." He shrugged.

She laughed. "All right. Now that you've succeeded in leading me off our original subject...do you feel any better?"

"I never said I felt bad."

"Not with words, anyway."

Taylor snorted. Just like Kay to know exactly what to say—a skill she and Sal had down pat, though Kay relied more on logic and her perfect memory, while Sal made much more use of her feminine arsenal, even in combat gear and strapped into a crash seat.

Salayla returned his glance with a smile and a wink. She looked almost fragile beside Tonee's bulk. But that was as deceptive as her flirtations. Salayla could hold her own in any fight, and her gregarious personality and seemingly endless knowledge about cultures and etiquette, coupled with her training as an intelligence officer, gave her an advantage most people underestimated. He had yet to see somebody she couldn't enchant.

"FIVE MINUTES TO DROP."

Taylor's eyes flicked to the intercom. The pilot's voice sounded bored, as if announcing the next stop on a regular shuttle route. Having done this countless times, he might well have been. Kaydeen, on the other hand, was not. Her fingers almost left marks on Taylor's arm. She relaxed almost as quickly as she had tensed, but the damage was done. It took a sharp rebuke from Unit Commander Tess, seated at the front of the troop bay, to stop the ensuing remarks from some of the veterans.

Taylor was sharply reminded of how unwelcome the timing of their arrival in the unit had been. Nobody wanted to be burdened with an unproven team during a major mission, no matter how well they had performed at the Academy. He had heard rumors suggesting each teammate be assigned to a different squad, a severe insult to teams with even the slightest experience. But they were CHiTs—Combat Heroes in Training—and as such had no status within the unit, no honor to be sullied. They would have to earn it first, and their trainer at the Academy had said it took at least five successfully completed missions to earn an SF Unit's respect. Taylor intended to do it in three.

The instant the 'Ready' signal in the cabin activated, Taylor's hand was on the buckle of his crash webbing. He didn't release it. He didn't know why. No, he knew exactly why. His surroundings came into sharp focus as adrenaline rushed through his body. Minute details became snapshots, instantly dissected and analyzed as if his brain had hours to study them, not the moment it took his body to flood with the chemical. Something was wrong. It was a thought, a feeling, a certainty; but what, he didn't know. It didn't work that way. Just enough info to steer his next move, but not enough to explain it. He knew to trust it and follow its impulse. And right now, the last thing he wanted to do was unbuckle his crash webbing. His hesitation confused his teammates, but his instincts had proven themselves many times during training, and they followed his lead without hesitation.

"You guys sleeping?" Commander Tess called from across the cabin. The rest of the squad was out of their seats and prepping to jump.

"Looks like our Ace Cadets are nervous," Dieran, standing halfway between Tonee and Tess, jeered. "The real thing's different than the sims, huh?"

The words had barely left Dieran's mouth when an explosion in the cockpit rocked the ship, buckling part of the bulkhead and tossing people and equipment around like rag dolls. Commander Tess, who stood within arm's reach of the bulkhead, was thrown across the cabin and smashed with a splattering crunch against the rear access hatch where he hung suspended for a moment before slipping lifeless and broken to the floor grates. A gagging stench of burned metal, plastoids, and flesh filled the cabin as the ship tilted and started to tumble.

Taylor reached for his pack, but his chair's Active Protection System kicked in. His crash webbing tightened, pulling him deep into his seat and in the process nearly cutting off his air supply. The sudden impression of possible asphyxiation brought his attention, and limbs, back where they should be. As soon as his arms returned inside the APS' safety zone, its Softshell deployed, cocooning him into his seat. Sound and light still filtered through, but details were lost in the shield's opaqueness. For that, he would need to access the bay's cameras via his Heads-Up Display. His training kicked in. 'Arms across chest to loosen the Fast Capture System to a breathable setting, then check oxygen flow and HUD, and report your status.' He felt the airflow against his neck and cheek—the oxygen was flowing—but his helmet, which would normally block the air from reaching his skin, had not deployed. He retracted the glove around his right index finger and touched the side of the headband wrapping around his forehead, temples, and occipital bone, to activate the manual switch. The helmet deployed with quiet clicks that he felt more than heard as the links locked into place. His neck and the lower half of his face stayed uncovered. His visor, which looked like oversized eye protection, polarized to combat mode.

The HUD activated, but the Squad Net indicator blinked red, signaling the squad's network was offline. He switched to the UNet, the unit's network, which was also offline, and then to his team's network. Kaydeen, Tonee, and Salayla were all in the green. Hix, their Team Chief, wasn't listed. *What the—?* But Taylor didn't have time to ponder this oddity since he was busy refraining from ducking every time something impacted his seat's Softshell. It was easier said than done to stay upright and seemingly fully exposed to whatever was trying to punch through the malleable membrane less than thirty centimeters from his vital organs.

As the screech of mangled metal and the increasing whistle of the wind overpowered the screams of the injured, Taylor could only guess whether the impacts were caused by objects or people.

2

CHAOS

Commander Dean Richards stood stunned as the large communication screen turned to static.

As Intergal's liaison to the Tinaree Resistance Movement, or TRM, Dean had spent the last two years laying the groundwork for this mission. First, by contacting and organizing the planet's resistance, and then, by helping to plan and coordinate its liberation from its two-year-long Traverse occupation. His hard work had finally paid off, and the Task Force had been dispatched. On board the flagship, the battlecruiser *Cartage*, Battle Group Commander Kilrian, leading the Task Force, had invited him to observe the mission's progress from the BCC, the Battle Coordination Center. As SII Commander, Dean held the same rank step as Kilrian, although not the same command authority, but his operational authority as mission advisor and TRM liaison should have given him automatic and unrestricted access to the BCC and not required an invitation. However, shoving one's rank or position into people's faces rarely facilitated positive work relations—though it did get the job done at times.

A hush had fallen over the BCC. Not five minutes before,

everything had been going according to plan. Now, all was in shambles, and 431 of Intergal's best-trained troops were either dead or in enemy hands.

The mission had begun as expected. The fleet had stayed at the edge of the solar system while its advance forces, composed of the 215th, 315th, and 415th Special Forces Units traveling in their specially equipped frigates, had easily made it to the planet's moon. From there, each unit's three commando squads had used Stealth Infiltrator Landing Craft, SILCs for short, to reach the planet. The squad-sized ships were fast, highly maneuverable, and equipped with the latest stealth technology Intergal had to offer and could easily slip past passive and active sensors and visual scans. Everything had gone well, and the ships had been past the planetary defenses and approaching the assigned HALO drop zones when the proximity alarms had sounded. With only seconds to react to the sudden missile attacks, few of the pilots had been able to maneuver, and none had escaped. The missiles had hit the nine ships almost simultaneously and either destroyed them on impact or damaged them enough to cause them to crash. Onboard computers from only five of the SILCs were able to send damage reports to their frigates.

The mainframe of the 315th SF Unit's frigate had received its squads' reports at the same time as its sensors had registered a large number of Traverse starfighters, bombers, and other small attack craft. Comparing threat level to defenses, maneuverability, and escape vector, it had calculated the probability of escape at 3.937 percent and crew survival at 9.738 percent, warranting the commencement of emergency protocols. So, 0.263 seconds after receiving 1st Squad's report, it had opened a communication channel with the *Cartage's* BCC, dumped all data in its memory banks, and proceeded to transmit ongoing battle reports. The battle had been over within minutes, the sheer number of attacking ships overwhelming the three frigates like ants swarming over a piece of candy dropped on their hill. The 315th had held out the longest, its last transmission reporting critical system failures in shields, hull, and life support right before its communication link to the *Cartage* cut off.

Battle Group Commander Kilrian, standing beside Dean, cursed quietly. Under normal circumstances, nobody but Dean would have heard it, but in the dead silence, everybody did. It broke the spell that had fallen over the BCC and loosened an avalanche of activity and noise as everybody jumped to the task of figuring out what happened and why.

"What the hell just happened?" Kilrian shouted over the chaos. "Where did these ships come from, and why didn't we see them? I want answers, and I want them five minutes ago!"

Dean stepped out of the way as Kilrian charged past him, shouting orders and instructions, and made his way to the BCC's exit to work his assets. The hatch didn't open—of course not. The ship, and the fleet for that matter, had gone to Full Battle Alert. Now, the question was whether Kilrian had given him unilateral access as he had indicated during their last meeting. Dean waved his hand over the hatch access panel to activate the embedded ID reading sensor. If he had full authority, the motion should override the lockdown and allow him access to the panel.

It stayed dark.

Dean sighed. So much for working on equal footing. It seemed that having someone of equal rank, but technically outside his chain of command, run loose on his ship intimidated Kilrian more than he had let on. Well, he wasn't the first and wouldn't be the last. Dean settled into the corner next to the hatch and pulled out his comm. He would have to do his job the hard way—nothing new there, either.

~

THE SILC BOUNCED, tumbled, and skidded violently before coming to a smoldering stop. The Softshell retracted, and Taylor, spitting out a glob of blood, was out of his seat before the ship had fully settled. Seeing Kaydeen up and moving without hesitation or impairment, he turned to scan the nearly destroyed cabin.

It was hardly recognizable. Loose and even some previously tied down equipment was mangled and scattered among buckled or collapsed bulkheads, dislodged seats, and storage bins. Blood and bodies, or parts thereof, were everywhere—some obviously dead, others, possibly still alive. The air had taken on a milky consistency, a yellowish haze that stung his eyes, scratched his throat, and thickened as it oozed to the lower parts of the wreck, making him wonder about its toxicity as he breathed. He focused on the equipment icon in the lower right corner of his HUD to deploy his helmet's fullhead mode and lock it into his armor to provide a self-contained environment, but the icon was grayed out. He tried the manual switch, but it didn't work either.

Shit.

No time to troubleshoot. He moved on. The noise finally subsided. The screaming and screeching of the crashing ship had given way to the creaking and hissing of the settling wreck and other more subtle and less distinct sounds—some possibly human-generated. Noting the locations of potential survivors, he continued searching for the familiar forms of Salayla and Tonee. His HUD marked both as alive, though Tonee's indicator was blue, implying he was impaired. That could signify anything from being knocked out to having a broken bone or other wound. At least it wasn't tinged purple, as that denoted critical wounds or dropping vital signs. He tried to raise them on the comm, but that was offline, too. Maybe there was something actively interfering with his system.

Kaydeen, who had moved away from him, spotted Tonee at

the same time he spotted Salayla. They quickly climbed over the rubble to the debris pile where the two were buried, still strapped into their seats. Unlike Tonee, Salayla was conscious and had already manually retracted her seat's Softshell. They soon had enough debris cleared to allow her to slide out of her seat and crawl out of the pile. Tonee, on the other hand, was not as easily freed. The teammates had to remove most of the debris around him before they could reach the external access hatch of his seat's control panel. Taylor had barely opened it when he heard the rumble of an approaching vehicle. He twisted toward the only visible exit from the wreck, a jagged hole in the bulkhead that used to be the access hatch to the cockpit, and watched Salayla look outside. Her tensing posture told him their chance of escape was dwindling before she signaled the arrival of a tracked Tinaree Guard Troop Carrier. Most likely, they were mercenaries the Traverse had hired to replace the original Tinaree Guard personnel.

He turned back to work the manual controls without waiting for her report on how many disembarked. It didn't matter if it was five or fifty, it would take only one shot into the ship's fuel cells to bring all resistance to an instantaneous and fiery end. No, if they wanted to fight and survive, they needed to escape the wreckage before they were surrounded or vaporized. But first, he had to get Tonee on his feet.

"Commander Kilrian requests your presence in the Situation Room, sir."

Dean looked up at the young man in front of him. He was in his late twenties and looked like a typical staff officer who had never seen a battlefield in person.

"Thank you, Mr. Bastogne, but I need to check in with my team."

"You can do that from the Sit-R, sir."

Dean knew that but preferred to talk to them in private first. Commander Kilrian obviously had other plans. Bastogne didn't budge, so Dean followed him across the BCC to the adjacent conference room.

His concern that he wouldn't be able to vet his information and reactions before presenting it to Kilrian and his staff was short-lived. The Sit-R was nearly empty. Only two officers occupied the alcove workstations surrounding the large central display table. Dean couldn't see their insignia, but he guessed they were intelligence specialists gathering and sifting through the information that wasn't readily disseminated by the personnel in the BCC.

Bastogne followed his gaze. "They're Intelligence Officers supporting the BCC staff," he explained, mirroring Dean's thoughts.

"Only two?" Considering the myriad of minor battle and intelligence details the BCC personnel didn't have time for or outright ignored because they didn't seem important at the time, Dean would have had at least a team of IOs in here.

"The Intelligence Section handles the rest."

Dean raised his eyebrows, "Do they, now?"

"Yes." Bastogne nodded. "Commander Kilrian receives regular reports."

"I'm sure he does."

Bastogne bristled at his tone. "Those reports are objective and inclusive."

"I'm sure they are." Dean smiled at Bastogne's misinterpretation of his comment, though his tone wasn't as friendly. His tolerance for people jumping to conclusions without verifying facts wasn't very high.

Flustered, Bastogne showed him to a comm station and asked for his team's comm codes. Transferring the codes to his handheld without so much as a second glance, he left Dean alone to stare at the blank terminal screen.

Within moments, the screen came to life with the list of his team members and the message 'Active and notified' blinking beside each. The first to check in was his assistant, Robert Teak, who had been making his way toward the BCC. Since a call to Battle Stations included sealing all hatchways and shutting down lift tubes to unauthorized personnel, his progress had been slow. However, his S9 rank and training as a Psychological Operations Specialist had, as usual, gotten him where, by regulations, he had no authority to be—three decks up and within four hatchways of the BCC.

It took only a few minutes to update him on the status of events and lay out their next steps. Robert signed off, and Dean leaned back and stared at the blinking status indicators on the screen in front of him. Five names, two of which, Teak and Nick Torrents, a cyber specialist on loan from the battleship *Cooley*, were the only ones Dean could trust the status indicator was correct about. The other three were located on Tinaree; high-ranking members of the Tinaree Resistance. And, while the comm signal might have gone out to them, Dean had no way of knowing if it had made it to the ground. For that, he needed Torrents, and the slicer took his time checking in. Robert had warned him about that. Less than a year out of the Academy, the nineteen-year-old had already been repeatedly flagged, getting himself into trouble even while still at the Academy. But he was one of the best in his field, and that was exactly what Dean had been looking for.

3

WRECK

Taylor was pulling the last of the crash webbing out of the way, when Tonee finally stirred. "About time you chose to join us." He grinned. "I was starting to think you expected us to carry you out of this thing."

"You wouldn't be able to lift me." Tonee touched the contusion above his right temple and flinched. His helmet was mangled but had probably saved his skull from being caved in.

"We would've managed, but I'm glad we don't have to." Taylor pulled the pain patch Kaydeen had handed him from his pocket and carefully applied it to the bruise.

Tonee closed his eyes, and his face softened as he relaxed back into his chair with a sigh.

"Better?" Taylor asked as he stole a glance at Salayla.

"Much. The hammer in my head is shrinking rapidly." Tonee's previously glassy and unfocused eyes had cleared up. "Why aren't we moving?"

"Because we crashed," Taylor answered, a smile playing around his mouth.

"Of course, we crashed," replied Tonee, "we were shot down." He looked at the pile of rubble beside him. "They knew we were coming." He tried to sit up, but Taylor didn't budge. Frowning up at him, Tonee lay back down. "They'll be looking for survivors."

Taylor nodded slowly.

"Then, why am I still on my back?"

"Because we need to make sure you'll be able to get up without passing out." Taylor scanned his body for visible wounds one more time. "I need you able to move without help."

"We can do the slow rehab later." Tonee tried to push past Taylor again. "Right now, we need to get—" he broke off, his brown gaze flicking from Taylor to the pile of rubble, and then to Kaydeen and Salayla. "How much I cost you?"

"Cost?" Taylor didn't have to follow Tonee's gaze to know he had correctly put together the clues around him—the moved debris pile, the single exit, and Taylor's unhurried demeanor. They had not become and stayed the top-scoring Academy team without being able to quickly and correctly interpret each other's moods, signals, and actions. But this skill was failing Taylor now, because he had no idea what 'cost' Tonee meant. "What are you talking about?"

"How long was I out?"

Taylor shrugged. "Didn't time it."

Looking back at Taylor, Tonee said quietly, "This isn't funny."

"I'm not laughing."

"How long?"

"Long enough."

Tonee's eyes widened. "They're already here?"

"Arrived a few minutes ago," Taylor answered. "Some big mouth is barking orders."

"Are we fighting?"

"No."

"Why?"

"Because we're in no shape to fight, have no weapons to fight with, other than our sidearms, and are inside a highly volatile tinderbox with only one exit."

"So, we're just going to give up?"

"No," Taylor scoffed, "we're going to do whatever it takes to survive, as per SERE protocols." He jumped off the chair and grabbed Tonee's hand. "Let's get you on your feet."

Once Tonee was steady, Taylor released his grasp to step back, but Tonee's vice-like grip pulled him closer.

"You should've gotten out."

"And leave you behind?" Taylor frowned. "I don't think so."

Tonee's eyes took on intensity as he gazed at the debris pile beside them.

"It took too long to dig me out. Because of me, you missed your chance to escape. You shouldn't have allowed that to happen."

Tonee's words hit Taylor like a frozen sledgehammer, filling him with an ice-cold, almost physical, pain. He shoved it down, forcing it into a corner of his consciousness, and poured heat onto it until the cold dread burst.

Only inches from Tonee's face, his voice turned quiet and precise, his eyes cold. "We are a team. We live as a team. We fight as a team. And we will die as a team, if necessary. But we will never leave a teammate behind. Whatever comes, we will go through it as a team."

A sensation in his neck brought him to a sudden stop. Like dipping into a pool of water on a hot summer day, it spread slowly through his body, filling him with a cooling, calming comfort as alien and strange as it was familiar and safe—and utterly Salayla. He could feel her, smell her, taste her with every part of his body, inside and out, and knew instantly that he hated this sensation as much as he loved it.

Behind him, Salayla said quietly, "Calm yourself." Inside,

he felt as if she screamed every word into his very being, "This is not a time or place for anger."

"Anger?" With his face still only inches from Taylor's, Tonee looked at Salayla, "He looked intense; felt, first ice-cold, then scalding hot; and had me locked down—still does—but he didn't seem angry."

Taylor released Tonee's wrist and shirt. He hadn't even realized he had grabbed them. "I wasn't angry."

He felt Salayla's disagreement slam into every fiber of his being, as if all the oxygen was sucked out at once. Unable to breathe, Taylor's knees weakened, and he struggled to remain upright and coherent. "What...are you...doing?"

Her regret and apology flashed through their contact as quickly as her disapproval had. He liked them much better.

"I'm Sharing your pain, your anger."

My anger? He could've sworn the anger, if that was what had just ripped through him, had originated with her, not him; but he didn't argue the point, he didn't need a repeat demonstration. "I didn't know you could do that."

"It is a more intimate Reading, usually reserved for Mates," she explained. "Anger and pain might not have been the correct terms to use, but they are the best human expressions to describe the manifestations I sensed."

He wanted her to elaborate, but a *thud*, followed by a surprised yelp, brought their discussion to an abrupt halt.

"Whatever happens, don't fight them," Taylor instructed as he slid past Salayla and moved around the debris pile. Her astonishment at the ease with which he pushed her out of his mind and slipped from her grasp surprised him. His steps faltered.

He saw the soldier crouched behind a piece of debris a few feet past the opening at the same time the man's targeting laser lit up his chest. Cursing himself for letting Salayla's reaction distract him, Taylor spread his arms to his side, palms facing forward, and froze. He hoped his footing was as stable as it looked.

The soldier didn't move or speak and neither did his weapon, but others with him did. Taylor picked out four distinct voices, two right outside and two farther away, or maybe one farther away and one coming through a comm unit —it had a clanky sound to it. He didn't understand what was said, couldn't even identify the language or region it came from, and he didn't dare turn to check with Salayla, their language expert.

He waited. It didn't take long. More voices approached, some sounding agitated, and then the opening darkened as someone ducked through. Taylor noted the targeting laser never wavered from his chest.

THE MAN—HIS crumpled uniform's insignia identified him as Juvak but didn't give a rank, position, or unit—was in his late thirties and rough looking, as if he partied too hard and lost too many fights. Yet his posture stated he won more fights than he lost, and his mannerisms hinted at a highly educated background. His olive skin was a sharp contrast to his light hair. Taylor had no idea what to make of him. The man's appearance contradicted his presence to the core.

The L-Slugger he casually aimed at the ground as he scanned the wrecked cabin was an older model fixed-rate laser pulse rifle that discharged a powerful, and deadly, projectile-like burst of energy. A targeting laser built into its trigger-control improved its accuracy but made careless handlers accident-prone. If the weapon pointed at him was the same, Taylor hoped the gunman had steady fingers and didn't get a cramp.

Juvak's eyes took in the scene and then flicked to the others momentarily before settling on Taylor with a smile as if happy to see him.

"Look who has returned," he said in excellent Trade, as if discussing merchandise with his favorite customer.

Taylor frowned. Traverse and their mercenaries were not usually fluent in the commerce language of the Free Galaxy. Juvak's smile grew wider, though now it reminded Taylor of a back-alley drug dealer watching a first-time customer take a sample of his special concoction.

"And the boy brought new friends." His facial expression iced over as he paused. "Follow instructions, and we'll be fine."

Taylor knew Juvak was goading him, leading him on, feeling him out. It was Battlefield Psychology 101, to unbalance and take control. But even knowing what it was and how it worked, didn't help him shake its effect. He felt as outmatched as he had the first time he had faced the close-combat instructor on the mat. Back then, his stubborn refusal to quit, to cede the fight and leave the mat, had earned him a grudge from a trainer and a trip to the med ward. Now, it could cost him much more. But, like then, backing down or giving anything less than his best wasn't an option. It would only make him weak and his teammates targets. He'd simply have to deal with whatever came their way.

Taylor straightened, met Juvak's gaze, and nodded. The time to evade and escape was past, and resisting was not yet an option. That left only one objective of the SERE protocol—the most important one—for his team to survive.

"Good." His smile friendly again, Juvak motioned with his weapon. "Drop your kit and then head out one at a time." He pointed at Taylor. "You first."

Taylor released his battle harness and, after disconnecting the armor actuators on his limbs and around his neck with a quick twist of the wrist, he added the separate pieces and his helmet to the debris pile by his feet. As he did so, he tempted the laser burning an imaginary hole into his chest to glance at his teammates and, using the sign language they had learned at Basic and later refined for their use, reiterated his earlier instruction. He wasn't sure if Juvak, whose gaze was locked on him, recognized or understood his signal but seeing his expression unchanged, thought he might not have. He was wrong.

As he moved forward, he sensed Juvak's arm twitch an instant before the rifle slammed into the side of his knee. It was such a small, quick movement, he wouldn't have been able to dodge it if he had tried. As it was, he gasped in pain and went to his knees. The targeting laser never wavered from his chest.

Behind him, Tonee, in the process of lowering his own kit, started forward but stopped before taking a step. Taylor froze. He didn't have to look to know Tonee was ready to pounce, to smash that maggot in front of them. The smallest sign or even a wrong move, and he would explode into motion with a speed most people didn't expect a man his size to be capable of.

Juvak did. An expectant smirk played on the corners of his mouth as the strange man eyed them. He knew exactly what Tonee, or any of them for that matter, was capable of. And he was ready to take him down—possibly permanently.

Juvak stepped beside Taylor and leaned down. "I don't think your friend got your message."

But his gaze was on Tonee, his eyes boring into him, daring him to move, to so much as twitch a muscle. Taylor willed his friend to see the situation for what it was—a non-contest he could neither win nor lose because either would be detrimental. He was outmatched. They all were. And this battle of wills was not to test Tonee's resolve, but Taylor's. It was a thought, a fact, as clear and true as the sharp pain shooting up and down Taylor's leg.

"Got it," Taylor said, as much to Tonee as Juvak.

It broke the spell.

Juvak's forehead twitched. *Respect or contempt?* Taylor wondered. The man held Tonee's gaze a moment longer and then stepped back.

Taylor knew the blow was coming before it did. One last move to demonstrate where the base of power lay—for now. Sharp pain exploded across his lower cheek as his blood splattered across the debris, but all he could think of was for Tonee to not take the bait. He didn't. He held his peace and watched as if memorizing every instant.

Taylor swallowed the coppery fluid pooling in his mouth and picked himself up. His knee throbbed as he straightened it, but he refused to let the pain reach his expression. He wouldn't give Juvak the satisfaction. Plus, he couldn't allow it to influence his teammates' actions. They would each have to fight an uphill battle already, no reason to add to it. Breathing through the sharp pain shooting up and down his leg with each twisting step, he picked his way around oozing puddles and unstable debris. As he approached, he saw that his earlier approximation of the opening's location had been correct. The top part of the cockpit hatch was still visible above, but the ragged inward-blossoming edges of the slightly taller than wide hole gave him the disturbing impression that, if he turned around, he would find a pilot's chair embedded in the opposite bulkhead.

He banished the unpleasant image from his mind and pressed on. Why worry about the dead when there were still living to take care of? The closer he drew to the outside, the more he realized how toxic the air around his team was. No wonder Juvak had taken only a few steps into the wreck.

THE COMBAT BOOTS he saw on each side of the opening were his first hint he wouldn't be allowed to walk of his own accord, the hand grabbing his neck, his second. After that, everything happened so fast, he was barely able to keep his wits about him and his feet below him.

Pulled from the hole and then shoved forward, he caught his balance long enough on the edge of a broken piece of bulkhead to realize the rifleman crouched below was ignoring him. The man didn't even flinch when a hard kick propelled Taylor over his head and onto a teetering slab of cockpit control panel. Landing in a partial crouch, his hand shot out for balance at the same time as the acrid stench of still smoldering electrical circuits bombarded his senses. His hand was faster. Grabbing a handful of wires, he immediately felt the stinging burn of electricity course through his skin.

His resulting hiss drew a snicker from his right. He looked up in time to see the butt of a rifle coming his way and started to dodge, but remembering his own instructions, he turned his shoulder into it instead. It didn't hurt, at least not much. The two meaty fists meeting his chest and slamming him into a tangle of cables and rods did, though. He wasn't sure what hurt worse: his front, his back, or everything in between. He didn't have the time to contemplate the question since he was immediately hauled to his feet. Still fighting to get air back into his lungs as he stumbled along, Taylor tripped over a sharp, jutting piece of metal that would've cut deeply into his ankle had his boot not been in the way, and barely caught himself before his face slammed into the jagged end of a broken piece of bulkhead. Yet to take a full breath, he was grabbed again and shoved down the embankment of the furrow the wreck had carved. His knee gave out, and he landed face-first in the dirt a few meters from the Tinareean transport.

Moments later, Salayla landed beside him. He chanced a glance at her, but the butt of a rifle slammed into his neck and shoved his face back into the ground before he could get a good look. The weapon's owner leaned over him, increasing the pressure painfully. Taylor didn't understand the barked orders coming from the direction of the transport but was happy to feel the soldier push off him. His relief turned to dread when the snickering man aimed the gun's barrel at his face and slowly squeezed the trigger, causing the red targeting laser to light up his cheek. Another barked order, this one from Juvak, caused the soldier to pull up the barrel right as the weapon discharged.

The bolt hit the ground inches from Taylor's face. The dirt absorbed it instantly. Had it hit rock, he would have felt much more than the tingle of intense heat passing by. He squeezed his eyes shut, ignored the soldier's laugh and obvious snide remarks, and concentrated on getting his racing heart back under control.

After a short but vocal argument, two soldiers grabbed his arms and dragged him toward the transport. By the time he had his feet under him to walk, they had stopped in front of a pudgy middle-aged officer, whose insignia identified him as the commander of this group.

The officer studied him, nodded, and gave an order. A third soldier stepped up and helped the first two strip him of all insignia and uniform pieces identifying him as an Intergal trooper. They pulled him back to his feet for another inspection. Satisfied, the officer nodded and turned away. The soldiers bound Taylor's wrists, pulled a cloth sack over his head, and tightened its cord around his throat.

Blind and barely able to breathe, Taylor was unable to cushion his fall when the soldiers dragged him up the transport's ramp and threw him in. Landing hard, he groaned in pain and reached for the cord around his neck, but his wrists were pulled above his head before he could touch it. He tried to pull free, but the constant battering and lack of oxygen left him too weak to do more than slow the motion. Nevertheless, even this minute resistance was immediately repaid with a blow to his side. Taylor screamed and curled up, jerking his wrists free as he did so. His tormentor grabbed his shirt and pants, picked him up, and slammed him onto his back. Out of air, Taylor lay were he landed and groaned.

4

PUZZLE PIECES

After signing off with Commander Richards, S9 Commander Robert Teak accessed a ship terminal to locate S3 Technician Torrents. The ship's communications system tracked everybody's location, though Robert would not have been surprised to find that Torrents had hacked into his comm's transponder and changed or turned off its signal.

He hadn't.

It took him a while to cross the ship, but Robert found Torrents exactly where his comm signal said he was—in the temporary quarters he had been assigned for the duration of this mission. The slicer was busy working on his terminal, his personal comm silently flashing the contact alert beside him. He had clearly gotten the notification; the audible alert could not be turned off until it was acknowledged—unless, of course, Torrents had hacked it.

"The comm signals aren't reaching Tinaree," Torrents said without so much as a greeting or acknowledgment of the superior officer's arrival. "So, either they're blocked groundside, or the relays are out." He didn't give Robert a chance to reply. "I'd prefer a problem with the relays, 'cause if it's groundside, then we've been hacked, and the guys down there are in for it."

He turned with his last words and, remembering protocol, added a quick "sir" and jumped to attention.

Sharp, intelligent brown eyes framed by curly ash blond hair barely within regulation length watched as Robert's studying gaze ran over his disheveled uniform, which looked like it had been stored crumpled in a ball. Torrents' skinny frame didn't help the matter, and his lack of concern to do more than meet regulations didn't, either. No wonder he kept getting flagged. Military discipline wasn't in his blood, though looking at his pedigree, it should have been. Tenth generation Intergal—his family had served pretty much from the day the Intergalactic Freedom Defense Force was founded. His grandfather had been a retired Senior Force Commander. Something went wrong in the boy's track and maybe someday Robert would have the time to figure out what it was. But for now, he had more urgent concerns.

"The relays. You're talking about the relay satellites?"

"Yes, sir."

"Can you check them?"

"Yes, sir."

"Then do," Robert instructed with a nod.

Torrents jumped to it, his fingers flying over the virtual keyboard before he had settled into his seat. Robert picked up the still-flashing comm.

"You overrode the sound but not the visual?" He acknowledged the alert to shut it down.

"So I don't forget to answer it," Torrents answered without apology.

Robert wondered if he had forgotten or ignored the fact that tinkering with a comm was against regulations and considered a breach in security.

"You do realize it had a 'Highest Priority'?"

"Yes, sir," Torrents answered while keeping his attention on his screen. "I figured Commander Richards was looking for answers, so I wanted to have them before I commed."

"And you knew what answers he was looking for?"

"Well, it was obvious from what happened." Torrents slowed as he realized his mistake. His fingers stopped moving for a moment, then he drew a resigned breath and continued, "I watched the live feed." He added a "sir" with the slightest pause, as if hoping it might buy him leniency.

"From here?"

"Well, yeah, it's not like I'm authorized in the BCC."

Robert said nothing and merely watched as Torrents' fingers continued to fly over his keyboard, bringing up screen after screen, sending out commands and responding to results. While keyboards weren't quite obsolete, most people accessed the screen directly or used voice controls. Not Torrents, he preferred to use the virtual keyboard. Even with this, what many people would consider a major handicap, he worked faster than anybody Robert had watched before, and with better results. Now, if he could stay within regulations and stop accessing data he wasn't authorized for, he could fly through his service time with his pick of assignments and duty stations or be set for life in any civilian market.

"I can show you a replay," Torrents ventured, "so you can see it firsthand."

"You recorded it?" Another security breach.

"Well, yeah, so we can study it in detail to figure out what happened."

"We could study the official recording."

"But then we'd have to go through all the bureaucratic stuff and ask for access. This way, the unedited raw footage is all here, ready to go whenever the commander wants it."

"And that's why you did it."

"Of course," he replied without missing a beat. "Mission first, whatever it takes."

"Right."

Another screen appeared above the ones Torrents was working on, angled to optimize Robert's view. It showed the Infiltrator craft leaving the three frigates and then jumped ahead to right before the attack. As he watched the replay, Robert considered that some would see this as an attempt on Torrents' part to mitigate negative consequences by making Robert an accomplice to his breach. Thankfully, Torrents wasn't that conniving yet, which was why he kept getting caught and flagged. But, if his deceptiveness ever caught up to his slicing abilities, he would have to be watched. That would be somebody else's issue, though. *I do need to check and tighten the security setting on my personal logs and data.*

"Well, this is interesting," Torrents mumbled beside him.

TAYLOR WASN'T sure how long they had been in the transport. He remembered hearing distant gunshots and then a loud explosion before feeling the floorboard vibrate with stomping feet as the mercenaries boarded, kicking and stepping on their prisoners without regard. The transport had rumbled to life, and Taylor had been jostled around with every bump and hole in the ground. Every time he moved, he had received another kick or punch, until a barked command had brought him some respite, at least until the transport had stopped and the mercs had piled out, again leaving their boot prints all over him. Then the transport had fallen quiet, the only sound coming from his teammates' ragged breathing and his feeble attempts to get oxygen into his own lungs. He had finally found a rhythm of shallow breaths that let him stay conscious without too much light-headedness when he felt a presence behind him.

At first it was tentative, as if someone was trying to sneak up on him without knowing how to go about it. Then, fingers ever so softly touched his neck in search of a pulse, then the rope. After a short and unsuccessful struggle, he heard the scrape of a blade coming from its sheath and then felt its cold metal gingerly push under the rope and twist. He hoped the blade was single-edged, or at least, not too sharp. A jerk, and suddenly air and precious oxygen flooded his lungs. He breathed deeply and immediately coughed.

"Shhhh. No, don't. You have to be quiet, or they'll find us."

Taylor barely heard the young, Tinareean-speaking voice over his coughing fit. Hands struggled to turn him over and remove the cloth over his head, but even if he'd had any mind to follow the softly spoken instructions, his body wanted no part of them as it tried to purge the carbon dioxide from its cells while taking in as much oxygen as possible.

The boy—at least that's the impression Taylor had of the person beside him—finally got the hood above Taylor's mouth, which increased the amount of air Taylor could take in but did nothing to quiet him. Voices sounded from the outside. The boy turned, as if looking over his shoulder, then pulled the hood back over Taylor's face.

"I'm sorry. I'm so sorry. I'll come back. I promise."

And he was gone.

Taylor, finally able to control his coughing fits, heard metal scraping on metal. A compartment door?

Someone rushed up the ramp, pulled him onto his back, and slammed a large meaty hand over his mouth.

"Shut up, asshole."

Hot breath, carrying an aroma of sharp spices and meat he couldn't identify, assailed Taylor's nostrils.

A second hand latched on to the back of his neck, as if readying to snap it, while a shin landed across his midriff. With his hands still tied above his head, Taylor lay pinned to the floor.

The voices faded away, but his assailant didn't move. Eighty-three heartbeats later, steps sounded on the ramp. Taylor's assailant turned, shifting his weight across Taylor's chest, then pushed himself up and walked out. No words were exchanged.

Silence fell over the transport, bringing his teammates' breathing into the foreground. Three sets, slow and regular. It should've been four, because the person who had come up the ramp hadn't left. Taylor could sense his eyes studying him. He was sure it was Juvak, though he didn't know why. He didn't move and simply sat there, watching. Taylor forced his body to relax. Tense muscles now would only cause problems later.

"WHAT'S INTERESTING?" Robert looked from the battle replaying on the screen in front of him to Torrents.

"A camera on a telecom sat," Torrents answered without looking up.

"Come again?"

"Civilian telecom sats don't have cameras," Torrents explained as if stating the obvious. "I wish they did. I could have so much fun." His eyes defocused. "All the things I could do with them, and they're so easy to get into." He pulled himself back to the present. "But governments are stingy and unwilling to pay for stuff that isn't necessary." His words tumbled out faster as he went on. "Now, GPS and mapping sats, they need them, and military sats use them, too." He rocked his head from side to side. "Of course, the military puts cameras on everything, so that's kind of a no-brainer." He shrugged. "But civilian TCs don't need them, and since they're paid for by the government, which always goes with the lowest bidder, they don't have them." He paused. "But this one does."

His fingers continued to fly over his keyboard. "And it's not the only one."

"Okay, stop." Teak held out his hand to slow Torrents down. "Start from the top. Why are you looking at civilian telecom satellites?"

Torrents drew a deep breath and exhaled slowly as he regarded Robert.

"All right. The defensive satellites never activated. The orbital defense platforms are still pointed outward, away from the planet. So, once the SILCs made it past them, they were out of the game." His speech sped up again. "Of course, there're still the defensive satellites in lower orbit and the groundside emplacements, plus the fighters that can be scrambled. But none of them made so much as a byte of noise. So," he drew out the word, "for all purposes, it looked like the SILCs made it past the defensive net undetected. But then, they all got shot down." He extended his fingers explosively in front of his face and then wiggled them as he lowered his hand. "We don't have much data. Some of the visual files we received show incoming missiles the pilot-view cameras picked up. So, where did they come from? And why didn't any of our other passive sensors pick them up?"

"Stealth tech?" Robert asked.

"On missiles?" Torrents frowned. "I guess it's plausible, but damn expensive. Why would they go through that effort?"

Robert felt like he was tracking an erratic ball bouncing inside a spherical polyhedron—and he'd now given it a new direction to explore.

"No," Torrents said after a few moments of consideration and shook his head. "I think they dumbed them down."

"Dumbed down high tech?"

"Actually, it's not all high tech." Torrents turned back to his terminal. "I mean, yeah, the armor and the CCS are high tech to prevent the scanners from picking us up, but we also use low tech like gliding in without propulsion and running silent with everything shut off."

"So, the sensors are shut off, too? That would explain why the missiles weren't detected."

"The active sensors are. The passive sensors don't have emissions, so they're up and running."

"Passive sensors?"

"Yeah, like audio and visual sensors that pick up EM waves that are already out there. They don't send anything out, so there's nothing to give them away. I think that's what they did with the missiles."

"But our passive sensors should've picked up their propulsion system."

"Not if they didn't use one. They could've pushed the missiles in the direction they wanted them to go and then let them glide in, like our SILCs did. Then, when they came within visual range, they linked up to an operator who fired up the propulsion system and guided them in remotely."

"Running silent until they made contact would explain why the SILCs didn't pick them up," Robert agreed. "But how did they locate the SILCs in the first place?"

"With cameras on civilian telecom satellites."

The visual of the space battle on Robert's screen changed to a view of clouds in the sky. The screen split in half and another view of sky came to life, this one without clouds.

"What am I looking at?"

"The camera feeds from two civilian TCs." Torrents explained. The right view zoomed in on a cloud formation. "I found a total of forty-eight civilian satellites with cameras they shouldn't have or need. All of them seem to be looking at clouds or empty air." Torrents looked up from his screens. "Every so often, a camera zooms in on an atmospheric disturbance. When it does, comm traffic kicks in. They're speaking

Tinareean, but I've run a translation on most of them. Here's a sampling."

The screen changed to a single visual feed overlaid with audio of two male voices.

"Control, potential target. Sending visual feed," the first voice said.

"Received feed. Evaluating visual." The second speaker paused while the camera view zoomed in on a moving cloud formation. "Negative. Natural phenomenon."

Torrents played three more clips with similar conversations identifying sightings of possible targets.

"I've run a location comparison," Torrents said after the last clip finished. "Every one of those non-standard cameras was monitoring a space of atmosphere that covers, or is close to the flight path of, one of our SILCs." He paused. "So far, I found thirty comm exchanges where Control positively identified a sighting as a possible target."

Robert looked at him in shock. "They located the SILCs through atmospheric disturbances?"

Torrents bobbed his head up and down. "They've outdumbed our stealth tech."

"They what?"

"They used low tech to beat our high tech," he explained, sounding impressed. "We use the CCS to—" He broke off at Robert's questioning expression. "The Chameleon Camouflage System," he clarified slowly. "We use it to spoof visual scanners, and the stealth system to bring our emissions to zero. In effect, scanners have nothing to pick up, which is a giveaway because the SILCs leave a hole, an anomaly of nothingness. Computers and AIs usually accept those anomalies as part of the scanners' failure rate. That is, if the amount or size of the anomalies doesn't set off the established alert protocol, the anomalies are ignored. That's why you send only a minimum number of SILCs spaced as widely as possible across a target zone. While the machines ignore the anomalies, they do record them, so if presented with other evidence, like a CCS ghosting, the AI or human controller can go back and use the recorded anomaly to validate a presence."

"What is a CCS ghosting, and how do you know all of this?"

"My parents are Combat Developers in Intergal's Research and Development section. Discussions on the latest technological advancements, or non-classified details of whatever program they're working on, are commonplace fare at the dinner table and beyond." Torrents shrugged. "Aural osmosis at its best," he grinned. "At least, if you like tech. I did. My sister, not so much." His smile turned rueful and then sobered. "Ghosting is a known problem of the Chameleon Camouflage System. While we can spoof sensors and eyes into not seeing the SILC itself, there is nothing we can do to prevent the physical effect the mass of a SILC has on the atmosphere it touches. The ship will move dust particles and even water and air molecules. While they don't leave contrails, they will disturb clouds or any other visible particles in the air. But the chance of someone looking at the right spot at the right time, with enough attention and knowledge to recognize what they're seeing, is a statistical improbability so small, it hasn't been considered an issue.

"For them to have found one SILC, much less all nine of them, means they knew when and where to look, with enough warning to repurpose civilian sats and hire and train enough monitoring personnel to do so." Torrents left the words hanging in the air.

"They knew we were coming."

"Not only that," Torrents' voice grew serious, "they knew when, where, and how we were coming." His voice softened as he looked at the commander. "They knew everything."

5

AFTERMATH

Taylor woke to the rumble of the moving transport. *Damn.* He knew better than to let himself fall asleep like that. Now he had no idea how long they'd been on the move this time. Not that it made a difference since he had no way of telling which direction they were heading or how fast. But he also didn't know if his teammates were still with him, or if the boy was still on board. Something, maybe a leg, touched his side. So, at least one of them was still here. He thought it was Salayla. He had heard her groan when the mercs dumped her next to him at the crash site. Or had that been outside, after they'd been dragged from their ship? He couldn't remember. Events blended. Lack of oxygen sucked.

The transport stopped. Somebody unlocked his wrist bindings from the floor and pulled him to his feet. A few minutes later, he stood in a room with a large desk taking up about a third of it. A couple of uncomfortable-looking chairs sat about four steps from where he and his teammates were lined up. He had looked around when his hood was pulled off, but a rod slapping his back had stopped the motion. He had glimpsed five men spread out behind his team, but he had not been able to tell if they were mercs or belonged to the grossly out-of-shape man sitting in the overstuffed chair behind the desk.

On the desk lay a small pile of hard currency—local, from the looks of it. Beside that lay four large metal rings. Juvak, who had just finished shaking the weighty man's hand, reached for one of the rings as Weighty pulled out a remote and pushed a few buttons. The ring in Juvak's hand sprang open, revealing a hinge and electronic lock. Small electrodes lined its inner edge.

Juvak approached him.

The lock re-engaged with a resounding click.

Juvak pulled Taylor close. "Let's see if you can live up to your promise, kid." He released his grip.

The edges of the metal dug into his collarbone as the ring settled around Taylor's neck.

Juvak stepped back, eyes still on Taylor.

"Let's make sure we understand each other." The fat man smiled. His Trade was broken, obviously not a language he spoke regularly. They were the first words he'd spoken that Taylor understood.

"We," he pointed at himself and the people behind Taylor and his team, "say what to do. You," he pointed at the team, "do it." He paused. "If not..." He raised the remote and pushed a button.

Sharp agony coursed through Taylor. It jumped from the electrodes into his body, surging along nerves, blood vessels, and bones, touching and smoldering every piece of him. His body was on fire, burning from the inside out.

And then, it was gone.

He was on his knees, catching his breath, willing his heart to stop skipping every third beat. He didn't remember screaming, but his sore throat said otherwise. Slowly, the sounds around him overtook the ringing in his ears.

A struggle. Tonee cursing. Salayla, trying to calm him down. And Kaydeen, calling his name—*his* name.

"Taylor."

Juvak still stood a few steps away, observing him, not with malice or glee, but curiosity, as if studying him, watching his reactions and testing him. Taylor sucked in his breath, pushed off the floor, and stood. Juvak smiled ever so slightly in approval. Taylor twisted around, his fingers moving as fast as his bindings allowed.

'Stand down. Don't fight.'

"I'm fine," he said aloud.

Kaydeen and Salayla immediately fell silent. Tonee took a moment longer. He had a split lip and a dark welt spreading across his left cheek. The two guards beside him looked worse. Their batons, the rod Taylor had felt across his back earlier, slammed into the back of Tonee's knees, forcing him down. He complied without a struggle, his eyes whirling with anger and frustration.

'I need you alive.' With his hands still bound, Taylor's signals were crude. He doubted anybody could miss them. He was wrong. They all did, all but Juvak. But this time, no jab to the knee came. Instead, Juvak gave a smirk and a minute nod of approval as he untied Taylor's hands.

"You might live up to expectations." Juvak's tone had changed, a thoughtful contemplation replacing his indifference as if a mask had cracked and his true skin peeked through. "Good leadership shows in the discipline of your troops."

"They're not my troops."

"They are now." Juvak paused.

Taylor thought about pointing out that they were the same rank, but he was sure Juvak had had no problem reading the insignia on their uniforms before the mercs stripped them off.

"Rank has nothing to do with leadership," Juvak hissed, and the cracks were gone, buried by the iron mask. "You want them to survive, you lead them through."

Taylor had no idea what to make of the man.

He didn't have time to contemplate the questions in his mind. Jabs to his back propelled him forward, out the door, down a hallway, and into a lift tube. The door closed, the lift started downward, and the light faded away.

And he knew what awaited him: Absolute darkness and a long hard battle back to the light.

~

"THEY WHAT?"

The mid-grade intelligence officer, or IO, leaned back at Commander Kilrian's sharp tone but held his ground.

"To intercept all of our SILCs and ambush the frigates, they must've had specific strategic details," IO Carmichael explained. "We checked the data Commander Richards forwarded, and his slicer is correct. To pre-position that many ships and missiles, they not only had to have had specific details of our plan of attack, but had them with enough notice to set up the ambush before we arrived in system and circumvent alarming the Tinareean Resistance." He glanced at Dean. "Unless the Resistance was aware but chose not to warn us."

Kilrian stared at him as the accusation hung in the air; then both turned to Dean.

Well played, young man, Dean thought. *Redirect his attention, and possible wrath, onto someone else.* "And why would they do that?"

The last few hours had been a flurry of manic activity interspersed with spans of deadening stagnancy as officers had come together in the Sit-R to pool the data their different sections had compiled. It had effectively turned the two main compartments of the BCC into the Fleet's C4I, with Command and Control, or C2 as it was referred to, in the main compartment and Communication, Computing, and Intelligence, the rest of the alpha-numeric acronym, taking over the Sit-R.

In the chaos of the immediate aftermath of the ambush, Kilrian had aborted the second and third waves of the attack and ordered the fleet into a holding pattern at the terminus of their first micro-jump into the solar system. Unit Commander James Tagger of the 615th SF had contacted him soon after and requested his unit deploy as a Quick Reaction Force. Kilrian had denied the request. While an SF unit was best suited to act as a QRF, doing so would have left the fleet depleted of its Special Forces. Kilrian instead chose to send in two stealth scout ships and a handful of surveillance drones. The scouts made it back—barely. The drones did not, proving Kilrian's suspicion that the ambush was still ongoing and designed to deprive the fleet of all its SF capabilities.

While the scouts were out, Kilrian had ordered the data to be pooled within the BCC so he could have immediate access while allowing his specialists to continue working with minimal interruptions from briefings. He had also requested Tagger transfer to the *Cartage* to act as SF advisor to the C2. By the time Tagger had arrived in the BCC, the scouts had returned and reported the ambush that had been lying in wait for them. In response, Kilrian had kicked intel-gathering into high drive and ordered all rescue operations held back until further notice.

Data had flooded into the C4I, but progress had stagnated as the different sections had struggled to make sense of it. Then Torrents had finally reported in, or better, Robert had done so for him. It had been a highlight, as the slicer's data had kicked off one of the few instances when information fit together in a sensible string of events.

Dean remembered his earlier exchange with Bastogne. Allowing the Intel section to compile data into an abridged report might not skew the report toward this intelligence chief's opinion, but it sure as hell didn't always include all essential information in the correct order. Nobody but Torrents had thought to check the civilian telecom satellites, at least not in the timespan he did. They probably would have gotten around to it—once they had exhausted all other options.

"Could something have changed their minds?" Tagger asked.

He didn't voice it, but Dean understood his train of thought. If the Resistance had been compromised, its actors might have come under pressure from threats to their or their families' lives or freedom. The Traverse was notorious for making dissidents or their families disappear into the flourishing and vast slave trade in its territory.

"If they had changed their mind, they could've simply called this off." Bastogne, standing beside and slightly behind Kilrian, waved him off.

"Not necessarily," Dean interjected. "They're fully aware of what kind of juggernaut their request for help brought to life and how hard it would be to call off, especially once it got going. Not to mention what calling it off this late in the game would do to their chances of having future requests for aid answered. From that point of view, it would be better if this mission was aborted because of an external factor, like a mass casualty event during the initial phase of attack."

"Losing 434 troopers won't deter us," Kilrian said. "Quite the opposite."

"431, sir," Carmichael interjected.

"Excuse me?"

"Two mechanics of the 215th were injured during the loading preparations," the IO explained. "The Unit Commander decided to leave them behind on the *Cooley*. And a sniper was transferred from the 415th to Commander Tagger's unit."

Tagger shrugged when Kilrian eyed him. Pre-mission transfers were usually made to boost a deploying unit's personnel or specialties, not decrease them. "Commander Qauros requested a temporary transfer as a cool-down period," he elaborated. "There seems to have been a—" he paused to consider his words "—let's say, a conflict of personalities." He nodded with a frown.

"That bad, huh?" Kilrian tilted his head to the side and raised his eyebrows. He was clearly familiar with the unique challenges SF commanders faced when dealing with that many Type A personalities in tight spaces during the build-up to a mission and the organizational leniencies SF Units were afforded.

"Ash is a special case, all right." Tagger pursed his lips. "One of the best in his field, but he's on a whole 'nother level of Type A personality. And that 'A' doesn't stand for alpha."

"Ah." Kilrian nodded in understanding. "Well, that gives me three troopers less to weigh on my conscience, then." He turned back to Carmichael. "But I still won't abandon 431 of my people, dead or alive. We will finish this mission, and we will recover them."

He turned toward Dean. "In your estimation, what are the chances the leak came from the Resistance?"

"Slim to none. Quite a few of the details needed to set the ambush were need-to-know information—" he paused "—and the TRM didn't need to know."

"Do we know what intel was leaked?" Kilrian turned back to the IO.

"Not until we determine the extent and nature of the leak," Carmichael replied, "but we can make some educated guesses. From the areas and angles the satellites were monitoring, we can deduce that they probably knew only the SILCs' general flight paths. They positioned forty to fifty missiles across each of those target zones to ensure at least one would be within reach once the SILCs were detected. The satellites were probably equipped with AIs that were programmed to link up with an operator when they made visual contact with atmospheric disturbances that matched the parameters of CCS ghosting. If that link-up was a quick data burst providing the satellite's ID and the data from the suspect sighting, the SILC's passive sensors would have had a hard time picking it up. Once the operator positively ID'd the sighting as a ghosting, he could have sent an attack command or remotely fired up a missile's propulsion system and guided it in by hand." He paused before adding, "All that is conjecture, of course, until we have more data."

"An AI?" Bastogne asked. "Tinareeans don't use autonomous AIs. It goes against their core beliefs."

"But the Traverse have no such constraint. Slavery of AIs, humans, and other self-aware organics or non-organics is well documented and widespread in Traverse territory," Tagger objected.

"They didn't have to be full AIs," the IO clarified. "They could've been limited AIs, similar to our mainframes. The behavior they exhibited doesn't require autonomous decision-making and is easily programmed into any level of dumb AI."

"So, we can't determine if the attack was initiated by the Traverse or the Tinareean government," Kilrian said.

"Not yet, sir," Carmichael replied.

"All right." Kilrian folded his left hand into the crook of his right arm and tapped his chin with his right forefinger. "What else do you have?"

"We have some preliminary casualty numbers as recorded by bioskins and uploaded with the data dumps."

Kilrian nodded his understanding of what Carmichael was offering. "How reliable is it?"

"Extremely, but it's also incomplete since it shows only the health data of the SILCs and only up to the point when the mainframes initiated their dumps."

"Only for the SILCs?"

"Yes, sir. During a mission, the SILCs actively monitor and

record their troopers' activities, movements, and bioskins data. The frigates do not."

"Ah, of course." Kilrian nodded. "And what does that data tell us?"

Carmichael hesitated, glancing at Tagger as if only now realizing how this information might be received, then ventured ahead. "That the SILCs had a ninety-five percent casualty rate during the initial attack."

Richards' core turned icy at his words.

"Ninety-five percent?" Kilrian sputtered.

Beside him, Bastogne's mouth and eyes gaped wide open.

"Yes, sir." Carmichael pressed his lips into a thin line as he nodded. "They timed it perfectly." He stole another glance at Tagger, who had frozen in place, his face stoic. "Most of the squads were out of their seats readying to jump when the SILCs were hit, so their seats' APS would've been useless."

"And of those ninety-five percent, how many died?"

"Thirty percent of the bioskins reported flatlining of vital signs." Carmichael shifted from foot to foot but didn't break eye contact.

"And the rest?"

"Various degrees of injuries, from shrapnel to dismemberment."

"And only five percent made it through the initial attack unscathed?"

"Yes, sir." Carmichael nodded. "But that doesn't mean they survived the crash," he cautioned.

"That's not especially helpful," Bastogne put in.

"Actually, it is," Dean refuted him. "We now know the rescue missions will need to be medevacs, and that captives will most likely be held in or near medical facilities."

Carmichael nodded his agreement. "It also means few of them, if any, would've been able to escape on their own."

"So, you're saying we can expect most, if not all, survivors to be taken prisoner," Kilrian clarified.

"Yes, sir," Carmichael agreed. "That's our conjecture."

Kilrian nodded in acknowledgement as he digested the implications.

Not only had the strike force lost 431 of its people, but 431 of its best fighters. Those troopers represented three-quarters of their SF contingent, their best trained and most rounded warfighters.

It was a severe blow, one that would have far-reaching implications within the fleet and for the mission. Their current battle plan relied heavily on SF to seize and hold strategic locations and important infrastructure to help minimize the damage and maximize the fleet's ability to quickly turn over the planet to its rightful government. Intergal wasn't in the business of extended nation-building, but of keeping nations free and independent, after all.

Those plans would have to be redrawn, and not only to account for the leaked data. The one SF Unit the fleet had left didn't have the manpower to complete all the missions the original plans had assigned to SF teams. Either ground forces or Resistance fighters would have to complete some of those missions, which meant the mission profiles would have to be changed to fit the skillsets of the people executing them. But first, they had to sort out the leak, control its damage, and see how much of their original plan was recoverable. And that would take time—time the downed SF units didn't have.

"Okay, keep me apprised of all developments." Kilrian nodded in dismissal and turned toward the small-scale simulation taking shape above the compartment's central table. When Carmichael didn't move, he turned back.

"Something else?"

"Yes, sir."

"Then spit it out."

"It's sensitive, sir," Carmichael replied and showed the screen of his handheld datapad to the commander. Kilrian took the handheld and read the screen. Carmichael kept his eyes straight ahead and his posture locked, not at attention but in avoidance. Dean wondered if the young man realized how much his attempt to not divulge the subject of their conversation actually gave away.

Kilrian looked up from the screen.

"How conclusive is this data?"

"Enough to warrant dispatching security details. Due to the sensitivity of circumstances, Commander Herletogue wanted to inform you first and verify that all executives are secure."

Dean raised his eyebrows and scanned the compartment. Sure enough, a security team had entered the Sit-R while they'd been talking. They were mingling by the Sit-R's main hatch, trying to be inconspicuous.

Kilrian nodded thoughtfully as he handed the datapad back.

"And are they?"

"Not yet, sir. One is within reach of the target."

"Commander Richards." Kilrian turned to Dean, "We need to have a word." He looked around. "In private."

6

DARKNESS

Taylor wasn't sure what was worse, the ache in his knees from kneeling on the rough-hewn rock and his previous injury, or the spasms in his back from staying in a semi-upright position. His bruised face was a good contender too, and the total lack of light and the tricks his mind played on him because of it. It must have been hours since the last ray had disappeared with the closing of the lift tube doors. The lift had descended for some time, but without a reference point for its speed, he had no idea how deep they'd gone. It could have been a slow-moving five stories or a well-buffered thousand. Not that it mattered—his guards had kept full control over him. Using his new neck jewelry as a handle, they had dragged him from the lift tube and down a warren of passageways he hadn't been able to sense, but they had navigated with ease. Not to say that had kept them from letting him stumble into the occasional corner, wall, or boulder. Though, as painful as that trek had been, it had verified that the vision enhancement devices his guards were using were sophisticated ones. When his feet had found a nest of large rocks and he had tumbled into a ditch, they had grabbed their convenient handle on the first try and dragged him back to his feet. His throat still ached from the sudden chokehold the collar had put on it in that maneuver. Nothing as bad as the spasms in his back right now, but enough to stay with him. That fall had also confirmed his impression that they'd left the manmade building and entered a rough-cut tunnel.

Now that he'd had some time to sit still and attune his other senses, he could make out the distant *pings* of metal hitting rock, the scrape of rocks being dragged or rolled, and the *thuds* of muffled explosions. A mine? He'd never been in an active mine, but he imagined this was what it sounded like. That would explain the comments from the fat guy upstairs, the money on the table, the ring around his neck, and why he hadn't been interrogated or seen any Traverse. Juvak had sold them to a miner.

Somebody approached. Two somebodies. Their steps were too soft to make out if they were the same two who had brought him down. One stayed back while the other unclipped the cable holding him in place then grabbed the collar and dragged him to his feet. His legs screamed in protest, but it was either get his stiffened knees and cramping muscles moving or choke. He gritted his teeth and forced his feet to carry him.

Left, right, right, half-left, full back. He wasn't sure if they were trying to confuse his sense of direction or were simply lost. Either way, he'd have a hard time finding his way back to the lift tube on his own. At least his legs moved easier as they went along, and he was steered clear of any obstacles. That was a definite boost to his morale and overall wellbeing.

Then, they stopped.

"Kneel."

He had barely enough time to register the demand before the baton slammed into the back of his knees and forced him down. The hand on the collar switched to the top of his head and forced his neck to arch back.

"Open."

Again, they acted faster than he could react. One of them grabbed his jaw and shoved two fingers and a thumb into his cheeks.

Why are they even bothering giving me commands?

"Drink."

This one came at the same time as the liquid hit his mouth. He gagged and tried to spit it back out, but a hand grabbing his larynx made it clear that wasn't an option.

He swallowed. The consistency was more like a free-flowing gel than a true liquid, with a hint of flavor, although he couldn't pinpoint what it was. He waited for the burn, ache, or any of the other telltale signs of poison to set in. Nothing happened. The guards dragged him back to his feet and shoved him into a rectangular hole cut about chest high into the bedrock. A metal door slid shut, closing him into a compartment that was nothing more than a large casket, only not as comfortable.

He was able to extend his arms into a half push-up before his back hit the ceiling. *Not enough room to sit up, but plenty to roll over.* Next, he extended his elbows sideways and reached roughly a forty-five-degree angle before he hit the rock on one side and the door on the other. Reaching past his head, he discovered the compartment was longer than he was tall, but not long enough for him to stretch both legs and arms at the same time. Tonee would have a hard time fitting into one of these.

He rolled onto his back and took stock of his wounds. Split lip: dried up. Swollen and split cheek: also dried up but tender. Sore chest: probably a cracked rib or two, but he could breathe without a problem so no issues with his lungs. His knee was sore and swollen from the jab Juvak had given it, but it had held his weight, so that should be fine, too. His right palm had an electrical burn, but his reflexes were pretty fast, so he had probably let go before it caused any deep tissue damage. Everything else was soft tissue damage and lots of bruises, so he'd be sore and stiff for a while.

He ran his fingers along the edge of the collar of his bioskins, about two finger-widths above where the shock collar sat on his collarbone. The bioskins obviously didn't interfere with the transfer of the shock collar's current. Its conductors might have enabled the current to better spread across his body. Since the bioskins drew power from his body's movement and heat production, it wouldn't be too far-fetched to assume the discharge from the shock collar used the bioskins' pathways for a reverse flow of current. If that was the case, it might be a good idea to get rid of it. If it wasn't, he might be wasting a good piece of kit, although, at the moment, this high-tech piece of equipment wasn't much more than a base layer of clothing. Yet, its ability to regulate his body temperature might come in handy and having that extra—albeit thin—layer would absorb some abrasive damage, though it didn't do much for blunt trauma.

He checked the rest of his kit. His blouse was gone, stripped by the mercs at the crash site. With it, he'd lost the compact pieces of his emergency kit he'd tucked into the hidden seam pockets—compass, signaling mirror, cord saw, silk line, hook, and needle. The rest of his e-kit had been in a belt pouch, which they'd taken when they stripped him of his belt. His base layer shirt, slightly more than a long-sleeved t-shirt, was fine, as were his pants. Both had a layer of abrasion protection and monitored external conditions and his body heat to adjust breathability as needed. The temperature control was nowhere as good as the bioskins', but it would do in a pinch, and it was less of a conduit for electrical currents. He checked his thigh pockets. The left had been empty, but the right had held his blow-out kit as was standard procedure, so if he was shot or otherwise severely injured, anyone rendering first aid would be able to quickly locate it and not be forced to use theirs. Both pockets were empty. That left him with his t-shirt, pants, boots, and bioskins.

Well, better than having been stripped naked.

He considered his options. The compartment was a bit tight for undressing, but it was doable. And it would keep everything confined, so he couldn't lose anything in the pitch darkness—not that he had much to lose. But did he really want to strip naked just so he could lose the bioskins? What if the guards came back before he was done?

He was probably overthinking this, but it wasn't like he had anything else to do. And he didn't want to let his mind wander to what might be heading his way next.

"The BCC was breached," Kilrian said without preamble once the hatch of his operations day-cabin had sealed out the cacophony of the BCC. He walked to the desk separating the office space in the front of the compartment from the sleeping area in its back and sat on the desk's edge facing Dean before adding, "By a member of your team."

Dean had stopped a few paces away, with Carmichael standing to his left and slightly ahead, forming the third point of an irregular triangle. In the corner behind the two was a small sitting area, but Dean didn't expect to be offered a seat. As Kilrian's words and Carmichael's stiffened posture indicated, this was not to be a relaxed conversation.

"You don't seem surprised," Kilrian said.

"Commander Teak informed me when he relayed the intel Torrents dug up," Dean conceded.

Carmichael frowned at him, clearly unhappy to hear that Dean had chosen to hold back that information when he had forwarded Torrents' intel. At the time, Dean had considered the data's acquisition method secondary and known it would distract from the data's value. He still stood by that decision, but he was surprised it had taken the IOs this long to catch on to how Torrents had obtained the data.

Kilrian nodded in acknowledgement. "Could he be the leak?"

Dean considered the question and then turned to Carmichael. "What was the timeline of his breach?"

Carmichael looked to Kilrian for his approval before answering. "It started as the SILCs launched and ended a few seconds after the transmissions from the frigates cut out."

"How did you find it?"

"The files you forwarded included data from the BCC. Its metadata showed unauthorized access from a terminal outside the BCC. We backtracked the access to the terminal in Nick Torrents' quarters."

"So, you realized the BCC was breached when Torrents' files contained data he should not have had access to?"

"Yes."

"If he's able to access the BCC without you noticing, wouldn't he be good enough to cover his tracks after?"

"Everybody makes mistakes. His was to include his pirated data instead of officially released recordings when he compiled the files to be forwarded."

"I don't think that was a mistake." Dean shook his head. "I also don't think the BCC breach is the cause of your leak."

"No, but if he's able to breach the BCC, he would be capable of accessing the leaked data."

"As are many other people in this fleet, I'm sure."

"But none of them have a history of breaking into files like he does."

"That you're aware of."

"That we're aware of," Carmichael conceded. He glanced at Kilrian again, but the Commander was content to watch the discussion play out.

"Wouldn't it make more sense for a mole to hide his activities instead of putting them in the open like this?" Richards continued.

"Unless he is using his BCC breach to lead us off his trail."

"I'm not disputing that possibility, but I am suggesting you find true evidence instead of using a, albeit illegal, breach that aided the fleet as evidence of a breach that led to the ambush and possible death of dozens, if not hundreds, of our people. Careers and lives have been destroyed by much less serious allegations, so make sure the person you're accusing is the one who deserves the charge."

"We are."

"Yet, you've dispatched a security team already." Dean frowned. "So, you're using circumstantial evidence to justify arresting the person who, so far, has made the most headway in figuring out the turn of events and might be your best chance to quickly find the actual perpetrator?"

"I have to agree with Commander Richards," Kilrian said before Carmichael could reply. "I want Torrents and his ID closely monitored but left to work as Commander Richards sees fit."

"Sir," Carmichael addressed Kilrian. "What if his goal is to interfere with our investigation?"

"Then you'd better stay on top of him," Dean interjected. "Or are you saying you don't have anyone who can match his skills?"

"Of course, we do." Carmichael bristled at his suggestion.

"Then that shouldn't be a problem."

Kilrian nodded his agreement, input his new orders for the different department heads, and sent Carmichael on his way without further delay.

~

"You like to rock the boat, don't you?" Commander Kilrian motioned Dean toward the sitting area and then retrieved a bottle and two glasses from a cabinet sunk into the bulkhead by his bed.

"If that's what it takes to keep them straight," Dean replied as he settled into one of the two armchairs facing a couch across a low table.

"Is that what you were doing?" Kilrian chuckled. He filled two-thirds of each glass with the bottle's amber liquid, handed a glass to Dean, and relaxed into the corner of the couch with the other. "How's that working with your team?"

Dean half shrugged. "He's getting results."

A sweet-and-tangy undertoned cinnamon spiciness assaulted Dean's senses as he brought the glass to his lips and allowed the liquid to roll over his tongue. It burned its way to the back of his mouth and down his throat before spreading warmly throughout his stomach. He smiled in appreciation. It had been a long time since he'd had some of his home world's specialty export.

"Yes." Kilrian nodded after savoring a sip himself. "But at what cost?"

Dean looked at him. "Are you planning to have him charged?"

"For his breach of the BCC data stream? No, not unless he's connected to the leak." Kilrian shook his head. "But that's not what I'm talking about. You're setting a dangerous precedent."

"Oh?"

"Allowing him to get away with this will only encourage him, setting him up for future failure. Not everyone is as unconventional a commander as you."

"He has a history of breaking into files, as Officer Carmichael pointed out. You expect me to fix your problem?"

"My problem?"

"He's under your command."

"He's assigned to the *Cooley.*"

"Which is under your command."

"You do realize how many layers of commanding officers are between him and me?"

"Is that your excuse?"

Silence fell as they stared at each other. Dean drew out the moment, wondering if he'd been wrong about Kilrian. Was the commander too rigid in his traditional views and style of command?

"He's obviously come to your attention before." Dean softened his tone.

Kilrian studied him a moment longer before nodding his concession. "What would you have me do?"

"Ensure his CO doesn't bury him like your intelligence officer tried to do."

"Well, that's only going to work while the *Cooley* is part of the Task Force. She's not part of my permanent command." He paused. "And here I thought you were working me up to push for a transfer release."

"I don't have a slot for a slicer."

"That doesn't seem to've stopped you before."

"Oh?"

"Robert Teak, for example. A Psychological Operations officer is an interesting choice for an adjutant."

Dean shrugged in dismissal. "I can take care of my schedule and communications, and I do know how to dress myself. Might as well fill the position with skills I don't have."

Kilrian smiled at the off-handed ribbing.

"And why would I want to add him to my roster, considering the trouble he keeps getting himself into?" Dean asked.

It was Kilrian's turn to shrug. "With your unorthodox operations and a PsyOps officer handling him, I'm sure you'd keep his activities in check, or even make them legitimate, considering your history with his grandfather."

"His grandfather?"

"Force Commander Alan Sutton." Kilrian took another sip, but his eyes, and attention, were on Dean. "You worked for him?"

"Yes," Dean readily admitted. "I was assigned to his command for a few years after I graduated." He let his eyes defocus. "But that was long before he became a Force Commander." He refocused on Kilrian's face without offering further details.

"Assigned? He personally pulled you under his direct command and held onto you for five years."

"You've looked at my record?"

"You haven't mine?"

"A little deeper than a cursory read."

Kilrian shrugged in dismissal. "I like to know who I'm working with."

"What else have you learned?"

"That some of your files are sealed." Kilrian raised his eyebrows. "SII, huh? Right. Our support branch has become a convenient catchall."

Dean simply looked at him.

"Is your rank step at least correct?"

Dean nodded. "I am a Step II Commander."

"Good. I wouldn't appreciate that kind of deception."

Kilrian met and held Dean's gaze, then leaned forward, grabbed the bottle off the table, and refilled both of their glasses as if the interplay hadn't happened. But his message had been clear, his tolerance defined.

This wasn't Kilrian's first go-round.

7

ENCOUNTERS

Taylor startled awake. His knee throbbed, his body ached, and he felt damp and chilled. *Still in the box.*

He hadn't dreamed it, then. Other details flooded in—the cold, hard rock around him, the sweet, moist air tasting of dust and destruction, and the distant and muffled sounds and voices. *Are they coming back?*

He hoped so. He wanted out of this box.

He hoped not. It meant more pain and misery.

He wished himself asleep, into a nightmare. He could wake up from those.

"If you find yourself in a tight spot, narrow your focus," his mother had often said when he'd struggled with one of her challenges. "Sometimes, the smallest step, or even holding your ground, is progress. Focus on your situation and set yourself goals you can accomplish. Your body can endure an amazing amount of pain and abuse as long as your mind doesn't lose its focus."

A *clunk* and a *swoosh* were all the warning he got before hands grabbed him and pulled him from the box. Taylor twisted to get his feet under him, but only succeeded in softening his landing with his hands and knees. Pain shot through his injured knee, blotting out the sting in his palms. He muffled a scream.

Don't show them what works.

Rocks crunched beside him. He tried to stand but was forced to his knees. The same two guards who had brought him down forced water down his throat and then dragged him through the tunnels again. After a short walk that was more a stumble and limp for Taylor, the guards forced him to his knees, connected a chain to the back of his collar, and left. Taylor listened to their receding steps, wondering what they had in store for him next.

At least with them gone, he was able to move. He needed to get the weight off his screaming knee.

Shifting the knee while it was carrying weight was out of the question. He couldn't roll back to sit on his heels. Taylor bent at the waist. The collar dug into his throat, keeping him from reaching the ground with his hands. He leaned to his left. The chain allowed him to do that. He leaned further, reaching his hand out for the ground. In the pitch dark, he had no idea what he'd find. For all he knew, the floor dropped off and he'd hang himself. The chain slid down his left shoulder. He lifted his right leg for balance. Carrying the weight of his lower leg hurt like hell. His fingertips touched rock. Ground, not a hole or major dip. He breathed a sigh of relief. After some maneuvering, he finally sat. The pain in his knee eased, but not by much. Wrapping it would help, but the guards had left him with only his boots, pants, and shirt, and going shirtless down here appealed to him less than leaving his knee unsupported, even with the bioskins still on.

He reached behind him for the chain tying him to the ground. It was made of large, heavy, metal links, which explained why it pulled the collar into his throat. He considered different options to keep it from cutting into his trachea, but in the end simply lay on his back.

Able to breathe and swallow without strain, his heart rate and breathing soon settled and, with the internal quiet, his external senses kicked into overdrive. He allowed their impressions to wash over him. He couldn't see, at least not to the degree that his brain could make sense of the visual input, but he wasn't in complete darkness. He could differentiate shades of black, shadows among shadows. Not enough to maneuver by or even see his hand in front of his face, but enough to get a sense of his surroundings—the ground above him forming his ceiling, too far to touch but not impossibly out of reach, and the rock forming the walls around him. He wasn't in a tunnel; it was more like a chamber or cave. No, caves were natural. This was man-made, or man-dug. He sensed openings, sections where the rock gave way. Tunnels? Or alcoves? He couldn't tell. The guards had left in a different direction than they'd entered, so there were at least two tunnels, but he was sure there were more. The distant mining sounds he had identified the day before seemed omnidirectional, or maybe the chamber's acoustics transferred them that way. Water dripped into a puddle close by. Pebbles fell, dirt scraped, and the breeze he hadn't noticed before suddenly stopped.

TORRENTS DID his magic and wormed his way back into Tinaree's network nineteen hours after the attack. His explanation of how a marker he had left in the system during his original infiltration allowed him to open a proxy connection and piggyback authorized signals between Tinaree and the comm nodes at the edge of the system sounded like a string of gibberish to Dean, but obviously made sense to the Intel Section's comm specialist, as the young woman nodded enthusiastically. The two looked like a perfect match, feeding off each other as they talked across the small workstation crowded with their equipment, like VR addicts comparing notes on their discoveries in the latest game.

They're probably star-spaced on stimulants.

Dean looked around the small compartment that served as Torrents' quarters. Two bunks across from each other, each framed by lockers, and a small workstation Torrents and S4 Technician Conti had pulled from the far wall to maximize its available surface was all there was to it. Robert had been lounging on the left bunk when Dean entered. The right one held a scatter of mess hall meal carriers, one of which was being used as a depository for empty stim vials—small containers of stimulants that could be added to drinks or food. He didn't see any full vials.

Dean looked at Robert. "Did they max out their stim allowance?"

Robert nodded. "And mine."

"Yet, you're nowhere near as animated."

"That's because I haven't had any," Robert explained. "I've been taking naps in between their enthusiastic, and loud, exultations." He yawned.

"Ah." Dean nodded slowly. "So, I can expect to receive a formal complaint from the medical department and the CO of a certain comm tech in the near future?"

"The stim will be worn off long before she returns," Robert replied. "With all the hours she's putting in for us, the least we can do is make sure she gets a good, long rest period before she returns to her regular duties."

"Sir," Torrents broke in. The previous high-pitched, adrenaline-rushed excitement had left his voice.

Dean turned to look at him. Even the young man's demeanor had sobered.

"I've accessed the media network."

Conti, sitting across from him, blanched as she stared at her screen. Dean stepped over to get a better view of what she was seeing, Robert was right on his heels, but Torrents hit a few keystrokes on his virtual keyboard, and a large screen in the bulkhead over the desk sprang to life. It showed a smoldering wreck sitting at the end of a deep furrow in the ground. A group of armed people swarmed over the area and, every so often, aimed and discharged their weapons at something out of sight of the camera. The clip changed to a close-up view of a piece of armor plating with clear marks identifying the wreck as an Intergal craft—one of their SILCs. The screen changed again. It continued to do so, stringing together a series of short clips that showed different views of wrecks and squads of Traverse and hired mercenaries scouring the crash sites and seemingly shooting survivors. Sometimes, it showed bodies and, once, even a row of bodies lying beside each other as if, while still alive, they had been lined up and shot execution-style.

"How reliable is this data?" Robert asked.

Dean wet his suddenly parched throat and looked at Torrents.

"Well," the slicer answered slowly. "I'm still scouring it. So far, I've found multiple clips that show the same wreckage, just different angles and timespans, but the footage is cut and arranged to give the impression those clips show different wreckage sites. Of course, the report doesn't outright claim that, as the data is part of Tinaree's public domain, so anybody willing to put in the effort could easily access the data and prove how they spliced it together."

"So, they could simply be waging a PR war and tilting the news, so people draw the conclusion they want them to?" Dean asked.

Conti's face lit up at the prospect.

"What are the chances people will actually put in the effort and dig deeper than the headline?" Dean asked Robert.

"For the general public, probably slim to none," Robert replied. "The public domain rights have become so ingrained in Tinaree's cultural fabric and its infrastructure that most people won't even consider that there's a need."

"You'd think that after the Traverse's attempt to introduce privacy laws backfired so spectacularly, the people would be a bit more skeptical," Conti said.

"That's just it," Robert said. "Having such a severe change to their public domain laws brought the whole planet to a grinding halt within days, and, facing a societal collapse, the Traverse reluctantly reinstated the previous laws. The upheaval was powerful, but too short to have a lasting effect on the public consciousness. Once the status quo returned, so did the people's thinking."

"What about footage from the space battle?" Dean asked. "Have you found any of that?"

"Yes, but it only shows the attack and its immediate aftermath, nothing after that," Torrents replied. "And since that footage came from Traverse ships, and therefore does not fall under Tinaree's public domain laws, the Traverse control what data is released."

"So, since clips of survivors being picked up during recovery efforts don't correlate with the message they want to convey, they didn't release the full data," Dean said.

"But that doesn't prove they recovered survivors. They could have still killed them," Robert said.

"Yes, but they showed the slaughter on the ground, so why not also show it in space?" Conti asked.

"There are too many unknowns and too big a chance the Traverse are feeding us misinformation through manipulated data." Dean shook his head. "We need firsthand reports from boots on the ground."

"Working on that." Torrents nodded. "We've scrubbed our previous comm protocols and are in the process of devising new ones. Once they're in place, we'll have to verify our backdoors are still free of markers and then circumvent any new NABs they've added."

Dean looked at him. "Nabs?"

"Network Antibodies," Robert supplied. "Defensive hunter-killer programs that keep the network clear of things that shouldn't be there, like backdoors or covert communications." He nodded at the slicer to continue.

"While they can be a pain in the ass to get around," Torrents said, "I already have tracers in place that'll help ID them. It might slow us down a bit, though."

TAYLOR'S HEARTBEAT QUICKENED, and his neck hair raised, tingling with alert energy. He wasn't alone. Somebody to his right was watching him. He turned his head. Black on black. Did that darkness move? Or was his imagination playing tricks? He calmed his breathing, willing his heart to slow and his useless eyes to pierce the darkness. It moved, slowly, smoothly, closer. He heard it—no, he sensed it—there was no sound. The movement was too smooth to be one of the guards, the body too lithe.

His mind conjured up a memory of Salayla on one of her scrounging expeditions, gliding smoothly through the mess hall, evaluating its occupants and then angling for her target. He didn't remember what Salayla had been hunting for that time, probably a piece of equipment they had lost or broken. It was a favorite ploy of the trainers to keep the trainees short on supplies to test their resourcefulness and ability to adapt and overcome.

A scraping sound snapped his attention back to his

surroundings. It—she—wasn't alone. With her came two more, but heavier, bulkier... Males.

How did he know that? He couldn't see, and nothing he heard could account for his conclusions. It was more like a presence, an energy that left a specific impression in his mind. She approached slowly but not timidly, reaching out. He tensed, fighting the urge to get into a better defensive position, but the chain wouldn't let him rise higher than his knees. He'd have more room to maneuver if he stayed flat.

She meant him no harm. Again, it was a feeling, an impression—this one more familiar, like that special sense or gut feeling he so often relied on.

He started as she touched his cheek. The men split off. One crouched by his feet, the other by his head.

A foot settled on the chain with a crunch, further restricting Taylor's movement. Her hand moved down his cheek. He flinched as it touched the bruise Juvak's rifle had left, but that didn't stop her from exploring. His arms and legs would probably be restrained the moment he reached for her. She moved his head to the side as if taking a closer look, then moved down his body. Although he couldn't see her, he turned his head to follow her movement. The moment he did, a knee landed on his temple and forced it back to the side. The rocky ground crunched in his ear, shooting sharp pain into his left cheek. As he grabbed for the knee, the foot attached to it slid back, taking the chain with it and settling the man's weight on Taylor's temple. The pressing pain in his cheek turned into a cutting pain punctuated by a sudden struggle for oxygen as the chain pulled the collar into his throat. Taylor tried to bring up his knees, but a heavy weight fell across his shins, forcing his feet down and out. The sudden twist in his injured knee shot agony up and down his leg. He screamed, but with his windpipe nearly cut off, he was unable to produce much sound.

He stopped struggling. The pressure on his windpipe eased.

He gasped for air, fighting off the roaring fireworks the lack of oxygen had thrown against his closed eyelids and into his eardrums. By the time he had full control of his senses again, the two men had pinned his arms and legs. His feet were shoulder-width apart, with shins draped over his own. The guy's feet were between Taylor's and his knees on the outside, which meant his crotch was exposed—a perfect target for a nicely-placed punch. Not that Taylor had a free hand to follow up on that. His arms were arched around his head, wrists restrained by the other guy's hands with at least half his bodyweight behind them. At least the knee had come off Taylor's temple. The restraining grips were tight and might have been effective on somebody without much fighting experience.

Taylor immediately thought of ways to slip out and take down his opponents, especially Open Crotch Guy. The other one was a bit trickier since he still had the chain under his boot. Taylor lifted his head, and the collar immediately bit into his throat. *Not quite amateurs, then.*

Their lack of restraining material meant they hadn't expected the need to restrain him. Or, they hadn't expected him, which meant he might be a victim of opportunity. *Opportunity for what?*

The female was back. Actually, he didn't know if she'd ever left. He was pretty sure she hadn't taken part in the struggle, but he could be wrong. Lack of oxygen could do that to you.

Her fingers explored his sore cheek again, more tenderly this time. She sat back on her haunches, and he heard her pull something from a bag, or a pouch, or pocket? She leaned back over him. Her warm breath flowed over his face. A cold gelatinous liquid touched his cheek, then spread across his wound as she carefully draped a cloth over it. A sharp, pungent smell attacked his nostrils. He tried to move his cheek out of the way, but she followed his motion. It wasn't like he had much room to maneuver. The pain in his cheek suddenly subsided. The tingling telltale of numbness set in, but after a moment, that was gone, too.

Her hands moved down to his chest, exploring his ribcage and abs with her fingers, carefully pressing into muscles and onto bones, searching for wounds. She found multiple. From there, she moved down his legs. A few moments later, she came back up and pulled his shirt over his head so it was bunched up around his elbows. The guy released his wrists and proceeded to kneel on the shirt between his head and elbows, practically locking Taylor's arms in place. They then proceeded to pull his pants down to his ankles, locking his legs down in similar fashion. His bioskins took more effort as they were compressed against his skin. After a short struggle, she used some kind of cutter to slice them open, fully exposing him.

The female treated his contusions like she had treated his cheek, minus the cloth, and then went to work on his knee. When she was done, his knee was tightly wrapped and nearly pain free.

She wasn't done.

Her fingers moved over his body again as if looking for more wounds. He soon realized she wasn't looking for wounds. She moved away. He heard cloth rustle and then she returned, straddled him, and proceeded to take her payment for his treatment. The two guys tightened their grip on him.

When she was done, she stood and stepped away. More cloth rustled, presumably her getting dressed. Meanwhile, the guys wiped him down, cleaning off the residue, medical and other. If it weren't for the rocks digging into his skin, he could almost have conceived of himself in a health parlor. Place the parlor in the personal pleasure section of town and he could probably obtain the exact sequence of treatments he'd received, including the rocks digging into his back and the restraints, if that were his thing.

The guys stood, and moments later, all three were gone.

Taylor pulled the tattered bioskins out of the way and dressed, trying hard not to think about what had happened.

Health parlor...health parlors are a good thing...and according to Botch and Tooley, the seedier the better. So, seedy health parlor it is...

His body was pain free. He wondered how long this effect would last. The cloth was still stuck to his face, a thick layer of gel keeping it in place. He rolled over onto his hands and feet and tested his knee. It could hold his weight with hardly a pinch, at least as long as the weight wasn't directly on it. Kneeling was still out of the question. Still, that was major progress. He might be able to walk without having to conceal his painful limp.

He sat, letting the chain hang into his lap, and pulled the cloth off his cheek. It was still thick with gel. The edges were folded-over adhesive strips. Between them was a smooth backing with raised symbols on it. He recognized the center symbol almost immediately—it was the standard medical symbol Intergal used on all their medical equipment. This was a med patch, a fricking Intergal med patch. But the odor was wrong. That's why he hadn't recognized it when she applied it to his cheek.

Med patches were reusable, so she'd probably loaded her version of med gel into it. It still had some gel on it, so the patch was still viable. On a whim, Taylor applied the patch where the collar had bruised his throat. The moment he did, the collar started to beep. He jerked the patch off, but the sound continued. Quiet and steady, each interval was accompanied by an ever-increasing ripple of current, about three heartbeats apart. The second was a tingle, the third a hiss, the fourth a gasp, and the fifth a curse.

And then it stopped.

Some time later, the guards returned, force-fed him, and locked him back into the box. By the time he was alone again, the ache in his face and the pain in his knee had returned, but neither was anywhere near as intense as before.

8

PROSPECTS

The daily pattern repeated itself ten times, three of which included a revisit from the female and her two friends.

Each of the female's and her friends' visits was a near mirror image of the previous one, minus the foreplay of her hands exploring Taylor's dressed body. The guys laid him flat if he wasn't already and restrained him. She stripped off his clothes, treated his wounds, and then took her payment out of his sperm count. The guys wiped him down while she dressed, and then the three disappeared again. Taylor would dress and sit back up, marveling at the healing and pain reducing properties of her med gel and ignoring the rest.

Each time, she reused the wrap and med patch she had left on him the first day, and each time, she knew exactly which pocket he'd stuffed it into. At first, he suspected they kept him under surveillance, but when she knew where to find the patch even after he had switched it to a different pocket while in the box, he concluded that whatever she used to navigate the tunnels must have the capability to detect the patch or a substance it contained. Miners often used scanners to detect minerals and ore, so it wasn't too far-fetched for some of the workers to use some kind of advanced vision system. He wondered if her boss knew how she put company equipment to use.

After their fourth visit, the trio didn't return. Taylor almost missed their interaction with him. At least it had kept his mind occupied and off his growing dislike of darkness, tunnels, and being alone. Plus, her medical care had been excellent. His injuries were healed, including the suspected broken rib and his cheek, his burnt hand could grab things with only minor discomfort, and his knee complained only when he twisted it too sharply.

After his tenth session in the tunnel, the guards took him to a lift tube.

Taylor couldn't tell if they were going up or down, but then the lift stopped, and the door opened. They'd gone up. The light was blinding. Before his eyes had a chance to adjust, the guards pulled him out of the dark tube and into a courtyard of painfully bright sunlight. Taylor instinctively pulled back into the shadow of the door, shielding his eyes.

He realized his mistake the instant he felt the bones crunch against his neck. The guard holding his collar cursed loudly. The other guard, who had lost his grip on Taylor's arm, turned around, swinging the baton he carried in his other hand. Taylor tried to duck to protect himself, but the hand still stuck under his collar kept him from moving far. Sharp pain exploded as the baton landed against his ribs. His arm clamped down instinctively, and he was halfway through a body twist to pull the stick from the guard's grip when his instructions to his teammates flashed into his mind.

'Don't fight. Survive and escape.'

The guard jerked forward with the baton's movement. The other guard finally pulled his hand free and shoved Taylor away. Taylor released the rod, dropped to the ground, and curled into a ball, shielding his head as best he could from the incoming onslaught.

The baton's blows were quickly joined by kicks from the injured guard. Taylor took them as best he could, breathing through the pain as his mother had taught him, repeating her mantra, 'It will pass.' He had taken beatings before—it was part of the SF training—but nothing like this.

It will pass.

He tasted blood.

It will pass.

The world closed in on him.

It will pass.

He couldn't breathe.

It will pass. It will pass...Please let it pass...

The world finally faded.

It took seven days to re-establish contact with the TRM.

Torrents bounced the comm signal all over the planet, pinging not only TRM members' comms, but also hundreds of comms of other people living on the planet. To most, the message would look like gibberish or a random connection, he'd explained, as if somebody were pranking them or a glitch in the system had caused it. But when received by a comm with the correct decryption key installed, it would clarify into a message—a seemingly random one that was anything but.

Then, the waiting game started.

On day seven, Aksel Mitalius, Richards' main contact within the TRM, finally replied. The news was as catastrophic as the news clips had shown. Squads of Traverse and hired mercenaries had scoured every crash site and executed all survivors on the spot. No ships had been launched to recover survivors in space. Recordings of the slaughter had been broadcast on the Tinaree Media Net for days.

Richards was stunned by the revelation. 431 people dead, wiped from the universe, many murdered in cold blood while they were defenseless. It was a new low the Traverse had sunk to—never in the nearly two hundred years of ongoing conflict had there been such a massacre.

Dean looked at Torrents. "Who has access to this?" His mind raced with damage control and possible ways to keep the rumor mill in check. *Every member of the Intergal fleet is going to scream for Traverse blood.* But that might be exactly what they were aiming for.

"Just you, Commander Teak, and me."

"Nobody else?" Dean frowned. Kilrian's intel section had a standing order to monitor Torrents' activities.

"Well, the intel section is keeping tabs on me, but I haven't released it to them yet."

"You haven't released it—" Dean looked at Robert, who raised his eyebrows in an 'I told you so,' before turning back to the slicer. "Are they aware you're controlling what they see?"

"Of course not." Torrents scrunched up his face. "They'd have a fit if they did. But I'm not really controlling it as much as I'm delaying it." He paused to consider the two commanders. "I'm kind of sending it the long way around. You know, like going from here to the BCC via every mess hall and lounge on the ship."

"How long?"

Torrents shrugged. "A few minutes or so. Why? You want me to send it on another loop?"

"Yes." Dean headed to the hatch. "How long can you give me?"

"How long do you need?"

"Long enough to allow me to be in place to prevent a

rushed attack that's ill-prepared or based on the previous battle plan," Dean said over his shoulder as he left the compartment.

"You got it, sir," Torrents called after him as the hatch slid shut.

Commander Kilrian agreed with Richards. Instead of moving forward with the attack, he pulled the fleet further into deep space and put it on total lockdown until the operational security of every person, computer, and piece of equipment was vetted and new battle plans were drawn up.

"What timeline are we looking at?" Kilrian asked.

"At least four or five months," IO Carmichael replied.

"You expect the survivors to hold out that long?"

"Per the reports, there were no survivors."

"Have you seen a body count? No? Then let's give our people, and their training, a little more credit than that."

"Yes, sir," the officer said, chastised.

"You will account for every last one of them."

"Sir, considering the damage done to the ships, there is no way we'll recover all the bodies."

"Understood." Kilrian nodded curtly. "But non-consequential."

The officer stared at him.

"We'll do the best we can to give you a full report of every trooper's death or whereabouts," Carmichael said once he recovered.

"See that you do." Kilrian dismissed him with a nod.

"He has his work cut out for him," Richards said, nodding toward the back of the retreating officer.

"Considering how long we expect them to last, it's the least we can do for them."

~

Taylor woke up sputtering, fighting to take in air past the painful stream of water assaulting him. A few moments later, the water stopped. He lay in a puddle, coughing, trying to catch his breath. He hurt all over. Somebody grabbed his collar and dragged him across the floor in a lopsided, knuckle-supported scrabble. Soon after, he was flying toward a cacophony of voices. The floor came up fast, but a flurry of arms caught him and landed him against a warm body.

They rolled him onto his back.

A goofy grin accompanied by a gaze that should be restricted to visitors of a med ward's intensive care unit filled the round face looking down on him.

"What the hell did you do?" Tonee asked.

Damn, it was good to see the big guy.

"Broke his fingers coming out of the lift tube," Taylor mumbled past his pain. "I think it pissed him off."

"You think?"

Taylor tried to grin at Tonee's nonchalant answer, but only succeeded in grimacing.

A loud staccato of metal hitting metal startled Taylor. He flinched. Tonee looked up.

"He needs medical attention," Tonee said in broken Tinareean.

"He's got you, don't he?" a voice answered from behind Taylor. It belonged to the guard who had dragged him to the cell.

"We aren't medical personnel," Tonee shot back.

That's a lie.

Kaydeen was a full-blown MO, after all, and Taylor a combat medic, but the guards wouldn't know that. At least, Taylor hoped they didn't.

"Not my problem."

A moment later, a door closed with a *thud*. Taylor hadn't heard the guard walk away but considering the overload of messages his pain receptors sent up his nervous system, that wasn't surprising.

Kaydeen leaned into view. Her fingers flew expertly over his wounds, inspecting the damage and diagnosing his injuries.

"Couple of broken ribs, cut on the temple, probably a concussion." She pulled up his shirt. "Contused abdomen." She looked up at him. "You don't do anything halfway, do you?"

"It was worth it." Taylor shrugged and winced, immediately regretting the move. Kaydeen shifted her attention to his shoulders.

"Move." She motioned for Tonee to loosen his grip and grasped Taylor's left arm.

He grabbed her wrist, stopping her attempt to move his arm.

"Don't think so." He shook his head and immediately regretted that move, too.

"It's dislocated. I need to set it." She looked at Tonee. "Get him flat."

Tonee complied, and with Salayla's help, lifted Taylor off his lap while Kaydeen steadied his shoulder.

Taylor hadn't realized Tonee was below him.

Nerve damage? Peripheral system? Nervous system?

He remembered fighting for breath the moment the guard grabbed his collar. It had cut deep into his throat. Dragging him like a dog, the guard had kept him too low to get his feet under him but too high to push off with his arms. Or maybe that was when his shoulder had gotten dislocated. He vaguely remembered getting some distance from the floor and then losing it when the guard rammed him into a doorframe. He'd nearly passed out from the sudden pain shooting through him. After that, the floor had rushed past, then changed to this rough gray canvas of dark circles. He'd assumed the lack of oxygen was playing tricks on his mind. Air had flooded his lungs again as the guard shoved him forward, but it hadn't kickstarted his brain fast enough. As he had tumbled, falling, scraping, or possibly even flying across the floor, he hadn't had time to dread his landing. He'd registered surprised yelps, then a bunch of hands, and finally a body sliding below him as he landed. And those stupid circles again. So, he had registered Tonee below him—it had simply taken him a while to process it.

He turned to look at the floor, nearly rolling out of Salayla's grip in the process. Kaydeen tightened her hold on his shoulder. He screamed in response. Salayla adjusted her grip, and his vision rolled back onto the ceiling. There were circles up there, too. No, those were holes. Who would put holes in a ceiling?

"What are you doing?" Salayla's oval face blotted out the holes.

"Looking at circles."

"Excuse me?"

Tonee had slipped out from under him and rolled to his knees. He slid his arms under Taylor's body and nodded to Salayla. She let go, and while Tonee lowered him to the floor, touched her hands to each side of Taylor's neck.

"Relax." Her face blotted out everything again. He'd never seen eyes that dark blue. "You're confused."

You can say that again.

She had that calm singsong in her voice that he absolutely hated but couldn't remember why. Then he felt her invade his mind and remembered—he didn't like her Reading him.

"Shh. This is going to hurt, but I'm going to help you through it."

It felt nice, feeling her...her...her what—Essence?—filling him. What was not to like? A sharp pain brought everything back into focus.

"Whoa, shit." Nope, his nervous system was still functioning, at least the part connecting his shoulder to his brain. And he definitely didn't like Salayla muddling his senses. He shoved her out and tried to sit up. The first one worked, the second didn't. Tonee held him pinned to the floor.

"We're not doing that again." Tonee leaned over him to catch his gaze. "This time, you hold still until she's done."

The severe concern in Tonee's gaze was gone. Not completely, but some of his humor was nudging its way back in. "I'm not taking another bloody shower."

Taylor remembered the incident Tonee referred to. They had been together only a few weeks, and Taylor had still been coming to grips with suddenly controlling only a quarter of his grade and having to depend on his teammates for the rest.

It was the first day of advanced hand-to-hand combat training. Trainer DeMacia had called Taylor onto the mat and told him to give it his best try. DeMacia had intended it to be a quick, eye-opening demonstration. But Taylor hadn't gone down as easily as expected and then he'd refused to stay down. He kept getting up, no matter how many times DeMacia beat him down. In the end, DeMacia told him to submit. Taylor refused. The next time Taylor landed off the mat, he had a broken arm and dislocated shoulder. DeMacia commented that if he came back again, he'd be shipped home in a box. Taylor tried to get back up, but his teammates stopped him. DeMacia sat on the mat and watched.

When Taylor stopped struggling, DeMacia nodded at Kaydeen and said, "Your teammate's finally stopped trying to kill himself. So, what do you do next?"

"Get his injuries treated."

"Then treat them."

"Sir, his arm is broken and dislocated."

"You're a medic, aren't you?"

She was, but barely. Kaydeen had completed a few civilian first responder courses before she joined Intergal. Although nowhere near qualified as a medic, the courses, and her near perfect memory, gave her a leg up on her training. She had breezed through the basic infantry medic course and was finishing up her intermediate certification. By the time they graduated, she was not only an SF commando with sharp-shooter qualifications, but also an advanced SF medic capable of minor surgeries.

But at the time of Taylor's brawl with DeMacia, she hadn't been.

"Sir, I'm not yet qualified to treat a break."

"But you are qualified to treat a dislocation."

"Yes, sir, but I might do more damage to his break."

"That'll be his problem, not yours. You want to get him to medical? Then set his shoulder."

She did, and she would have done it well, but the pain brought Taylor's reflexes into motion. He pulled out of their grip and in the process turned his clean, closed break into an open, gory wound that had doused Tonee in blood.

They had ended up confined to quarters for two weeks for his defiance. The trainers took teamwork to the letter. Each trainee team ate, slept, trained, and was punished together, no matter whom the perpetrator or what the infraction was. DeMacia stayed pissed at him and rode him hard the rest of training. That little bloody temper tantrum of his, as Tonee liked to call it, might have earned him a trainer from hell, but it had done wonders for his teamwork capabilities.

TONEE LOOKED AT SALAYLA, who had backed away. "You okay?"

"Yes," she answered with a frown. "He pushed me out again. This is very disorienting."

Tonee scanned the room before returning his gaze to Salayla.

"I thought humans were helpless against Readings?" His voice was scarcely above a whisper.

"Not helpless," she replied, keeping her voice equally low. "Some are able to resist. A Primary's Reading is harder to resist than a Minor's, but it's not unheard of." Salayla frowned. "When it comes to a struggle though, Din will win, which is why a human, once a Din has entered his mind, cannot break the contact."

"But Taylor just did."

"Yes, he did."

"Maybe you weren't all the way in, or something?"

"Tonee," she admonished, barely raising her voice above the whisper she'd been using, "This is a gift we are born with." She spoke as if addressing a small child. "It refines and strengthens as we grow and reaches its full strength by the time we become sexually mature."

Tonee rolled his eyes at her. They'd heard that speech many times before.

The day they had met, Salayla and Kaydeen had introduced themselves as Din. Descended from humans who settled the planet Dinai, Dinai's Children, as they called themselves, evolved differently than the rest of humanity. While they looked the same, Din had the ability to 'Read' other people's feelings and thoughts and were much more open in their sexual relations. Or, at least, that's what most people knew when asked, which explained why Din usually didn't announce themselves. But Kaydeen and Salayla, thinking openness and clarity was the way to become the best team possible, had immediately cleared up any misconceptions Tonee and Taylor might have had about Din. Yes, they could Read feelings. No, they couldn't read thoughts, at least not in the commonly understood way. Yes, their society encouraged sexual activity, and yes, there was no chance of pregnancy since Din were infertile until they Bonded. But Readings needed skin-to-skin contact, usually hand to neck, and gave only feelings and a general impression of surface thoughts. And no, Din didn't have an insatiable sexual appetite. They simply didn't perceive sex as intimate and emotionally attaching like humans did. Sex was another developmental step to be practiced, like walking and talking, and a tool to find a Bond-Mate, become fertile, and have children.

Seventeen at the time, the boys had received a crash course in Din physiology and psychology which left no question about what they could and could not expect from their female teammates. At least, until the girls had pointed out that the closer their relationship grew, the easier and deeper Readings would get, and the better the sex would be.

"How far a mind can be entered into," Salayla continued, pulling Taylor back into the present, "or how much a mind can be influenced, depends on the strength of the Gift in the individual Din."

Taylor waited for the punch line.

"But even Minor Din can easily use it on humans, as Kaydeen has often proven to you. Saying I cannot tell if I have fully entered his mind is like saying you cannot tell if your penis has entered my vagina." She cocked her head at him.

"Okay, got it." Tonee closed his eyes. "And I really didn't need that visual."

"It helped clarify my point."

"That it did." He shook his head. "So, why was he able to kick you out?"

"I do not know."

"I'm right here, you know."

Tonee looked down at Taylor. "So you are. How's that shoulder?"

"Well, I can move it and feel my arm again. May I sit up now?"

"Nope, not until she's done with you." Tonee looked at Kaydeen. "And?"

She had finished inspecting Taylor's shoulder.

"Doesn't feel like there's any permanent damage, but I need to take a closer look at those contusions on his abs."

Tonee shifted his weight out of her way, then looked back at Taylor.

"About time you joined us. Started to wonder if you were snubbing our company." He grinned. "So, what the hell happened to 'don't resist?'"

When Taylor stared blankly at him, he elaborated, "Tico's hand. I assume that was your work?"

"Yeah, felt the tendons pop and his knuckles crunch against my neck. Never felt anything better." Taylor grinned, then hissed, as Kaydeen found a sore spot over his kidney.

"It wasn't worth this beating," she said without looking up.

"Yes, it was." He chuckled, then thought better of it—too painful.

Kaydeen shook her head.

He looked back at Tonee. "Tico?"

"The guy whose hand you mangled. He and his running partner, Tristan, the guy giving you flying lessons, have been providing us with these lovely accommodations." He motioned around him.

The room was square and about four times bigger than their cell. As Kaydeen moved down his side, Taylor saw the only two doors leading out. One, oversized with two sliding sections sealing it shut, was in the center of the wall. The other, person-sized, hinged, with a small window in its top half, was closer to the right corner. Four equal rows of ceiling-to-floor bars made up their cell in the middle of the room. He didn't see a door into the cell. He had gotten in, so where...

"They're the only ones we've seen," Tonee continued, drawing his attention back to their conversation.

"How long have you been up here?"

"Two or three days. Kaydeen came up first, then Salayla, then me a shift later. We still work the mine separately, but they let us sleep up here together. Been waiting for you to show up. Now, we know why they took their time. What happened to no fighting?"

He's not going to drop it.

"I wasn't fighting. I jerked back when the light hit my eyes. Not my fault he had his hand wedged tight inside my collar."

"Those damn reflexes again, huh? Gotta get control of them." Tonee smirked, then became solemn. "Before you end up with another DeMacia."

"I'll deal with it."

"I hope you can," Salayla put in quietly, "Tico can be a mean S.O.B."

Taylor looked at her, then at Tonee whose eyes had widened at her choice of words—Salayla didn't curse. Kaydeen nodded her agreement but made no comment. Taylor wondered what had happened but didn't press them for details. They would repay him in kind, and he wasn't ready to talk about his time in the dark.

Instead, he changed the subject. "Work the mine?"

"Yeah, move ore, push carts, empty and fill hoppers." Tonee paused and tilted his head. "They haven't put you to work?"

Taylor's headshake ended with a hiss as Kaydeen found another sensitive spot. She raised her eyebrows at him as he controlled his breathing. "You might have internal damage."

"I'll be fine. Just sore."

She didn't believe him.

She finished her exam, then motioned to Tonee. "His shirt needs to come off." She moved to open his pants, adding, "And so do these."

"No." He grabbed his pants, shoving her hands out of the way, and pulled his shirt back down.

She froze and looked at him.

"You are wet," she enunciated, "and have early signs of shock. We don't need to add hypothermia to the mix. Let's at least get your shirt off." He saw the questions in her gaze, but she didn't voice them. She slowly pulled his shirt up but stopped at his chest, all the while watching his reaction.

Salayla had moved by his head and leaned into his view.

"You can have mine until yours is dry." She pulled off her shirt and dropped it beside him. "It is dry and preheated." She wasn't wearing bioskins.

She grabbed his back and pulled him into a sitting position. Pain lanced through his abdomen. By the time he caught his breath, she'd pulled his shirt over his head and leaned into him to slide it down his arms. Heat radiated from her bare chest into his back like two directional hot pads, amplifying the low temperature of the rest of his body. His shivering worsened, shooting spasms of pain through his abdomen. He groaned and tried to curl up but couldn't—Salayla's tight grip kept him upright. They got the dry shirt on him.

When she released him, he curled into a ball to ease the pain, but the shivering spasms continued. Tonee grabbed him from behind, pushing an arm and a leg below his body, lifting him slightly off the ground. Kaydeen slid in from his front, using her back to wedge him onto Tonee's chest. Then Sal's essence enveloped him, pushing his ever-present pain into the background. She didn't explore, only held him and filled him with warmth and peace. He wondered why he'd ever hated this feeling. He was warm, inside and out, safe, and not alone. He drifted into blissful nothingness.

9

INTEL

He woke sore and aching, his arm and shoulder asleep. The door to the cellblock had opened. Tonee and Salayla got up immediately. Kaydeen stayed beside him a moment longer to indicate for him to stay down.

Tristan and Tico entered the cellblock, calling for them to get up. Tico's hand was wrapped, but he moved it with only slight hesitations. So, they had access to regen-tech for medical treatment. While Tico stayed back, Tristan approached the cell. He motioned for Kaydeen to move away from Taylor.

She hesitated.

"He's in no shape to work," she protested in close to fluent Tinareean, but she moved when Tristan pulled out a small control pad.

As soon as she did, bars rose from the floor between her and Taylor, cutting their cell in two.

So that's what those circles and holes are for.

As soon as the new wall of bars locked into the ceiling, a set of bars in front of Tristan lowered to give him access to Taylor's half.

"Get up," Tristan ordered as he approached and kicked Taylor's foot for emphasis.

The first kick didn't hurt. The second left a bruise. Taylor didn't want to find out what the third would leave, so he pushed himself off the floor. With one shoulder partially asleep and the other painful from the dislocation, it took him a moment to get his feet under him. He tried to straighten, but his abs refused to relax.

Kaydeen jumped on his halting movements immediately.

"He can't even stand. There is no way he'll be able to work. He needs to rest and heal."

Tristan stepped closer, within easy reach of a quick jab to the throat, but that would have been counterproductive. Plus, Taylor wasn't sure if his injuries would allow him the speed and power he needed to take down the guard and get out of the cell before Tico could step back to the control panel and close it. Instead, he hunched his shoulders, ready to take whatever Tristan had in store for him. It wasn't much, at least nothing too painful. Tristan grabbed his good shoulder and shoved him. Taylor stumbled back, only half pretending, then the injuries to his core took over. He couldn't keep his balance and fell to the floor, hard. He groaned.

Kaydeen continued to reason. It was her specialty, laying out facts to prove her point and using logic to drive home the conclusion she aimed for. It didn't always work, but where Kaydeen's logic failed, Salayla's flirtations or Tonee's knowledge of rules and regulations could usually pick up. At least, that's how it worked in Intergal territory.

It wasn't hard to see where she was heading. A non-injured worker could provide a much better work output than an injured one. And allowing the injuries to heal first would yield a higher output faster than working him while injured. Plus, the chance of permanently disabling him was lower, therefore increasing his overall production. She laid it out in nice cold facts, appealing to the greed of the mine owner and the benefit Tristan and Tico could gain from delivering the strong workforce the team could provide. Taylor wasn't sure he liked the promises and fringe benefits she hinted at, but at the moment he merely wanted to be left alone. His tumble had hurt more than he had expected and let on. He wanted to curl back up and concentrate on ignoring the pain.

The scrape of moving bars sounded again, then the sliding door, and then the cellblock fell silent. They'd left. He didn't remember hearing Tristan or his teammates move away. Maybe he'd blacked out. He was thirsty. He lifted his head—the cellblock spun as if he were in a free-floating vortex shaft. He lay back down. Water could wait.

The next time he woke, Kaydeen was beside him, lifting his head and touching a soft cup to his lips. Cool water flooded his mouth. He drank greedily. Next came a metallic pouch with a gel-like substance. Salayla helped empty it into his mouth. He gagged at the overly honeyed richness of it, but Kaydeen clamped his mouth shut to prevent him from wasting the only food they'd been able to scrounge for him. A few more cups of water, and they settled him against Tonee, whose large chest was much more efficient in transferring body heat, even clothed.

I'll take that over Salayla's bare breasts any day, Taylor thought as he drifted off to sleep and vowed to never let either in on that thought.

The next morning was much like the previous one, minus Tristan forcing him to stand. Kaydeen made sure he drank a few cups of water before the guards came, then he was left alone. The pattern continued day after day, or at least what they established as day after day. Without a way to tell time, it was hard to estimate whether their work and sleep shifts truly added up to a full day.

He slept for most of the first five days, waking only long

enough to swallow the water and nutrient gel Kaydeen and Salayla poured into his mouth, or whenever Kaydeen poked a sore spot too hard. He usually fell back asleep soon after they left him alone. Kaydeen found the wrap around his knee on day two and used it to wrap his ribs. He had enough presence of mind to remember and point out the med patch he'd stashed in his thigh pocket. The next day, she applied it, freshly loaded, to his shoulder. He wondered where she'd acquired the med gel but didn't have the energy to ask.

After day five, Taylor stayed awake longer, usually only sleeping at night and when he was alone. It took him another two days before he retained most of the information his teammates told him.

"WHAT DO YOU MEAN, it's peculiar?" Taylor asked as he finished the latest food pouch his teammates had brought him.

"Only about one-third of the workers are collared. The rest are uncollared, but we don't think they're fully free, and we don't think they're all Tinareeans," Tonee answered. He stood in his customary spot, leaning against the bars, blocking the view from the door. "The collared workers aren't locals, either. It seems they're from all over the planet." He crossed his arms over his chest and pulled his right foot up, leaning it against a bar beside his left knee.

"Which is why you haven't been able to pinpoint our location." Taylor finished the cup of water Kaydeen handed him, then lay back down. His ab muscles were still too sore to keep him in a seated position for any extended period.

Kaydeen pulled up his shirt and started her daily prodding routine. She was happy with his recovery so far, though he was nowhere near able to work the mine yet.

"Correct. I'd say we aren't far from where we crashed. Of

course, our out-of-control tumble probably put us way off course from our objective."

"How far off?" Taylor looked at Salayla, who sat with her arms wrapped around her knees, a few feet to Tonee's left.

"Hard to say." She returned his gaze, deep in thought. "I would say we were in tumbling free fall for roughly twenty to thirty seconds. Considering a SILC's average speed of descent and our time and altitude allowance for drop prep, that could put the crash site multiple hundred klicks from our target."

"Twenty to thirty seconds?" Tonee put in. "It felt more like a few minutes."

"The only way to explain a time lapse of multiple minutes between the attack and the crash would be that our descending flight path was not only thrown off course but halted or even negated for some time. Any kind of non-descending lateral move could have thrown us thousands of klicks off course."

"When you put it that way," Tonee said, "I like the first option better, but it sure as hell felt a whole lot longer."

Taylor had to agree with Tonee but was acutely aware how adrenaline could affect one's internal sense of time. He looked at Kaydeen, who had moved down his leg and was checking his injured knee's range of motion. He wanted to hear her opinion. With her near-perfect memory, he hoped she'd be better at estimating the passage of time. She returned his gaze and then looked at Salayla and Tonee while considering her answer. She looked back at him, released his leg, and sat back on her feet with a sigh.

"We've discussed this already. Repeatedly." She studied him, tilting her head.

We have? He remembered intangible snippets of conversations but had considered them dreams.

"How often?"

"Four times."

"Ah." He nodded. "Well, can we go over it one more time?"

"You going to remember it this time?"

"Yes."

"That's what you said last time."

Ah. "Okay...then let me change that to maybe."

She smiled. "You'll do."

"I'll do what?"

She laughed at his question but didn't answer it.

"Okay." She took a breath. "To answer your question, no, I do not have an internal atomic timekeeper."

My question? I guess we have had this discussion before.

"So, I cannot tell you exactly how long it took before we hit dirtside," she continued, "and even if I could, what does it matter?" She paused to look at the others in turn. This seemed to be a subject they had already discussed.

"Finishing our mission objective has moved down our priority list, or at least should have. We have other and more worrying concerns right now, I would say."

Taylor nodded his agreement. "It would still be nice to be able to at least approximate our location, so we know what to expect topside."

"Agreed, but for that to be of any help, we need to get free and to the surface."

"I'd say we're at the surface right now. So, we've reached half of that objective." Taylor smiled.

"Yeah," Kaydeen returned, "now we need to get out of this box. And I don't think that's going to be all that easy."

"Whoever said any part of our job was going to be easy?"

"Nobody," the others replied in unison, grinning. "If it was easy, GFs could do it."

Taylor smiled at the familiar jab at Ground Forces troopers. It was good to see their enthusiasm was still intact. Now, they needed to keep it up. "Tell me more about the people down below. Do the collared and uncollared get along?"

"Mostly, but there's a faction of uncollared the others seem to be wary of," Kaydeen answered.

"Guards?"

"No, there are no guards. Only workers. Most of the collared are Tinareeans, with the odd off-worlder thrown in. The uncollared have a larger portion of off-worlders."

"Traverse?"

"Possibly, but not military."

"Civilian Traverse? Tinareeans are considered civilian Traverse right now."

"Not the same. Tinaree is still under forced occupation. They are not, or at least, have not been long enough under Traverse rule to have accepted their lot."

"Ok, so the Traverse have brought in civilians, or allowed civilians to immigrate." Taylor paused. "Why?"

"To work the mines," Kaydeen supplied.

"Mining has been part of Tinaree since it was founded," Salayla interjected. "Tinareeans have become well acquainted with the subject and have their experts. Why bring in outsiders?"

"To undercut a rebellion or the Resistance?" Taylor asked.

"That's what the collars are for. To control the work force," Kaydeen said.

"So, what do the off-worlders bring that the Traverse can't find here?" Taylor asked.

"Good question." She smirked.

"Let me guess. I've asked it before?"

"Yup."

"And I assume we haven't come any closer to an answer."

"Nope."

"Okay." He considered what he remembered from their previous conversations. It wasn't much.

"Why don't you give me what we know so far?"

Kaydeen raised her eyebrows at him.

"Humor me one more time," he pleaded. "Please?"

She shook her head with a grin. "Only one?"

He shrugged.

"Ah, hell," Tonee put in. "It's not like we have anything else to do."

So, they hunkered down and filled him in—again.

The mine was a thriving community where collared workers toiled hand-in-hand with free workers, Tinareean and Traverse. Guards weren't present, at least not in the sense of controlling the workers and their activities. The few people who weren't actively working the mine were more concerned with supplying food and water and moving the workers from location to location as needed. They didn't enforce the workload or the rules, the miners did.

Foremen assigned daily duties to be completed in set amounts of time. Regular water breaks and one meal break cut the monotonous work into endurable chunks and provided time to socialize and trade.

This was the time when Salayla was in her element. Although they worked in a different area with different workers every day, she was always able to scrounge extra food and med gel for Taylor. He didn't ask where she acquired them or what she used as trade since he probably wouldn't have liked the answer.

Ten shifts later, things changed.

10

NEW NORMAL

The guards pulled Taylor from his cell in the middle of the day and cuffed him to a set of chains hanging from the ceiling. With a push on the control pad, the chains tightened and pulled him onto the balls of his feet. Tristan pulled up Taylor's shirt, securing it over his head, then loosened his pants. Tico, meanwhile, paced in front of him like a predator waiting to pounce on his prey. When Tristan stepped back, Tico's leer broadened as he pulled a curl of cabling from the small of his back. He unfurled the neural whip with a grin.

Taylor recognized the device immediately. They'd studied it at the Academy. He remembered its statistics clearly—the type and levels of pain it provided and the damage it could do to his nerve endings, especially if applied wrong or overused. The instructors had even given each trainee a taste of its bite, dialed down, of course.

What he felt then was nothing compared to what he felt now. Each lash hit his back, then curled around his side to bite into his front. Some came in at angles, at times coiling the whip's tip over his shoulder and onto his throat or around his hips and into his groin. He tried to hold in his screams, clenching his teeth against the pain, but could do so for only a few blows. By the time Tico let up, Taylor hung in the cuffs, barely holding onto consciousness.

Tristan slapped him across the cheek to get his attention, then leaned closer. "Tell the big guy to reign in his curiosity. It's not good for your health."

His breath, gliding over Taylor's shoulder, felt like sandpaper scraping over an open wound.

They left.

Taylor tried to get to his feet. He couldn't find them. He couldn't feel anything below his hips but could feel everything above them. Every nerve ending was on fire—if not from a direct hit from the whip, then from its electric discharge. And it didn't end with the whipping. His pain receptors continued to fire at the slightest stimulation.

The door opened again. His teammates entered the cellblock, and with them, a cool rush of air that set his skin ablaze. A scream formed at the back of his throat, but he swallowed it. He needed his voice to keep them from touching him. They rushed to him, a jumble of movement and sound, each bringing its own gust of air, lashing him anew. But they didn't touch him. The air settled and, with it, the pain calmed. He opened his eyes. Tonee and Salayla stood a few steps away, ready to spring into action but waiting on Kaydeen's instructions. Kaydeen was closer, studying his wounds as she slowly circled him. She didn't speak. She even breathed shallow and into her hand, but he felt the air move as her fingers formed a message to the others. She had recognized the cause of his wounds and was taking care to cause him the least amount of additional pain.

She was only halfway around him when the cuffs opened. He fell. She caught him. He screamed. Salayla and Tonee were instantly by their sides, Tonee cursing loudly. Kaydeen told him to shut up, then directed their movements as they carried him to their cell and settled him to the floor. Salayla lay next to him, her hand between the floor and his throat. Pain flared up from her touch and the floor against his stomach, hips, and shoulders, but then was drawn out into her hand. Her mind entered his, her essence pushing between his presence and the pain, forming a buffer. The pain was still there, but at a distance—he could sense it and taste it, but it was as removed as somebody grabbing his arm through a double layer of insulation foam. He was able to breathe, and think, and turn his head to look at her. She smiled at him, but her eyes stayed the dark swirling black-blue he had seen so often lately. He wondered if he would ever again see her fun-loving bright blue sparkle.

"Tonee." Taylor croaked as he looked over her head to where Tonee leaned against the bars.

Tonee pushed off and came over. He had placed himself to interfere with a clear view from the closed door to the cell and continued to stay that way. As of yet, the guards didn't know Salayla's and Kaydeen's true nature, and the team planned to keep it that way. The old argument to not use their gifts during captivity because of the high chance for discovery fell, as expected, on deaf ears. Their ability to ease pain and stabilize emotions and moods was too valuable during a high-stress situation like this.

Taylor pushed up onto his elbows as Tonee approached. Salayla's hand rose with him. Tonee crossed his legs and sat. Salayla immediately took the opportunity to use his knee as a pillow. It was a typical action for Din—the urge to touch, to be close to others, especially people they felt connected to. It was an action the Academy instructors had encouraged in all teams, to dull the sexual innuendoes some humans connected with touching, and to allow Din to blend in and better obfuscate Readings. The best way to hide a Din's nature was in the open with teammates who were so comfortable with each other's proximity, they didn't seem to notice.

“What happened down there?”

Tonee scrunched his forehead at the question, “What do you mean?”

Taylor repeated the message Tristan had given him.

Tonee cursed and then explained, “I talked to an uncollared miner, a Tinareean. Was trying to find out what’s going on outside. You know, political, social, the mood out there, what people’s thoughts are on things, what happened to the Intergal attack, why the hell the Traverse are still in charge—but I didn’t get much, barely got past his family. Shit, Taylor, if I’d known they’d do this to you, I never would’ve asked.”

Taylor waved him off.

“They do avoid speaking about their private lives or anything outside the mine,” Salayla put in without lifting her head. “It seems to be taboo.”

“He had no problems talking about his family. Chatted my ear off about his beautiful wife and smart kids.” Tonee shook his head. “If it’s taboo, then he didn’t know about it.”

“Or he was testing you to see how far you would push it,” Salayla suggested.

“Well, if it was supposed to be a trap for me, it didn’t work that well. He was the one who didn’t shut up. Once I got him going, I couldn’t get a word in anymore. Shit.” He nodded toward Taylor’s back. “It definitely wasn’t worth that.”

“Maybe it was,” Kaydeen said. She sat on Taylor’s other side, carefully spreading med gel on the welts on his back. “It shows that life down there is more controlled than they’ve been letting on.”

“And the collared aren’t as unmonitored as they seem,” Taylor added. “That was worth finding out.”

“Not at that cost.”

“You didn’t expect to be punished?”

“I expected them to punish me.”

“Then it was worth it.”

"Worth getting your skin flayed over it?"

"If that's what it takes."

"Taylor..."

"From the way they've been playing things, it doesn't look like I'm going to get out of here anytime soon." Seeing Tonee's questioning frown, he explained, "Keeping me locked up ensures you come back. Not providing me with food ensures you work harder to earn an extra ration. Now, they're taking the next step, figuring out how to keep your tongues in check."

"Don't show them what works." Kaydeen repeated the mantra their SERE instructors had used over and over during the 'R' section of their 'Survive Evade Resist Escape' training.

Taylor smiled, "So they said."

"I keep stepping on that mine, don't I?" Tonee asked.

"They never explained how to avoid it."

"What if they keep beating you?"

"They will. And I'll keep taking it."

Tonee stared at him as if Taylor had stepped into a blazing fire and announced it was warm.

"And you will keep digging. The Traverse are obviously still in charge, at least in this area. So, our SILC might not have been the only one shot down. If it was a concerted attack, or even a mass ambush, dirtside might be one massive battleground or, worst-case scenario, the fleet might have never made it planetside."

"Then, where did they go?" Kaydeen put in. "Or are you suggesting they took out the whole Fleet?"

Tonee slumped. "If they did, then we're shit up the Vortex."

"Either way," Taylor replied, "we need more intel, and then things will fall into place."

Tonee shook his head. "It's not that easy."

"I didn't say it would be easy on you."

"On us?" Tonee exclaimed. He glanced at Kaydeen and

Salayla, who had stayed quiet during the exchange. "You're the one who's—"

"Me?" Taylor stared at him. "I got the easy part, Tonee. All I have to do is sit up here and take what they dish out. They're not going to kill me or maim me to the point where I need serious medical attention. That would be counterproductive. So, I'll heal. You guys are the ones busting your asses down there, working extra to keep me fed, trading who knows what for meds, and then spending part of your sleep cycle taking care of me. And the whole time you worry about what your actions will do to me. Don't you think I can't see that? You're tearing yourself apart over something you have no control over."

He paused to catch his breath. Arching his back to meet Tonee's gaze quickly drained what little energy he had left.

"I screwed that one up. I showed them what works when I came out of that lift. I moved when I shouldn't have. I set myself up as their punching dummy. That's on me, so I'll take it. The good part is that they're leaving you guys alone, so you can work the intel and, when the time finally comes for us to make a move, you guys will be on top of your game."

Taylor looked at Tonee a moment longer, then lay back down.

Tonee's eyes met Kaydeen's, who shrugged. "It's not like we have anything else to work with."

Tonee looked at Salayla, who had been cradling Taylor's neck in her hand.

She met his gaze, held it for a moment, and nodded.

Taylor felt her reassurance. She agreed with his plan, though it was clear she didn't like it. An instant earlier, her disapproval had shot through him, along with the knowledge that she had sensed the part of his plan he hadn't voiced—his decision to make sure none of them would ever take his place. It was his obligation to see them through this, even if it cost his life. He would do whatever it took to keep the guards' attention, and their wrath, on him and off his teammates. It wasn't a thought or a decision, but a fact of his being.

DEAN SELECTED the next name on the long list displayed on his screen. As the personnel file opened, his comm pinged with a direct visual connection request. Dean smiled. Only one person would have the audacity to comm him with a direct visual this late at night. Most people would request an audio connection or send a message requesting a visual connection so a rote acceptance wouldn't catch him in an inopportune situation or attire. He considered ignoring or denying it but knew that wouldn't help. If there was one trait deeply imbedded into his assistant, it was determination.

Dean accepted the request and set it to display on half of his computer screen.

"Why are you looking at profiles?" Robert asked, not even bothering with niceties or protocol. Dean didn't mind. He preferred direct, straight to the point conversations over the social dancing most people's sense of etiquette or protocol called for. That was one of the reasons he had chosen Robert Teak as his assistant. Another one was his Psy-Ops background. It was always helpful to have a leg up on evaluating the people Dean regularly dealt and negotiated with, unless Robert was using his skillset on Dean.

"And how do you know I'm looking at profiles? Are you tracking my activities?"

"I am not," Robert replied. "That would be a breach of regulations." He kept a straight face. "I have, however, set a marker tracking access to the personnel files in the MIA list."

"Ah, and that's different, of course."

"Correct." Robert grinned. "So, coming back to my original question..."

"I'm filling my idle hours with a useful activity. It's not like I'm swamped with exhaustive work right now."

"Idle hours, my ass. It's the middle of your rest period, when you should be going in and out of REM sleep, not personnel files."

Dean smiled. Robert was always good at keeping him grounded.

"It's as good a time as any to familiarize myself with the people I lost."

"You didn't lose them. If their loss is anyone's responsibility, it's Kilrian's. He's in overall command of this mission."

"They were part of a mission I set in motion, based on my legwork, so they each deserve to be known and remembered."

"Turning a list of anonymous names into people with faces and lives opens you up to guilt."

"Not guilt. Mourning and recognition. I didn't cause their death. I initiated the mission that gave them the opportunity to come here and fight an oppressive regime. They chose to join this fight fully aware that they might not make it to the other side."

"So, you feel no guilt at all?"

"Don't twist the meaning of my words." Heat rose from the pit of Dean's stomach. "Of course, I feel guilt, but second-guessing myself after the fact only sullies their memories and efforts. We need to know what went wrong and make sure it doesn't happen again." His words had become clipped, his tone sharp. "And we have to honor and remember those we've lost to the cause." He paused and took a breath to cool the internal heat burning his scalp. "You know this is how I deal with the losses and make them bearable. We've had this conversation before. Repeatedly. How often are you planning to bring it back up?"

"As often as you sit down and open a new batch of personnel files," Robert calmly replied.

"Making sure I stay emotionally stable?"

"That *is* what I'm here for."

"You're here to work for me, not on me," Dean replied wryly.

"All in a day's work."

"And if you ever found evidence of my stability slipping?"

"Then I'd have to start working on you, not for you."

"Well." Dean smiled. "Until then, why don't you keep working on Torrents. I think the young man is going down the wrong trail."

"Oh? Something I should know?"

"No, I would prefer you look at it with an unbiased mind."

"Don't I always?"

"Do you really want me to answer that?"

Robert smiled.

"One more question," he said before Robert could log off. "How many names are supposed to be on the MIA roster?"

"431," Robert replied. "Why?"

"That's what I thought. But there are only 427."

TAYLOR'S PREDICTION came true twelve shifts later. This time, they didn't pull him out of the cell. Tico came in and beat him with the baton he always carried on his belt. No words, no explanation, just a thorough beating and then he left. It wasn't too bad, as far as beatings went. The welts from the lashing were mostly healed, and Taylor was able to protect his most sensitive body parts. A few blows got through, though, so he ended up with a split lip on top of the contusions on his arms, legs, and back, but no broken bones or dislocations and not as much internal pain as the first beating. By the time his teammates returned from their work shift, he was even able to sit up again.

"Did you get anything useful?" he asked as Kaydeen started working on his latest batch of wounds. He was getting pretty good at keeping his pain from showing and only hissed when she touched an overly raw spot.

"Well—" Salayla hunched down in front of him "—the good news is that we seem to have exhausted the number of crews they can assign us to work with."

She offered to help him with the pain, but he waved her off. No need to push their luck and risk being discovered if they didn't have to.

"We were back with Coparoda's crew today."

They'd fallen into the habit of naming the different crews after a person who'd been a good resource for them.

"The bad part is that Coparoda has been reassigned."

She pulled out a meal pack, ripped it open, and handed it to him. He stared at it, resisting the urge to snatch it from her hand and guzzle it down. As usual, he was starving.

"They moved him a few shifts after we met him."

He finally took the food and forced himself to nurse it.

She grinned and waved him on. "Go on, I have a feast for you today."

She pulled out three more packets. His eyes widened, but not wanting to let on how starved he really felt, he played it off as a reaction to her previous words.

"Moved him? Where?"

He didn't fool her. She opened the next pack and held it ready for him.

"Nobody knows, but nobody seems concerned, either. While it doesn't happen often, workers do get shifted around."

As soon as he took the second pack, she opened the third.

"Although, recently, it does seem to be happening more often."

He paused to look at her and then hissed when Kaydeen touched his shoulder where Tico had kicked him. He closed his eyes to get the pain under control before continuing his conversation with Salayla.

"Why?"

"We aren't sure." She ignored his reaction to Kaydeen's ministrations. "Nobody was willing to elaborate."

He looked at Tonee, who had stayed silent throughout their exchange. As usual, he leaned against the bars, blocking the view from the door.

Tonee shrugged. "We'll find out. Today was the first time we reconnected with workers. Some of them were skittish and reluctant to talk to us, which might be from something that happened with this crew, or it might be bigger. I'd like to hope for the latter as an indication of things happening topside, but until we know more, it's smoke in the wind." He looked up and around. "I guess smoke in the stale air would be more appropriate." He grinned and pushed off the bars. With Taylor refusing Salayla's Reading, there was no reason to block them from view. He walked over and settled beside them.

"If we truly have met every crew, then we'll soon find out if this sudden skittishness is more widespread."

Salayla nodded her agreement. "Now, eat." She indicated for him to finish the packet in his hand and opened the last one. "We're fully aware your food has been meager in the last few days, so stop pretending you aren't famished and dig in."

He grabbed the last pack. "I'm not starving anymore."

"Good. We plan to keep it that way."

They soon found out that other crews had lost members, too. Most workers chalked it up to normal personnel movement, although some made the connection, like the team did, that almost every removed person had either had contact with them or had been overly curious about them. Most of those workers were understandably reluctant to talk, and oftentimes tried to segregate the team from their crew. But not every crew was affected, and not everybody who was friendly or helpful disappeared. It was enough to make the teammates even more cautious.

The beatings continued, coming every few days. Sometimes, they took place in the cell, but oftentimes, the guards strung Taylor up by the cuffs they had used for the lashing. They never used the neural whip again. Taylor counted his blessings for that, but they came up with many other ways to make him scream.

As the days started to run together, Taylor lost track of how many of Tico's special treatments he'd been subjected to. Kaydeen could probably give him an exact count, with a detailed list of the wounds he had suffered during each, but it didn't matter. He would take whatever they handed him—one day at a time, one interaction at a time. The human body could take a shitload of punishment and adjust to its new normal. It was up to him to make sure his mind adjusted with it.

It took some time, and quite a few raw throats, but his training paid off, and the pain lessened, or at least his perception of it did. He was finally able to tune it out, and his lack of emotion the next time they strung him up pissed off Tico to no end. Taylor smiled.

It's the little things in life...

Tico beat him harder. He didn't care. Even the smallest victories could feel like planet-shattering conquests.

Tristan and Tico left. Taylor breathed a sigh of relief and grimaced in pain. They'd left him hanging in the cuffs, but at least this session hadn't been nearly as long as the others. His victory was short-lived, though, as the two returned soon after, released him from the cuffs, and dragged him to the far corner of the cellblock. There, they activated a new cell around him no more than ten paces square. They'd found a new torment.

Watching the other cell retract and reform as far away from

his as the large room allowed tightened his chest. He would be alone again. But he'd be damned if he'd show them what worked. He fought down the tremors and was glad his latest beating concealed their true cause.

By the time his teammates returned, he was able to play off their separation as another ploy by the guards to keep them in check. The upside of the separation was that the guards brought him a daily ration of food and water, so his teammates didn't have to provide for him any longer. The downside was the guards didn't provide him with meds or care. He downplayed his wounds and the toll the continuing torments took on his body and mind, and even got up to prove he was fine when, previously, he would have curled into a ball and kept upbeat on their situation and chances of escape. He knew they'd get out, but he wasn't sure what shape he'd be in when they did.

11

FRIENDSHIP

"Taylor."

Tonee's voice was like an annoying insect, buzzing his face again and again, each time a bit sharper and more demanding.

Taylor finally gave in.

"What?" He intended to say, but his tongue stayed stuck to the roof of his mouth. He wasn't sure what actually came out.

"When is the last time you drank water?"

From the parched feeling of his mouth and throat, it had been a while. He should probably drink some, but the bucket was across the cell, and he hadn't yet come up with the energy to cross those two meters.

"You need to stay hydrated," Tonee said.

Yeah, well, I'm working on it.

Taylor rested his forehead on the crook of his arm. He wanted to go back to sleep. Tico had visited him the day before, shortly after Tristan had been in for Taylor's daily duty to empty the waste buckets and refill the drinking buckets with fresh water and to give him his food ration. Tico had been pissed, but he hadn't beaten Taylor. No, he had decided to take charge of the weekly shower Tristan usually made Taylor take during one of his visits. But, unlike Tristan, who used the water hose in the cellblock and allowed Taylor to use soap, Tico had used the high-pressure hose in the courtyard by the lift tube—and a hydro massage it definitely hadn't been.

"Taylor!" Tonee's bark brought him back to the present. "Hydrate!"

Taylor looked at the bucket. *Yup, still hasn't moved any closer.* He lowered his head again.

"Move!"

Fine.

He did. Slowly, one limb at a time, he dragged himself toward the bucket. His body was lethargic and stiff and still aching from this newest set of bruises. What little energy he had drained like water running through sand. He wanted to pause, needed to rest, stock up energy, but every time he stopped, Tonee barked at him. So, he continued, the circles in the floor moving past at a snail's pace, until he felt the bucket.

Finally. He leaned his head against the rim. *Just a moment.*

"Drink!"

Taylor started up again. *Shit. He's not going to drop it, is he?* He pushed up onto his elbows and leaned over the bucket.

Whereas the rest of the cell smelled of dirt, piss, and blood, the inside of the bucket smelled fresh and clean. He filled the cup floating in the water and brought it to his lips. Cool, refreshing liquid flooded his mouth, unsticking his tongue in the process. He repeated the process three more times, savoring every sip, and then allowed the cup to slip from his grasp. Leaning his forehead against the opposite rim of the bucket, he waited for the water to do its magic on the rest of his body. With the water so close to his nostrils, filtering the air, he could almost imagine himself in a different, better, place.

"You trying to drown yourself?"

Tonee's humor edged out some of the worried urgency in his voice. *There he is.* Taylor smiled and closed his eyes.

TONEE SAT on a boulder beside him. His booted feet dangled in the pool of water in front of them, but it was clear that he wasn't happy with the prospect of making his way through the underwater obstacle course the trainers had set up in the simulated pond.

"Drown myself?" Kaydeen replied. She'd just finished her leg of the obstacle course relay on their training schedule that day. "You realize I'm floating, right?"

"Yeah, but you keep sticking your head under water."

"Tonee," Kaydeen laughed, "I'm using a rebreather."

"So? Your face still gets wet."

Taylor had been following Salayla's progress through the course and had been barely listening to their exchange, but Tonee's comment turned his head.

"What does a wet face have to do with drowning?"

Tonee shrugged. "Sounded good."

"No, it didn't." Taylor frowned.

"Yeah." Tonee grinned. "But it made you come out of your 'win all or die' mode. This *is* only a practice session, you know."

"So, I'm not supposed to take it seriously?"

"Nah, but not to this life and death stress level you keep taking it to."

"I'm not stressed."

"Of course not. You're shoving that off onto everybody else."

"You're not stressed, either."

"That's beside the point." Tonee wrinkled his forehead. "But it would be nice, every once in a while, to do something other than study and train. That's all we do, even in our free time, as if that's all our life revolves around—training and learning."

"It does. We're at the Academy."

Tonee shook his head. "Don't confuse me with facts."

The seriousness with which Tonee delivered those words brought Taylor up short. Tonee held his gaze.

"We've been together for two months now." Tonee traced a circle with his palm facing his chest. "And you don't even know how to read this." His expression stayed serious as he shook his head then threw up his arms. "Dude, you don't know me, and I don't know you."

"I got that. What do you want? Handholding sessions where we shell out our deepest secrets to each other?"

"It'd be a start." Tonee shrugged. "But I'd be happy with you loosening up a little. We've been working hard—busting our asses, more like it—and I think we—" he indicated himself, Kaydeen, and Salayla, who was about halfway through the course "—have done enough to prove we're worth trusting." He held Taylor's gaze while he paused. "So, why don't you?"

"I do."

"With the missions, training, and teamwork, yes, but not with yourself. Open up. Let us in. Stop guarding every fucking word and action. I need to be able to tell if what you're saying is truly what you mean. I need to be able to read you. Right now, I can't, like you can't read me, because you keep yourself shut away and protected. That hurts both of us, and our team's performance."

"Okay, so what do you want me to do?"

Tonee stared at him, then scrunched up his face and looked at Kaydeen, who was climbing out of the water on his other side. "Isn't that what I just told him?" He turned back to Taylor. "Are you really that dense?"

"No." Taylor glanced at the water. "Unlike you, I can actually float."

Tonee stared at him. "You made a joke." His face broke into

a grin. "And a good one at that." He punched Taylor on the shoulder.

"Who says I was joking?"

"Aw, dude, come on, my hopes for you were starting to rise." He shook his head. "Why'd you have to shoot them down like that?"

Taylor chuckled.

"Kaydeen," Tonee deadpanned, "get a medic."

Taylor looked up in alarm, searching for Salayla in the water. She was fine.

"He cracked his face with a smile," Tonee continued.

Taylor closed his eyes and drew a deep breath before looking back at Tonee, who was grinning widely. Behind him, Kaydeen shook her head.

"You know," she said, "he has a point." She looked back and forth between them. "Both of you." She looked at Taylor. "While I don't think it's hurting our performance too much, it would make things easier if you'd allow us to get to know you a little more, to see through your defenses. Not everybody is as good at reading people as Salayla and I." She eyed Tonee as if indicating a handicap. "Some people need more visual clues."

"Hey," Tonee protested.

"But Taylor is right, too." She ignored Tonee's scowl. "You don't float because you tighten your muscles too much. You're not afraid of the water, and you swim as well as anybody here, even better than some, so it shouldn't take much to learn to relax enough to float. Our bodies are mostly made up of water, so it could be considered a natural habitat for us."

"If water was supposed to be my natural habitat, I'd have gills."

"I don't understand your aversion to water."

"Blame my parents. It's their fault I grew up as an Intergal brat."

"What's that got to do with it?"

"Their duty stations were exclusively space-based, so I spent time dirtside in nature only during family leave or on visits with my grandparents."

"Most space stations and large carriers have real and virtual water features for recreational and training use."

"Hey, stop using facts to confuse my truth."

"TAYLOR!" The concern had edged its way back into Tonee's voice. "Get your face out of the fucking bucket." His cursing had picked up over the last three years, but at least he'd stopped calling Taylor 'dude.'

Ah well, it was good while it lasted.

Taylor took one more, long whiff of the clean water, dismissed the memory it and Tonee's words had invoked, then rolled onto his back. He still felt sore, but at least the cobwebs had lifted from his brain. He stared at the ceiling, resuming his habit of counting its holes, and listened as Tonee tried unsuccessfully to settle himself into a comfortable sitting position. His breath was ragged and shallow and accompanied by the occasional grunt.

"What happened?"

The movement cut out, but Tonee's breathing stayed shallow. "You were dehydrated and nearly drowned yourself in the bucket."

That's not what I'm asking about, and you know it. But Taylor allowed him the deflection.

"I can see your obituary now: Mark Taylor, top graduate of SF Class 7.68.174, drowned during his first mission while attempting to drink from a bucket." Tonee's snicker was cut short by a sharp intake of air.

Taylor continued to wait.

"I bruised my side a little," Tonee finally relented. "It's no big deal."

"I'd say that's more than a little bruise."

"How would you know?"

"You're favoring your side, breathing shallow, and holding your breath whenever you move your torso."

"You haven't even looked over here."

"Don't have to. Your mass displacing the air generates enough sound waves to not need a visual."

"In other words, my fat ass is making too much noise."

The one thing your body mass does not consist of is fat. And you'd be the first one to graphically point that out to anybody claiming otherwise.

"I would've said that my hearing is that good, but fat ass works, too." Taylor grinned, waiting for the rebuttal. It never came.

"How bad is it?"

"A couple of bruised ribs and a cut across my side."

"What happened?"

"A miner tripped in front of one of the automated hoppers. I pulled him out of the way but didn't move fast enough to avoid a piece of ore sticking over the rim. We ended up at the bottom of a waste rock dump."

"Any cracked ribs?"

Tonee stayed silent.

"Tonee, if it truly was nothing, you wouldn't be sitting here talking to me. You'd be below, working."

Tonee sighed. "No, no cracked ribs, but the ore sliced me open pretty good, and the tumble ground dirt and tailings into the cut. I lucked out, though. The miner broke his leg and cracked his head open on a boulder."

"Did they treat you?"

"Yeah, they cleaned the cut and sealed it. They also scanned me for internal damage, which came up clean, so no broken ribs. I'm off the labor rotation for two days to make sure the seal takes."

They fell silent, each disappearing into their separate thoughts.

"How are you holding up?" Tonee broke the silence a few minutes later.

Taylor stopped himself from giving his reflexive answer. That wasn't fair to Tonee—he wanted to know the uncolored truth, the same as Taylor had.

"I'm sore and stiff, but all right. Haven't received a beating in a while."

"Then what are you sore from?"

"Got a shower yesterday from a high-pressure hose."

"Shit. I'd call that a beating, too."

"It wasn't too bad. I've had worse. Tico is merely trying to get to me. Guess he's still pissed that I broke his hand."

"So, how are you holding up in that department?"

"In what department?"

"Yeah, you know—mentally, emotionally. And don't say this shit's not affecting you."

"Okay, I won't."

"You won't what?"

"Tell you this shit's not affecting me."

"Are you saying it isn't?"

"Is this a trick question or something? You told me not to tell you that." Taylor smiled. Usually, it was Tonee who led the conversation in circles. Unless, of course, he was trying to be serious—like now.

Tonee harrumphed, clearly aware that Taylor was using Tonee's tactics against him.

"You know we're going to get out of here." Taylor didn't like the direction Tonee's thoughts seemed to keep wandering.

"That's what you keep saying."

"Because it's the truth."

"Yeah?" Tonee's voice turned incredulous. "When? And how? We've been here for weeks, if not months, and haven't come any closer to an escape plan." He paused in frustration. "We haven't even been able to determine what's going on out there or what happened to the Fleet."

"We haven't been handed over to the Traverse," Taylor soothed.

"No? Then what do you call this shithole?"

"I don't know." Taylor kept his voice level and low but resolute. "But it's not Traverse."

He felt Tonee's gaze on him.

"What makes you say that?" Tonee's voice had lowered a few octaves. Good.

"Well." Taylor looked at his friend. "We haven't seen any Traverse soldiers, nor have we been interrogated." He paused. "Have you gotten any closer to figuring out how long we've been here?"

"117 work and sleep cycles, by Kaydeen's count, though we're still not sure how long a cycle is. A Tinareean day is slightly shorter than nineteen standard hours and divided into twenty-five hours, which makes a Tinareean hour a little over forty-five standard minutes long. From what we've gathered, workers are expected to put out ten hours of labor a day, but with the different breaks, we haven't been able to figure out how long each shift is. We can't ask straight out, so it's hard—"

"Why not?" Taylor interrupted him.

"Because Tristan made it clear that if our presence raises so much as an eyebrow, he'd allow Tico unrestricted access to you."

"Unrestricted? Are you saying he's restricted right now?"

"Tristan told him straight out that he couldn't use the whip again, and it seems he's also keeping him from doing other things Tico has come up with." Tonee paused. "That bastard wants to break you," he continued quietly. "He's even gloated that by the time he's done, you'll drop your pants at the sight of him and beg him to fuck you."

"Did he."

"Those were his words."

"Why haven't you told me?"

"What good would it have done?"

True, but it would've still been nice to know. "He's not going to break me."

"Yeah, I know." Tonee's voice lacked conviction. "But I'd prefer he not get the opportunity to put effort into it. Not with all the shit he's already doing to you."

As would I, my friend. "I'll be fine," Taylor deflected. "I know you guys have my back."

Tonee snorted. "How can we have your back when we're down below while you're up here?"

"Exactly as you are. We're still a team, pieces of the whole, each with a specific role. Mine is up here, keeping Tico's attention. Yours is down below, collecting intel. We keep at it; we'll beat them and get out of here."

Taylor felt like one of their trainers giving an overblown pep talk. From Tonee's huff, he sounded like it, too.

"We are each excellent at what we do. As long as we work together, we're unbeatable. We both know that."

"Yeah," Tonee scoffed, "at the Academy, where the worst we had to face was a bad-tempered trainer with a grudge while completing controlled challenges that had been run so many times, the trainers had the risks and possible damage of every step and kink memorized."

"And they gave us all the skills we need," Taylor rebutted. "We simply have to translate them into the here and now." He paused to let his words sink in. "I'm a scout. As such, I'm not supposed to be with you, but out finding the way and clearing your path. That's exactly what I'm doing. The more Tico focuses on me, the less Tristan can focus on you guys, allowing you to find and do what you need to get us out of here."

He met Tonee's gaze.

"No one ever said this job was going to be easy or without sacrifice. I'm fine with that. I know you'll pull me out on the other side. You always do."

Tonee looked at him sharply.

Oh, come on, big guy, do I have to map it out for you?

"You're our powerhouse, Tonee. You drive us through whatever comes." Taylor couldn't believe Tonee had never realized that. "I only point the way. You're the one who gets us there."

Tonee stared at his folded hands and rubbed his thumbs across each other. "What if, by the time we find the right intel, you're unable to work it?"

"You don't need me to work it. You have the best two minds with you."

"What if he breaks you?"

Damn it, Tonee, get out of that fricking dump of despondency. But Taylor knew that was what had been on Tonee's mind all along. It had taken this roundabout conversation for him to put it into words. It was a fear that would paralyze his confidence if he allowed it to run wild.

"Then you fix me."

"How?"

"You'll know."

"What the hell is that supposed to mean?"

"Exactly what it sounded like."

"There you go again, going all cryptic on me." Tonee threw up his hands.

"Telling you that I trust your instincts is cryptic?"

"No, being vague and mysterious is. Like a Seer."

"I'm not a Seer. I can't see the future. I only have a knack for picking the right direction and timing."

"Yeah, but you sure as hell sound like one. I'm your drive."

He snorted. "And what, Sal keeps us stocked and balanced, and Kay makes us whole?"

"That's not what I said." *Though it does sound right.*

"Close enough. The gist is that it leaves you in the shithole."

"Well, deal with it," Taylor replied, a little sharper than he intended. "I am."

Tonee fell silent.

An image of a kicked puppy came to Taylor's mind. He looked over at his friend to verify his words hadn't done what his mind had imagined. Tonee stared into space, lost in thought. He didn't like hearing the truth of their situation, but he would deal with it. A few moments later, he returned to the present and met Taylor's gaze. Yes, he would deal with it, and he would do his damnedest to ensure they all came out the other end—Taylor didn't expect anything less.

12

VISITOR

Voices intruded into his dark oblivion and pierced his mind like daggers. Sick and nauseated, his stomach churning and burning as if acid ate through its walls, he slowly became aware of his surroundings. And with it came the pains and aches the beatings had left behind, although he could handle those much better than the chemicals eating his insides. His hope that the voices were in his imagination and would disappear again didn't hold out.

"He picked himself the day we pulled him out of iso." The voice belonged to Tristan, the younger and less volatile of their two guards. Not too long ago, his words would have caused Taylor to pay close attention. But now, Taylor was too preoccupied with the sensory input from his nerves to puzzle through something that didn't cause him pain.

He wasn't sure how long he'd been lying like this, sprawled on his back, right arm flung wide, left twisted under his back. From the lack of feeling in his left arm, it had been quite a while. He vaguely remembered hearing the guards come for Tonee, Kay, and Sal, so it had been all night and at least part of the next day. At least, he hoped this was still the next day and not two or more days later—that would be unhealthy for his arm. Not that this place was healthy for any part of his body.

"How so?"

The low rumble of the second voice was vaguely familiar, but Taylor couldn't pinpoint its owner. He was sure it didn't belong to Tico, the reason he was in so much pain again. He couldn't even remember what Tico had punished him for this time. Not that it mattered—Tico hadn't needed a reason, lately.

"He was the last one up, and when we pulled him out of the lift, he jerked back so fast Ticos' fingers got caught."

"Jerked back?"

"From the light, of course," Tristan answered. "After their time in total darkness, the light hurts their eyes. We use it to show 'em who's in charge. We bring 'em up and pull 'em into the light. They jerk back, we rough 'em up, they get the picture, and that's it." Tristan paused. "They all jerk back. Even his three buds did, but I've never seen anybody move as damn fast as he did.

"He pulled right out of my grip. Tico had him by the collar. His hand got caught in it, and it pulled him right off his feet. Tico was so pissed, he didn't even realize his fingers were broken until after he had beaten him into a bloody pulp."

"Did he fight back?"

A picture finally rose to Taylor's mind. Rumpled uniform, olive skin, light colored hair—a rough-looking man who was so much more than he pretended to be: Juvak.

JUVAK FOLLOWED Tristan into the cellblock. With its retractable bars forming only two cells, it looked mostly empty. The larger cell, in the room's front right corner, was unoccupied and open. The smaller one in the far-left corner was not.

"That would've been the day." Tristan snorted. "I don't think he would've survived if he had."

"You'd be surprised."

"No, I'm telling you, Tico would've killed him, no matter what you, the Boss, or anybody else would've said or done. I've never seen him so pissed. I could barely stop him. By the time I did, he couldn't move. After I cleaned him up, I had to help him to the cell." Tristan looked at the empty cell. "His three friends were all over him. You should've seen it. The big guy even cradled him in his arms like a baby." Tristan shook his head with a snort. "That's what decided it. That, and the fact that he was already injured. It would've been stupid to pick one of the others and then have two workers out."

He looked back at Juvak, who had stopped to look at the cable hanging from the ceiling, and followed his gaze to the dark stains below, but didn't offer an explanation. When Juvak continued to walk, Tristan stepped back—a little too fast—keeping his distance at two arm lengths.

Juvak ignored him.

"So, Tico is still holding a grudge." Juvak approached the small cell and studied Taylor.

"Tico's got a grudge all right, and a big one at that. He wants to break him so badly, *I* can taste it."

"He won't."

"I wouldn't be so sure." Tristan shook his head and walked to the control panel by the door.

"So, you let him play with drugs?"

"Not real drugs." Tristan punched the necessary keys to open the cell. "Just dryroot."

A section of cell bars, wide enough to give easy access, retracted into the floor. Tristan looked back up, but, seeing Juvak's gaze boring into him, showed no inclination of approaching. Juvak held his gaze a moment longer, then walked into the cell.

"How much of the root did Tico give him?" Juvak asked as he leaned over Taylor.

"It wasn't just the root." Tristan inched forward but stopped a few paces from the cell. "It was a mix of all three parts of the plant." His words quickened when Juvak's back stiffened, "The flower's healing properties neutralize the stem's poison. Together they enhance the root's psychedelic effect, that's all. It's just a new twist on an old drug."

"A new twist that increases the potency of the drug and the possibility of killing a first-time user."

"Not locals. They just have a bad ride."

"Just because he's lived here before doesn't mean his body is still used to the local flavors."

Tristan flinched at Juvak's sharp words and raised his hands as if ready to ward off a blow, but Juvak ignored him. Instead, he leaned closer to Taylor's face.

"Not today, kid," he whispered. "Too many people have given their lives for you to give up now."

He straightened, pulled out a med scanner, and scanned Taylor from head to toe. After reading the data, he put the scanner away and rolled Taylor onto his side.

"Hold him."

Following Juvak's instructions, Tristan knelt and held Taylor from behind, keeping his upper body leaning over the floor.

"What are you doing?"

Standing in a half crouch, Juvak grabbed Taylor by the jaw, jammed his forefinger and thumb into his cheeks, and forced his mouth open.

"Emptying his stomach," Juvak answered as he shoved his fingers into Taylor's mouth.

Limp and unresponsive until now, Taylor's eyes flew open, his knee shot into Juvak's side, and he grabbed for Juvak's wrists, almost breaking Tristan's hold in the process. Juvak took the blow with a grunt, tightened his grip, and shoved his fingers deeper. Taylor gagged. Juvak held him a moment longer before releasing him and stepping out of the way of Taylor's stomach contents splashing onto the floor.

As soon as Taylor stopped heaving, Juvak grabbed his face again and repeated the procedure. He continued until Taylor vomited only bile.

"I think he's done," Tristan said as he held Taylor's trembling body over the latest puddle.

Taylor's last few heaves had come up dry, a good indication that this round was over. Preparing for a new round, Tristan tightened his grip and was astounded to feel the other man's muscles tense again. It wasn't much and would've been laughable had they not known how depleted Taylor's strength had already been when they'd started half an hour ago.

"Can we stop now? His stomach is obviously empty, been empty for a while now."

Juvak smiled. "Why? Don't you enjoy this?"

"No." Tristan looked at Taylor before meeting Juvak's gaze again. "I commed you to save his life."

"No," Juvak scoffed, "you commed me because you were afraid of what might happen to you if he died." Tristan averted his gaze as Juvak paused. "You were fine with whatever Tico did, as long as it didn't affect your health or your paycheck." Juvak's voice cooled multiple decrees. "And as soon as it looked like it might, you came running."

Tristan's head snapped up. "As you said, the drugs could've killed him."

"That's debatable." Juvak shrugged and pushed off the cell bars he'd been leaning against. "Pull him back."

He motioned with his hand until Tristan had pulled Taylor multiple arms' length from the mess on the floor.

Tristan started to lay Taylor on the floor, but seeing Juvak shake his head, pulled him into a sitting position against his knee. Juvak forced Taylor's mouth open again and jammed a thumbnail-sized pellet down his throat. Taylor struggled and tried to spit it out, but Juvak leaned on him and clamped his mouth and nose shut.

"Swallow if you want to breathe," he whispered as he stared into Taylor's widening eyes. Taylor made a couple more, feeble attempts to get free, but to no avail.

When he was sure Taylor had swallowed the pill, Juvak released his grip and met Tristan's gaze.

"Go clean up."

Juvak took Taylor's limp form from Tristan and motioned with his head at the mess on the floor. Tristan nodded and stood.

Juvak propped Taylor against the wall and pulled the water bucket over.

"Your mother would be very disappointed to see you give up like that." He pulled a vial out of his pocket and added its contents to the water, stirring it in with a finger. "She trained you better than that." He filled the cup floating in the water and lifted it to Taylor's mouth, slowly feeding him the water a sip at a time. "We all did."

Taylor grabbed the cup with both hands to stop its progression and looked at him, brows furrowed.

Juvak studied him for a moment then refilled the cup.

"Drink. It'll help you get stronger."

Taylor grabbed the cup again but didn't stop its movement.

"You really don't remember me, do you?" It was a musing more than a question. "Maybe it's better that way."

After Taylor emptied the second cup, Juvak dropped it back into the bucket and turned to Tristan.

"He needs to stay warm. Turn on the heat in the corner."

Tristan looked at him in surprise. "There's no..." He started to argue but stopped. Shoulders slumped, he walked to the smaller of the two doors and entered the cellblock's control room.

Juvak turned back to Taylor. "It's almost over. Draw on your training and your instinct, and you'll get through this without a problem." He paused. "And remember, if you don't make it, neither will your friends. You're the only reason they're still alive."

A whistling of air drew Juvak's attention to the corner of the cell. He stood and walked over. Feeling the floor with one hand, he used the other to signal Tristan. The whistle quieted. Satisfied, Juvak came back and helped Taylor move into the corner. Warm air flowed out of the gaps around the bars sunk into the floor, warming an area that was barely large enough to curl up in. Juvak set the bucket of water next to him and then walked out. Tristan joined him at the door. Within moments, Taylor was alone again.

TAYLOR DIDN'T KNOW what to make of Juvak. The man had captured them, then sold them as forced labor, and now, he pretended to be his benefactor. His surprise that Taylor didn't recognize him had seemed genuine, and he hadn't been talking about their encounters since the crash. Tristan's fear of him had also been genuine. Juvak hadn't threatened him, verbally or physically, yet Tristan had flinched from him. It was a side of Tristan that Taylor had never seen. He wondered if Juvak had the same effect on Tico.

The burning in his stomach subsided, and the fog in his head lifted. He considered Juvak's and Tristan's words about the drug and his locality. It made no sense. He wasn't from here, had never lived or visited here—at least, not that he remembered. His mom's job had moved them to a new location every few months, and being spaceborn, he didn't consider any one place home or himself a native of a specific planet. And how would Juvak know, anyway? A bluff then, to hide that he and his team were Intergal? That would explain why they hadn't been handed over to the Traverse, but to what purpose?

And Juvak's promise of freedom?

Taylor had sensed, and believed, its sincerity and from the fear the man had generated in Tristan, he likely had the power to fulfill his promise. They needed to lay low and keep the guards off his back, so he could heal and regain the strength Juvak had hinted he would soon need.

But how could he explain this to his teammates? Throughout their training, he had oftentimes seen their confusion and inability to understand the reasons for his actions, but they had come to trust his hunches. Lately, though, their trust had been overshadowed with concern about his mental and physical health.

Juvak was the enemy. Anything he said to dispute that now would bring up those doubts. And neither Din would be able to verify that he wasn't suffering a mental breakdown.

He owed them an explanation, one he couldn't give at this distance without giving himself away to the guards. As the warm air and his exhaustion pulled him into sleep, he resolved to give the guards what they wanted. It would devastate his teammates, but he would finally be able to get them out of this hellhole. He fell asleep, amazed by how nice it felt to not be chilled. He knew that, with time, he'd recover.

13

FREEDOM

A low rumble in the distance startled Tonee awake before dawn. At least, he thought it was before dawn. Kept inside the cellblock or underground, he hadn't been outside since their squad's ship had crashed and only assumed their work shift started in the morning.

Kaydeen and Salayla had moved closer to him sometime during the night and were using his arm and shoulder as pillows. Less than a year ago, he would've been ecstatic to wake with two girls in his arms. Now, he wondered how long it would take to get circulation back as he carefully untangled himself and stood.

He massaged his shoulders as he moved to the metal bars separating them from the rest of the dimly lit cellblock. Even the dark couldn't hide the bleakness of his surroundings. Gray on gray—the bars, walls, ceiling, floor, and door—everything was made of the same material and color. The only thing breaking up the monotony were the retractable bars outlining the two cells and the circular seams hinting at hundreds of bars still sunk into the floor, able to raise and lower at the guard's whim to adjust the cell block's layout or to torture its captives.

It took him only a moment to locate Taylor. As had become the norm, he was lying curled up facing the far corner of his cell. Tonee didn't try to rouse him. He knew Taylor wouldn't respond. He hadn't responded since the guards had pulled him and Kaydeen out of their cells one night. When the guards had returned them, hours later, Taylor hadn't been able to walk. Dumped into his cell, he lay where he'd fallen.

Kaydeen had been quiet and withdrawn. Staring at Taylor, she had refused to talk about what had happened and had refused to let Salayla Read her. After a while, they'd finally been able to get her to lie down and fall asleep in Salayla's arms.

Kaydeen had felt better the next morning, though she still refused to say what had happened. Taylor, on the other hand, had been the same as the night before. At first, Tonee had thought that Taylor might be in too much pain to move—or possibly unconscious—and was glad when the guards had left him alone, hoping a full day's rest would help him recover. His hopes were dashed when Taylor had remained unresponsive that evening, and even more so when he'd ignored the guards' arrival the following morning.

It had been the same ever since. Curled in his corner when left alone, Taylor only moved when the guards ordered him to. Every so often, they had been able to elicit a reaction or gotten Taylor to drink water, but even then, it had taken repeated barked orders, and Taylor never acknowledged them, only crawled to the bucket and took a few sips of water. But lately, not even that worked.

Tonee lowered his head against the bars and closed his eyes. He didn't want to consider what Taylor's behavior signified.

Taylor had been their rock, had held steadfast in his belief that Intergal would return, and they would get out, had refused to let them give up hope, and now...

Another rumble interrupted Tonee's thoughts. It sent a shiver down his spine and his heart on a beating frenzy as if it were trying to jump out of his chest.

Suddenly, he was nine again. Standing with Grammy at the window, gazing at the city center with its high-rises all lit up and sparkling their nightly light show as lights in offices and condos turned on and off. Playing their bedtime game of finding as many shapes as possible in the continuously changing light combinations and wondering what the strange distant rumble was that sounded so much like thunder but totally different. Seeing Grammy's hand go to her mouth and her eyes and mouth open wide in horror when the sky suddenly lit up with bright oranges, yellows, and reds. Hearing Papaw scream to get to shelter just as part of the city center exploded into a huge fireball. He'd been in the stairwell when the house shattered with a roar and was the only one that day who survived a direct hit in the bombardment of his grandparents' home planet.

When the noise stopped, Tonee turned with a start. "Kaydeen, Salayla, get up." Seeing both move, he turned back. "Taylor, even if you only hear me this once, please—you need to get on your feet and out of that corner, away from the walls."

Salayla and Kaydeen came up beside him. "What do you know?"

"You hear the rumbling? Somebody's hitting this place from above, way above." He paused to let his words sink in. "And the Traverse wouldn't bomb a planet they're already holding, would they? No. It's gotta be our guys. Now, all we have to do is survive the damage they're going to do to this place."

Salayla raised her eyebrows, "Is that all?"

A deafening roar drowned out the rest of her words. The floor shook and, for a moment, Tonee envisioned ordnance hitting the mineshaft. How far would the explosion spread? To a tunnel, a level of tunnels, two levels, all levels? He didn't know. He knew explosives, had trained in them. He knew how to take out a vehicle, a building, even collapse a tunnel, but he had no idea what the munitions designed to destroy surface installations from orbit would do to this network of mining tunnels. He didn't even know if there were tunnels below them, or if there were, how far below they were.

Air pressure popped his ears. A new threat, a new rumble, this one more felt than heard. From below. The tunnels? No, much closer. He felt the vibration. But not from the trembling ground. This was much smaller, faster. The bars. The metal bars in the floor were vibrating and hot. The heat burned through the soles of his worn boots. A blast of hot air suddenly erupted from around the bars, pushing up his legs, his body, and past his face, as if somebody had opened the door to a furnace under pressure and released a fiery hot wind, shriveling the hair on his skin.

He realized two things the instant it was over: he was unharmed, and he was crouching halfway across the cell from where he had been, facing in the opposite direction. Salayla gasped behind him. He spun around and, barely noticing the rubble on the floor, made his way back to her and Kaydeen. The dense cloud of dust hanging in the air scratched his throat and stung his eyes, but it did nothing to hide the pile of rubble filling the far corner of the cellblock, right where Taylor had lain.

He inhaled sharply. Dust covered his mouth and throat instantly. He coughed, hard, but every new inhalation brought in more grit. He bowed over, then went to his knees, eyes tearing up. He tried to swallow, spit out the crud, but he couldn't find enough saliva to unstick his tongue from the roof of his mouth.

Damn, he hadn't survived this hellhole only to suffocate from the side effect of his escape route.

A hand covered with a wet cloth landed on his face.

"Slow down."

Kaydeen knelt beside him and wiped his face then repositioned the cloth and covered his nose and mouth with a clean section.

The moist, dust-free air entering Tonee's lungs was bliss. He inhaled deeply.

"Better?"

Tonee cleared his throat and spit out a gob of gunk before answering her. "Much."

He looked up, first at her face, then her chest, then at the cloth in his hand, and finally back at her face.

"Good."

She grinned, grabbed her shirt from his grasp, and pulled it over her head.

He got to his feet and scrutinized the pile of rubble. He couldn't see any sign of Taylor. Maybe he'd gotten out. The hole the collapsed wall had left behind was big enough for him to fit through. But wouldn't he have said something? Told them where he was heading? No, not in the state of mind he'd been in. He probably panicked and ran. They needed to get out and catch up with him before he came across guards or Traverse and got himself killed.

Tonee looked around for a way to escape. The bars were still solid, but the quake had opened a hole in the ceiling. It was too small for him or Kaydeen, but Salayla's tiny frame might be able to squeeze through. He helped her climb onto his shoulders then steadied her to test the fit. Sharp metal edges pushed at her from all directions. She twisted and turned to get around the worst of them without cutting herself to pieces. He slowly lifted her higher, supporting her feet with his hands until she was able to pull herself through. She disappeared. A moment later, her face looked through the hole. He couldn't believe she'd been able to fit through it.

"I'm in a cavity between the ceiling and the roof. The roof is still solid, but I see light from below that might be outside the cellblock. Sit tight."

"Actually, I was thinking of going to get a cup of coffee. Meet you over there."

Her face had already disappeared, but it returned. "Very funny."

He spread his hands and looked up at her. She shook her head with a smile and was gone again.

"A coffee sounds like heaven," Kaydeen mumbled by his side.

He looked down at her. "I'll get right on it."

"Don't make any promises you can't keep, big boy."

It didn't take long for Salayla to return. The door into the cellblock opened a crack, then a little more, and finally far enough for her to step through. She put her back against one side and her feet against the other and pushed it open until a large piece of rubble that had been leaning against the outside of the door fell in to block it from closing. She jumped out of the way and turned to the control panel. It was dead. She went through the smaller door into the control room and operated some levers. The hissing release of air pressure sounded, and the bars retracted, not under power, but by gravity. They stopped at different heights, but multiple were low enough for Tonee and Kaydeen to squeeze through.

They met Salayla by the door.

"I came down in a hallway running behind the cellblock." She pointed to the hole in Taylor's cell. "It seems to run along a battery of cellblocks. Taylor was about halfway down. He acknowledged me and signaled for us to follow but didn't stop to wait."

At Kaydeen's inquiring gaze, she added, "He seemed fine. At least, he was moving like his old self."

They made their way through the door into the intersecting antechamber. The door across led to an interior courtyard and the lift tube they'd been taking to the mine tunnels. The door to the right was locked. They went through the left door into a crossing hallway. To the right, the passage went straight for some distance and then turned right. No other turnoffs or doors were visible. Salayla led them left. Following the passage around their cellblock, they came to the breached wall of Taylor's cell. Salayla pointed down the continuing hallway. Intersections branched off at regular intervals, and the dust on the floor indicated it hadn't been used in quite some time. A single track of boot prints led to an open door at the end, which was presumably where Taylor had gone. They made their way down the hall, slowing at each intersection to verify that the connecting passages were clear of threats. The doors at the end of each were locked. The place was deserted.

The open door led to another, smaller hallway, not as industrial—more like an office building than a warehouse. No dust here. Tonee checked the hinged door. It had no signs of tampering, so it had been unlocked. This seemed too easy, as if somebody was leading them along. He looked at Salayla and Kaydeen. Kaydeen cocked her head at him.

'Too easy?' he signed.

They both agreed.

THEY PROCEEDED WITH CAUTION, checking every door and clearing every room. It slowed their progress significantly, but it had the advantage that they would flush Taylor out if he had gone to ground.

The first few rooms were quarters—three rooms with three double bunks each, a community bathroom, and a kitchen/lounge combo. Then came three more rooms with two bunks each. The rooms were empty of people and personal gear but had clearly been lived in. They moved on. They passed a couple of quarters set up as apartments, with a kitchen/lounge combo branching off into a bedroom and a bathroom. It looked like they were moving up in rank. These were also abandoned. Next came storage rooms and, as the hallway wound around some corners, offices. The door to the second office was open, with noises floating out.

Tonee pushed himself against the wall and glanced around the doorframe. Shelves lined the walls to the right and left, and a large desk took up the far half of the room, with slightly taller cabinets on each side. A large chair was pushed back behind it, and two smaller chairs were neatly lined up in front of it. Taylor's head popped up from behind the desk.

"About time." He jumped to his feet, grinning broadly. "You ready to get rid of your neck jewelry?" He displayed a remote in his hand as he bounced around the cabinet beside the desk. Salayla and Kaydeen slipped past Tonee through the door. Tonee stopped three steps into the room.

"What the hell, Taylor?" Tonee stared as Taylor bounced from Kaydeen to Salayla, removing their collars.

Taylor seemed fine, other than acting like a toddler on three energy bars who'd just found candy land. Taylor dropped Salayla's collar and bounded toward Tonee.

Tonee backed up, raising his hands. "What happened to you?"

Taylor sidestepped and tried to skirt him, but Tonee turned with him. After a full rotation of Taylor dancing around him, Tonee finally had enough and grabbed him by the shoulders.

"Stop."

He wanted to shake him to get some sense back into him, but that would probably encourage his fidgeting. Instead, he held him in place.

Taylor finally paused and looked at him, the energy draining from his body as if he had sprung a leak. He lowered his gaze and handed the remote to Kaydeen, who proceeded to remove his collar and then moved behind Tonee to do the same. When Taylor looked back up, Tonee could nearly taste the exhaustion in his friend's eyes. Taylor looked like he was standing through sheer willpower. Tonee's angry flare-up over what Taylor's behavior and refusal to communicate had done to them evaporated.

Tonee crushed him against his chest. "I thought we lost you."

Taylor stood stiffly, mumbling something about protecting the team.

Kaydeen slipped the collar off Tonee's neck and thumped the back of his head. Tonee looked up at Salayla's moving hands.

'Cease and desist,' she signaled. 'Later.'

Tonee's chest tightened. This wasn't the time or place to get emotional. And this definitely wasn't the time to throw Taylor for another loop.

Taylor's behavior was out of character. So what? If that's what it took to function, then they would work with it.

Tonee pushed Taylor to arms' length, but before he could say anything, footsteps sounded from the hallway.

Taylor slipped out of Tonee's grasp and past him to the door. Back to business—calm and collected, without an inkling of exhaustion showing—he signaled them to hide and be ready. It was scary how quickly he snapped back and forth, but this wasn't the time to ponder the implications of Taylor's behavior.

Tonee took a position behind Taylor.

Somebody approached the room carefully but carelessly loudly. It sounded like only one person or whoever was accompanying them was much better at concealing their presence.

Taylor shot out the door. A surprised yelp, a tumble of bodies, and a figure with hiking boots, dark trousers, and a white shirt landed in the middle of the room. Tonee slipped into the hallway, going right. Kaydeen, right behind him, split off in the opposite direction.

"No, no, no, I'm here to help!" The Tinareean-speaking voice coming from the room cracked, slipping multiple octaves.

Finding the hallway clear, Tonee returned to the room. Kaydeen met him at the door, signaling 'all clear.'

A boy lay on his back in the middle of the room, blond, shoulder-length hair in disarray and fear written over his dirt-streaked face. Taylor crouched next to him, studying him with a tilted head. Salayla stood off to the side, allowing Taylor to take the lead but ready to jump in if needed. The boy couldn't have been older than fourteen or fifteen. He had pushed himself into a half-sitting position, leaning on one hand while warding Taylor off with the other.

"I'm a friend," he stuttered, "not your enemy." Seeing no further aggressive moves, he relaxed. "I was looking for you, trying to get you out." He talked slowly, forming the words carefully as if he wasn't sure they understood him.

"Trying to get us out?" Kaydeen repeated.

"Yeah." He perked up at Kaydeen's accent-free reply. "After they left yesterday, I figured it was safe to go looking for you. I couldn't get in until now."

"They?"

"The miners and the Traverse," he clarified. "They all left yesterday."

"So, how did you know we were in here?" Salayla asked, also in perfect Tinareean, perking up the boy even further and speeding up his speech.

"I didn't see you come out when they loaded everybody in the transports."

"And you knew to look for us, why?" Tonee asked. His accent was heavier, but he'd had enough time in the mines to become fluent enough to hold a conversation.

"You were in the transport when they brought us here,"

Taylor interrupted the questioning. His accent wasn't quite as heavy as Tonee's, but he wasn't as fluent. Tonee wondered where and with whom he'd had the opportunity to practice.

The boy looked at him. "Yeah." He dropped his head. "I couldn't help you, though..."

"We noticed," Tonee commented.

Salayla shot him a look. Tonee shrugged.

Taylor grabbed the boy's wrist and pulled him to his feet.

"What's your name?"

"Mica."

"So, how do we get out, Mica?"

"The way I came in." His face lit up. "And we need to hurry, before they level this place." He started for the door.

"Who?" Taylor called after him.

Mica stopped and turned around. "Intergal, of course. They're leveling all Traverse strongholds before setting down this time." He waved them on impatiently. "And this place is on that list."

Tonee and Taylor exchanged glances. The boy obviously had more information than he had divulged so far.

Taylor motioned for Mica to show the way and then nodded at Kaydeen and Salayla. Tonee was about to follow them out the door when he realized Taylor had turned back to the desk. He stopped.

"You're going the wrong way," Tonee said, switching back to Trade. Since he was addressing Taylor alone, there was no reason to continue speaking a language neither of them had fully mastered yet.

"I'll be right there. Go ahead."

"I'm not leaving you behind."

Taylor stopped rummaging through the drawers and looked up. "I'll catch up."

Kaydeen stuck her head back through the door. "What are you waiting for?"

Taylor stood triumphantly, brandishing a pistol and two extra power clips. He hurried to the door and handed the weapon to Kaydeen, their best shot.

"You have the lead. I'll bring up the rear."

Kaydeen nodded and sprinted to where Salayla was waiting with Mica.

"Sal and Tonee, take center."

The lineup surprised Tonee. He usually brought up the rear while Taylor took the lead, but he didn't argue. He could already see that Mica would need some extra guidance—he kept trying to get in front of Kaydeen. The boy had no tactical training or intuition.

A few minutes and multiple piles of rubble later, they finally saw the opening Mica had entered through. A floor collapse had cut a hole in the wall, separating the hallway from the enclosed driveway into the compound. All they had to do was jump the two-meter abyss and avoid the metal girders sticking out of the remains of the wall. Taylor waved them on, his attention on the open door beside him.

Kaydeen jumped across, verified the area was clear, and waved Salayla across. When Mica was across, Tonee turned back. Taylor had disappeared. Tonee went back to the door that had drawn Taylor's attention and found him inside an office. He recognized it as the office where Juvak had sold them to the miner. Taylor was rummaging in the desk drawers.

"Not the time for treasure hunts."

Taylor looked up. "Looking for intel."

"Really? Now? You have noticed that the explosions are closing again, right?"

The rumble had been in the background ever since the compound had first been hit. Most of it had been distant, more like an echo of a dream, but every so often, it had gotten close enough to reverberate through the compound. In the last few minutes, it had built to a cacophony again, as it had when it foreshadowed the last hit on the compound. Tonee wanted to be as far away as possible from this place when the gunners upstairs finally realized Mica's prediction.

"Go. I'll be right behind you."

Tonee shook his head. Taylor huffed in exasperation but let off his search.

They jogged down the hall to the exit. Salayla stood past the gap in the wall, waving them on.

"Time to go." She looked to her right with a worried glance.

"Go. Get to cover." Taylor waved her on. "We're right behind you." He motioned Tonee ahead.

Tonee jumped the gap and landed easily. Taylor backed up to get a running start. Tonee scanned the compound. The tunnel he stood in opened into a large courtyard. In its center stood a low building surrounded by a half wall—a magazine, a common way to store mining explosives. The half wall directed accidental detonations upward to protect the surrounding area.

Over the roof of the building on the courtyard's far side, he could see treetops and mountains and the incoming strikes of a capital ship rail gun. The gunner was manually zeroing in his shots on this target, or he was walking his shots over multiple targets. Either way, they were coming this way.

Taylor was just starting his run when the ground shook violently. Another section of the floor crumbled, widening the hole to two-and-a-half meters. He caught himself on an exposed girder and slid to a stop.

"They're hitting the mineshaft." Tonee looked back at the magazine and shook his head. As long as the half-walls stayed intact, the force of the exploding magazine would be directed up, but if the walls were damaged first, the design and safety features of the magazine would be compromised, and all bets would be off. They didn't want to be anywhere near that thing when it lit up. And this tunnel might funnel the blast like the barrel on a rifle.

"Go," Taylor told him as he backed up again. "You're no use to me here and will only slow me down once I get across."

Tonee hesitated. Their gazes met. Taylor wasn't ready to die, that was clear. Tonee nodded, turned, and ran.

The tunnel dumped him into an open area separating the compound from a settlement of high-rises. Ahead of him, he saw Salayla cut into an alley behind the first building. She stopped and looked back, waving him on. He was between the buildings when he turned to glance back. Taylor was only now coming out of the compound. Behind him, the compound was backlit with explosions. Tonee wondered what was back there for the gunner to walk his gun back and forth like that. The strikes reached the compound, shooting debris into the air. Tonee stopped by the alley and turned around. Kaydeen pulled him behind the building. He shook her off and leaned around the corner. Taylor reached the building. Tonee thought he would make it, and then the magazine exploded.

14

REST

Tonee pressed his back against the wall then pushed off again. *Taylor.* The thought had barely surfaced when a shadow appeared next to him. He didn't think, only reached out. He felt cloth, closed his fist around it, and pulled. Taylor swung around him like a pendulum and landed flat on the ground. Kaydeen was on top of him instantly. At first, Tonee thought she was putting out fire, but realizing there were no flames, he finally registered that she was checking him for wounds. She ran her hands up his legs and under his shirt. Coming out clean, she checked the back of his neck and then pulled him to his feet.

"Got to keep moving."

"I got him." Tonee grabbed his shoulders, pulled him up the rest of the way, and pushed him ahead. Taylor stumbled, landing on his knees. Tonee tightened his hold and pulled him back up. They followed the others, but Tonee did most of the steering and balancing to keep Taylor on his feet. They ran from alley to alley, moving in a zigzag pattern through the settlement until Mica disappeared into a building. They followed but stopped at the stairs. Mica was halfway up to the first floor.

"Whoa, stop," Tonee called out. Realizing he'd used the wrong language, he switched to Tinareean. "Where are you going?"

He handed Taylor over to Kaydeen, who sat him against the outside of the stair railing.

"Upstairs." Mica had stopped and started back down.

"I see that. Why?"

"We have a safe place up there where we can wait out the bombardment."

"We're in the middle of it and need to get out of it."

"They won't hit us here. They're only targeting the mine, and Intergal gunners are really good, so we'll be fine."

Tonee raised his eyebrows. "Are they, now?"

"Yeah, and their guns are all sophisticated and stuff, so they won't miss."

"Riiight." Tonee wondered what dream world the boy had gotten his info from.

"No, really." As if to prove his point, the rail gun staccato suddenly quieted, the rumble becoming more background noise than active attack.

"I think a break would be a good idea," Kaydeen put in.

Tonee looked at her in surprise—she knew better.

She pointed at Taylor, who was leaning on his knees, shaking his head and squeezing his eyes shut as if trying to clear his senses. Given the way he had stumbled, Tonee realized, something was messed up. Kaydeen agreed, and although her voice was nonchalant, her hand signals made it clear they needed to stop.

"Plus," Salayla added, "we need a plan, supplies, and intel." She indicated the boy with a meaningful gaze. "Why not take the advantage and security this building might offer while we accumulate what we can?" She didn't add comfort to the list, but Tonee could see it was on her mind. He smiled. It was on his, too. She winked at him.

"Fine," he relented, "we'll stay."

"And rest," Kaydeen added as she pulled Taylor back to his feet.

Tonee took him again and sent her up ahead. She pulled the pistol from her belt and ran up the stairs with Salayla.

Taylor tripped on the first step. Tonee caught him and pulled him upright.

"Steps, Taylor. We're on stairs." He had switched back to Trade.

Taylor didn't answer, making Tonee wonder if his hearing had been affected, too. His body was tense, but that could be an effect of the adrenaline rush they'd experienced and were still experiencing to a degree. His frustrated huff, though, was surely due to his sensory problems. Tonee had never seen Taylor display any type of frustration. Doing so wasted energy and time that could be spent on solving the problem. At least in Taylor's opinion. Tonee found punching something oftentimes helped marvelously to clear his mind, or to focus on the problem, or on the pain, for that matter.

Taylor nodded and tried again. He still stumbled every so often, but they made it up the steps. As they rounded the next landing, Kaydeen and Salayla were heading for the next flight of stairs where Mica was waiting. Kaydeen went ahead, taking two steps at a time, while Salayla paused long enough to give Tonee a status report.

'Floor clear, all doors locked,' she signaled, then followed Kaydeen.

They repeated the process three more times, with Kaydeen and Salayla running ahead to clear each level, while Tonee and Taylor followed at a pace Taylor could handle without needing too much help. At first, Mica was exasperated at their slow speed. He didn't see why they had to clear the building when he and his friends had used it for the last six months without incident. But he did as he was told and waited at the top of each flight until Salayla gave him the go-ahead to move on to the next.

By the time Tonee and Taylor reached the fifth floor, Kaydeen and Salayla stood on each side of a door with Mica holding a keycard at the ready. At Tonee's nod, Salayla signaled him to open the door. Kaydeen and Salayla entered first, while Mica stayed with Tonee and Taylor. It didn't take long until Kaydeen opened the door wide and motioned them to enter. They stepped into an L-shaped living room/kitchen combo with two bedrooms on the right and a short hallway leading to a large bathroom and laundry on the left. Kaydeen pulled Taylor to the couch and pushed him down. He sat but refused to lie back.

"We need to keep moving," Taylor said in Trade.

"You're in no shape to keep moving," she replied as she picked up his feet.

He pulled them out of her grip. "I'll be fine."

"I know, but for now, we're not going anywhere, so you might as well rest." She put her hand on his chest and pushed.

He shoved it out of the way. "We need to—"

"Taylor," she snapped, allowing the medical officer to come out in full force, "lie down."

"Yes, ma'am." He allowed her to push him prone. As primary team medic, she had the responsibility and authority to take charge of any injured. Not even a commanding officer had the authority to overrule or ignore the orders of the Medical Officer in Charge. At least, that was what it stated in the regs. Real life and especially combat usually weren't as clear cut.

"Now rest." Kaydeen softened her voice again.

Taylor was asleep within seconds.

She covered him with a blanket Salayla had retrieved from one of the bedrooms and rose with a sigh.

Tonee stood by the large window, looking down the alley they'd first entered. He had a perfect view of the entrance into the mine compound and was up high enough that he could see out without being seen himself. He turned to meet Kaydeen's gaze.

"And?"

"His equilibrium is off."

"No shit. I would've never guessed."

She gave him a dirty look. "What do you want me to say? I'm a medic, not a healer who can sense internal damage. Get me a med scanner, and I'll tell you why he can't keep his balance."

They looked at Salayla, who spread her arms wide.

"I can only procure what is available." She looked at Mica and switched to Tinareean, "Does this settlement have a medical clinic? We need a med scanner."

He nodded, then shook his head. "Yes, but they emptied it a while ago. We might be able to find some basic medical supplies in the apartments, but I doubt anybody here owned a med scanner."

"You have access to other apartments?" Tonee asked.

"I have a master keycard. Leer's dad heads the maintenance crew here, so his access card opens every door."

"Heads? So, he's still doing it?"

"Well, yeah, just because they're empty doesn't mean they don't need to be kept up."

"And the personal belongings?" Salayla pointed at the blanket.

"We weren't allowed to take much. The maintenance guys have been bringing stuff out, but there's not much room on their trucks, so it's been a slow process. I'm not sure how far they've gotten in this building."

"You said we?" Kaydeen beat Tonee to the question. "You used to live here?"

"Yeah, my dad used to be a foreman in the mine. This was our apartment. When the Traverse came in, they kicked everybody out and put their people in charge. Then they gave us an hour to clear the plateau and told the new mine manager he could have anybody lagging. Most got out in time, but not everybody did. A lot of people disappeared. We found out later that they'd been collared and taken to the mine to work off their trespassing conviction." He pantomimed quotation marks with his last words.

"What about the kids?" Tonee asked. The collared mineworkers they'd encountered had all been adults.

Mica shrugged. "If they were too young to work the mine, they were shipped off, supposedly to a state home, but we've not been able to find them. Mom thinks they've been taken off-planet." He looked down and shook his head.

Salayla walked over and put her hand on his shoulder. He inhaled deeply and looked back up. Tears glistened in his eyes.

"They were good kids, you know. They didn't do anything wrong. None of them did. Not their parents, either. They didn't tell us what would happen after the hour was up. If they had, we would've told them—we would've made sure everybody made it out before we left. But we didn't know." He shook his head. "We didn't know."

Salayla pulled him into her arms and talked to him quietly as he sobbed into her shoulder. Kaydeen motioned for Tonee to back off.

He didn't need to be told. He hadn't intended to bare the boy's emotions like that. Tonee could empathize. The boy felt guilty for making it out when others hadn't. Tonee had gone through it himself when his grandparents had died.

No words were going to help that, but distraction would.

"Tell me about your friends."

Kaydeen shot him a sharp look. He ignored it.

"Leer and..."

"Nitus." Mica pushed away from Salayla. "They're my best friends." He wiped the tears from his eyes. "They've been helping me keep an eye on the mine." His voice was still shaky, but he was getting himself back under control. "My parents didn't believe me when I told them about you guys, especially since they brought you to the mine. That's where civilians are punished. Intergal activity must be reported to the garrison in the valley since they're in charge of anything to do with the military. And then came the news that the Traverse had ordered everyone killed and your ships destroyed. They showed it—"

"Wait, what?" Tonee interrupted him. "They killed everyone?"

"Yeah," Mica answered with a nod. "They pulled out all the bodies, shot all the survivors, then blasted everything in place. They even shot down the big ships behind the moon. They had it on the news for days." He fell quiet.

Salayla and Kaydeen looked as shocked as Tonee felt. He lowered his head, pressing his fist against his mouth, and turned away.

Everyone was dead. He couldn't believe it. He'd assumed that...he didn't know what he'd assumed. That theirs was the only SILC that had been shot down? But that didn't make any sense. If that had been the case, the attack would have continued, and they would've been freed soon after. But they weren't, so the attack had to have been aborted. And Intergal didn't abandon their people, so the rest of the advance forces had been pulled out, or there had been nothing left to pull out. The possibility had always been in the back of his mind, but he'd avoided thinking about it.

Tonee combed his fingers through his hair—it was way too long. He wanted to punch something, but that wouldn't help.

He should've punched their guards, snapped their necks. That wouldn't have helped, either. Plus, they were civilians—sadistic civilians, but still civilians. They had nothing to do with the kill order.

He drew a deep breath, fighting down his anger. It was another point on the list. One day, he'd get the chance to cash in that list, and he'd enjoy every minute of it.

He'd been pacing, walking off his steam. He stopped and looked back at the others. Mica had withdrawn to the entry door and was playing with the control panel. Salayla and Kaydeen stood where they'd been, keeping their distance and giving him space. They'd dealt with their pain, he was sure of it, though he didn't know what that might look like for a Din. They had feelings, like humans, but they felt and dealt with them differently.

Salayla had tried to explain it one day soon after they'd met. Human emotions were hot burning impulses that were allowed to reign free, to control the body's actions, she had said. Taylor and Tonee had immediately disagreed, but she had continued to explain that Din emotions could be as strong but weren't allowed to override the brain. They were dealt with, Bled off, or Shared. Tonee had never quite understood the difference between Bleeding off an emotion and Sharing it—both involved Readings—but he'd never asked her to clarify that point. Probably because her insinuation that humans were emotional apes compared to Din had rankled him. The important part was that Din were more calculated with their emotions and didn't lose their temper.

Kaydeen looked at him. 'You good?' she signed.

He nodded and took a closer look at what Mica was doing with the control pad.

He was in the security app, but that was as far as Tonee could understand the symbols. He hadn't learned to read Tinareean during their train-up, at least not past the most basic info he'd needed for the mission. Salayla could probably make sense of it. As interpreter, she had learned the language almost fluently. But it was much easier to just ask.

"What are you doing, Mica?"

The boy didn't turn around. "I'm tapping into the building's security system. We've already set it up to alert us whenever somebody uses one of the doors into the building or approaches the apartment. I expanded it to all entries into the building. If anyone opens any of the doors or windows, we'll know about it."

"Good thinking."

"Thanks. My dad's been working security, and with the Resistance, monitoring our surroundings has been a high priority."

"Your dad is in the Resistance?"

"Yeah, we all are." Mica finished his work on the control pad and turned to Tonee. "Nitus' dad started the local chapter, or cell, I guess. He came across Dad while we were trying to find out what happened to the missing miners. He also helped with trying to locate where they'd shipped the kids, but even his connections couldn't locate them. That's why Mom thinks they were taken off-planet."

His eyes dropped to the floor, and his shoulders drooped again. Tonee needed to change the subject.

"So, Leer's dad gave you access to these buildings, your dad taught you how to use the security systems to your advantage, and Nitus' dad gave you the intel you needed to find us and get us out. And you said they didn't believe we were here?"

"Well, not quite. Leer took the keycard without his dad's knowledge, I learned to work security systems by helping my dad on the weekends, and we knew about the attack because they told us to stay home and wait until they sent us info about our evacuation."

"Evacuation?"

"Yeah, Intergal agreed to evac families of volunteers who did the jobs you guys were supposed to do six months ago." He waved his hand to encompass Tonee and his teammates. "Leer and Nitus were tagged as runners—you know, to let everybody know when and where they'll be picked up, since that can't be put out over the comms. When they're done, they'll come here."

Tonee, Salayla, and Kaydeen asked a few more questions before breaking to run a security check on the building. After they ensured the building was as secure as Mica thought and the monitoring program ran as he promised, they explored some of the apartments. They didn't find a med scanner but were able to put together four decent survival packs. They also found clothing that was close enough in size to fit each of them.

Once they'd scavenged the supplies, they returned to the apartment and took showers. The bathroom was luxurious, with an oversized shower with sauna, steam, and dry settings. Multiple showerheads sprayed from all directions, with adjustable water pressure and additives. Tonee didn't even have to move—he simply stood in the center and was massaged, soaped, rinsed, and dried. It felt like heaven, especially compared to the ice-cold water hose showers the guards had provided them with in the mine. The clothing they had found fit all right, though the shirt was a little too tight across his shoulders and way too colorful, but it was much better than the clothes the guards had supplied them with once their uniforms had worn through.

TWO HOURS LATER, Leer and Nitus showed up. Leer was a cocky sixteen-year-old with a wrestler's physique, while Nitus, at fifteen, had spent more time in front of a screen than in the outdoors. At least he wasn't as full of himself as Leer, who immediately tried to impress everybody with his experience as 'war zone runner.' Mica called his BS, pointing out that their town had no military value and only the standard Enforcement Officer presence to keep order, and therefore hadn't been on Intergal's target list. Leer tried to smooth over that point, but when Nitus jumped in on Mica's side and told how easy it was to get out of town and come here, Leer segued into fawning over Salayla and Kaydeen and the hardship they'd experienced. Salayla, always up for a good flirtation, took him right on. Tonee wondered if the boy realized how outclassed he was in experience and capabilities—that the woman he offered to protect could snap his neck in an instant.

Kaydeen ignored him and checked on Taylor. He was still asleep.

After the initial meet and greet and sizing up, the boys settled down enough for Salayla to debrief them, although she worded it more eloquently.

Tonee settled back by the window to listen.

The boys thought the attack was going well. At least, that was how they interpreted the 'all is well' message Nitus had received when his dad had commed to give him his 'homework'—a descending list of the founding families and their length of rule. Leer's smart recitation of the instructions made Tonee wonder what he missed. He looked at Salayla. She had no clue, but Mica immediately rattled off names and numbers.

As he did, Salayla's face brightened. When Mica was done, she turned to Tonee and Kaydeen to explain.

"The founding families are an important part of Tinareean history. Their reign during the settlement period was the only time the planet's leaders were preordained and not elected. It's a common belief that their leadership was the reason Tinaree was such a successful colony and was able to pay off its debt and earn its independence within two hundred years of its founding." She paused in her history lesson.

"Considering the speed of space travel at the time," Kaydeen put in, "two hundred years from touchdown to independence was record time."

Salayla nodded. "It's such a matter of national pride that every history book on the planet starts with the account of the settlement period."

"And every school kid memorizes it," Mica added. "Everyone knows the names and the dates."

"So, how does that translate into meeting locations and times?" Tonee asked.

"Easy," Nitus answered. "Every region has one plaza named after each founding family. Their years of reign—each less than twenty-five—indicate the time of day, and their order of reign, the day the pickup will happen." He grinned broadly. "So, in descending order, the last family to reign would indicate the first pickup: today, at fifteen hours in Parilo Plaza, which is our home plaza." He looked at his wrist comm. "It's past sixteen hours, so we missed today's."

"But we knew that when we got the list," Leer continued. "The next closest is Totiga Plaza at ten hours on day four. That's in Mannahe. We should be able to make that." He looked at Taylor, who hadn't moved since they arrived. "Shouldn't we?"

Kaydeen shrugged. She wasn't going to comment on Taylor's condition in front of the boys. Tonee nodded his agreement. He had no intention of letting Leer or his friends in on every detail, even if the teenager seemed to expect them to. And neither did Salayla.

"Walking?" She smiled and batted her eyes. "That depends on the terrain, the exact distance we have to cover, and what we encounter on the way." She appeared friendly and accommodating, but that didn't mean she was. "Do you have a map?"

Tonee smiled. Their little social butterfly could be the biggest predator of them all.

The boys produced multiples. The team grabbed a printed

regional map and a digital map with satellite overlay and got to work. They spent the next hour poring over the maps and quizzing the boys on what they might encounter on the way. They had no vehicles, other than the single-seat trail runners the boys used to get to the mine, so they planned on walking the distance and possibly using two of the trail runners to carry a litter with Taylor.

When they were done, Kaydeen went to check on Taylor while Tonee and Salayla dug through the kitchen cabinets for food. Kaydeen joined them a few minutes later, frowning. Tonee paused, but she answered his questioning look with a noncommittal shrug.

THEY WERE in the process of going through the food packs they'd found in the cabinets when Taylor started awake. He was fully alert, his body tense and ready to fight, his focus on Leer and Nitus, who sat with Mica on the floor two meters from the couch—easily within his reach.

"Whoa, Taylor. Stand down." Tonee dropped the packet of mushy meat substitute he'd been wrinkling his nose at and darted around the island.

Kaydeen beat him to it and slid in front of the boys. Taylor looked at her, then at Tonee and Salayla, and relaxed.

He swung his legs around and sat up. Kaydeen motioned for him to stay seated and examined him. Satisfied with what she saw, she told him to stand. After another examination, she told him to drop. He looked at her.

"Give me some pushups," she instructed. "Drop."

He did. The moment he was on the floor, she ordered him back up. He jumped back to his feet. She held a finger in front of his face and moved it back and forth. His eyes and head followed its motion.

She shook her head. "You're fine."

"Yeah." His brow creased. "Is that a problem?"

"No." She shrugged. "Merely unexpected."

He frowned at her, but she didn't elaborate, and he didn't ask her to. Instead, he pointed at Leer and Nitus, who had moved to the other side of the room.

"Who are they?"

"Mica's friends," Tonee answered as he stepped closer. "We'll explain after you wash up." He wrinkled his nose. "You stink."

"We procured clothing that should fit you," Salayla added.

Kaydeen nodded her agreement. "And by the time you're done, we'll have some food ready."

He eyed Tonee's colorful shirt. "I'm hoping not quite as bright?"

Tonee spread his arms and puffed out his chest. "Hey, better than the rags you're wearing. This, at least, has style." He grinned.

"That's one way to describe it," Taylor replied as he followed Salayla down the hall.

Tonee waited for them to be out of earshot before turning to Kaydeen.

"So, what's the diagnosis?"

"He's fine." She walked back into the kitchen.

"I see that." He followed her. "Yet, you don't seem happy about it."

"It's not that I'm not happy about it, only confused."

"You know, it'd help if you elaborated. It's kind of hard to hear your brain rattle from out here."

She looked at him and then glanced at the boys who had returned to their games.

"The blast seemed to have injured his vestibular system, with his symptoms pointing to a possible traumatic injury of the labyrinth," she explained, "but that makes no sense. Not without corresponding injuries and symptoms."

She paused, probably wondering if she'd lost him. Unlike Kaydeen and Taylor, Tonee's medical training didn't go far past the rudimentary battlefield first aid every trooper learned, but he knew his explosives and with that came the knowledge of what his favorite toys could do to a person.

"Ok, so secondary and tertiary blast injuries are out. He was neither hit by shrapnel nor slammed about by the blast wind, but what about primary ones? The blast wave could've scrambled his insides."

"And injure only his inner ear?" She frowned. "Although primary blast injuries are hard to diagnose without a scanner, they do have physical symptoms. Plus, those symptoms get worse with time, not better. He seems to have healed in a few hours what should have taken days, if not weeks." She shook her head. "It makes no sense."

"So, maybe it wasn't as bad as he let on."

She looked at him, "Are you suggesting he faked his injuries?"

Tonee didn't reply. He didn't know what he was suggesting, or thinking, for that matter.

TWENTY MINUTES LATER, Taylor still hadn't returned. Tonee went to check on him. The bathroom was filled with steam. The fresh clothing they'd found for him was lying on the floor, probably damp from the moisture by now, and his dirty clothes had been dropped right beside them. Taylor was still under the shower, leaning against the wall, letting the hot water run over him. His back was to the door. His skin was blemish free. Taylor turned to look at him. Tonee couldn't see any of the lesions or welts Taylor's body had sported for most of their time in the mine. Kaydeen's fear that without regen tech, the damage from the neural whip might leave permanent scars, had obviously been unfounded.

"Dinner is ready." Tonee motioned at the clean clothes on the floor.

Taylor tilted his head. "Say that again."

"Dinner."

"No, the whole thing."

"Dinner is ready?"

"Yeah. One more time." He grinned. "Come on, indulge me."

He made Tonee repeat himself twice more and then laughed.

"Damn, that sounds good. Almost normal."

Tonee laughed and walked back out.

Salayla looked up. "Share the jest."

"I had to tell him dinner was ready four times."

Kaydeen frowned. "He had problems hearing?"

"No." Tonee shook his head. "It sounded so good, he couldn't get enough of it."

Taylor came out of the hallway pulling his shirt over his head. His hair was still dripping.

Salayla grinned at him. "You think dinner sounds good?" she asked. "Wait until you taste it."

Taylor grinned in return. Damn, it was good to see everybody cutting up again.

They sat to eat.

Kaydeen warned them to take it slow. After six months of gelatinous food substitutes, their stomachs weren't used to real food. Tonee didn't consider the reconstituted meal they'd prepared real food, but he heeded her warning.

His taste buds exploded. His jaw instantly locked in response. He didn't remember ever tasting anything so good—

the flavors were more intense than anything he'd ever eaten fresh from the market.

His parents had always proclaimed that the first meal after an extended deep space mission was the best one could taste. He'd never believed them. Now, he did.

They spent the next two hours nibbling their food while bringing Taylor up to speed on the current situation and clarifying their plans of action. They would spend the night in the apartment and then head out at first light. With Taylor's unexpected recovery, they should be able to get into the valley by late morning. Mica had told them about a hiking trail leading directly into the valley that was much smaller and steeper than the path the boys usually took with their trail runners but would cut their travel time by a third. It also had multiple locations with views of the valley and Mannahe, the largest city in the region, where Totiga Plaza was located, so they'd be able to get a view of what lay ahead of them. The team decided to take the trail, although it meant they'd have to leave the trail runners behind.

Leer suggested that he, Nitus, and Mica could take the trail runners and meet the teammates down in the valley. Taylor rejected that option. The trail runners were fast and could be used for scouting, but they were also loud and bulky. The last thing they needed was some overzealous teens zipping around, bringing attention to them. Leer bristled, but Salayla smoothed over Taylor's bluntness by explaining that they could only protect each other if they stayed close enough to support each other. Her subtle reminder of Leer's earlier promise did the trick, although Tonee could see she'd have to continue to work her magic on him. Taylor watched the interaction with his head tilted but said nothing.

After dinner, they rehashed their plan, its contingencies, and their emergency protocols one more time with the boys before calling it a night.

The boys slept in the back bedroom, Nitus in the single bed and Leer and Mica on camping mats on the floor. Tonee claimed the couch and first guard and sent the others into the front bedroom with its oversized double bed. When Taylor offered to take the couch and the first shift since he'd been sleeping most of the day, Tonee waved him off.

"I've been sharing with them for months." He nodded toward the bedroom Salayla and Kaydeen had disappeared into. "It's your turn to keep them warm."

Taylor studied him for a moment, shrugged, and disappeared into the bedroom.

The apartment fell quiet. Tonee grabbed Mica's datapad and settled onto the couch.

A MUFFLED sound roused him two hours later. He'd fallen asleep—bad choice to sit on a couch reading when he'd felt nothing other than hard, cold floor below him for months. He stood and listened. The double door to the front bedroom was closed, but he heard Salayla's and Kaydeen's voices filtering through it. They sounded concerned. He opened the door.

Taylor tossed and turned on the bed. Kaydeen was sitting on him, restraining his arms and legs, while Salayla crouched next to her, clasping his neck between her hands. Kaydeen looked up as Tonee entered. A purple mark marred her left cheekbone.

"We can't wake him. Salayla can't even read him. He's totally shut her out."

Tonee took Salayla's position and grabbed Taylor by the shoulders, motioning for Kaydeen to back off. As Kaydeen released him, Taylor started to fight Tonee, but his movements were too uncoordinated to do more than rumple the sheets below him. Tonee shook him while calling his name, then slapped him across the face. Taylor continued to struggle. Tonee slapped him again. The third slap finally seemed to get through to him, but not in the way Tonee had intended. Taylor raised his arms protectively and cowered in fear. Tonee called his name again.

Taylor froze.

"Tonee?" His voice, barely over a whisper, quivered.

"Yeah," Tonee answered, unsure what else to say.

Taylor reached out a searching hand as if he couldn't see Tonee leaning over him. His other hand continued to guard his face protectively. Tonee pulled him up. The moment Taylor's hand found Tonee's shirt, he latched on. Tonee wrapped his arms around Taylor's trembling body.

"I got you."

He looked from Kaydeen to Salayla, who shook their heads.

"We were asleep when he started to whimper then toss and turn," Kaydeen explained. "When I touched him, he attacked, but it was nothing he would normally do. More like he was afraid of me and trying to get away. Salayla pulled him off me and then tried to Read him, so he started fighting her. I restrained him, but she still couldn't get in."

"His mind blocked me," Salayla expanded. "I've never seen a human do that before. I couldn't get him to recognize me."

"Then you walked in," Kaydeen took over again, "and here we are." She peered around Tonee's arms at Taylor's face. "He recognized you, but I don't think he's awake."

"What do you want me to do?" Tonee stopped rocking.

"See if you can lay him back down."

Tonee tried, but Taylor continued to cling to him. "He has a death grip on my shirt."

"Then lie down with him," Salayla suggested.

She and Kaydeen slipped off the bed. Tonee rolled onto his side, bringing Taylor with him. He continued to tremble but didn't resist the prone position Tonee pushed him into. It took another ten minutes before Taylor relaxed enough for Kaydeen to declare him fully back asleep. Tonee released him and tried to slide away. As soon as he did, Taylor's grip on his shirt tightened. He reminded Tonee more of a frightened child hiding from the monsters in his dreams than the self-assured teammate Tonee had come to know over the last three years. Tonee shook his head. *What the hell did they do to him?*

Salayla waved him off and motioned for him to stay where he was. He nodded and settled in for the rest of the night—it looked like he wasn't getting his time alone after all. *Ah, well. At least I got the comfortable bed.*

15

CONFLICT

Kaydeen was rummaging through the kitchen in search of breakfast when she noticed Taylor sliding out from under Tonee's arm. He looked at Tonee's sleeping form and then to the couch where Salayla slept and frowned. Kaydeen started to speak, but then clamped her mouth shut. What could she say? *'Hey, nice to see you fully awake. Are you aware that you have some underlying angst that caused a tussle last night?'* If he remembered, this wasn't the time to delve into it. If he didn't remember, it still wasn't the time to open that box. She needed him as close to his top form as possible. Discussing psychological wounds or dragging them into the open wasn't the way to get him there.

After a few moments, he stood and came into the kitchen. He stopped a few steps from her, started to speak, stopped, started again, and then looked around with his mouth working as if unable to put words to the puzzle in his head. She had never seen him so confused, at least not in such a contemplative, serious manner.

Behind him, Salayla had woken as he had crossed the living area and now watched quietly from where she lay.

Tonee woke, looked around, and jumped up. Taylor reacted to the noise behind him but didn't turn around. Tonee entered the living area, taking in the scene. His muscles tensed and his movements smoothed as he moved closer. He was readying to pounce. Kaydeen wanted to signal him to back off and let her handle it, but there was no way to do so without Taylor noticing.

"Taylor," Tonee called quietly. He was about ten paces away.

Taylor's eyes refocused. "I'm fine."

Tonee continued to approach. "Then let them Read you."

"No." Taylor stiffened. "I said I'm fine."

"Bullshit." Tonee stopped a few paces behind him.

Salayla stood and approached, slowly and carefully, as if sudden movement might cause irreparable damage.

This was surreal. What was Tonee going to do? Physically force Taylor to submit to a Reading? Even if that worked, what if Taylor blocked it again like he had last night? Not that it should be possible for a human. But what kind of damage would that do to the team? And why was Salayla so tentative? After all they had gone through over the last six months and last night, needing some time to process things was understandable, wasn't it? Kaydeen wasn't sure, but she did know one thing. They didn't need a fight right now.

Before she could say anything, Tonee spoke again. "You need to let her Read you."

Taylor's eyes locked on Kaydeen's chest.

Kaydeen had never seen him like this before—backed into a corner, preparing to fight. The escalation was imminent and obvious. Why was she the only one who saw it? But, despite all her insight, she had no idea how to stop it.

She didn't have to. Tonee's next words did.

"We are a team. We live as a team. We fight as a team. And we will die as a team, if necessary. But we will never leave a teammate behind." He repeated the words exactly as Taylor had spoken them so many lifetimes ago, then added, "Physically or otherwise."

Taylor's resolve collapsed. The pain, so clearly visible in his face, nearly tore apart her heart. She had no words...could only watch as he crumbled.

Salayla was suddenly behind him. Kaydeen hadn't seen her move. She reached for Taylor's neck but stopped before touching him and looked at Kaydeen.

Her silent question hung between them.

Before Kaydeen could answer, Taylor nodded, lowered his head, and leaned into her. His weight pushed against her in surrender. She moved a leg back to brace herself, put her arms around him to keep him upright, and felt utterly inadequate to carry him. But he was finally ready to let them in. Kaydeen smiled at Tonee. Today, Din weren't the only empaths with the right words.

Salayla gave her a quick nod and touched the right side of his neck while Kaydeen reached for his left. A shiver ran through Taylor's body, physically manifesting their mental contact. They didn't push, didn't force their way, but hovered, waiting for him to open. At first, he seemed like a fortress, dark, brooding, and sealed shut. They waited patiently.

"Taylor." Tonee spoke as if addressing an injured animal. "Let them in."

Salayla must have signaled him, or maybe Tonee had learned to recognize when they entered another's mind.

Taylor's presence shifted. It was still dark and brooding, but the energy had softened and swirled. With the swirls came the pain. It wasn't physical pain, but a twisted, inside-out jumble of emotions that was wearing him down and grinding his spirit to dust. The first time Kaydeen had sensed it, it had taken her breath away. Luckily, her audile gasp had easily been explained by their physical activity at the time. This time, she was ready for it.

Salayla covered her surprise well. As Primary Din, her gift was stronger, with better and subtler control. A quick glimpse of shock and pain, and then release. As Salayla relaxed, so did Taylor. The tension left his body. His full weight was still on her, but it wasn't as heavy or burdened. The pain moved away... not forgotten, but set aside, to be examined from a safe distance. Salayla opened her eyes and smiled. A sad one, but a smile. She released Taylor's neck, nodded at Kaydeen, and turned to talk to Tonee. She wouldn't be able to tell him what happened to Taylor—they couldn't read minds or touch memories like psychics, so that was still Taylor's story to tell—but she could reassure him that they'd help Taylor deal with it and keep him balanced.

Now, it was Kaydeen's turn to tend to Taylor. She dropped her hand around his shoulder and settled in.

He didn't move, not for a long while. But that was fine. Salayla had taken Tonee into the bedroom and would give them the time it took.

Taylor's breath was slow and steady, almost as if he were asleep. Kaydeen knew better. He needed time to sort things out and come to grips with what had happened.

Readings affected people differently. Some welcomed and even yearned for them. Others were indifferent, but all understood their benefit, especially after a Reading was performed. Taylor, on the other hand, avoided them. Not that he disliked them...he simply didn't want them. He understood their benefits—the ability to release pain, both physical and emotional, and gain distance could be invaluable, especially in combat. But he thought it a crutch, one he shouldn't need or want.

Kaydeen waited for him to settle and reboot. He would be

fine, she knew. She could feel it. His presence was changing back to calm and collected and absolutely sure of himself.

He straightened and looked at her in calm attentiveness, seeing every detail, every emotion, without giving away anything of himself. She returned his gaze, studied him in turn. Yes, he was back. The only thing missing was the twinkle in his eyes, only visible to those who knew him best. She couldn't begrudge that. Too much had happened in too short a time, to them and between them. She laid her hand against his neck but didn't attempt to Read him again. He was open to her, but she didn't join his mind. Instead, she savored the warmth of his skin, his being, and his presence.

"Kay—"

She laid her fingers on his lips to stop him, "Shh."

"I had no choice." He wasn't talking about last night.

She shook her head.

"They would've killed you if I hadn't—"

"You are the one who was hurt, not me," she interrupted him, pressing harder against his lips. "What they did doesn't matter," she whispered. "What we did, does, and I wouldn't want to have missed it." It wasn't quite the truth. She *had* felt pain and disorientation when they had ripped him off her and shattered their link.

He frowned. She continued, "Nothing they did can, or will, take that away." After a short pause she added, "Ever."

That Sharing had been nothing like any she'd ever experienced before. It had been beautiful and intense...and hurried...and incomplete. The pain when they'd pulled him off her had been excruciating, as if a piece of her had been ripped away. It had disoriented her for hours. But he didn't need to know that.

He held her gaze, studying, imploring. Humans were so fragile in this subject, always second-guessing. She wished they could be a little more like Din—enjoy the exercise without attaching all the emotional baggage. Then, she sensed his decision. Closure.

Finally.

“Sometimes you can be so human.”

He looked at her, knitting his eyebrows. “I am human.” The side of his mouth quirked up, ever so minutely.

“Exactly. But I’m not, so human conventions and emotions don’t apply. At least, not fully. Don’t flinch over what doesn’t injure me.” She touched her palm to his chest. “They can affect this—” she raised her hand and touched the tips of her two forefingers to his temple “—and this, only if you let them.”

“My mother used to say that.” The sparkle in his eyes almost returned.

“She was a wise woman.”

“She also said attachments are a hindrance.”

Kaydeen shook her head. “That’s one saying she had wrong.” She paused. “I like your version better. We are a team. We live as a team, we fight as a team, and whatever comes our way, we will deal with it as a team.”

He still had a long way to go, but he was well on his way to his old self. At least, his old self adjusted with these new experiences.

THE DOOR to the back bedroom flew open. Mica walked out, fully dressed, stuffing his rolled up sleeping bag into his pack. Behind him, Nitus hopped on one leg, desperately trying to aim for his half-pulled-up pants with the other one. Leer sat on the edge of the bed in his underwear, rubbing his face.

“I thought we were leaving with first light,” Mica said as he closed his pack and swung it onto his back.

Tonee came out of the other bedroom. “First light is past.”

“Why didn’t you wake us?” Nitus asked. He had finished

dressing and was stuffing his loose sleeping bag into a pack already bulging in all directions.

Tonee started to answer, but Salayla stepped around him, cutting him off smoothly. "Because you needed the sleep."

"Oh." Nitus paused to look at her. "We could've gotten up earlier. We have alarms."

"Then why didn't you set them?" Tonee asked.

"We did." Mica dropped his pack by the door and then returned to Nitus and helped him pack his gear correctly.

"So, we don't have to hurry?" Nitus handed over his pack without hesitation.

"I want to be on the road by eight," Taylor answered and grabbed one of the packs they'd prepared yesterday.

Nitus asked, "Why eight?" at the same time Leer demanded, "Who made you the boss?"

Taylor didn't look up as he moved the pack to the middle of the floor. "Because that gives us an hour to get going and fifty-two hours to travel thirty klicks." He crouched over the pack and opened it. "Nobody."

His voice didn't rise. Ignoring Leer's challenge, he simply stated a fact. Typical Taylor.

Leer, fully dressed, strutted out of the bedroom, puffing out his chest and trying a little too hard to be casual about his posturing. Being taller and more muscular than Taylor and seeing the man crouched on the floor seemed to bolster his confidence.

"Then why do we have to do what you say?" He stopped halfway across the living area and smirked at Nitus and Mica as if trying to impress them with his boldness.

The two paused, looking from Leer to Taylor and back. Leer's behavior obviously wasn't new to them.

"You don't." Taylor inspected each item as he emptied the pack. "You can leave whenever you want to."

He had yet to look up.

"We had a deal," Leer huffed. "You can't renege what they agreed to." He stomped closer, spreading his elbows.

A picture of a bull readying to charge came to Kaydeen's mind. She stifled a laugh. If Leer thought Taylor—who looked closer in age to the teens than his teammates—was a peer he could push around, he'd be unpleasantly surprised when he hit that brick wall. Taylor might appear to ignore him, but his muscles had tensed, and his movements had become too precise, too calculated to be casual. No, Taylor knew exactly where Leer was and how to take him down.

Leer wouldn't be the first to underestimate Taylor. They'd seen it on a regular basis at the Academy as other recruits had tried to knock him off the pedestal the trainers kept putting him on. As the top-ranked trainee, he already had a bullseye on his back, but the trainers had made sure it was clear and sharp for the rest of the class to target. Taylor hadn't been fazed, though, and dealt with whatever was thrown at him, sometimes with unconventional methods. He could be brutal and blunt, using the smallest advantage to destroy an opponent mercilessly, but he could also be helpful and supportive. He readily handed out praise or advice if approached, and wasn't above admitting when he stepped wrong—although he never apologized for his actions.

"Then I guess you'd better leave with us." Taylor finally looked up and met Leer's gaze, stopping the boy in his tracks.

The room fell silent, as if holding its breath. Taylor was still on his knees. Leer towered over him in comparison. It didn't matter. Taylor's presence dominated, turning the bull into the sheep he truly was. Leer didn't like what he received but was smart enough not to test it. He turned, huffed, and stormed back into the bedroom to retrieve his gear. Kaydeen shook her head and continued prepping breakfast while Salayla and Tonee helped Taylor with the packs.

THE MOMENT THEY STEPPED OUTSIDE, an acrid stench of burning fuel and plastoids assaulted Kaydeen's nostrils. It hung in the air and clung to every surface like soot from a fire, leaving a bitter taste in her mouth. She scraped her tongue across her teeth but was unable to rid herself of the nasty tang. They quickly made their way out of the village—Taylor in the lead with Mica, and Tonee bringing up the rear. Leer gravitated toward Salayla, smoothly directed there by her attention, leaving Nitus for Kaydeen to manage. To the boys, it seemed like a natural formation of their choosing. It was anything but.

As they left the settlement and entered the forest, the air improved, replacing the pungent stench with a musty, woodsy scent that had a citrusy hint with sweet undertones. Kaydeen inhaled deeply—nature was so amazing. Her eyes agreed. Vibrant greens and browns in every shade imaginable jockeyed for dominance, attempting to drown out the colorful palette of flowers, mosses, and fungi hidden throughout, as tall deciduous trees with an understory of low ferns and shrubs followed the natural dips and rises of the descending mountainside. Kaydeen smiled. There was nothing like being locked into a color-deprived prison to remind the senses of how brilliant nature was.

The dirt trail they followed was easy going at first, the slope not very steep. Ample enough to easily pick their way around washed-out roots and rocks, although not quite wide enough for two people to walk side-by-side, it wound around patches of knee-high shrubs dotted with small round fruit. Where the shrubs spread across larger areas, the trail split into a web of smaller paths, crisscrossing through the plants in a seemingly random fashion.

Kaydeen's enjoyment was soon curtailed when the cool

damp mountain air started to seep into her bones. She closed the light jacket she had found and was glad she had grabbed it. Being locked underground for six months had done nothing to acclimate her to the temperate weather of the region. The boys had said the valley was warmer. She hoped so, or the coming nights would be miserable.

The hiking trail quickly became narrow and steep, at times winding in serpentines, at others, angling straight down the mountain. Roots and partially buried rocks served as natural breaks for their momentum, while tree branches and boulders offered handholds for balance. They made good progress. Nitus was much more used to this type of activity than he'd previously let on. He huffed and puffed and slipped on loose gravel and wet ground, but with a few pointers, he easily picked up the tricks to navigate the alpine footing.

The first outcropping was covered in fog, inhibiting their view of the valley. Distant rumbles bespoke the destruction the milky wall kept hidden from their view. They didn't stop. Fog tended to obscure the distance and origin of sound, but it did nothing to hide their bodies' signatures from airborne sensors. When they reached the second outcropping an hour later, the fog had lifted, and the valley opened ahead of them.

At 178 klicks wide, the valley's other bordering mountain range was only a shadow in the distance. Mannahe spread in its center, surrounded by blocks of colorful agricultural fields dotted with smaller towns and villages. The scene would've been beautiful if not for the plumes of smoke rising like fingers reaching for the sky and the aerial craft zipping around like gnats over an open sore, dropping their deadly armaments or coming in for landings to discharge their living, but equally deadly, payloads. The fighting was concentrated over the large city, leaving the fields and smaller towns mostly untouched. Mica pointed out a tall comm-array tower that poked into the sky from the city's center like a skinny needle and explained that Totiga Plaza, their destination, was about half a klick beyond it. Roughly 30 klicks of open fields lay between the bottom of the mountain and the edge of the city. Although that part of their route was untouched by the fighting, the sensors of any aerial craft passing within 70 klicks would easily notice their movement. If they were lucky, an Intergal patrol would come to investigate and give them an opportunity to identify themselves as friend or foe. If they were unlucky, a patrol—Traverse or Intergal—would decide to shoot first and ask questions later.

Mica, Nitus, and Leer fell silent as they watched the destruction spreading below them. Taylor motioned for everybody to retreat into the tree line for a break, but soon after, he and Tonee moved to a better vantage point to quietly discuss how what was going on below might affect their continuing route and progress.

Kaydeen and Salayla stayed with the teens, keeping them occupied and their minds distracted from the events playing out below. Twice, Taylor called on Mica to identify locations or infrastructure, but he waited for Mica to return to the others each time before he continued his conversation with Tonee. Throughout their discussion, their hands signed a running transcript of their conversation for Salayla and Kaydeen. It was a habit they'd gotten into during their captivity to keep each other informed or hold obfuscated conversations. Sometimes, they'd spoken about mundane subjects, filling the air with inconsequential noise while their hands had done the real talking.

"I think Taylor wants to change our route," Mica said as he sat beside Salayla.

"What?" Leer's head snapped up from the comm he'd been engrossed in. "Why?"

Kaydeen was surprised he'd heard Mica. His face had been

glued to the handheld ever since he sat. He saw her gaze and laid the comm screen-first in his lap. She wondered what he was hiding but then dismissed the thought. His movements had been so natural, the boy probably hadn't realized he was doing it.

Mica shrugged in reply. "I think he thinks it's a bad idea."

"A bad idea? It's the shortest route. We discussed that last night." Leer huffed. "We all agreed it was the best route."

"He wasn't part of that decision."

"His fault he slept through it. That doesn't give him the right to change our decision willy-nilly."

"What decision did I change?" Taylor asked as he and Tonee approached.

"Who says we're talking about you?"

Tonee raised his eyebrows at Leer's snappy retort and looked at Salayla, who shrugged. The boys were under stress—they all were—but unlike the teammates, the teens had no training in how to handle it. Using somebody else as a lightning rod was probably Leer's way of dealing with it.

Taylor seemed to blow off Leer's attitude, which was probably a good thing.

"Who says you weren't talking about me?" He said it lightly, with a shrug and a flutter at the corners of his mouth.

Leer huffed again. "And if we were? What's it to you?"

He didn't get up, clearly trying to imitate Taylor's body language from this morning and failing miserably.

Tonee inhaled deeply but said nothing. Taylor was quite able to fight his own battles.

This time, Taylor smiled fully. The image of a tiger allowing a kitten to stalk and pounce on his paw came to Kaydeen's mind.

Taylor shrugged. "Just wondering." He turned to the others. "Are we ready to move on?"

The boys frowned at him. They had clearly expected a bigger confrontation.

Taylor didn't oblige them, nor did he seem to pay attention to Leer's smug posturing.

16

TUSCOONY

An hour later, they entered a tight foothill valley that took them into the small town of Tuscoony. It was quiet and empty. Nitus explained that most of its residents were probably at the market on the central square. Holding to old tradition, all villages and small towns still held a market day to sell local produce and goods and to distribute information. Although the information dissemination was mostly done over the Net nowadays, people used the market to mingle and socialize and, since the Traverse invasion, to distribute info that was blocked or forbidden on the Net.

"Produce?" Salayla looked past Leer at Nitus. "As in raw food from a farm?"

"Yeah." Nitus nodded.

"That might not be such a good idea," Kaydeen put in, easily following Salayla's train of thought. "We've been eating nothing but nutritionally balanced manufactured slush. Eating something naturally grown will probably give us some gastric side effects we don't want to deal with right now."

"Oh, come on," Tonee said from behind them. "Think about

biting into an apple, or whatever their version here is called. The smell as you bring it to your mouth, the resistance as your teeth break through the skin, the crunch as you bite into the flesh, and the flavor as the juice floods your mouth." He closed his eyes. "Hmm, my mouth is watering just thinking about it."

"Yeah, and your gastrointestinal tract might thank you with cramps and diarrhea later."

"Might be worth it." Tonee smiled. "Plus, the food from the apartment hasn't given us any issues."

"The food from the apartment is also manufactured."

"But based on real food, not chemicals. I read the ingredients lists."

Kaydeen shook her head and smiled at his insistence. "We don't have money, anyway."

"We can charge my ID," Mica said over his shoulder. He was still walking point with Taylor. "Or, if you prefer—" he turned to walk backward "—Leer usually has cash on him."

"Cash?" Taylor asked, glancing back. He continued to walk forward but slowed to match Mica's speed.

Leer shrugged as the group's attention turned to him. "Don't like to hand out my ID. Not everybody needs to know who I am."

"Yeah, it's an off-worlder leftover," Nitus explained. "We've been trying to break him of it, but old habits die hard." He grinned and punched Leer in the shoulder. "Don't they?"

"Hey." Leer frowned and rubbed his shoulder. "I've lived here longer than anywhere else, so I'm not an off-worlder anymore." He made to punch Nitus back. "Plus, not my fault Dad pays me my allowance that way."

"Ooh, some people get an allowance," Nitus mocked as he danced out of the way.

Kaydeen smiled. It was good to see the boys relaxed enough to play and tease each other.

Leer started after him. Nitus slipped around Kaydeen and

behind Tonee, nearly grabbing the latter to use as a shield. But he stopped short and moved on to grab Mica instead. Their antics went on for a few more moments as the group followed the street into town. Mica was quickly drawn in, but the boys avoided doing more than using the teammates as moving obstacles. The fun ended when Leer put on a spurt of speed to circumvent Mica and wrapped his arm around Nitus' neck. Forcing the younger boy to bend at the waist, he rubbed his knuckles across Nitus' head and then released him.

"Yeah, sure." He grinned as he fell back in beside Salayla. "I have cash you can use. You can pay me back later." He dug in his pocket for some coins and handed them to her.

IT DIDN'T TAKE LONG for Nitus' earlier prediction to be proven right. As they followed the street into the center of the town, the team encountered more and more residents coming or going. Soon after, the street opened into a large square filled with stands and people. The teammates looked at each other in surprise. Nitus' description hadn't prepared them for the hustle and bustle they saw and the seeming ignorance of the fighting going on around them.

Stands with colorful sunshades arranged in neat rows surrounded a central seating area with greenery and trees. Scents of roasted meats and fresh-baked bread hung in the air as people bustled from stand to stand, filling their baskets and bags with fresh foodstuffs, small household items, and the occasional piece of clothing. Clusters of people gathered in front of a few stands that sold food and drinks and mingled as if this were a normal day. It felt surreal. Not 40 klicks away, people fought for their lives and the freedom of this planet against the Traverse oppression that had gripped Tinaree for the last two years. Here, people acted as if they didn't have a care in the world.

The team split up to cross the plaza. Taylor and Mica skirted to the right, Kaydeen and Nitus to the left, while Salayla, Tonee, and Leer crossed through the center of the market.

Walking along the outer row of stands, Kaydeen soon realized the people weren't quite as nonchalant as they appeared. A nervous vibe hung in the air—people talked in low voices about the fighting in the region and especially in Mannahe. Few were sure of its cause, but many doubted it was more than a regional routing of dissidents. These people seemed to have accepted the new reality of their life under Traverse rule. Kaydeen hoped it wasn't too late to turn this mindset around. If enough of the populace considered the Traverse their valid government, then Intergal would land on slippery footing. This attack was supposed to be the boost Tinaree needed to throw off its oppressors and stand on its own again, not an invasion and occupation to force a mindset down the collective throats of unwilling people. That was how the Traverse operated, and why Intergal had been founded in the first place. But, if the Traverse weren't considered oppressors, then Intergal would be received as invaders.

KAYDEEN AND NITUS were about halfway across the square when she noticed two Local Enforcement Officers cutting across the market toward Taylor and Mica. Unlike the rest of them, Taylor had opted to stay outside the market's footprint and walk along the perimeter of the square. He and Mica were 30 meters from the street they would follow out of town when the LEOs intersected their path. Taylor dropped his hands to his side and loosened his stance as they approached. He was preparing to fight but held back as Mica stepped forward. It wasn't optimal, but Mica, being a native, would probably have a better chance of talking their way out of this situation than Taylor.

While Mica talked to one of the LEOs, the other eyed Taylor. They were too far away for Kaydeen to hear what was being said, but it looked like the officer thought Taylor might run. She knew better. Taylor wouldn't turn his back on a threat like that. Kaydeen resisted the urge to rush over. Whatever was about to play out would be finished before she arrived. Considering how leery the second LEO was about Taylor's change in posture, her sudden approach would probably ignite a confrontation, not soothe it.

She scanned the square. Two more officers waited in line at one of the food stands, and another two stood with some locals an aisle over from the cross-aisle she and Nitus had passed. None of them were paying attention to what was transpiring with Mica and Taylor—so far, so good. She also couldn't see any drones the local enforcement agencies used to support their officers, but with the eight cameras she'd identified in the square so far, the drones didn't need to be present. They could be docked somewhere, ready to swoop in when needed or called.

Kaydeen picked up her pace, motioning for Nitus to keep up. He did so without objection and immediately started to scan the area. *Good boy. He's trainable.* Stands and people blocked their view of Taylor and Mica as they weaved through the market, so it took him a moment to figure out the reason for her sudden urgency. Meanwhile, Tonee, Salayla, and Leer had turned off the central aisle and were using cross-aisles to make their way toward Taylor and Mica.

"Oh no," Nitus mumbled beside her.

Mica, Taylor, and the LEOs had come back into view. The officer watching Taylor had visibly relaxed, although his hand rested out of sight by his belt. The second officer had pulled out a scanner and was aiming it at Taylor. If Mica had been trying to keep the officer's attention off Taylor, it obviously hadn't worked. The officer looked at his scanner, then at Mica, and finally at Taylor. Kaydeen was still too far away to make out their words, but Tonee and Salayla were almost on top of them.

Salayla suddenly pulled Tonee into a stand and made a show of pointing out some merchandise. A moment later, Kaydeen saw why. Taylor was signaling them to stand down and meet up later. She slowed and scanned the plaza to make sure they hadn't drawn attention.

Taylor pulled out a blade and handed it to the officer hilt-first. He then glanced across the square, making eye contact first with Tonee and Salayla, then Kaydeen. It was only a minuscule pause, but long enough to confer his intent to not fight. Turning back to the speaking LEO, he nodded to instructions Kaydeen was still too far away to hear and walked in the direction the LEO indicated.

"I didn't know he had a blade," Nitus commented as they watched the four retrace Taylor's and Mica's steps. "The scanner probably picked it up."

"What scanner?" The pistol in the small of Kaydeen's back suddenly felt oversized and prominent.

Scanners had been mentioned during their pre-mission briefing, but only as they pertained to their mission specifics. It had been more important to Commander Tess to stress that Tinaree LEOs, who most often were the people behind the scanners, were sticklers for enforcing the standing law until it was officially changed, revoked, or put on hold, but were not to be considered enemy combatants. They could shoot at you, but you couldn't return the favor, at least not with deadly force. "Neutralize them," Tess had said, "but keep them alive. They'll be the people who keep Tinaree safe once our job is done."

"The security scanner at the Magistrate building." Nitus pointed to a building with a wide stairway at the far end of the plaza. Taylor and Mica had passed it shortly after the group had split up. "It scans for weapons as people are going up the stairs to enter the building, but sometimes it bleeds into a wider area and picks up people outside the checkpoint." He looked at her hand that had inadvertently moved to verify the back of her jacket was still hanging loose. "Nah, you're good. That's why I took you the other way around the plaza." He waved her off.

"Are there other scanners?" She suppressed a smile at his boisterous claim. Adrenaline was pumping through the boy.

"Not in a town this small."

"Okay, good." She paused as another memory from the pre-mission briefing floated to the foreground. "The LEOs are chipped?" She knew the answer the moment she voiced the question.

"Chipped?"

"They have implants providing an AR overlay to augment their vision with data."

It wasn't the only augmentation possible, but it was the one most often used by law enforcement and said to be standard equipment for all LEOs on Tinaree, even before the Traverse had invaded.

"Yes."

"Do you know what kind of data they can draw on? Can they access the sensor at the Magistrate building or the cameras in the square?"

Nitus thought for a moment. "Not sure about the sensor, but I know they can access the cameras and the drones."

"So, although the other LEOs in the square look like they're not paying attention, they could be watching us via the cameras."

Nitus looked at her in surprise. "Why would they be watching us?"

"Because it would be prudent for them to know if Taylor

had friends who might cause trouble." She sped up her steps. "We need to move."

"So, how would they know to watch us?"

"Hopefully, they don't. But I'm sure the cameras in the square aren't the only ones in town, so they could've picked us up walking together."

Tonee and Salayla fell in beside her as she passed their stand.

"Four more LEOs and eight cameras for them to access."

"I counted ten cameras," Tonee replied.

"And three drones," Salayla added. "One just lifted up from the magistrate's roof, one sits in the large tree in the plaza's center, and one came out of the street we came in from."

"You think they've been tracking us?" Nitus asked from behind.

"Why would they?" Leer asked beside him.

"Do the drones have sensors?" Tonee asked in return.

"Some do, but not all."

"So, the drone in the street could have scanned us as we passed it," Kaydeen clarified.

"Then they would've picked you up, too, not only Taylor," Tonee replied. "Plus, I doubt they would've allowed us to enter the crowd." He shook his head. "No, I still think the drones are coincidence or standard procedure."

He and Salayla had obviously discussed this subject already. Kaydeen shrugged. They'd find out soon enough.

"And I'm sure you guys marching as though you're in a military parade has nothing to do with drawing attention," Leer commented with a chuckle.

Sure enough, they'd fallen into their Academy habit of marching in step—a rookie move. Kaydeen switched her step pattern immediately while Salayla fell back between the two boys and hooked her arms in theirs. Tonee harrumphed in annoyance.

By the time they entered the street, Taylor and Mica were about halfway to the Magistrate building. Kaydeen kept expecting Taylor to bolt, in a surprise dash to get away, but he didn't. Instead, he stayed ahead of the two LEOs and aimed straight for the Magistrate building, without another glance at his teammates.

She felt like they were abandoning him.

Tonee must have sensed her hesitation. He looked at her and then motioned with his head back to the square, giving his silent consent. She would stay behind while the others headed out of town. As he started to jog away, she turned around to head back. Salayla nodded at her and then ushered the boys forward to catch up with Tonee. They would meet up at their fallback point outside of town.

Nitus made to stay with Kaydeen, but Salayla grabbed him by the arm and dragged him with her. It was better that way. Kaydeen could move faster and take more risks without him. Plus, if the LEO network did pick up on her being armed, anyone with her would automatically be targeted with a warrant.

Kaydeen crossed the street to the opposite corner and leaned against the wall. Better to be in plain view and seem nonchalant than peeking around a corner like a thief.

She quickly picked out the LEOs in the crowd. All four were standing together, chatting while eating. The drones were harder to find. The one in the tree would have been easy to miss had she not known where to look, the second one was just turning up an alley on the far side of the little park, and the third had settled back atop the Magistrate building. It looked like an odd-shaped weathervane, with its elongated body and two stubby wings, sitting on top of a pole on the peak of the roof. Taylor and Mica climbed the stairs and disappeared into the building. Kaydeen continued to wait and watch, hoping against hope that Taylor and Mica would soon come back out.

After what felt like hours, but couldn't have been more than fifteen minutes, Mica came out alone. Kaydeen's heart sank as he raced down the stairs and along the edge of the plaza. Kaydeen scanned the area for anybody tracking the boy's movement, but with the cameras and the drones, the person doing the tracking didn't have to be visible. She waited until Mica saw her and then walked down the street. The cameras would make it impossible to keep them from being seen together, but she could at least make it look as casual as possible. Mica caught up with her moments later. They continued walking toward the edge of town.

"What happened?"

"Taylor...got...arrested." Mica was breathing hard from his sprint, pushing the words out in quick bursts. "I didn't know... he had...a blade on him. The scanner...picked it up...and... alerted the LEOs."

Kaydeen motioned for him to stop talking. "Take a moment to breathe." She moved her hand up and down in front of her body, coaching him to slow his breathing. "We saw what happened but couldn't hear what was said. The LEO scanned both of you. That should've set off alarm bells but didn't seem to surprise him."

"Well, no." Mica's breathing had slowed enough to speak in complete sentences. "Taylor's ID was clean."

"Excuse me?" She stared at him.

"Yeah, it didn't mention that he'd joined Intergal, 'cause that would've definitely set off alarm bells." Now that he'd caught his breath, the words tumbled out in rapid-fire succession. "But I thought he was older. I mean, doesn't it take more than a year to train you guys?"

"Yes."

She was still processing what he was telling her. Although her perfect memory allowed her to speak Tinareean with hardly an accent, it still took her a moment to translate the words. At the speed he was firing them off, she was playing catch up.

"Then, how can he be only seventeen? I thought you couldn't start the Academy until you're at least sixteen?"

"You can't, and he isn't." She held up her hand to keep his words in check. "Are you saying the scanner IDed him as a seventeen-year-old Tinareean?" Mica's head bobbed up and down. "What name?"

"Mark Taylor."

"That makes no sense." She frowned.

"Why not?"

"Because he is neither Tinareean nor seventeen," she answered.

Taylor was spaceborn and claimed no nationality, but he had lived on dozens of planets all over the galaxy. While he'd told them he'd never been on Tinaree, the frailty of recall most people suffered, especially of early childhood memories, could mean that he simply didn't remember. It was feasible, therefore, that he had been here and that, during that time, his bioprint was entered into the system and mistakenly assigned a permanent ID. Somehow, she doubted the explanation was that simple, especially since it didn't explain the age discrepancy.

"But that buys us some time." She turned back to Mica. "They arrested Taylor for having a blade, which is considered contraband, but they let you go?"

"He said he found it on the mountain and that I didn't know he'd picked it up." He shrugged. "And I really didn't see him grab it on the trail."

"Because he didn't." She'd felt it on him the day before when she'd checked him over in the alley.

Mica frowned at her, but she didn't elaborate.

"What happens now?" she prompted.

"He has to go before the magistrate."

"When?"

"In about two hours."

"That gives us some time." She nodded then looked down the street. "Let's catch up with the others."

TAYLOR LOOKED around the small room the LEO had deposited him in. It was a standard confinement cell with blank walls and a single bunk in the far corner. The lack of a sink and toilet, or access hatches for such, indicated it was intended for short-term use. The lack of visible monitoring devices implied he was meant to feel like he had some privacy. Not to say that he wasn't being monitored—audio, visual, and scanning equipment could easily be hidden within the door, walls, or bunk, or miniaturized to the point of near invisibility.

Our body cams are only detectable with scanners, after all.

Oversized or visible surveillance tools, like the cameras throughout the town, merely served as a reminder of their presence.

He sat on the hard-looking bunk and was surprised to find that it conformed to his body's shape and temperature. He leaned back and looked up at the glowing ceiling. Confinement cells weren't usually intended to be comfortable, but here, even the light felt natural and soothing. He wondered if this was a Tinareean standard or a tactic to lower his guard.

Well, nothing to do but wait and see.

His bioscan had come up with an ID. It shouldn't have, but it did. Some people might call that luck, but he knew better. Someone had added his bioprint to the system and then changed it to make him appear three years younger than he was.

Who would do that, and why?

The obvious answer was Intergal or one of its agents, so

he didn't get identified as a foreign operator if he was captured. But that still made no sense. Had he been captured while executing the mission, his gear, his squad's presence, and the squad's SILC would've been a dead giveaway that he wasn't a local. Unless the bioscans of the whole squad had been added to the system as a contingency plan...but Commander Tess would have mentioned that during the pre-mission briefing. It's a bit hard to use a contingency plan if you don't have all the details. Maybe the IDs weren't meant for the troopers' use but for Command's, as part of their tracking and recovery system. That sounded a little far-reaching and involved. He also doubted his teammates' bioprints were in the system.

Why me? What is so special about me?

It was a question that had kept cropping up since landing on Tinaree.

The sound of the door lock mechanism brought Taylor out of his contemplations. He looked up to see the LEO who had arrested him.

"Your dad is here."

"My dad?" Taylor jumped to his feet. *Shit.*

"Well, dad isn't quite the right term." Taylor recognized the second voice before the door had slid open enough to reveal the man. "Guardian is more like it," Juvak said as he stepped into the cell.

He wrung his hands with hunched shoulders, but Taylor could see through the act even before his hard, evaluating gaze hit him, bespeaking the lie of his insecure voice. Taylor was sure that was intentional since Juvak drew out the moment just long enough. It was a message, a warning. Juvak was in control, at least for now, but he needed Taylor's cooperation. Taylor considered his options, but before he could respond, Juvak turned to the LEO who had raised his eyebrows at Taylor's reaction.

"We've had some differences of opinion lately." Juvak cringed in apology. "You know, growing pains."

He shrugged and looked at the floor, his hands still fiddling with each other. He put forth the perfect picture of a man trying to explain something he was too embarrassed to admit. And the LEO fell for it.

"I have a teenager myself." The LEO nodded with a knowing smile. "They can be a handful."

Juvak glanced at him with a shy smile. "Yeah, they can." He looked at the floor again before snapping his head up with a bright gaze, as if suddenly struck by an idea. "Officer Cameron —" he paused as if searching for the right words "—would you mind helping me make a point?"

"Sure." The LEO nodded. "What do you need?"

"Could you please explain what would have happened if Mark were older?" Juvak paused. "Let's say nineteen or twenty?"

"He would have gone straight to jail," Cameron replied, "and we would've had to report him to the Regional Guard."

Juvak nodded his understanding, giving Taylor a poignant look.

"And if his ID had come up as 'not found?'"

"Not found? Why would it come up 'not found?'" Cameron frowned.

"Humor me, please, Officer," Juvak appeased. "As I said, I'm trying to make a point."

Cameron studied Juvak, as if evaluating his reply. "All right." Cameron glanced at Taylor before addressing Juvak again. "If he'd been found to be an illegal, meaning his ID scan had come up empty or as tampered with—" he glanced at Taylor with a raised eyebrow "—he would've gone straight to the Regional Guard post."

"To be handed over to the Traverse?"

"Illegals are considered enemy combatants and are to be

treated as such." He turned toward Taylor. "Son, tampering with your ID is going to get you into a shitload of trouble neither your dad, here, nor anybody else would be able to get you out of." He nodded in emphasis. "You don't touch your ID. Ever. Understood?"

He looked at Taylor expectantly. Beside him, Juvak raised his eyebrows and motioned for Taylor to answer. Surprised to see Juvak use a standard Intergal hand signal, Taylor took another moment before he did.

"Yes, sir," Taylor acknowledged with a curt nod.

Juvak tilted his head, the ends of his mouth twitching with a satisfied smirk that disappeared as soon as Cameron turned to him. A handshake and a few more pleasantries later, the officer left the room. Juvak turned to Taylor, fatherly concern wiped off his face.

"What were you thinking, picking up contraband and bringing it into town?" His body language had shifted, though his tone of voice hadn't, at least, not until after his wrist comm *dinged*. He looked at his comm. "Don't answer that. I might not like finding out how bad a screwup you are." He spoke Trade without a hint of an accent.

He looked back up. "Arrested by a village LEO for possession of military contraband." Juvak snorted. "All that money they spend on your training, and you couldn't even make it past your first encounter with civilization." He shook his head. "No wonder he said you needed my help."

Taylor frowned. "Who?"

Juvak ignored him. "If you can't make it through the first pokey dump village, how do you plan on making it into the city?"

"The city?"

"Mannahe. You know, the big collection of buildings crowding the center of the valley. The place Mica is leading you to."

Taylor's heartbeat flooded his eardrums. He forced it back down and refused to allow his lungs to follow through with its sudden spasm. Taylor was reminded of his first encounter with Juvak and how outclassed he'd felt back then. But he would not, could not, allow this old man to keep ripping the footing from underneath him like that.

It was a logical conclusion that their objective was Mannahe since it was their best chance to contact Intergal troops. Mica had been with him when he was arrested, so his name would have been easy to obtain. And that they were using the boy as their guide could also have been a logical deduction—Mica was a local, after all.

Taylor shrugged.

"I guess it's a good thing I added your ID to the system." Juvak smiled.

Of course. "You expect me to thank you for that?"

"Oh, I don't know." Juvak folded his arms across his chest. "Where would you prefer to be? Here or at the Traverse garrison?"

Taylor looked at the door. "Well, that might still be where we're both heading."

Juvak followed his gaze.

"Nobody is listening. They're bound by law to allow us our privacy."

"Somebody is always listening, especially in a place like this." Taylor indicated their surroundings.

"This is Tinaree, not Intergal."

"Under Traverse rule," Taylor countered.

Juvak looked at the bunk. "You'd be surprised how much autonomy the Traverse allows its member nations." He said it grudgingly, as if unwilling to admit the statement.

This man makes absolutely no sense. "What do you want?"

"You."

What the fuck? "Why?"

"To keep you out of Traverse hands and get you off this dirtball."

Taylor frowned. "I don't know you."

"So you keep saying."

"You think I should."

Juvak simply looked at him.

"Why?" Taylor repeated. "What will happen once you get me off-planet?"

Again, Juvak didn't answer.

Fine. "How are you planning to get me off-planet?"

"I'm not."

Fucking bastard.

"You're contradicting yourself."

"With Intergal in full invasion mode, we're not going to get off-planet, not with you fighting me every step of the way."

"You expect me to come willingly?"

Juvak obviously did, though he continued to refuse to explain.

This makes no sense. "You're not Intergal."

"I'm not?" Juvak raised his eyebrow at him.

Finally, a reaction. "You wouldn't be here alone, undercover, or at least not without identifying yourself."

"I wouldn't, huh?" Juvak asked. "And you're the expert who knows all of Intergal's nuances and intentions?"

Taylor's heartbeat jumped back into his throat like red-hot embers flaring to life and then quieted to near stillness. "Intergal sends in rescue ops to pull its people out of shitholes, not lock them into them." Tightness rolled off his neck, like a triggering wave that loosened his compacted muscles and locked joints.

"My actions saved your life and that of your friends," Juvak hissed.

"Your actions castrated our chance to fight and locked us

underground to be drugged, tortured, and fucked," Taylor spat as he stepped forward.

Shock flashed across Juvak's features. Taylor didn't care. Juvak's intimidation factor had been nullified. He'd take this asshole down and beat him to a pulp. Then it registered that it had been his words, not his actions, that had caused Juvak's reaction. He hesitated as Juvak brought up his arm, his index finger pointing up as if to admonish him while his other hand motioned the standard sign for 'surveillance.'

"Watch your temper, boy. Their cameras are still active."

Taylor released his anger in a slow, drawn-out breath.

"Anger is good for a quick, overpowering strike, but bad for a full battle." Juvak spoke calmly.

What, now you're my fucking teacher? But Taylor knew the truth in those words. He'd heard them often enough—from his mother.

"This isn't the place for it," Juvak continued. "You have a mission to complete, a team to lead, and charges to protect. That, right now, should be your only priority—to get those you're responsible for through to the other side. You can't do that if you're stuck in here. So, play your part."

"Charges?"

"The boys are non-combatants—" Juvak paused as if catching himself. "The cameras showed three teenagers traveling with you," he backtracked. "I'm assuming they're still with your teammates."

Not a good recovery, old man. And how the hell do you know we're teammates?

"What do you care what happens to them?"

"They're innocent kids playing war, and you're dragging them along, straight to the front line." All mockery and superiority had left Juvak's manner. His voice held true concern. "They might think this is fun, but you know better. You should've never allowed them to come along." He paused, his gaze turning fierce.

And so, the table turns. How far are you going to go? "So," Taylor asked, "taking payment for medical treatment out of their sperm count is out of the question, then?"

Juvak stared at him, frozen in place.

Come on, react, or give me a fricking sign. This is taking way too long. And he was way too close. *Shit.*

Juvak exploded into motion. He grabbed Taylor by the collar, slammed him sideways into the wall, then pinned him with an elbow across the throat.

"Let's make this clear," he hissed. "Something happens to them, it's on you and you alone." He paused. "Shit happened to you. I got it. They'll pay. But this is war. And this is exactly what you were made for. You'll be all right. Fall back on your training—all of it—and you'll be fine. But these boys, they won't be, so it's on you to make sure they are."

The door slid open, and Cameron burst in, followed by three other LEOs. "All right, Dad, that's enough." They rushed the first few steps but then slowed to a more careful approach.

Juvak held Taylor's gaze a moment longer before whispering, "Play your part."

He pushed off the wall, raised his hands beside his head, then turned his head toward the LEOs.

"I'm sorry." The insecure father was back in full effect. "He knows how to push my buttons." His voice quivered. "I didn't mean to hurt him."

"Let's step away from him. Nice and slow." Cameron laid a hand on Juvak's shoulder and guided him into the arms of two of the other LEOs, who led him toward the door. Once Juvak was out of the way, Cameron turned toward Taylor.

"Are you all right?" He reached for Taylor's left shoulder.

Taylor swiped Cameron's arm to the side distractedly, his mind still picking apart Juvak's words. "I'm fine."

Cameron used a roundabout motion to circumvent Taylor's arm with his hand, grabbed his shoulder, and pushed him back into the wall—forcefully. Taylor reached for Cameron's forearm, but Cameron was ready for him. He grabbed Taylor's wrist instead, twisted it out of the way, and shoved his other forearm into Taylor's chest. Taylor was pinned against the wall again, although this time he could breathe.

"Boy," Cameron admonished, "settle down."

Taylor nodded and spread his arms to his side in surrender.

"Good." Cameron released him. "Now, let me look at your face."

He touched two fingers to the side of Taylor's chin and gently guided his head to turn. "That looks like a pretty good bruise."

Taylor hadn't realized his cheekbone had slammed into the wall. It started throbbing the moment he did. "I'm fine." He lifted his chin from Cameron's fingers to look at him.

"Is he okay?" Juvak asked from the door. He was resisting the two LEOs guiding him out of the cell. Or at least, resisting the way the person he was pretending to be would probably resist. "I didn't mean to hurt him," he reiterated. "It all happened so fast. And the wall was so much closer than I expected." The words tumbled out of his mouth. "I really didn't mean for him to hit it."

Bullshit.

"He's fine," Cameron reassured Juvak. "His ego probably took the bigger beating." He turned and nodded to the door. "You go and get yourself sorted out. It looks like this messed you up more than him."

"Oh, okay." Juvak looked at the LEOs in turn. "I guess I better go, then." He met Taylor's gaze. "I'll be waiting. When you're ready, I'll pick you up." He winked, turned, and walked out with the two LEOs.

Cameron shook his head and turned back to Taylor. "Sit

down. The magistrate isn't quite ready for you, yet." He looked at Taylor's cheek again. "You want an ice pack for that?"

Taylor shook his head. "I'm fine."

"Okay." Cameron shrugged. "It'd probably do you good to learn some respect for your dad."

Taylor watched Cameron walk out of the cell. *And it would do you good to learn to read people better.*

The man had no inkling of how badly Juvak had played him.

17

REVELATIONS

Kaydeen had yet to see anyone following them, but even with leaving the town and its cameras behind, she took her time and a few detours to get to the small, wooded area where the others would be waiting for them.

It was one of the fallback points they had chosen while planning their route the day before, in case they were separated. This one was an old garden or orchard that hadn't been taken care of in a while. The fencing was overgrown and down in multiple places, and the evenly spaced fruit trees were slowly being overtaken by underbrush and saplings. In the middle of it was a small, prefabricated building covered in vines. She wasn't sure where the others would be waiting, other than somewhere on the lot, but the old garden shack would be a good place to start looking.

She was right. Tonee opened the door, or what was left of it, as they approached. Salayla came in behind them a few moments later.

"Clear," Salayla reported. "No drones or people in sight."

That didn't mean they weren't being watched, only that

nobody was being obvious about it, and that no person or machine was within the immediate area. So, they had a little breathing space.

Tonee nodded and motioned them to the center of the room where Nitus and Leer sat. He settled into the back corner between the two windows looking out the side and back of the shed. Salayla stayed by the door, squatting eye-level with a gap overlooking the overgrown clearing in front of the shed.

"What will happen when Taylor sees the magistrate?" Tonee asked after Mica finished repeating what he'd told Kaydeen.

"His infraction will be dismissed, judged, or deferred," Salayla explained. As interpreter and cultural specialist, her train-up packet would have included local social and regulatory norms, just as Kaydeen's packet had included pertinent medical information.

"Being caught with a weapon never gets dismissed," Nitus put in.

"Even with war knocking on the door?" Tonee asked.

Nitus shrugged.

"Can't. They don't have the option to dismiss contraband charges," Mica explained. "That's why the LEOs couldn't confiscate the blade and let us go. He said that since it had been recorded on us, he would have to take us in. But he did say it should be only a formality, considering what's going on."

"Okay, so judged or deferred." Tonee frowned. "I'm assuming deferred means his hearing is pushed back?"

Salayla and Nitus nodded.

"What kind of judgment can he expect?" Kaydeen asked. She knelt by the boys, watching the windows. Her distance from the wall restricted her view outside, but Tonee, who had slid into a crouch, easily covered the angles she couldn't.

"Don't know," Nitus answered. "Guess that depends on his record." He shrugged.

"Mica said his ID came back clean," Tonee ventured. "So, they're looking at a minor without a record who found a blade he couldn't let be although he should've known better." He paused as his eyes defocused.

His mind was probably picking the situation apart from the viewpoint of the LEOs. It was one of his specialties and favorite pastimes—to dissect rules and regulations and pinpoint the mindset of enforcers.

"Yeah, the blade is considered military contraband." He shrugged. "But it's his first offense, and with the fighting going on, they don't want to keep him in their custody and be responsible for his safety." He considered for a moment. "They could push him off to the local garrison. But, again, they think he's a local teen. A hormonal, brain-farted teen, but still one of the local kids. They're not going to hand him over to the Traverse, not with what happened to the miner kids." He looked at Mica. "That is general knowledge, right?" He barely waited for Mica's nod before continuing. "No, they'd want to keep him out of harm's way, not put him closer to it." He nodded. "They're sticklers for enforcing the law, but that's how they protect themselves and their people. And for now, they think Taylor is one of their people." He paused to look at the others. "Let's hope it stays that way."

"Hormonal, brain-farted teen?" Nitus asked.

"That's all you got out of my speech?" Tonee looked at him.

"Well, no," Nitus stammered, shrinking into himself.

"Don't call us that." Leer rolled onto his knees, positioning himself between the two.

"Actually," Tonee turned to him, "I called Taylor that. But if you want to claim the title..." The corners of his mouth slowly lifted.

"I think," Salayla put in, smoothly cutting the sudden tension, "Tonee is using an expression he's heard a few times himself." She eyed him.

Tonee chuckled. “Once or twice.”

Kaydeen shook her head as Leer settled down. Leave it to Tonee to not miss an opportunity to rile an easy target.

“How will we find out the magistrate’s decision?” She brought the discussion back to their immediate problem. “I assume we won’t be able to enter the building without an ID scan.” She looked at Mica.

“Don’t have to,” he replied. “We can watch the hearing from here.”

“Watch it from here?”

“Yes.” Mica elaborated, “Since the magistrates are part of the public domain, the hearings are too.”

“And that helps us, how?” Tonee asked.

“Because anything in the public domain is accessible over the Net,” Leer clarified.

“So, we can access it with your comms?”

“Yes,” Leer dragged the word out, “that’s what that means.”

Tonee looked at him for a moment before breaking into a grin. “Good one,” he conceded with a nod.

Leer grinned in return and pulled out his comm. Nitus and Mica did the same.

Mica’s was the largest at twice the size of Nitus’. Its edges slid out to increase the screen another 50 percent and allow for comfortable two-handed use of the screen’s virtual keyboard. Leer’s was half the size of Nitus’, fitting comfortably into the palm of his hand, but it could unfold twice to increase its screen to the size of Mica’s collapsed comm. Both Leer’s and Nitus’ comms had holographic keyboards that needed a flat surface to be used. In the team’s world, the gadgets would have been called datapads, but whenever the teammates had used the word, the boys had given them blank stares—that word wasn’t in their vocabulary.

Kaydeen watched over Nitus’ shoulder as he brought up the magistrate’s office on the public Net, then narrowed it to the Mannahe region, and finally to Tuscoony where Taylor had been arrested. A few taps later, he had the list of upcoming hearings. Taylor's had begun a few minutes earlier. The screen quartered, showing an overlapping view of the room as seen from its four corners. It looked square with a door in the center of each wall and two rows of benches, separated by walkways, surrounding an open space with a large desk. A uniformed man sat behind the desk looking at Taylor standing in front of it. The two LEOs who had arrested him sat on the bench behind Taylor. Otherwise, the room was empty.

"...have planned to do with the blade?" the magistrate was asking as the sound cut in.

Taylor shrugged, his eyes flicking to one of the cameras.

Kaydeen did a double take. "Can you zoom in?" she asked Nitus as she squinted for a better look.

"No." Nitus shook his head. "Sorry."

"His left cheek looks bruised." Salayla squinted at Leer's comm.

"You see it, too?" Kaydeen looked at Mica's datapad, where Tonee was watching. Mica's larger screen gave a better view. "Yup, that's a contusion."

"You think he mouthed off?" Tonee asked.

"Taylor?" Salayla frowned at him.

"No way." Kaydeen replied at the same time.

"Did he look at us?" Mica asked. "I mean, I know he looked at the camera, but it seemed like he knows we're watching."

"How would he know we're watching?" Leer scrunched up his face.

"There, he did it again," Nitus agreed. "I think Mica is right."

"Do you know how stupid that sounds?" Leer shook his head. "They aren't going to let him see the login screen."

Kaydeen looked up in alarm, as did Tonee and Salayla.

"Login screen?" She looked at Nitus. "They can tell who's watching?"

"Well, yeah." Nitus knitted his brows. "But not by looking at the cameras. They don't have screens to display that."

"But the system tracks who's watching," Tonee clarified.

"Well, yeah," Leer mocked. "Public domain, remember?"

Tonee ignored Leer's derisive tone. "Can they see us and where we are?"

Mica's face brightened in understanding. "No." He shook his head. "And yes." He raised his hands at Tonee's exasperated huff. "No, they cannot see where we are by looking at the room's logins," he explained. "For that, they have to actually ping our location." He shook his head again. "And they can't access our comms' cameras without our approval. So, they can't see who's watching."

"If they attempted to, you would get a pop-up requesting permission?" Salayla clarified.

"Yes."

"But that could be bypassed?"

Mica shrugged. "Anything is hackable."

"Yes, sir." Taylor's sharp reply drew their attention back to the screens.

The magistrate had been reprimanding him to pay attention, meet his gaze, and give audible answers. But the magistrate's next words caught everybody off guard.

"No wonder your dad lost his temper." He raised his hand to forestall any argument Taylor might offer. "I don't want to hear the 'he's my guardian not my dad' BS, you seem to have successfully fed him. You might not be blood, but he took care of you, kept you safe, and he continues to sacrifice his time for you. He got you where you are today. In my book, that makes him your dad, and you owe him respect for that." He paused. "Is that clear?"

"Yes, sir." Taylor stood frozen at attention, his face a mask, not betraying an inkling of his thoughts about the magistrate's words.

Kaydeen knew his posture well. She'd seen it—or whatever variation was called for at the time—often during training. Standing at full attention in the heat, carrying a rifle over your head while running in gale force strong winds, or holding the push-up ready position in biceps-deep surf. They had done it all, and Taylor had always been the one to last the longest, without fail, and without showing one emotion. He could shut out the world and keep going through sheer force of will.

The magistrate stood and walked around his desk, studying Taylor with narrowed eyes. Taylor's eyes followed him, to hold the magistrate's gaze as he had been ordered to.

"Shit." Tonee's exclamation startled her.

She scanned the windows, then the door, before looking at him. His eyes were on Mica's datapad, tied to the events playing out only a few klicks away but so untouchable they could be happening in another star system. Tonee looked as helpless as she felt.

"You've been to a military school?" The magistrate turned the statement into a question at the last syllable.

Taylor's posture tightened, the only visible sign of his reaction. Easily overlooked unless you knew him well enough to recognize the telltale signs, or you were watching him closely from a few steps away. The magistrate raised a finger as if to forestall an answer.

"No, you wouldn't have," he answered his own question. "At least not in the last two years, and before that, you would have been too young." He abruptly walked back around his desk and sat. "I'm going to defer my judgment." He moved his hands as if accessing a desktop terminal, but none of the cameras were angled to pick up the screen sunk into the desk's surface. "You will report back to me in two weeks." He paused. "No, let's make it one month. That gives you enough time to show a change in your behavior." His eyes flicked to the LEOs in the background before returning to Taylor. "Be forewarned, your warrant will stay active. I will make sure of that. I want to see you back here after all this is over and hear the rest of your story."

He held Taylor's gaze a moment longer before dismissing him with a wave of his hand. Taylor turned and followed the LEOs out of the room. The magistrate continued to watch him with the same studious, pinched gaze. A few moments after the door closed, his eyes flicked to the cameras, then back to the door, and then finally to his terminal. He leaned forward and punched commands.

"Shut it down," Salayla ordered. "Shut down the connection."

The boys looked at her but did as she instructed. An alert sounded on Mica's datapad. A moment later, Nitus' comm went off.

"How do you shut down the tracking?" Tonee asked. "Will powering them down work, or are they pingable while off?"

"Theirs are," Leer said. "Mine's not."

"Destroy them."

"Why?"

"Because the magistrate wants to know who is watching," Kaydeen explained.

Tonee nodded. "And if we don't answer, we'll have LEOs breathing down our necks."

"Wouldn't destroying the comms be more suspicious and send them out faster?" Nitus asked.

"Can they differentiate between the comm losing the signal and being destroyed?"

"Okay," Tonee conceded at Nitus' nodded shrug. "What do you suggest we do, then?"

"I could answer it," Mica suggested. "They already know me, anyway."

"The moment you answer, he'll know where you are," Leer said.

"Yeah, but he probably knows that already." Mica shrugged. "And why would I want to hide where I am, anyway? I mean, I simply want to know what's going on with my friend." He grinned.

Kaydeen, Tonee, and Salayla looked at each other. None of them liked it, but it was the best option they had.

"Okay." Salayla nodded. "Verify that no one else is in camera view before you answer, give as little information as possible, and remember that he will be able to see you looking at us."

Tonee leaned forward. "So, don't."

Mica nodded, drew a deep breath, and tapped his datapad.

The conversation was short and seemed innocent. The magistrate verified that Mica was all right, asked if he was waiting on his friend, and then elicited the promise that they would get home as quickly as possible, but it left a bad feeling in the bottom of Kaydeen's gut. She wasn't the only one.

Mica stared at the datapad, frozen in place. Seconds ticked by. Kaydeen slid forward, unsure if the comm was truly disconnected. The screen was blank. Tonee nudged it from behind, almost flipping it out of Mica's hand, and breaking the spell on him. He looked up with a start.

"You okay, bud?" Tonee studied him.

"Yeah." Mica nodded quickly. "Yeah, I'm fine. I just—" He glanced at Leer and Nitus.

"You've never lied to an officer before, have you?" Tonee smirked.

Mica shook his head.

"Don't worry." Tonee grinned. "It don't get easier. You just get better at hiding it."

"I think—" Salayla pulled the datapad out of Mica's shaking hand "—we're going to leave these here."

She motioned for Nitus and Leer to hand over their comms. Nitus did so, but Leer shook his head.

"They can't track mine."

"Hand it over anyway."

"But—"

"As Mica said, anything is hackable." She grabbed it out of his hand.

They buried them under a pile of junk in the corner and then went to the edge of the tree line to await Taylor's arrival.

TAYLOR APPEARED A SHORT TIME LATER, jogging across a fallow field and surreptitiously scanning his surroundings. Considering how quickly he appeared, he must have been running the whole way.

"You okay?" Kaydeen asked as they stepped out of the tree line to meet him.

"Yes." Taylor nodded as he slowed to a walk. He wasn't even out of breath. "Let's keep moving." He motioned in the direction of Mannahe.

"What happened?" Kaydeen indicated the welt on his cheek as she fell in beside him.

Taylor touched his cheek, his eyes losing focus. "A small altercation."

"With your dad?" Tonee asked, raising his eyebrows as he elongated the last word.

"You watched the hearing." Taylor looked around again. He didn't seem surprised to hear they'd accessed the cameras in the hearing room.

They crossed through the overgrown border of a manmade water channel and into a dry depression. It wouldn't prevent scanning equipment using different wavelengths from detecting them, but it would make it harder for somebody using only the visual band. Plus, it gave them a sense of security, albeit a false one.

"So?" Tonee brought Taylor's attention back to the subject. "Who is your dad?"

Taylor stared into the distance with a frown. He scanned their surroundings one more time, breathed as if steeling himself, and then stopped to look at his friends.

"Juvak."

Juvak? Kaydeen looked at him in surprise. *The opportunistic merc who preferred to make some quick cash over following orders?* He'd been the last person she expected. From what Mica had told them, the merc's greed had probably saved their lives, but that had been a lucky chance for them, not an intentional result on his part. Or had it?

"At least, that's what my local ID says."

Taylor met her gaze, then Tonee's and Salayla's, whose minds were working, like hers—probably with a similar thought pattern.

Leer was also staring at him, but with narrowed eyes, more suspicious than surprised.

"Who is Juvak?" Nitus asked.

Innocent curiosity. That was closer to what Kaydeen would've expected from the teens. Or Mica's intense scrutiny as he noted the teammates reaction to the name. Leer's reaction didn't fit.

And it disappeared the moment the teen noticed her attention. He looked at her, not embarrassed or defiant, but self-assured and assertive. It was a glimpse of the man the boisterous youth would become—and the man was far more guarded.

Taylor watched her interaction with Leer and then turned to Nitus. "That's a question I'd like to have answered, too." He looked around again, then indicated a depression in the water channel up ahead with the top of a culvert visible to its right. "Let's find some cover, and I'll fill you in."

The depression turned out to be a small basin where three water channels combined to drain into the culvert. A small stream of water coming from the channel to their left ran down its center into the culvert. Otherwise, it was dry. Tonee led the way and jumped the one-meter height difference into the basin to approach the pipe. It was slightly shorter than he, but wide enough to accommodate three people side-by-side—if the person in the center didn't mind wet feet. The pipe's surface was smooth, grayish-white, and unmarred, probably some kind of alloy or composite material to stand up to the water and debris.

Tonee ducked into the pipe and, after a short pause, proceeded into its shadows. Kaydeen waited for the others to precede her and then followed. Once her eyes adjusted to the sudden darkness, she saw Tonee had stopped a few meters in and was using a foot to prop himself against the tunnel's arching sidewall. He was looking expectantly at Taylor, who crouched partially up the opposite arch, his elbows resting on his knees and his hands folded one over the other with his chin resting on his outstretched thumbs. Taylor, in turn, was studying the boys as if evaluating their presence. When Kaydeen joined them, he met and held her gaze for a moment and then proceeded to tell them about Juvak visiting him in the mine. He didn't get very far when Tonee interrupted him.

"They fricking drugged you?"

Taylor shrugged. "Guess it was their pleasure of the week."

His answer sounded nonchalant. His expression and body language told a different story, and Tonee realized it. The rage bubbling in his eyes didn't burst forth. Instead, Tonee's gaze locked down, his attention as much internal as external.

Kaydeen had seen that expression before during 'team

bonding sessions' when they had to reveal their most painful experiences. While his teammates had been allowed to choose their subjects, Tonee hadn't been so lucky. With his whole life on record in Intergal files, the trainers had picked his subjects for him: feeling the bodies of his grandparents grow cold and stiff around him as rescuers dug them out of the rubble of their collapsed house when he was nine, and getting notified on his twelfth birthday that his parents had been killed in the line of duty, his mother during a mission and his father while returning to their home station with her body. That same rage of helplessness had surfaced during those retellings and been just as quickly compartmentalized, although for a different reason. Back then, to protect himself, this time, to protect his friend.

Taylor met Kaydeen's gaze again and then told them how Juvak had emptied his stomach and forced the antidote down his throat.

Juvak's actions had probably saved Taylor's life, but that didn't excuse him for putting them into that hole in the first place. She reprimanded herself. Juvak hadn't had to save Taylor, so he deserved her gratitude. She merely needed to decide if she would thank him before or after she killed him.

As Taylor continued, and it became clear his withdrawal had been a choice, not a psychological impairment, Tonee's jaw tightened.

Taylor paused and looked at him, clearly not surprised by his reaction. Neither was Kaydeen. Tonee motioned for Taylor to continue.

Taylor met her gaze a third time and then relayed what had happened at the magistrate's.

All in all, they ended up with more questions than answers. Not good in the chaos of war. It added another complication to an already overcrowded set of headaches. She had thought Juvak out of the picture. But now, he was not only back, but with the capacity to affect an unknown number of possibly random factors. Random, at least, until they could make sense of his actions, motives, and intentions.

TONEE WAS quiet for long moments, anger and pain vying for control of his face as he processed what Taylor had told them. Kaydeen knew he had agonized over Taylor's behavior during the last weeks of their captivity. He hadn't admitted it, though, and he had tried to hide his downtrodden and depressive lapses into despair. Kaydeen and Salayla had seen through it, of course, but they hadn't pressed him—humans could be funny when put on the spot like that—instead, they'd used their nightly sleeping arrangements to Share the burden and help balance individual low points. Tonee hadn't been the only one to benefit from those Readings.

"Why did you leave us in the dark?" Tonee's voice held more pain than anger when he finally spoke.

"You wouldn't have believed me," Taylor replied with a minute shake to his head. "Not without a—"

He didn't look at the three boys as he left the last word hanging, but his intent was clear. While he was willing to divulge what happened between him and Juvak, he wasn't as willing to reveal the presence of Din.

"Maybe." Tonee nodded in acknowledgement. "But we would have liked the opportunity to decide that ourselves—" he paused for just a fraction "—and the knowledge that you trusted us with that decision."

Taylor flinched at his words.

"And what if we hadn't believed you?" Tonee continued. "Nothing would have changed. Things would have played out the same way." He paused again. "Other than knowing that we weren't watching you slip away."

Taylor's eyes tightened. His gaze switched from focusing on

Tonee's face to staring through his chest as Tonee's words, and the emotions behind them, settled on him. The words were painful, but Tonee was right, and Taylor needed to hear it, although Kaydeen wouldn't have chosen this time or place to confront him. While he said the encounter with Juvak in the mine had been the only reason for his withdrawal, Kaydeen knew better. She'd sensed the dark abyss in Taylor. He might have intended to pretend he was broken, but it probably hadn't taken much effort to bring despair to the forefront. And she wasn't sure how much it would take before he was toeing that abyssal edge again.

Tonee studied Taylor in silence, and for a moment, Kaydeen thought he would leave it be. But then, Tonee went on the attack.

"When were you going to tell us?" He spoke quietly at first. "Or would you have told us at all if your arrest hadn't forced you to?"

Taylor's head snapped up. "Of course. I hadn't—"

"Oh, really?" Tonee drew out the words. "You don't think it might be advantageous for the rest of us to know a little detail like the possibility of Juvak hunting us before we head out? It's not like we're in Traverse territory, or anything."

"Juvak isn't Traverse."

Taylor's quick reply took Tonee aback. But not for long.

"Of course. That explains it all." Tonee's words dripped with sarcasm. "Or is there something else we don't know about?"

"Tonee," Salayla admonished.

"I'm not done giving him a piece of my mind, yet." Tonee waved her off.

"That's not helping," Kaydeen put in.

"What?" Tonee looked at her. "You prefer I just punch him?"

"That wouldn't improve the situation either," Salayla said.

"Well, it might improve my mood."

"Really?" Taylor frowned at him.

"Well, no," Tonee replied, "but it would get rid of my steam."

"All right." Taylor stood, shrugged off his pack, and spread his arms by his side. "Then punch me."

Tonee pushed off the wall.

"Guys." Kaydeen spread her arms to keep them apart. "This is neither the time nor place."

"Gentlemen," Salayla said, reaching for the teenagers, "back up, please."

She grabbed Leer by the elbow and pulled him toward the exit, motioning for Mica and Nitus to follow.

Tonee pushed Kaydeen's hand out of the way.

"He said I can punch him."

Kaydeen stepped in front of him. "And I'm saying you shouldn't."

"Oh, come on." Tonee grabbed her by her upper arms and lifted her to his eye level. "He's going to dodge, anyway," he whispered as he set her aside.

Before she could block him again, he crossed the runnel of water between the two men.

Taylor still hadn't moved.

Time seemed to slow as Tonee's right hook rushed toward Taylor's head. Kaydeen's mind screamed at Taylor to move. With the size and layout of the tunnel, he was quickly running out of options to avoid the blow.

Taylor's lack of movement surprised Tonee as much as Kaydeen, as was evidenced by his partial exclamation of "Fu..." as he barreled into him.

He punched the air above Taylor's head, stumbled, and landed hard on his knees.

"You fucking bastard," Tonee spat as he unfurled himself from around Taylor.

Taylor, laying on his back, halfway up the arch of the tunnel, looked up at him. "You missed."

"And you didn't fucking dodge."

"Then you would've definitely missed."

"Duh. I could've broken your fucking jaw."

"I doubt it. Not punching me like that."

Kaydeen exhaled in relief. *Idiots.*

Tonee sat back on his haunches. "Don't do that again."

"Not dodge?" Taylor asked as he sat up.

"That, too." Tonee grabbed Taylor's outstretched hand as he rocked back to his feet and stood.

Kaydeen grasped the side of Taylor's shoulder, slipping her hand under the loose sleeve of his shirt, and Skimmed him. True Readings were best, of course, but the four had built a deep enough connection that Salayla and Kaydeen could get a general feeling of their teammates' emotional status without having to enter their minds. That is, if Taylor wasn't actively shutting them out.

"I'm all right." Taylor waved her off but didn't avoid her studying gaze, or her touch—external or internal.

The teetering insecurity she had seen in his gaze earlier was gone, and the edge of his abyss, not even in the same solar system as the rest of his mind.

"Very graceful," Salayla commented as she walked up to Tonee.

Tonee shrugged. "Gotta do what I gotta do."

"Eloquence incarnate." Salayla slid her fingers up his arm and wrapped them around his biceps below his rolled-up sleeve.

He followed her motion and then looked at her. "Bite me."

Salayla held his gaze. "Promises, promises." She winked. "Are you finished?"

Tonee looked at her hand still touching his arm. "You tell me."

She smiled and then looked at Kaydeen. "Taylor?"

"Not yet," he replied and turned toward the boys. "Mica, what happened the first time you tried to free us?"

Mica flinched at Taylor's words. The guilt of not being able to get them out of the transport was written all over the boy's face. Taylor needed to work on his delivery. Even an unintended slap in the face stung.

Taylor's gaze sliced to Salayla, who was rolling her eyes and shaking her head at him, and then amended, "How did you get out of the transport, and how did you know where to find us?"

Mica swallowed his guilt. "I was in the transport until they took you to the mine. I hid in a storage locker and waited for a while. When it was quiet again, I tried to get out, but something was blocking the locker door, and I couldn't open it."

"Probably a good thing," Tonee said. "'cause after his little commotion—" he nodded toward Taylor "—they kept a guard on us." He snickered. "The guard was probably leaning against the locker when you tried to open it."

"Oh." Mica's eyes widened at the realization of how close he'd come to getting caught.

"You rode the transport all the way to the mine?" Salayla asked, cutting off Taylor's next question.

Taylor looked at her with calm indulgence. His expression hadn't changed much, at least not to outsiders, but his body language spoke volumes. Their silent exchange went over the teens' heads but not over Tonee's, who met Kaydeen's gaze with a smile. They hadn't had much to be happy about, but seeing the team's chemistry return was something.

"Yeah," Mica answered. "I waited for a good twenty minutes after the transport stopped and fell silent before I tried the door again."

Twenty minutes? Kaydeen looked at him in alarm. She was sure it hadn't taken twenty minutes for Juvak to hand them over and collect his money. But she didn't interrupt.

"And then?" Salayla prodded.

"That's when Leer's dad found me."

"Leer's dad?" Tonee asked at the same time as Taylor's gaze snapped to the bigger boy. "What was he doing in the transport?"

"I don't know." Mica shrugged. "He didn't say."

Taylor frowned. "So, he was aware of the transport, yet, he didn't believe you'd seen us?" When Mica shrugged again, he asked, "What does he look like?"

"Why?" Leer stepped forward. "What's that got to do with anything?"

Taylor tilted his head. "Wondering if we saw him."

"You accusing my dad of being Traverse?" Leer's nostrils flared.

"Juvak's not Traverse," Taylor said. "But if your dad was using his position to collect intel for the Resistance, we might have come in contact with him."

Leer shut his mouth since he couldn't argue with Taylor's logic. Although, if he'd known the only people they'd come in contact with had actively participated in their capture and enslavement, he probably wouldn't have given in as quickly.

"So, what does he look like?" Taylor reposed the question to no one in particular, but it was Mica who answered.

"I don't know. He's old, has light-colored hair and a tan, and always has tools on him."

"Do you have a pic?" Taylor looked at Leer, who shook his head. "I did, on my comm they made me destroy."

"We didn't destroy them," Mica retorted, "we hid them. We can go back and get it."

"That won't help. I wiped it," Leer added quickly.

"You did?" Tonee asked. "When did you have time for that?"

"It only takes a few commands." Leer shrugged. "I'm sure yours wipe as quickly."

"Yeah, but ours are military-grade with special features to

keep sensitive data out of enemy hands. Civilian models are set up to avoid easy data wipes, so they don't happen by accident."

"The Resistance has sensitive data."

"On your comm?" Taylor asked.

"Maybe," Leer snapped at Taylor. "But if you hadn't gotten yourself arrested, we wouldn't be having this discussion, 'cause I wouldn't have had to leave my comm behind."

"Whoa, buddy," Tonee soothed. "Shit can happen to anybody."

"Yeah, more so to the people hanging around him," Leer spat, indicating Taylor with a curt nod.

His venomous tone took Kaydeen aback, but his comment's insinuation threw her. If she hadn't known better, she would have said his tone was for effect, to distract from the idea he was sowing. But that wasn't something a hormone-driven, emotional teenager reacting to disliked stimuli in a stressful environment would come up with on the spur of the moment.

"Son," Tonee started.

"Don't 'son' me," Leer snapped at him. "You're not my dad." He paused before adding in a calmer tone, "Who, by the way, is not your enemy."

"Nobody said he was," Tonee replied.

"He did." Leer jutted his chin at Taylor. "At least, he insinuated it," he amended before Tonee could argue the point further.

Taylor's expression, unlike Tonee's, showed no reaction, positive or negative, to Leer's outburst. But his gaze stayed on the teen, studying, evaluating. As did Salayla's. She seemed as perplexed as Kaydeen by Leer's minefield of confounding behavior. Mica stared at his friend, while Nitus openly gaped, so Leer's reaction had surprised them, too. Maybe it was the stress of their situation, but Kaydeen doubted it was that simple.

Tonee fell silent. There was no sense in continuing the

argument. Doing so would only increase its volatility. He held Leer's gaze a moment longer, then turned to his teammates as if dismissing the boy. Kaydeen expected another outburst, but the teen's ire had dissolved as quickly as it had exploded. Tonee's words and actions hadn't produced the same reaction as Taylor's.

Tonee looked at Salayla and Kaydeen before settling his gaze on Taylor. With the discussion and its value having reached a dead end, it was time to move on. Taylor agreed with a nod, grabbed his pack, and headed to the tunnel's exit. As the others filed out behind him, Kaydeen noticed Leer's gaze glued to Taylor's back. It wasn't threatening or vengeful, but speculating. His calculating eyes were so much more mature than the teenager smiling at her an instant later. He played the awkwardness well, and were her memory any less immaculate, it might have worked in making her doubt her impression. As it was, it succeeded in raising her conviction that he was far more than he let on.

18

THE FIELDS

The blocks of color, as seen from the mountain trail, were large swathes of plants separated by lanes between two and five meters wide. Some of the lanes were paved, but most were compacted dirt. The plants were in full bloom, displaying an array of purples, greens, and blues topped with yellow, red, and orange flowers. Each field was a mass of the same plant arranged in rows for easy tending and harvest. Most were tall enough to impede their view in any direction but along the lanes. Taylor, who was in the lead with Mica, kept them out of the cleared areas and skimmed the edges of the fields, weaving in and out of the plant rows as the footing allowed.

About an hour into their march, Salayla passed Kaydeen and Nitus to walk beside Taylor. "Mica, would you and Nitus please walk with Leer? I would like to speak with Taylor."

The two dropped back behind Kaydeen and fell in with Leer and Tonee, who was bringing up the rear as usual. As they approached, Tonee slowed for a few paces until a good five meters of separation turned them into two distinct groups.

"Leer finds issue with you," Salayla said in Trade.

"I've noticed," Taylor replied without taking his gaze off their surroundings.

"He seems content for us to think your behavior incenses him. However, I don't believe that's his true sentiment."

He glanced at her, then looked at the ground in front of them before returning to his vigilance. "Have you tried Reading him?"

"And how would I justify that request?" She raised her eyebrows at him.

"What about that little hands-on thing you and Kay keep doing?"

Salayla laughed. "So, you *have* noticed."

"I wasn't supposed to?"

"Of course, you were." She grinned. "We wondered how long it would take."

"How long have you been doing it?" He looked from Salayla to Kaydeen suspiciously.

"Since you joined us in the cell."

"Ah, well, it took me a few months then." He seemed relieved.

"You do have some valid excuses."

"Have you been using it on Tonee?"

"Regularly," Salayla readily admitted. "Witnessing your plight and subsequent decline took a toll on him."

She didn't voice how much worse it had been in the last few weeks. She didn't have to.

"My choice was valid."

"For your state of mind at the time, probably," Salayla conceded. "But I agree with Tonee." She paused. "Now that you have your full faculties back, so should you."

Taylor inhaled deeply.

"But this is neither the time nor the place to debate this

point," she conciliated before he could reply, "and it isn't what I intended to discuss with you."

He studied her, clearly not ready to concede, but he did yield to her decision to drop the argument—at least for now.

"So, Leer doesn't like me." Taylor paused. "That's his prerogative."

"That's what he wants us to think."

"Are you saying he does like me but hides it behind animosity?"

"No. I'm saying that he's sending mixed signals. He also seems to have expectations of you. Sometimes you meet them, other times you don't."

"And he gets pissed at me when I don't?"

"Quite the opposite." She paused to let her words sink in. "It's like he has a previously formed opinion of you and is trying to decide if it's correct. However, I'm uncertain if that opinion is positive or negative, or which he would prefer."

"Previously formed? I've never met him before."

"Understood. However, memories are frail and malleable. At least in most people." She glanced at Kaydeen and smiled. "You have lived in so many places already, you cannot expect to remember every friend or enemy you have made. And he might not have been the person you interacted with, but a bystander or a relation of said person."

He looked at her doubtfully.

"You told us yourself that the earliest memory you have, in your own point of view, is from when you were nine."

He nodded. "The shuttle trip to the space liner that took us to Mom's next job. I slept through the takeoff and was so confused when I woke, I couldn't remember where we were or what we were doing. Mom had to jog my memory on almost everything." He shook his head at the memory.

"You know," Kaydeen put in, "a takeoff in a shuttle with

malfunctioning dampeners and shielding wouldn't affect a human's psyche like that, even a child's."

It had been the explanation Taylor's mom had given him at the time. Taylor had believed her until he had gone through the combat medic course at the Academy. "Yeah, I know."

He'd been disappointed to realize his mother had been wrong, but she'd had no formal medical training, so her explanation could have been justified as a layman's way to ease a child's panicked confusion. At least, that was what the teammates had reasoned at the time. It didn't explain what had caused nine-year-old Taylor's confusion and memory lapse, but with the Academy's isolation, they'd been unable to perform a thorough enough data search to find a plausible cause.

"The point I'm trying to convey," Salayla continued, "is that for reasons I cannot discern, he tries to convince himself you aren't worth his respect or liking, and he exerts himself to find faults in everything you do."

"Well," Taylor snorted, "those shouldn't be too hard for him to find, as you pointed out."

Salayla frowned at his deflection. "What does your Gift tell you?"

"My Gift?"

"Yes." She nodded. "Intuition, sixth sense, gut feeling—call it what you choose, but it is a Gift, nevertheless."

The corners of his mouth lifted at her reply. "Leer is no threat." He paused as his gaze turned internal and then added in a more subdued tone, "At least, not yet."

"What does that mean?" Kaydeen asked.

Taylor looked back at her. "He wants to hate me, but he doesn't." He shrugged.

"Yet, you're not concerned."

"Worrying won't change anything. He's not affecting the team's cohesion or its safety. Until he does, it's so much dust in space."

"And if he does?"

"Then he'll find himself outclassed. You three will take him down in a heartbeat."

Taylor's voice and demeanor had changed. He'd become a wall of smooth polycarbonate that sealed him in and locked them out. Salayla had noticed, too, and she reached out a hand to touch him. But he turned to look at Tonee. "Let's speed up and cut some distance."

"Sure thing," Tonee answered easily and looked at Mica. "You heard the man. Get going." He waved Mica and the others ahead as he studied his teammates' faces. He hadn't missed Salayla's aborted move. His eyes tightened, and his jaw set for an instant.

KAYDEEN FELL in beside Tonee as Taylor and Mica led them off the lane and into the next field.

"It's all good." She looked up at Tonee. "Trust is a finicky thing and takes a lot of work, especially when you've become so used to physical verification." She grimaced. "It's a challenge we need to remaster."

Tonee stayed silent for long moments as they walked between the first two rows of evenly spaced brambles growing along lines of wire. Smoke rose in the distance over Mannahe, bespeaking the destruction ahead of them. The fighting had intensified since they had seen the valley from the mountain trail the day before, but it hadn't yet reached the fields they were crossing. Kaydeen was glad about that. With only a single pistol and no effective cover against sensors, they wouldn't stand a chance. She hoped they could obtain more firearms before they reached the battle zone.

"What did he do?"

Tonee's question surprised her, at least his word choice.

Taylor had been in his view, after all, so Tonee had seen everything Taylor did.

"You've been around us too long." She grinned. "You're way too comfortable with our thought and speech patterns. Every other human would've asked about what he said."

"You're not as concerned about the words that come out as the words that stay in."

"And your true depth reveals itself."

His eyes danced at her jab, but he stayed on subject. "Well?"

"The usual." She shrugged. "He shut us out."

"That's it?" He pulled his head back with a frown. "You do need to come off the physical verification thing a little." He looked at her. "You're starting to display withdrawal symptoms."

She snorted. "It's not a drug."

"It seems to be with you two."

Her steps faltered as she stared at him. He continued but turned and pointed at his mouth. "Truth, right here."

She shook her head and slapped his arm as she caught back up.

Tonee's face sobered as she fell in beside him. "So, what else?"

Before she could answer, he raised his hand for silence and cocked his head. She looked around. The lane they were following curved slightly, allowing a clear view of no more than a few hundred meters in each direction. The sky in their vicinity was clear, too. She was about to ask what had alerted him when she heard the rumbling whine in the distance behind them. As she listened, it grew louder.

"Vehicle," Tonee called to the others. "From behind."

Taylor immediately stopped and motioned for everybody to seek cover. They spread out, ducking behind the thickest parts of the brambles.

Less than a minute later, a small, wheeled transport with a

cargo bed sped up the lane they had been walking on only a few minutes before. Had Taylor not chosen to cut into the field when he did, the team would have been caught in the open as the brambles were too tight to easily pass through, and the plants in the field across the lane were barely knee high. Within moments, the transport was upon them and then past. Six fully armed and armored Tinaree Guard members sat in the bed, three more in the cab. Kaydeen was glad they didn't have to test whether the patrol would find their group worthy of investigating. They waited a full two minutes once the transport's rumble had disappeared into the distance before Taylor stood to move on. Definitely a sign he agreed with her notion that this patrol wasn't something they wanted to be confronted by.

They continued, a little more careful and subdued. Half an hour later, another patrol sped by, this one in a larger troop carrier. Again, they sought cover in the field of plants, although this time they had to move in deeper to stay out of sight. After that, three more patrols went by, all heading toward the city. About an hour before dusk, Taylor stopped and pointed out a building with an A-frame roof across a few fields to their right.

"A barn?" he asked without preamble.

"Storage building," Leer answered, "for field equipment."

"Would it be locked?" Tonee wanted to know. "It looks like it has an upstairs floor with windows," he added. "Maybe a good place to spend the night."

Taylor nodded his agreement and looked at Leer for an answer to Tonee's question.

Leer shrugged. "Don't know, never been in one."

They turned onto the next cross lane and made their way to the building.

The building's walls didn't quite touch the ground. The metal sheeting left roughly a half-meter gap that granted them easy access to its interior. Inside, five brightly colored machines of different sizes took up most of the floor space. The smallest was close to the size of the cargo transport that had passed them earlier. The largest was six times its size. Thick cables running on overhead tracks connected each machine to a junction box hanging from the ceiling in the center of the building's front half. The back half had a loft with a catwalk running along each wall to a small platform above the large front doors.

The loft had no obvious access—no stairs, no lift. The power terminal in the far corner was dead, as was the control panel inside the man-size door in the back wall. They could sleep on the floor in between the machines, but if they suddenly sprang to life, the teammates wouldn't have much room to maneuver, and some of the machines' implements and dangling appendages could easily cut through flesh and bone.

Taylor had other ideas and proceeded to climb the largest machine. From its top, he used one of the cables to pull himself onto the track, which he then followed to where it was attached to the underside of the loft's floor. He stepped into the loft and disappeared. A minute later, he reappeared and motioned the rest of them to follow his route up.

The loft was a workshop with tools and spare parts to maintain and repair the field machines. It had six windows, two in each slanted section of the roof and one each facing out the front and back of the building, overlooking the surrounding fields. The windows were open, allowing the sun-heated daytime air to quickly be replaced by the cold nighttime chill Mica had warned them about when they had scavenged supplies from the apartments. The boys had brought well-insulated sleeping bags and mats to keep them warm, while the teammates used blankets and a large thermal sheet as a ground cover. The loft's floor space was at a premium, but after moving some of the equipment, they were able to open a large enough space for everyone to lie in its center. They ate some of the food they'd brought from the apartment and then settled in for the night. Tonee volunteered to take the first guard shift and instructed everyone else to rest. Taylor lay down beside Kaydeen—he on his back, she on her side—close enough to share heat, but not touching. Within minutes, he was asleep. Soon after, so was she.

PAIN BOLTING through her hand startled Kaydeen awake. Had she inadvertently touched some exposed wiring? The pain ceased the moment she grasped the thought. She opened her eyes. She was still on her side. In front of her, Taylor lay on his back, left hand clutching his right, rubbing his skin where it had touched hers. He had felt the current too, then. He rolled onto his side, clutching his right arm to his chest and tugging his left hand under his right shoulder so he wouldn't accidentally touch her again, but he didn't move away.

He looked at her. No emotion, no comment about what had happened, and no discussion of why. Their energies had collided. It was similar to what had happened that night in the mine, but back then, their energies had danced around each other and intermingled, not slammed against each other. He knew it. He'd felt it and identified it, too, then and now. Was he as confused as her? He closed his eyes.

His breathing stayed ragged for a while. She watched it settle, slow down, and even out. His skin glistened, and his warmth radiated, inviting her to touch him, feel his skin against hers. She fought down the urge. This was neither the time nor the place. What was going on? Bond-Mates often talked about how irresistible they had found each other from the moment they touched for the first time. But she'd touched him many times before—becoming comfortable with all your teammates' body parts, dressed or not, was part of the training. So, if they were destined to be Bond-Mates, it would've already happened. Plus, it wasn't supposed to be painful. The pain had felt like an electric current, similar but much stronger than the static discharge she'd felt when she'd touched him yesterday. At the time, she'd dismissed it as a side effect of being caught in the blast, but maybe it was a manifestation of his injuries. Although it wasn't a symptom she'd heard of before, it did follow the same pattern of worsening with time. And her physical attraction might be a result of biology and circumstance. Captivity wasn't conducive to satisfying one's sexual desires. So, the two probably had nothing to do with each other. She would have to keep an eye on his symptoms and take care to bleed off their effects so they didn't affect their performance.

A presence above her pulled her awake again some time later. Moonlight, filtering through the windows, bathed the workshop in a bluish hue that allowed her to easily distinguish the open spaces from the midnight-black shadows of the blocky equipment and the in-between shades of smaller and less solid shapes of gear and people. Or maybe the time in the mine had trained her eyes to pick out more details in low-light situations. Either way, she readily identified Mica as he stepped over her into the spot where Taylor had lain. He continued to where Taylor sat on a tool bench looking out the window.

Taylor didn't move, but his stiff back indicated he was aware of Mica's approach. Mica hadn't quite reached him when Taylor spoke quietly. "You should be sleeping." But he made room for Mica to sit beside him.

They sat in silence for a few minutes. Kaydeen was dozing off again when Mica's low voice pulled her back to the present.

"I'm sorry for what you had to go through."

"It wasn't your fault."

"I should've gotten you out of that transport. I should've moved faster. I froze when you started coughing."

"You saved my life."

"But I didn't get you out."

"You did yesterday."

Mica shook his head. "You guys were already free by the time I found you."

"We wouldn't have found our way out of the complex in time without you."

"Maybe, but if I'd gotten you out six months ago, it would've saved you a lot of pain."

"Don't dwell on the past." Taylor looked at him. "Everything happens for a reason."

Kaydeen perked up at Taylor's words. That wasn't a sentiment he subscribed to. He wasn't saying it out of his convictions, but because Mica needed to hear and believe it. Still, it wasn't something she would've expected Taylor to say. He preferred truthful bluntness over sparing someone's feelings with half-lies.

"You reached your goal," he continued. "Sometimes the road is longer and has twists and turns you don't expect, but you stuck with it, and you finally succeeded. That's all that counts."

"Still—"

"You saved my life back then," Taylor repeated with more emphasis.

"How so?"

"The cord around my neck was too tight and was slowly strangling me."

That was arguable, but Mica didn't seem to have enough medical training to know better.

"Oh."

"I had been struggling to stay awake. If you hadn't cut it when you did..." His voice trailed off, leaving the rest to Mica's imagination—and Mica imagined the worst.

"That's why you coughed so much...and I was trying to make you stop...if the guard hadn't come, I could've..."

"That wouldn't have killed me." Taylor sounded amused.

"But you were already choking, you said—"

"Mica," Taylor interrupted, "accept that you did well. Yeah, you didn't get the result you wanted, but you did help me. So, stop putting yourself down for failing. You didn't."

Kaydeen smiled at the exasperation in Taylor's voice. Self-doubt wasn't something Taylor had ever suffered from.

"The results you aim for are rarely the results you attain," Taylor continued, "but usually, they're the results you need. Stop focusing on missing the bullseye and see that you did hit the target."

Such wisdom for such a young age. Kaydeen cringed as the words popped into her head— in *The Father's* sagacious tone, no less.

She'd heard it often enough during the many hours she and Salayla had spent in the small group discussions the current head of their Family Clan had instituted long before he'd stepped into the role of *The Father*. He still led many of them himself—to stay grounded and in touch with the clan's future, he liked to say, though Kaydeen always had the impression he enjoyed the lively and open discussions an informal get-together with a gaggle of teenagers could produce. Through luck of proximity, Kaydeen's and Salayla's group discussions with *The Father* had always been in person, which afforded a much more intimate and personal experience. There was nothing like having such a mega-presence in the room with you to instill a sense of the trust and responsibility Mother Dinai conferred on each of her children when bestowing her Gifts. Especially when said powerhouse readily used his Gifts to demonstrate the negative effects that abusing one's power over others could have, and the responsibility they each had to protect others against such abuse.

"You aren't just saying this to make me feel good?"

Mica's voice pulled her back to the conversation at hand.

"I don't lie," Taylor said, "and it's not my responsibility to make you feel good."

No, my friend, you do not; but you've picked up some tricks from a certain member of our team about how to avoid telling the truth without lying. He would be quite proud to hear you talk like that.

The two fell quiet again. Soon after, Kaydeen fell back asleep.

19

MANNAHE

They entered the outskirts of the city the next morning following a maglev line. The rail system connected the towns and cities in the region and would've brought them to their destination in less than an hour if it were running. On foot, they could expect to take at least the rest of the day and part of the night to get there, if they didn't run into further complications.

From the thickening mantle of smoke and dust hanging over the city, easy and uncomplicated wasn't going to be on the day's agenda. A promise the wind underscored whenever it turned against them and delivered a whiff of the acrid stench of destruction and misery enveloping the inner city.

The suburb they entered was still clean and untouched, its housing lots widespread and abundant with greenery, but the streets and yards were deserted. Not even the occasional stolen glance out a darkened window like Kaydeen had spotted the day before was in evidence. People were hiding, probably waiting and hoping for this manmade storm to blow over soon.

Even Tuscoony, with its seemingly busy market, had given

evidence of that sentiment. In retrospect, more so than when they'd been there. Something had felt odd about the town. At the time, she'd thought it was the surreality of seeing people perusing the market's offerings in leisure while their world was in turmoil.

Now, seeing the opposite in evidence, she realized the market—a mundane, routine activity they knew and could control—had been how Tuscoony's residents had coped with the chaos their life had turned into. The people here obviously thought hiding, or maybe even leaving, was their best option.

"Was the city evacuated?" she asked no one in particular.

All eyes turned to her. It was Leer who answered. "No. There's too many people and not enough places for them to go."

"What about a curfew?"

"Nah." Nitus shook his head. "They don't really work, anyway."

Tonee raised his eyebrows. "They don't?"

Leer laughed. "Not here. People just apply for an exemption and go about their normal routine."

"Ah." Tonee nodded knowingly. "Every rule has its exception. Some have more than others."

"Your kind of place." Kaydeen teased.

Tonee grinned in reply.

As they traveled further into the city, the gardens became smaller and the architecture closer and more compact. Soon, the rail line disappeared underground. Taylor paused and then steered Mica to a side street.

"Where are you going?" Leer asked. "The fastest route is to follow the rail line to its stop under the plaza."

"Not a good idea."

"Why?" Leer asked. "Because it wasn't yours?" He looked at the dark hole of the tunnel. "Or are you afraid of the dark?"

Taylor considered him for a moment but then turned to the team. “Tunnel is a no-go, and with no one on the streets, it’s time to go the back way.”

Leer looked at Tonee. “You going to let him change our route like that?”

“Following the rail line was one of the possible routes, not the only one.”

“But all of you—” Leer included Kaydeen and Salayla with a motion of his head “—agreed it was the shortest and best choice.”

“If it’s clear.”

“We would’ve noticed if the trains had started running again.”

“The trains aren’t the only ones who might be using the tunnels,” Kaydeen put in. “If we see the advantage of using them, I’m sure others do, too.”

“But we won’t know that until we’re down there.”

“Exactly,” Tonee said.

“Leer,” Salayla interjected, “we discussed this.”

“Yeah, but I still don’t agree.”

“You don’t have to agree.” Taylor had stopped and turned around. “You just have to follow.”

Leer stared at him. The standoff lasted longer than the one in the apartment, but in the end, Leer gave in. He motioned Mica ahead. Taylor resumed walking without another word.

“What’s your problem with him?” Nitus caught up to Leer as they assumed their previous marching order, with Taylor and Mica in the lead and Tonee on drag.

“He’s an asshole,” Leer replied. “Don’t know why they let him bully them like that.”

Nitus looked at him. “Maybe to them, he’s a good leader.”

Leer mulled Nitus’ words over for some time before falling back to walk beside Tonee.

“Why do you follow him?” he asked the larger man.

"He knows what he's doing."

"Really? Seems to me like we're following his whims."

"You don't know him. While he has his quirks, I do trust his judgement."

"Even if he doesn't trust yours?"

Tonee studied him. "Trust is earned through deeds, not sentiment. And reciprocation shouldn't be a prerequisite."

"But it helps when it goes both ways."

"Yes, it does."

They walked in silence for a few minutes.

"So, you think he's a good leader?" Leer pressed.

"I didn't say that."

"But you still follow him."

"Just because I know when to follow him, doesn't automatically make him a good leader."

Nitus turned to look at him. "It makes you a good follower. Dad says, to be a good leader, you need to be a good follower."

"And he's right, but in our job, everyone has a specific set of skills, and situational need determines who calls the shots."

"That's not how the military works," Leer argued. "They have one person in charge, usually the highest-ranking one."

"In the regular forces, that's correct, but the SF is different. Our commanding officers know when to allow the person with the skill set best suited for the job at hand to take the lead. And right now, that's Taylor."

"So, he's not in charge."

"Actually, he is." Tonee smiled at Leer's attempt to undercut Taylor's authority. "We're the same rank, so we each could claim the title, but he's leading right now, so that puts him in charge."

"But what if you don't agree with his decisions?"

"Again, I trust his judgement."

Leer fell silent.

The buildings around them continued to tighten until

multistory, multi-housing monstrosities lined the street from intersection to intersection, with not one bush or tree in evidence. The ground level held storefronts interspersed with people- or vehicle-sized entrances that might give access to the upper floors or inner regions of the blocky buildings. Alleys and hidden byways that led to back doors, service entrances, and interior courtyards riddled the area.

Kaydeen was still trying to figure out how Mica knew the cut-throughs from the dead ends when Taylor raised his closed fist and pushed Mica against the wall behind him. Taylor glanced into the courtyard ahead and then motioned Salayla and Kaydeen forward. They slid up to him and peered around the corner. Two Tinareean Guard mercs were trying to open a door. Beside them was a cart filled with expensive-looking electronics.

"Looters," Taylor whispered, "and distracted. Sal, you're with me. Kay, cover us."

Salayla and Taylor crept across the courtyard. A few meters from the men, Salayla stepped into the open. Her hips swayed with each twisting footfall as the fluid motions of her body funneled all attention to her chest and backside. Kaydeen had seen her in action many times, and her mind always conjured a picture of a predatory feline in heat.

"Hey, boys." Salayla's voice dripped with sensuality. "What'cha doin?"

The two men turned around in surprise, bringing their rifles to bear. Or, at least, trying to. The one who had been actively working on the door was fumbling to slide his rifle from his shoulder. The other one was more successful—he did have his rifle in hand after all. Neither succeeded. The moment their gaze locked on her seductive prowl, the men froze as they tried to process the unexpected vision in front of them. Taylor shot from cover. He grabbed the rifle of the first man as he pivoted into a roundabout kick into the face of the second and then continued to roll over the first man's back without releasing the weapon. Since the sudden attack caused the man to tighten his grip, he was pulled around backward and off his feet. Taylor twisted the rifle from his grip, shot the first man in the chest, and then slammed the rifle's butt into the head of the second. The fight was over before Kaydeen had fully registered Taylor's motions. Salayla shot a glance at Taylor and then at Kayden as if she were asking her to verify Taylor's unexpected speed.

As Salayla and Taylor appropriated the downed men's weapons and other useful equipment, Kaydeen motioned the others forward and took the teens across the courtyard, while Tonee helped hide the bodies in a nearby dumpster.

When they continued, they had added an L-Slugger and a laser carbine, two power packs for each, two belts with an assortment of pouches, six rations, and two first aid blow-out kits to their equipment list.

THEY GAVE a wide berth to the next group of Tinaree Guard, eight men guarding a roadblock, by backtracking multiple blocks and entering a village the city had grown around. It was opulent with old, luxuriously adorned houses and peppered with small plazas and parks. Streets became tight, at times no more than arms' width wide, and wove around structures and in and out of plazas and courtyards as if the roadway had been an afterthought. The neat, linear construction of the rest of the city was nonexistent here. Houses were built in all directions as if expansions were added as the need arose and positioned in whatever direction was available at the time, often over roadways and on top of other houses. It was hard to tell where one building ended and another began.

Where previously they'd been concerned about the

squared-off alleys and roads not offering enough cover, now they had the problem of not being able to see far enough ahead.

Their progress slowed considerably as the team hung back to give Taylor a chance to scout. He jogged ahead and scanned the diverse alcoves, side alleys, and courtyards while they slowly caught up. Then he'd verify their direction with Mica before jogging ahead again. Tonee stayed further back and scanned the windows and doors for snipers and other surprises.

Taylor suddenly stopped, pushed himself into the corner of a small archway, and motioned for them to stay back. Through the archway, the alley opened into a plaza with a central square bordered by trees and shrubs. Taylor signaled for Mica to find a different route. Mica shook his head. This was the central square to which all the village's streets led. To reach the other side of the village, you had to cross the square. Taylor shook his head and signaled that they had to find another way—a Traverse patrol was occupying the square.

Mica considered for a moment, nodded, and waved to them to follow. They backtracked a hundred meters and then turned left. Weaving through even tighter alleys, some of which Kaydeen would've considered private entryways or hallways—or even maintenance shafts, had they been on a ship—they crossed to another roadway that also led to the square. They did this twice more, cutting in between or behind houses, using passages barely wide enough to fit them. They hopped from street to street, slowly circling the central square. Mica was approaching a gap intended for water drainage from the rooftops—not human access—when Taylor motioned for Salayla to take the lead while he went to verify the Traverse patrol's location.

Salayla slipped between the walls. Mica, Nitus, and Tonee, who barely fit, followed. Leer was next in line but turned to follow Taylor instead. Kaydeen grabbed his arm, but he twisted out of her grasp. When he reached the corner, Taylor motioned for him to turn around. Leer shook his head and looked into the square. His back stiffened, and he turned to Taylor. They exchanged words. Taylor shook his head and turned to leave. Leer watched him for a moment, shrugged, and walked into the square. Taylor cursed silently and followed him. Kaydeen ran after them. She was about five meters from the end of the alley when the blast from a discharging bolter echoed off the walls.

She skidded to a stop and glanced into the square. Taylor lay on his side about twenty meters away in front of another alley. A Traverse soldier marched toward him, aiming a bolter, a two-handed, pistol-gripped firearm that could shoot slugs or bolts, first down the alley and then at Taylor. A second Traverse stood within the greenery, partially hidden by a tree, covering his partner. Kaydeen stepped around the corner, aimed, nailed the first Traverse in the throat, and then adjusted her sight toward the second Traverse. He stepped from behind the tree. She shot and hit his chest—his armor absorbed the energy.

Laser-absorbing armor. These guys aren't regular Traverse. Spec-ops or, considering his size, possibly shock troopers. No wonder Taylor wanted to skirt them.

She rolled back around the corner into the alley, barely avoiding a return salvo from his bolter. A sizzling sound drew her attention to the small impact crater the bolter had created in the stone masonry across from her. Steam rose as a thick gel-like substance oozed down the wall, slowly carving a furrow into the stone. Plasma. She needed to get to Taylor. If a plasma slug had hit him, it was eating him alive.

She glanced back into the square. The second Traverse was gone. He'd either ducked behind the tree or into the alley past Taylor, which was probably where Leer was.

A door slammed open on a balcony above, immediately followed by an L-Slugger staccato of *thuds*. The Traverse staggered from behind the tree, laser bolts hammering his chest. The bolts did no damage since his armor absorbed the energy, but their concentrated impact kept him distracted enough for Tonee to charge him from the other alley. He barreled into the guy at full speed, throwing him to the ground and flinging his weapon wide. The Traverse rolled over his shoulder and came back to his feet, ready to meet Tonee head-on. The Traverse's armor absorbed some of the damage Tonee dealt him, but it also slowed him down. The two collided again.

Kaydeen ran to Taylor. He grimaced in pain, grasping his blood-soaked abdomen. She knelt and tore his hands and shirt out of the way while doing her best to ignore the fight behind her. Leer sat in the alley, wide eyes darting from Taylor to the dead Traverse to the ongoing fight. She yelled at him to get the blow-out kit. He didn't move. The wound was jagged and ugly, and pink foam bubbled to its surface. Salayla dropped from the balcony and ran past her. Kaydeen plunged two fingers into the wound. Taylor screamed and convulsed. She shoved him back down while yelling at Leer. "I need that blow-out kit!"

Her fingers burned. The plasma spreading into the wound was eating her skin. How much time had elapsed since he'd been hit? The slug was designed to push its contents into the wound over a period of sixty seconds. The expelled plasma reacted with oxygen in the blood, expanding as it ate away the flesh. If the slug emptied too fast, most of the expanding plasma would outpace the cavity created and be pushed out of the wound. The intent was to keep the plasma confined in the body for full effect.

A hologram of a body with an empty upper chest cavity flashed into her mind. It had been the result of one plasma slug entering the man's chest between the third and fourth rib. "That's why you wear armor," the instructor had said at the time, "and make sure it's correctly sealed."

Well, they didn't have armor. But unlike that poor guy's

medic, she was able to reach the slug and get it out. She only needed to find it.

"You are *not* dying today," she whispered through clenched teeth and pushed past Taylor's convulsing muscles.

Mica fell to his knees by Taylor's head and grabbed his shoulders, holding him down so she could work.

"Where's the blow-out kit?" Nitus asked.

He had dropped to his knees beside Mica and was reaching for her backpack.

She shook her head. "Not mine. His." She nodded toward the Traverse lying on the ground. "Check his leg pockets."

Nitus scampered to the body.

Taylor's hot, viscous flesh pressed against her burning fingers, but with Mica restraining him, it didn't impede her probing. She pushed deeper and finally felt the pain of the slug's hard metal pushing into the raw nerves of her fingers. She grabbed it, removed it, and then plunged her hand back into the wound.

Salayla appeared beside Kaydeen with the blow-out kit as she pulled out her cupped fingers again. White gelatinous plasma intermingled with red gore. Good, it hadn't yet expanded to its foamy consistency. She tossed it aside and plunged her fingers back in.

Salayla pulled out the neutralizer and opened it. Kaydeen pulled out another glob of plasma and then spread the wound open with her burning fingers.

"Pour it in."

Salayla did as instructed. Tonee appeared with another blow-out kit and handed Salayla another neutralizer. Kaydeen pulled her fingers out of the wound, let Salayla rinse them with neutralizer, and then instructed her to shove the rim of the bottle into the wound. She sat back and pulled a wound wrap from one of the open kits. She could barely grasp it. She fought down the tremors, willing the adrenaline to continue to course through her a while longer, and wrapped her fingers. Taylor had stopped screaming, she wasn't sure when. She checked his vitals with her good hand, pulled the painkillers from the blow-out kits, and injected one into her hand and the other into Taylor's neck.

Still fighting the tremors, she grabbed the other blow-out kit, removed the neutralizer bottle from Taylor's wound, and with Salayla's help, wrapped his abdomen.

"We need to find a medical facility." She sat back and breathed in deeply, looking around.

Tonee stood at the entrance of the alley holding Leer on his toes by the front of his shirt, probably giving the boy a piece of his mind. Judging by Leer's facial expression, it wasn't a nice piece. Nitus was further down the alley, leaning into an alcove and making retching sounds. Above him was a ladder connected to a row of balconies an arm's width or two apart from each other. The balcony closest to the square had a small metal table jammed against the metal railing. Not a door slamming open, then, but a table slamming on its side. She looked at Salayla beside her.

"He isn't yet stable."

Salayla studied her. "How about you?"

"I'll be fine. The painkiller is kicking in."

"Doctor Mitalius' office isn't far from here," Nitus informed them as he stepped out of the alley. His face was pale with a tinge of green, but the boy held it together. "He's a doctor and with the Resistance. I don't know if he's there, but his office has all kinds of medical equipment."

"I don't need the doctor, only the supplies." Kaydeen looked at Tonee. "Can you carry Taylor?"

Tonee's shirt was torn, his lip bloodied, and his face bruised, but he moved fine. His opponent, brains scattered across the pavement, looked much worse.

Tonee nodded.

He picked up Taylor's pack and threw it at Leer. "You carry that."

Not waiting for an answer, he shrugged on his pack and then had Mica and Salayla help him settle Taylor's limp form over his shoulders.

20

DR. MITALIUS

Salayla took the lead with Nitus, scouting ahead like Taylor had done, although nowhere near as thoroughly. Five minutes later, they were back in the symmetrical roadways and blocks of the rest of the city.

Whereas the village had been deserted, and the previous part of the city had lived in fear, this section didn't have a care in the world.

Don't these people know there is a war going on? That their planet is under attack?

People and vehicles mingled and hurried up and down the street, going about their business as if they didn't hear the rumbling and shooting in the distance.

Salayla waited for an opening and then waved everybody across the thoroughfare and into the side street Nitus pointed out. This one was emptier, but they still encountered people moving around. After roughly two hundred meters, Nitus turned into a deserted alley. He approached a door and waved his hand over its control panel. The door slid open without delay. Inside was a short landing with stairs leading up and down. Salayla motioned for Nitus to wait with the others and slipped into the building.

Kaydeen leaned against the wall and scanned the alley. It was dark and quiet, but clean. The distant rumble of war sounded the intimate drums of gunfire and explosions, but this place was still untouched, like the people they'd passed.

Salayla stuck her head out and waved them inside. Nitus ran up the short flight of stairs and banged on the door on the first landing. Salayla went past him and halfway up the next flight of stairs while Kaydeen stayed by the door they'd entered and kept an eye on the stairs leading to the basement. Tonee stood halfway up the steps behind Mica and Leer, who had followed Nitus onto the landing. Holding Taylor's arm and leg with one hand, he pulled the pistol from his belt and held it by his leg.

The door slid open to reveal a disheveled, middle-aged stalk of a man inside a small foyer. A blue headband wrapped around his forehead kept his brown curls in check and out of his face. He wore hiking boots, cargo pants, and a loose button-up shirt with sleeves rolled up over his elbows. His outstretched arm disappeared behind the doorjamb, right where Kaydeen would expect to find the door's control panel. He nodded at the teens but studied the others with narrowed eyes.

"What are you doing here, boys?" His eyes hovered over the stairs leading to the next floor, probably on Salayla's rifle.

"We need your help, Dr. Mitalius," Nitus explained, then stepped aside and pointed at Taylor's limp form. "Taylor was shot."

Dr. Mitalius started forward but thought better of it and, without moving his hand from the wall, leaned to look down the stairs. His gaze went to Taylor's form on Tonee's shoulders, then down Tonee's body to the hand holding the pistol, and finally past him to Kaydeen and the laser rifle she held at the ready. She lowered the barrel toward the floor and gave him her warmest smile.

Mitalius rubbed his hand over the stubble on his chin and then looked at Mica. "Are these the people you told your parents about last spring?"

Mica looked at him in surprise. "They told you about that? Then why—"

Mitalius raised his hand to stop him. "Are they?"

"Yes, sir."

"How do you know they're the same people?"

Mica started to speak, but Kaydeen was faster. They didn't have time to play twenty questions.

"He doesn't, and we can't be sure you're with the Resistance as Nitus said." She nodded at Nitus. "I really would love to take the time to verify each other's credentials, but I have a man dying here, so we're not going to."

He raised his hands in appeasement. "Of course, I'll treat your friend. Please come in." He ushered them into a short hallway. "What happened?" he asked as the door slid shut behind them. He motioned for them to precede him into the kitchen ahead. Salayla declined, eyeing the two closed doors at each end of the small hallway.

He hesitated and looked at the doors. "They're storage rooms."

When she didn't budge, he added, "You're welcome to check them."

At her answering nod, he raked his hand through his hair and slid past the others through the kitchen.

"A plasma slug entered his left abdomen," Kaydeen explained as they followed him.

The kitchen opened into another, longer hallway with three doors on each side and one at its far end. Pictures of children playing and medical holograms decorated its walls.

Mitalius stopped in front of the second set of doors and looked at her.

"Plasma?" His eyebrows arched up.

"I removed the slug and most of the plasma before it fully activated, and I neutralized the rest," she explained as he waved his hand over the access panel beside the door on the right. It opened and revealed a white exam room with a trauma table in its center and a full-size med scanner hanging from the wall. Tonee followed the doctor into the room and, with help from Mica, Nitus, and Leer, laid Taylor on the table.

Kaydeen looked back up the hallway. Salayla was in the kitchen, taking her time checking every door as she went along.

"What did you use to remove the plasma?" Mitalius asked as he powered up the room's control panel.

"My fingers."

He looked at her wrapped hand.

She indicated Taylor. "He's the priority."

Mitalius nodded and turned to the counter folding down from the wall. It revealed a line of recessed shelves holding an assortment of medical equipment. Above and below, the wall turned translucent, revealing doors behind which more medical supplies were stored. He pulled out a bottle and dumped its contents into a pan.

"Soak your hand in there," he instructed as he activated the med scanner.

Kaydeen unwrapped her hand and placed it in the liquid. It tingled her skin.

"Neutralizer?"

"Not quite," the doctor explained without looking up, "but close enough, especially since you already used neutralizer. This will kill the last traces of the plasma and start the healing process. You really stuck your fingers into a plasma-filled wound?"

He was impressed.

"Had to get it out somehow, or it would've eaten him alive."

He nodded his agreement as he studied the display. "You did good work. The plasma didn't get very far."

"But was it enough?"

"He's alive because of it."

Dr. Mitalius settled in treating Taylor, drawing on Nitus' help to hand him tools and supplies. Tonee left the room to help Salayla, while Mica and Leer stayed by the door watching the doctor. A few minutes later, Salayla entered the room, indicating the rest of the office was secure.

Dr. Mitalius looked at her. "It's nice to know I'm safe in my office."

"Yes, sir, it is," she replied with a smile. It never reached her eyes.

She looked at Kaydeen, her gaze flicking to the pan Kaydeen's hand rested in. She didn't voice her concern, but it came across loud and clear.

The plasma had eaten most of the skin, but none of the underlying tissue. Kaydeen was still able to move her fingers. Nothing a little regen tech wouldn't be able to fix.

"It doesn't look like the damage is too deep." Mitalius voiced Kaydeen's thoughts. "I'll be able to tell more once I scan it, but, considering she's able to move the hand, she should be able to regain full functionality."

Salayla nodded and then looked at Taylor. "And him?"

"That's a different story," Mitalius answered, "but a full diagnosis will have to wait until the rest of my scans and tests are complete." He paused. "Meanwhile, I have a few questions."

Salayla cocked her head at him. "Go ahead."

He studied her, and then turned to Mica. "So, these *are* the people you told your parents about."

"Yes, sir," Mica replied, "but I thought they didn't believe me."

"Just because they thought it wasn't plausible doesn't mean they thought it wasn't possible."

"Then why didn't you do anything about it?"

Mitalius held up his hand. "How do you know these people are who you saw back then?" He looked at Kaydeen, Salayla, and Tonee in turn. "I'm not implying you're imposters," he backtracked.

"Yes, you are." Tonee crossed his arms in front of his chest and leaned his shoulder against the doorframe, effectively blocking the door.

"Vetting identifications is a good practice," Salayla interjected. She looked at Tonee, then Mitalius, and then Mica. "How do you know we're the people you saw in the transport?"

Mica frowned at her.

"You didn't see our faces," Salayla continued, pointing at Tonee, Kaydeen, and herself.

"No," Mica answered, "but I saw his." He pointed at Taylor.

Mitalius nodded at him reassuringly and then looked at Tonee. "What unit were you with, and what was your mission?"

Tonee studied him. Could they trust him? Nitus had declared Mitalius part of the Resistance, but what if he was wrong? Tonee looked at Salayla and Kaydeen. His eyes mirrored Kaydeen's concerns, but they had to start somewhere. She nodded. So did Salayla. He returned their gestures in kind and turned to Mitalius.

"315th SF, 1st Squad," he identified their unit. "We were to secure a power plant in Heidene Valley."

Heidene was a small mountain valley four hundred klicks east of Mannahe. They had never been intended to come this far west, so they hadn't been provided intel on the city or its surrounding region.

"The Heidene power plant." Mitalius nodded. "What kind of power plant is it, and how were you supposed to secure it?"

Tonee shook his head. "The power plant is a hydromagnetic generator, and the mission details are classified," he answered without pause.

Not that he could give details if he wanted to. They hadn't been given any past their orders—protect the squad's egress and secure its Infiltrator's landing site.

Commander Tess hadn't been happy when he'd received four newly minted Academy graduates instead of the seasoned fighters he'd requested to fill his unit's empty slots for this mission. His command staff had been even less thrilled to hear that the four CHiTs, as veterans called unproven rookies, had earned the team assignment privilege. Graduating the Academy with honors and at the top of the class looked good on the screen, but in practice, it was a pain in the ass for the receiving unit. It was hard enough to break in individual CHiTs, never mind assimilating a fully formed team.

It had helped that Salayla and Kaydeen were Din, since everyone clamored for the opportunity to add Din gifts to their unit's arsenal. This, of course, had started the argument against upholding the promise of the team assignment privilege.

Commander Tess had understood that Din Gifts weren't communal tools to be assigned or used as a commander saw fit, and that most Din considered them an intimate and private part of their person. Yet, he'd never attempted to clarify that point for the more ignorant members of their unit. That job had fallen to Salayla when Hix and Tooley had loudly stated their opinion on the subject one day in the mess hall. "Excuse me, Chiefs," she'd asked in honeyed tones as she slunk her way around the two tables between them, "do you prefer to be serviced from the front or the back?" Her voice carried loud and clear across the hall, instantly muting its cacophony. "If my personal Gifts and talents are open for assignment and general use at your discretion, and I'm transferred to your team, it would be advantageous to know if I have the right plumbing or if it would be advisable for me to accessorize before I report for my incoming skills evaluation." She smiled sweetly. "And if I *am* assigned to your team, Chief Tooley, I would like to request you assign Dieran as my mentor, if I may. From listening to his stories, you seem to be making good use of his talent to keep up the ship's morale, so I think he'd be an excellent choice for me to shadow for a while."

Commander Tess, who sat a few tables away, had nearly lost his lunch he'd laughed so hard. XO Churec, from a more prudish society and almost on the receiving end of the food-spewing catapult, had not been as amused.

In the end, Tess had assigned them to his squad and Churec had made sure they always received the shitty end of the detail assignment list. 'To ensure they learned the value of teamwork,' as he'd put it.

But the commander had shown his prejudice, or finally given in to his command staff's pressure, when he'd ordered the CHiTs to guard the SILC and its landing site, a job usually handled by the SILC's crew without help. Even Tess, with his forward-thinking and supposed willingness to let each person and team prove themselves on their merits, hadn't been able, or willing, to shake the long-held tradition that CHiTs were incapable and unwarranted risks in the field.

Mitalius nodded at Tonee's answer but didn't press him for further details. He didn't offer any information about his connections with the Resistance, and Kaydeen was fine with that. The less they knew, the less they could reveal if they were captured. He finished treating Taylor and then turned his attention to Kaydeen's and Tonee's injuries.

"I don't have regen-tech for internal caustic wounds,"

Mitalius explained as he treated Kaydeen's fingers. Plasma wasn't acid, but the damage it caused was similar enough so it could be treated with the same regen tech. "Your friend will need extensive in-patient treatment, and I don't have the facility or the time for that. You'll have to take him to a hospital or your medical facilities. I suggest you choose the latter." He looked at Kaydeen, Tonee, and Salayla in turn for emphasis before continuing. "I gave him a sedative with a heavy dose of painkillers that'll keep him out for a few hours. The neighborhood is probably swarming with Traverse right now, so you'll have to wait until things settle down." He looked at a clock on the wall. "I can give you four more hours, then I'll have to leave. You're welcome to stay, but it won't change his situation. I'll give him X-3 before you leave and supply you with enough doses to make it to the next pickup point, but you're going to have to get there on your own. With X-3, he'll function well enough to do so, though you'll need to make sure he doesn't crash and doesn't overdo it. That shouldn't be a problem since he'll still be in pain. X-3 doesn't eliminate that completely."

"I didn't know civilians used X-3." Tonee eyed him.

Mitalius grinned. "We do when we're part of the Resistance."

MITALIUS GAVE Taylor an injection to counter the anesthetic sedative he'd given him earlier. Kaydeen reached for Taylor's neck, steeling herself for what might come. She hadn't felt anything while treating him in the plaza, but the adrenaline in her system at the time might have blocked the sensation. A tingle ran through her fingers the moment she touched his skin, but nothing like before. Either it was diminishing, or her control was improving.

His presence, his energy, was blocked off and distant, as if a wall had been erected around him. The deep sedative Mitalius had given him must have shut him down to the point that there was little activity for her to sense. As the drug took hold and slowly countered the sedative, Taylor's mind stirred. The wall became less tangible, like a haze or a thick fog. She pushed through, searching. Then his pain returned, clear as a beacon. He gasped. She zeroed in on him, pushing through the fog as if wading through gel.

Mitalius gave him a dose of X-3. The nanobots the serum carried took hold quickly, swarming over him like insects over a carcass. It felt wrong, unhealthy and deadly. But X-3 was there to help. It would take over some of his systems to help him function. It had to invade his cells to do that, to keep him from bleeding out and his organs from shutting down. X-3 was a good thing—it would help him survive and keep going.

Then why am I unable to shake the feeling of dread, the sense that his body is being invaded, dipped in a flood of deadliness intent on eating him alive? She shook off the notion and entered his mind. He wasn't as open as he'd been the day before at the apartment, but he welcomed her touch, her energy. She sorted through his feelings, drawing on the pain to Bleed it off.

He struggled to keep from drowning as the flood of X-3 took hold. It was a strange and unnatural feeling, as if another entity had entered his body and pushed him aside to watch from a distance.

Is this how it feels to be treated with X-3? She immersed herself in it, shared it between them, buoying him with her presence, and then sent her logic and reason to spread between them and overshadow his growing panic. He calmed, saw and understood what was happening, and took back control. He slowly came to, and the old comfortable and known feeling of his dislike for Readings returned. She smiled.

"You are Din," Mitalius announced in amazement.

Taylor's hand shot out, aiming for the doctor's throat, but the sudden pain shooting through his abdomen cut his reach short, and he settled for the arm. The doctor yelped in surprise. She reached for Taylor's outstretched arm, soothing him through their mental connection.

"It's fine. He's a friend." Her alarm mirrored his, but hers was for the doctor's safety, while Taylor's was for hers.

Their eyes met. He studied her, reading her in turn. *Friend or foe? Protect the team above all. Is it safe? Her true nature identified, compromised. A threat?*

No.

Taylor relaxed and closed his eyes, concentrating on controlling the pain. The X-3 hadn't fully taken hold yet, and the quick movement had been excruciating. His breathing was ragged, but quickly evened out.

"What happened?" Mitalius, who had stumbled backward when Taylor released him, approached slowly, watching Taylor warily.

"He thought you might be a threat."

"How? I've been treating him. I've done nothing to threaten him or any of you. I only thought you might be Din because of the way you're cupping his neck and looking at him. I've never seen a Din in action—I don't think I've ever met a Din in person, for that matter, or at least not that I'm aware of. But I've seen pictures, and that's what it reminded me of. I didn't think it was a bad thing to..." His voice trailed off and then he looked at Tonee and Salayla who had entered the room behind her. "Oh, unless you're trying to hide the fact that you are Din, and I blurted it out." His eyes widened, and he backed up a step.

"You're fine," Kaydeen soothed him. "Yes, I am a Child of Dinai, and yes, we've been hiding that fact." She nodded slowly, "Traverse have been known to do some bad things to my kind."

Mitalius raised his arms. "I'm not Traverse."

"I know you're not Traverse, that's why I didn't mind Reading him in front of you." She nodded at Taylor's prone form. "But he didn't know that, and he's a little protective of us." She motioned to encompass the whole team.

"I'd say it's more than a little." Mitalius nodded his understanding. "It felt like he would've ripped my throat out had he been able to reach it." He edged forward again.

"You're fine." She smiled. "Now that he knows that you're a friend." That was true, at least for the moment, though she'd sensed Taylor's alarm and his intent when he'd reached for the doctor, and it hadn't been to give him a hug. But the doctor didn't need to know how close to the truth his statement was.

Mitalius picked up the injector he'd dropped and removed the now-empty cartridge.

"The X-3 will take a little while to fully take effect. Adrenaline will hasten the process, but it's better on his system to go the slower route whenever possible."

He returned the injector to the pouch he'd pulled it from, closed it, and handed it to Kaydeen.

"What's 'a little while?'" Tonee asked from the door.

Mitalius looked at him. "Exact timelines depend on the wound and his physiology." He shrugged. "Each dose lasts three to three-and-a-half hours." He looked back at Kaydeen. "So, it's recommended you administer a new dose every three hours."

Kaydeen nodded. She knew all aspects of X-3 and its administration, but she didn't interrupt.

"Don't allow the doses to lapse," he instructed. "Once the serum's effect runs out, his body will crash, meaning, at a minimum, he'll be in severe pain and possibly unable to move. A crash could also cause unconsciousness, shock, and collapse of the nervous system, so it's highly recommended you discontinue the serum only under full medical support."

She knew that, too. Few people who crashed survived, and

of those, none had survived more than two crashes. X-3 did wonders for a wounded soldier's survivability but the moment the nanobots stopped managing the wound and the surrounding structures, the body lapsed back into its pre-X-3 status. The resulting shock was usually too much for an already weakened nervous system to handle.

She took the pouch from Mitalius and opened it. The foam bed inside the hard shell held nine fingertip-sized cartridges and a palm-sized injector, with an empty slot for the cartridge Mitalius had just used. She had enough for 30 hours of treatment. The pickup was in seventeen-and-a-half hours, so she had almost twice as much X-3 as she should need. Good. She verified that the command module embedded in the shell was powered and actively communicating with the nanobots, then closed the pouch again and stowed it in Taylor's right pant leg pocket. It fit perfectly in the spot for a blow-out kit.

Taylor's breathing had settled, but she was sure he wasn't asleep. When she was done, Mitalius handed her another pouch, this one holding a handheld med-scanner.

"Here. It'll help you with his treatment and any other injuries you come across." As she tested the med-scanner's functions, he turned back to the cabinets. "Let's get a med-kit together for you." He opened doors and pulled out supplies. "Do you have room in your backpack?"

She retrieved her pack from the hallway and rearranged its contents to fit the supplies he laid out for her. By the time she was done, Taylor was awake and trying to sit up.

"Whoa, buddy." Mitalius pushed him back down. "Let's take it slow."

Taylor stared at him blankly but didn't fight the doctor's motions.

"We need to do this one step at a time."

Using the med-scanner he'd given Kaydeen, Mitalius had

Taylor sit up, then stand, and then walk around the room, scanning him every step of the way.

Taylor flinched a few times, but that was to be expected. X-3 reduced the pain enough to allow full functionality but not enough to allow him to forget he was injured.

"I'm linking these readings to establish a bio ID for him," Mitalius explained. "Verify it is selected before scanning him, so everything syncs correctly, and make sure the medical facility gets this data." He handed the scanner back to Kaydeen. "It'll help them purge his system and get him back on his feet."

He turned to Taylor. "Take it easy. Even when you feel like a hero, don't be one, or you'll pay for it later."

Misreading Taylor's frown, he launched into a detailed explanation of how X-3 worked. As the team's backup medic, Taylor knew X-3's stats. But he didn't correct the doctor's misinterpretation of his expression.

He continued to frown, his attention turned inward. While they'd covered X-3 during their training, they'd never had cause to use it. Taylor didn't like what he was experiencing. As Mitalius finished his explanation, Taylor looked up and nodded at him. His gaze met Kaydeen's. No, he didn't like what was going on inside him. Kaydeen motioned to Read him. He shook his head.

"I'm fine."

He wasn't, but she didn't argue.

Taylor pulled on the shirt Mitalius handed him and then walked into the kitchen where the others were preparing to leave. His breathing was ragged at first, but soon settled and only caught when he moved abruptly or rotated his torso. He quickly adopted the habit of keeping his shoulders in line with his hips, rotating his whole body to turn. Other than that, he gave no indication of his injury.

Tonee studied him and then looked at Kaydeen. She nodded. He nodded in return and then closed his pack.

"All right." He stood. "We're going to travel at night and stay out of sight during the day. That gives us thirteen hours to get to Tortiga Plaza and find a place to hole up."

"We shouldn't have that much further to go," Taylor noted.

Tonee nodded. "No, but we're going to take it slow. I'm not carrying you again." He grinned.

Taylor didn't argue. Injured, his time to lead was over. He acknowledged Tonee's decision with a nod and stepped aside. Tonee continued his briefing. Nitus and Salayla would take the lead, Tonee and Leer the rear, while Kaydeen and Mica would stay in the center to cover Taylor. He went over their route and possible rest points and made it clear their priority was to keep under the radar and get to the rendezvous point. They would avoid contact with anybody but Intergal, if possible.

As Tonee talked, Taylor's gaze wandered across the group, coming to rest on Leer. Leer dropped his gaze. Taylor looked at him a moment longer and then returned his attention to Tonee.

"I can be productive," he said when Tonee finished, "I'm moving fine."

"For now." Tonee nodded. "We'll see how it goes. But the moment it changes, I want to know."

It would be typical for Taylor to push through the pain and keep going, but X-3 wasn't the drug to do that on.

Their gazes met.

Taylor's health wasn't the only thing on the line, as Leer's display of disobedience had shown. Salayla and Tonee had had a long conversation with the boy while Mitalius had treated Taylor. Leer had been repentant for having been the cause of Taylor's injury, but not for his actions leading up to it. He had seen no evidence that anybody was in the plaza, and Taylor had refused to explain why crossing the plaza was too dangerous, or what was making it so dangerous. Leer had thought Taylor was making it up. And he still did. Though, by chance, that time, Taylor had been right. Tonee had wanted to beat Leer but had restrained himself. Taylor's Gift, as Salayla had called it, was, after all, an uncanny but extremely accurate sixth sense. He couldn't explain it, but the teammates knew it worked; it had proven itself often enough. But Leer had no such experience or proof. From his point of view, Taylor's decisions had been capricious. Mitalius had sensed the tension, even commented on Leer's downtrodden mood, but they hadn't told him anything more than Taylor had been shot while pushing Leer out of the line of fire. For all Mitalius knew, Leer's repentance was survivor's guilt.

While Tonee, Salayla, and Kaydeen had worked things out with the boys, Taylor hadn't been part of any of the discussions, which made him an unknown quantity in the boys' eyes. Would he react with anger, like Tonee had? Would he treat Leer differently, blame him for his injury? And the big question, clearly visible in their expressions, would he accept Tonee's lead?

For a second, Kaydeen saw the same doubt cross Tonee's mind as his gaze locked with Taylor's.

It was amazing how different yet so alike the two were, and how much they needed and fed off each other.

"Remember our convo after I busted my ribs in the mine?" Tonee asked quietly. "You told me that, when the time came, I would know what to do. I would pull you through." He frowned. "Did those words have substance, or were they only warming the air?"

He paused to allow Taylor to answer. Taylor did, although not with words. Tonee understood him loud and clear.

"Then let me do what you said I would," Tonee continued. "You carried us for six months. In many ways, you still do—"

Taylor frowned and slowly shook his head.

"Hey." Tonee grabbed him by the crook of the neck, stopping the movement. "I got you, bro," he emphasized. "I will get you through this."

"I know."

"Good." Tonee nodded and handed him his pack. It was mostly empty, with only a blanket and a bottle of water. The rest of his supplies were divided among the team. Taylor checked its contents and then pulled it onto his back without comment.

They were back in the alley ten minutes later.

21

COMPLICATIONS

Mitalius had said the alley had no lights, but Kaydeen hadn't realized how dark a city could be when its power was reduced to emergency use only. Her helmet, or at least her eye-pro, with its night vision, would be handy right now.

The street wasn't as dark as the alley, but it was equally deserted. Without lights, the city's inhabitants preferred to stay within the safety of their homes. The team traveled without difficulty—the deserted streets made it easy to spot and avoid patrols and checkpoints, and they made good time, even while taking regular rests. At least, for a while.

The first signs were subtle. Slightly stiffer movements, an aborted inhalation, a slower pace...they were enough to alert Kaydeen, so when Taylor stumbled a few minutes later, she was in place to catch him. Yet, she was unable to prevent him from dropping to his knees. Mica was by her side instantly and helped her settle Taylor's trembling body against a wall while Tonee alerted Salayla with a low whistle and then gave Leer a crash course in the finer art of perimeter security. Kaydeen pulled out the med-scanner and indicated for Mica to retrieve the X-3.

Salayla appeared with Nitus a few moments later and relieved Tonee.

"What happened?" Tonee asked as he knelt next to Kaydeen.

"Increased pain, decreased coordination, and a few minutes later, he stumbled," Kaydeen replied. "I thought I had him, but he turned into so much dead weight, I couldn't keep him on his feet." She shook her head. "The progression of symptoms is right, but they happened way too fast."

"Did he crash?"

"No. But from the readings, he came pretty close."

"It's only been two hours," Mica pointed out.

Kaydeen acknowledged the boy's concern with a curt nod. "The first dose has to initiate the repairs, so it always expires earlier than subsequent doses. I simply expected a little more warning."

It was more complicated than that, but going into details about how the command module monitored and programmed the nanobots would only invite more questions she didn't have time to answer right now.

"He's conscious," she continued in Tonee's direction, "but unresponsive." Seeing Tonee's eyes tighten, she added, "And actively blocking my access."

She swapped the scanner for the injector Mica held ready and ignored Tonee's deepening frown. She had no answers for him. At least, not yet.

As she returned the injector to its slot, she switched the command module's alert system from tactile to audible. It was a calculated risk. The sound might alert nearby enemies, but since Taylor was either ignoring the warnings or couldn't feel the vibration, and she didn't have the proper gear for a direct comm link with the module, that was preferable to the alternative.

Tonee acknowledged her choice with a nod and stood to discuss the added complication with Salayla. When they moved on, Salayla kept them off the main thoroughfares as much as possible. Her paths through the bowels of buildings or inner courtyards of the blocks weren't always the shortest routes and often required the team to wait while she verified a particular alley or series of courtyards was clear before they proceeded, but they had the benefit of adding short rest periods Taylor would otherwise argue against.

The Command Module shattered the silence of the alley they were passing through approximately two-and-a-half hours later. It wasn't the short *chirp* Kaydeen had expected to hear first, signaling that the nanobots were starting to reach the end of their lifecycle, but the ascending riff warning that the nanobots were approaching critical levels.

Kaydeen studied Taylor. The pain had set in again.

"Why didn't you say something?" she chided as she moved to his side.

"It just started." He slumped against the wall of the alley they were in and looked at his trembling hands.

She frowned. That made no sense. The physical symptoms were supposed to appear gradually and before the audible alerts. She administered the third dose and downloaded the nanobot activity log into her scanner. Analyzing the concentrations of nanobots would give her a better understanding of the state of his injuries.

Taylor was back on his feet a few minutes later. He moved fine again, although as they continued, his attention was more often introspective than situational.

The next two doses also lasted two-and-a-half hours each, which was shorter than Kaydeen would've liked, but at least the symptoms and alerts followed a more standard progression.

Her larger concern was that Taylor took longer to recover from each consecutive injection and never fully regained his previous level of vitality.

While the team waited for Taylor to recover from the latest injection, Kaydeen initiated a Reading. "What are you doing?" Mica asked.

He'd been watching her every move.

"Reading him."

"You can read his mind?"

Kaydeen smiled at the common misconception. "More his emotions than his thoughts."

"What are you reading now?"

"Pain and confusion."

"What's he confused about?"

"The foreign substance invading his body."

"You're talking about the X-3? I didn't know you could feel it working."

"You can't." She looked at Taylor's hunched-over form. He was sitting against a wall with his knees drawn to his chest and his forehead resting on his crossed arms. "At least, you shouldn't be able to. X-3 works on the molecular level like your immune system. The nanobots are no bigger than T-cells, and you can't feel those working and moving inside you."

Salayla looked at her, then moved closer and laid her hand against Taylor's neck. Taylor moved his head and opened his eyes to look at her. Salayla's eyes defocused as she initiated the Reading. A moment later, her eyes refocused with a start.

"A battle is taking place inside him and both sides are drawing on his energy reserves, draining him."

Kaydeen nodded.

"That is what's killing him. Not the damage to his body, but the X-3 and his immune system fighting each other."

"Then stop giving him X-3!" Mica exclaimed.

"I can't." Kaydeen smiled sadly. "He wouldn't survive the shock to his system."

"But it's killing him."

"Yes, but at a slower speed, buying us time to get him to medical."

Taylor didn't comment. He was fully aware of what was happening, and how much it slowed their progress.

A little under two hours later, Taylor stumbled, hissing in pain as he threw out his arm to catch himself. His shirt was wet. Kaydeen was already by his side when the alert sounded from the Command Module.

"I need to take a look," she told him.

He nodded and turned to give her access to the med patch Mitalius had placed over the wound. It was discolored with blood seeping from its edges.

"Well?" Taylor said.

"The nanobots are failing early."

Mica looked at them. "What does that mean?"

Taylor studied Kaydeen as she administered the injection and then turned his gaze to Mica. "Nothing good, but it doesn't matter. We need to keep moving."

Kaydeen didn't argue. The bleeding had already stopped, so they might as well continue while Taylor was able to do so.

About an hour-and-a-half later, the critical level alert sounded again without warning. Kaydeen injected the X-3 and then looked at Salayla. "We need to find a place we can stop for a while."

"We need to keep going," Taylor rebutted.

"You need rest," Tonee replied.

"It hasn't helped so far." Taylor lifted his hand. While the last injection had decreased his pain and increased his coordination, it hadn't eliminated the tremors like the previous doses had. "So, we might as well get it over with."

Tonee grabbed his shaking hand. "We'll get you home. I'll carry you, if I have to."

"Not quite yet," Taylor smiled, "but you will."

Tonee's eyes tightened. He looked at his hand grasping Taylor's, then touched Taylor's neck with his other. "Kaydeen, he's burning up."

Kaydeen pulled out the med-scanner and took a reading. She frowned. "Fever is not a standard side effect of X-3."

Tonee looked at Salayla. "Find us a spot to rest."

Salayla nodded, indicated for Nitus to stay with the others, and disappeared.

"I'd prefer to keep moving," Taylor insisted.

"Understood." Tonee looked at him. "But not happening."

Taylor snorted. "At this pace, we'll miss the RV."

Salayla returned a few minutes later to lead them to a hidden alcove in a back alley.

KAYDEEN SIFTED through the med-scanner's data for the umpteenth time, trying to figure out what she was missing. The X-3 cartridges were dosed to last three-and-a-half hours. Of course, the severity of the wound and the drug tolerance and metabolic rate of the injured could affect that timespan in either direction. Adding the uncertainties of a battlefield and the importance of avoiding a crash caused the medical establishment to set the recommended interval of administration at three hours. So, logically, the window for each succeeding injection was two-and-a-half to four hours. But two, or even one-and-a-half? Plus, X-3 was designed to lose its effectiveness gradually, so the medic had more than a few minutes to administer the next dose. After all, X-3 was designed for the battlefield, not the med ward.

A *thud* pulled her attention from the screen to where

Salayla and Leer stood watch. Leer returned her gaze sheepishly as he straightened from picking up the bottle he'd dropped. Behind him, Salayla shook her head with a smirk. Luckily, their security wasn't dependent on silence, or they never would've made it this far. Kaydeen smiled ruefully. The teen was trying hard to do everything right. All three were.

Mica, Nitus, and Tonee sat against the wall a few meters away, leaning against each other with their eyes closed, although Tonee wasn't relaxed enough to be fully asleep.

Kaydeen's gaze wandered to Taylor, lying curled in the boys' latest attempt to improve his comfort. This iteration resembled a nest more than a bed, but it got the job done. Taylor finally slept, something he hadn't done during their previous breaks. His disheveled black hair lit up in blueish-black hues as the morning sun found its way across the alley floor via the city's ingenious architecture. Some strands hung over his eyes, almost long enough to reach the tip of his nose. She liked the look. It gave him a less stark, more approachable air. His skin was still glistening, but now with a gray-tinted paleness that belied his peaceful expression. No, it wasn't peacefulness she saw, but stillness—deadly stillness.

Kaydeen rolled onto her knees toward him and touched his cool and clammy skin. He didn't react. She shook him. No reaction. She initiated a Reading.

Nothing. No resistance, no block...only emptiness.

"Oh no, you don't." She shook him harder.

"What?" Tonee opened his eyes, fully alert.

"Salayla," Kaydeen's voice rose an octave with each syllable. "I can't reach him."

She ripped off his covers with her free hand and dug for the X-3 pouch in his leg pocket.

Salayla crashed to her knees by Taylor's head and wrapped her hands around his neck. As her presence permeated his mind, Kaydeen was finally able to sense him—barely. He was so far away.

Salayla reached for him with brute force, her Gift reverberating through him like an unrestricted torrent. Kaydeen wasn't the target, yet still she felt battered and bruised as Salayla's will latched onto Taylor and snatched him back.

Taylor's eyes flew open with a gasp. The two stared at each other for unending moments. Finally, the panic-filled swirls calmed, returning his eyes to their usual green pool. Salayla rocked back onto her feet and leaned against the wall beside Nitus.

Taylor sat up, but Tonee, holding the discharged X-3 injector in one hand, halted his motion to stand.

"Let me up."

"No way. You're in no—"

"I need to stand."

Tonee looked at Kaydeen for guidance.

She nodded, too exhausted to speak. Salayla didn't look much better.

Tonee pulled Taylor onto his feet. Once he verified Taylor could stand on his own, he returned the injector to its pouch and handed it to Taylor, who slid it back into his pant leg pocket. Taylor seemed as fit as he'd been when they had left the doctor's office.

"What happened?" Tonee asked.

"He crashed," Kaydeen answered as she heaved herself to her feet, "and nearly let go."

Taylor looked at her, uncomprehending.

"I'm fine."

"Yes, now, but a few minutes ago, you were so far gone, I couldn't even sense you. If Salayla hadn't been here, I wouldn't have been able to pull you back."

'Dying' wasn't the correct word, at least not from a Din's point of view. It was too simplistic, bespeaking only the physical act of the body shutting down, and not accounting for the person's essence and will.

"Maybe I slept a little deeper than intended, but I'm fine, really."

"How *dare* you continue to feed us that line." Salayla pushed off the wall and stalked over. "It might have been justified the last few months, but not now, not here, and not us," she hissed through gritted teeth. "We are a team. Those were your words, were they not? They were a promise, an oath, a demand. We've lived by them—made them our mantra, our ethos. They've become our truth." She huffed. "It is time they become *yours*. You *will* continue to fight, and we *will* keep you going. Period. That is what teammates do. They see each other through to the end. The promise you made to get us out wasn't yours alone. You know better. And you will not throw that away. We will get you home. Together, as a team." She paused. "Is that clear?"

Taylor nodded. Tonee stared at her.

Salayla turned to Kaydeen. "Are you all right?"

Kaydeen nodded, as amazed as Tonee at this new, severe side of Salayla.

"Good." Her voice softened. "I apologize for not shielding you. There was no time, and I am unsure if I could have done so." She smiled.

"I'm fine," Kaydeen assured her. "Thank you. I thought I had lost him."

"Why?" Salayla frowned. "You kept him from leaving."

"Me? I couldn't even sense him."

"You must have, otherwise I couldn't have reached him." Seeing Kaydeen frown, she elaborated, "Without your link, I wouldn't have found him."

"My link?"

"You mean like Bond-Mates?" Tonee asked.

"No, nothing like a Bond." She hesitated. "Although, it did seem like a permanent connection."

"You realize you're not making any sense, right?" Tonee said.

"What is a Bond?" Nitus asked.

"The Din version of finding a lifemate," Tonee said. "It involves pheromones and ritualistic sex, and sometimes more than two people."

Nitus screwed up his face as his imagination turned Tonee's exaggeration into the worst kind of mental pictures. Misconception-building at its best—one of Tonee's specialties.

Mica took something completely different from Tonee's words.

"I didn't realize you were Din," he told Taylor.

"I'm not."

"Then how..."

"It's rare, but not unheard of," Kaydeen said. "Our basic biology is the same, and Mother Dinai did leave us backward compatible." She directed the last part at Tonee.

"How nice of her," he replied dryly.

Kaydeen grinned.

"A Bond is a sacred, lifelong commitment between two people," Salayla explained. "Usually Din. However, as Kaydeen mentioned, it isn't unheard of for a Child of Dinai to Bond with a human, or other near-human race, although it is rare. It is invoked during sex, yes, but not with any kind of strange ritual, as some people like to make it sound." She eyed Tonee, who grinned in reply. "The best human term to describe a Bond," Salayla continued, "is soulmate."

"With the difference," Tonee added, "that humans don't need to find their soulmate to become fertile."

"Correct."

"Mother's way to keep the population in check," Tonee quipped.

"We have evolved past the need for mass propagation." Salayla smiled at him.

"Kay and I are not Bonded." Taylor brought the subject back on track.

"Then, what other kind of permanent connection is there?" Tonee asked.

"None that I'm aware of," Salayla replied.

"Again, you're not making any sense," Tonee complained.

"It's unlike anything I've ever sensed."

"DEAN."

Commander Richards looked up at the sound of his first name. There weren't many people who knew it or would use it, at least not in public, and even fewer belonging to the Intergal military. But then, he wasn't on board a ship anymore, but dirt-side on Tinaree. He looked down the cross-hallway he was passing and immediately identified the lanky stature of Doctor Aksel Mitalius bouncing toward him. As usual, the doctor's chestnut hair stood on end, his wild locks barely contained by one of the wide, colorful headbands he seemed so fond of.

"Aksel," Dean greeted him. "I'm happy to see you made it. After you missed the pickup points we had set up for yesterday afternoon, we grew concerned that you might have had problems moving through the city. There's still a lot of Traverse activity."

"No, no, I'm fine. A few patrols stopped me, but even the Traverse understand that a doctor needs to be able to travel, so I had all the required clearances to pass through the checkpoints I did encounter." He paused. "Although, I wish you hadn't restricted my pickup to only my person."

"Well," Dean replied as they continued down the hallway, "as you said, your occupation gives credence to your need to travel, but having others tag along might raise suspicion. Plus, getting one person out is much easier than multiple." He paused. Bringing friends along didn't seem to be what Mitalius was referencing.

"Do you mind my asking why you missed the first two pickups?"

"I was treating one of your Special Forces troopers."

"One of ours?" Dean stopped to look at him. "We didn't have anyone near your location, or we would've had them escort you out."

"No." Aksel shook his head. "One of your missing guys. From the first attack."

Dean's brows drew together. "Did you get his ID?"

Aksel shook his head. "Sorry. I didn't think about it. They showed up late morning while I was getting ready to leave. Surprised the hell out of me when the back door rang. Couldn't see much through the camera feed—the boys had inadvertently placed themselves to block my view of the stairway. All I saw was that somebody was standing behind them, but not who or that they were armed. And the other two had kept their distance, so seeing them on the landings above and below mine, armed with rifles, was a shock. And then finding out that the patient had been shot with a plasma slug and that the medic had dug the plasma out of the wound with her bare fingers..." He trailed off. "You know I'm a pediatrician. I treat tummy aches, colds, broken bones, and such. I'm not used to handling acid that eats its victim from the inside out. And I'm definitely not used to first responders who willingly stick their bare hands into other people's abdomens to scoop that shit out."

"Slow down, Doctor. Let's find a better place to talk—"

"There's no time," Aksel interrupted him. "The young man was dying. I stabilized him and gave his friends the supply of X-

3 I had on hand to keep him going, but he needs to be evacuated."

"Understood." Dean nodded. "But if they made it until now, they can make it a little longer. And right now, I don't have a clear enough picture to start a rescue mission. Let's find a quiet corner so you can tell me exactly what happened."

Aksel stared at him for a moment, as if deciding whether he could be trusted to not waste his time, and then reluctantly nodded.

"Fine," he huffed. "But something better get done. And I don't want to hear the same excuses the other officer gave me."

"Who did you talk to?" Dean led Aksel back in the direction they'd come from. This issue clearly had to be resolved before Aksel would be willing or able to concentrate on the upcoming planning meetings he was scheduled to attend. And the hustle and bustle of the hallway wouldn't be conducive to calming the man down.

"I don't know. Some know-it-all who was trying to herd me to the conference room. He absolutely refused to call you, even after I told him who I was. He kept saying I could talk to you at the meeting. I don't know if he purposefully ignored my point that this couldn't wait, or if that got lost in translation."

Dean led the way to an office that served as a workstation and resting place for him and Robert while dirtside. It was a little cluttered with the two cots they had added to the desk, cabinets, and three chairs already filling the small space, but being spacefaring, they'd made themselves comfortable in much tighter quarters before. Aksel, on the other hand, was clearly used to more spacious accommodations. He looked around in confusion, taking note of the personal bags lying on the cots.

"Somebody lives in here?" He carefully moved through the cramped space, taking care not to come too close to the cots.

"Yes," Dean replied. "My assistant and I."

"Oh. Well. Then I guess it's okay for us to use it." Aksel visibly relaxed.

Dean smiled. Leave it to a Tinareean to be oversensitive about possibly invading someone's sanctum.

He went to the makeshift drink station on the corner cabinet behind the desk and poured two glasses of water.

"Is water okay?" he asked over his shoulder.

"Water?" Aksel's tone rose an octave. "Of course."

Dean grabbed the two glasses and placed them on the desk, then motioned for Aksel to sit in one of the chairs in front of it while he took the other.

Dean spent the next half-hour getting every detail of the encounter in Aksel's office.

22

RENDEZVOUS

The team encountered more Traverse patrols as they approached the Rendezvous point and diverted through a building. They found the building's access point to the rail system unlocked and decided to follow the tunnel to the station under Tortiga Plaza. In the tunnel, they encountered an even larger Traverse presence. With their path forward blocked, the team returned to the building and made their way to its third floor, the lowest of its ten housing levels. Since the blocks in the area were all similar heights and connected via skyways at diverse levels, the team would be able to reach the plaza by staying aboveground.

Kaydeen took point, while Salayla scouted ahead, and Tonee stayed on drag. Taylor's condition continued to deteriorate, and he often stopped to catch his breath or used the walls for support. Two blocks from the plaza, Taylor had weakened to the point of needing continuous support. Kaydeen called for a rest. Taylor refused—they were too close to stop now. Tonee settled the argument in Taylor's favor. Kaydeen wasn't happy but relented. They moved on.

As they entered the last block, Salayla returned with the

news that a Traverse squad was crossing into their building via a lower skywalk. The team had planned to cross this block through its center courtyards, which would also have given them direct access to the Plaza. But with an enemy force with thrice their fighting capability and guns roaming the floors below them, Tonee decided to continue using the upper floors. Taylor's head snapped up as if ready to argue, but he didn't voice it. Instead, his eyes tightened and flickered to the teens. On anyone else, Kaydeen would have called the expression apprehensive. Before she could ask him about it, he pushed off the wall he'd been resting against and started in the direction Tonee had indicated.

Tonee stepped out of his way and watched as Mica hurried to duck under Taylor's arm and settle it across his shoulders. Tonee's gaze hovered on the clammy, pale skin of Taylor's trembling hand before looking at Kaydeen. He didn't put words to it, but his concern was clear. She wholeheartedly agreed—they needed to get Taylor to a medical facility as soon as possible. He was declining rapidly, and none of the doses she'd administered since his crash had done more than slow the process by a fraction.

"How many doses do you have left?" Tonee asked as she stepped beside him.

"One."

WHILE MOST OF Intergal's ground units were fighting Traverse forces, Commander Chick-Chara's unit was charged with evacuating personnel the Intel section had designated as essential to Tinaree's future stability, their families, and family members of frontline Resistance fighters.

The unit used four troop transports—heavily-armed and armored ships able to quickly move a squad and their equipment—to reach and secure each RV point during its designated time slot. Perimeter guards allowed only unarmed people to approach and used scanners to verify their identities before approving them to approach a transport.

Two transports carrying evacuees would take them to battlecruiser *Lima* for further vetting while the rest of the unit moved on to secure the next RV.

The evacuations were going as smoothly as could be expected in the middle of a war zone, and they were able to keep to the set timetable without much delay—until they reached Mannahe.

The large city was a cesspool of pitfalls. Small units of Traverse and mercs popped up throughout the city, giving Intergal a hell of a time trying to clear it. Tortiga Plaza promised to do the same for Chick-Chara's unit.

This close to the city center, the blocky buildings averaged fourteen stories tall, which turned the streets into tight canyons crisscrossed with skywalks that connected neighboring buildings at different levels.

His pilots were good, but the transports were too bulky to maneuver this maze with speed. That approach would turn them into lumbering behemoths that would give the enemy more than enough time to notice and target them. Instead, they'd opted for a vertical landing, which his pilot had turned into a free-fall ride from hell.

It had taken a few deep breaths for Chick-Chara to sort himself out and verify that his internal organs were in their correct locations. The pilot's stupid, broad grin came across loud and clear when he commed to report all systems in the green and inquired about the location of his CO's breakfast. That, at least, explained why Chick-Chara had been under such scrutiny since they'd entered atmosphere.

Luckily, they were on a private channel, so their exact exchange should stay off the unit's gossip band. But from the smirks around him, his tart grumble of a reply would not. *Whatever it takes to keep up the troops' morale.*

Chick-Chara shook off his seat's crash webbing and stood. Weapons ready, the advance team was already heading down the still-opening ramp with the next team ready to follow. A few minutes later, the perimeter was secure, and the defenses set. Different location, same process. Not one order was needed, as each trooper knew their—and probably everybody else's—responsibility by heart. Although Chick-Chara was sure there was plenty of communication going on as his troopers kept each other informed.

"RV is secure," the unit's XO, Stell, reported. "As expected, the first sensor scan barely penetrated the buildings lining the plaza. The techs are working on going deeper. 3rd Squad made contact with the first evacuees and is vetting credentials."

"How long until the scans will penetrate the required minimal distance?"

"Unsure. There seems to be some interference—"

Chick-Chara's head snapped up. "Physical or signal?"

"Also unsure. The techs aren't getting a clear picture."

That got Chick-Chara's attention. The continuing development of new tech to either nullify or beat the opposition's tech was a constant in any war, and this one was no exception.

After Intergal had gained air dominance and grounded all non-Intergal air traffic the day before, the Traverse had used the Tinareean comm system for cyber attacks on the infrastructure. They'd also thrown some malware against Intergal systems connected to the local Net. Intergal had replied in kind, so the cyberwar over the local data streams was in full swing and the Tinareean comm network essentially out of service for the duration.

As a result, the Intergal units within atmosphere had to rely on an ad-hoc web built by the comms of individual personnel and vehicles within reach of each other. This restricted who one could talk to and how far a unit could spread out. The buildings around them didn't help the situation.

In the beginning, they'd been able to use the well-established net of cameras that gave good coverage of all public spaces, but with the public comm net shut down, the cameras were also out of service. Drones helped, but it took a lot of drones to extend the ad-hoc Net into the buildings. His ships' sensors had become Chick-Chara's preferred method for scanning the buildings around him.

It wasn't a simple "scan once and see everything" type of deal. It was more of a "scan, evaluate, adjust, and repeat" type as there were far too many solid surfaces made up of different materials, but the time it took to build a clear picture of the immediate surroundings was within acceptable limits.

However, if the Traverse had found a way to interfere with those scans or the scanners themselves...

"I want Two back in the air," he told Stell. "Let's see if they can punch through from an angle."

"You want them to fly over the courtyards for visuals?"

"No." Chick-Chara shook his head. "If the interference is coming from Traverse, then that's an ambush waiting to happen."

KAYDEEN TOOK point again as they made their way through the housing level toward Tortiga Plaza. Meanwhile, Salayla continued to scout their surroundings to keep an eye out for Traverse patrols and to locate an egress point to the plaza. She found the latter in the form of a series of alcoved, multi-tiered patios that stepped down to the first floor. From there, it would be a short climb to reach the plaza.

She directed them to the correct hallway and then took off on a last scouting run. The hallway zigzagged past a dozen or so residential doors before T-intersecting with a wider hall that dead-ended in a glass wall.

The glass turned out to be the far wall of a 90-degree turn in the hallway, which wrapped around the patio on three sides. It was made up of large, retractable panes that allowed the hall and patio to combine into one large, open space. Only one pane, situated at the head of the U-shape, was open.

Once outside, the tiers Salayla had told them about came into view. They were connected by short stairs, with planters bordering each drop-off. Each floor had two or three tiers, none of which were laid out in a straight line. Not even the stairs were lined up with each other, and the plaza didn't come into view until they reached the second floor. Salayla met them on its top tier.

"Traverse are assembling in one of the larger inner courtyards of this block."

"What about the plaza?" Tonee asked. They had yet to glimpse it.

"The RV point is set up and taking in refugees, but they seem to be unaware of the Traverse."

"The sensors probably don't reach that far."

"That would be my guess."

"We're running out of time," Taylor said.

"We'll get you down there."

"We're too slow and too big a target."

Tonee and Taylor locked gazes. Not in opposition, but in synchronization.

"Nitus, Leer, Mica—" Tonee looked at the teens in turn "—I need you to get yourselves down there."

"We're not leaving you," Leer replied.

"You're not. You're getting a head start down that wall, so it doesn't become a choke point for us. Once you're in the plaza, I need you to alert the troopers guarding the RV point that we're coming in with wounded and Traverse hot on our heels."

Nitus and Leer nodded and turned to leave, but they stopped when Mica didn't follow.

"Mica, come on," Nitus urged.

Mica shook his head. "I'm staying here to help Taylor."

"I got him," Tonee assured the boy.

"Then you won't be able to shoot."

"I'm not planning on running slow enough to be able to aim."

"Crossing the plaza, maybe, but what if somebody attacks before you get down there?"

"Mica, come on," Leer demanded. "They can handle it."

Mica shook his head.

"You need to go with them," Taylor implored. "Now."

Still, Mica refused. Taylor grimaced and closed his eyes. A moment later, his head snapped up.

"Go," he told Leer and Nitus.

"But—"

"GO. NOW."

The two boys jumped at Taylor's vehement bark but followed his order.

"And don't slow down for anything," he called after them.

The teammates studied him, surprised at his strong reaction. Again, his gaze flickered with what Kaydeen could only identify as apprehension. She lifted her hand to Read him, but he waved her off.

"You don't want to know." Seeing her hesitation, he added, "It'll cloud your choices."

His deep green eyes lingered for just a moment before he turned toward the next set of steps. They needed to keep moving. Kaydeen stared after him as Mica helped him down the stairs. No, it wasn't apprehension, but his gift at work, and he didn't like what he saw.

By the time the team made it to the bottom patio, Nitus and Leer were sprinting across the plaza.

And then all hell broke loose.

THE DOCTOR'S information was nowhere near as much as Dean would've liked. No names, no units, no bio IDs. All he had to go on were physical descriptions of four young people in civilian clothing who said they were Intergal. That one of them might be Din gave some credence to their claim. Since Din were visually indistinguishable from humans, though, and anyone could pretend to go through the motions of a Reading, only participants or fellow Din were able to tell the difference.

But Dean wouldn't dismiss Aksel's account as easily as the officer the doctor had previously talked to. Not if there was the slightest possibility there were survivors. Even if their survival and captivity in a mine, of all places, sounded a little out there, that didn't mean it wasn't true; improbable was not impossible, after all. And he would not ignore that chance, however minute it might be. Plus, he'd promised the doctor he'd look into the situation and keep him updated. It had been the only way to get Aksel to focus on the upcoming meetings.

"Robert," Dean said after he cued his comm. "Do you still have access to Torrents?"

As soon as he'd spoken, he realized how absurd the question was. The slicer had returned to his unit only two days before.

"Of course, you do," Dean said. "I need him to dig through the files of the MIA SF Units and see if the doctor's descriptions pull up anything."

"And what makes you think I'll be able to get approval for diverting his efforts for this new project?" Robert replied.

Dean didn't bother to respond. They both knew Robert would get it done. It was what he did.

"Are we restricting the search to members of the same team?" Robert asked.

"No. Let's open the board. Do not tie the description to the same team, squad, or even the same unit."

"You realize that having four SF from different units being captured together and kept in a mine as labor force is more improbable than four crash survivors being from the same team."

"I do," Dean said. "What's your point?"

"Never mind." Robert paused. "This goes back to the four IDs disappearing off the MIA files, doesn't it?"

"Possibly."

"You know something or have a hunch," Robert mused. "Care to share?"

"Maybe. I knew someone who had people disappear like that, but he's long dead."

"Are any of his students still around?"

"At least one," Dean answered, "and I know for a fact he didn't do it."

"All right." Robert mulled over Dean's reply. "Well, if it's the same signature, and they're as good as you think, then it will take more than a simple search to find them. Much more."

"I'm aware."

"You're really intrigued by this."

"I am."

"Well, as long as you don't allow it to cloud your judgement."

"Isn't that what I have you for?" Dean signed off.

He walked into the comm center and asked the nearest officer, "Has today's RV in Mannahe already started?"

He knew the answer, of course. The evacuation progress of the TRM families was something he followed closely. The fighting members of the Tinaree Resistance Movement weren't professional soldiers, but civilians pushed by circumstance to employ extreme measures. They fought for their homeland, but mostly for their families. Having honest status updates—preferably positive ones—at the ready, was the best way to keep them, and their minds, in the fight and willing to take that extra step to complete a mission. And with three SF units missing in action, Intergal needed the local specialists' help more than ever.

The young comm officer saluted briskly. "Yes, sir. It started five minutes ago."

Dean nodded. "Which comm station?"

"Three-Two, sir," the officer replied. He pointed Dean in the right direction and hurried on his way. Dean walked over and settled in to listen.

TWELVE MINUTES INTO THE RV, the first transport, with the ten evacuees they had taken in so far, was preparing to take off and join the one Chick-Chara had left in the air. The plaza was large enough to hold all four transports, but landing and taking off at the same time would put each of them within four meters of at least one of the surrounding buildings. That was a little too close for comfort. Plus, with all the cover provided by the surrounding buildings and the network of tunnels below ground, Chick-Chara preferred to keep at least one of his major weapon platforms mobile—especially since the sensor techs hadn't been able to reach the minimum required scanning distance.

One of his new Team Leaders approached him.

"Commander." The young man skipped the salute, as was standard in a battle zone.

Chick-Chara acknowledged him with a nod.

"What is it, Tipson?"

"Sir, I received a report of a group of seven evacuees still making their way here. Four of which are ours."

"Four of ours?" Chick-Chara asked. "Who reported that?"

"One of our forward observers," Tipson answered.

"We don't have any forward observers in the area."

Tipson looked at him in surprise. "Isn't the 615th backing us up?"

"Son, the 615th is the only SF unit we have left for the whole fleet. So, yes, we have one of their squads assigned to back us up, but they're also backing up every other unit, not only in the city but in this entire region. You really think they dropped one of their twelve precious specialists to be a forward observer for this pickup? Sounds more like somebody is trying to play us."

"But what if they *are* ours?"

Chick-Chara looked at his comm. "They have three minutes to get here." He signaled Stell to prepare for lift-off before looking back at Tipson. "If they don't make it, the four troopers will have to take care of the civvies a while longer."

"But, sir," Tipson said, "it sounded critical that we take them."

"Why?" Chick-Chara looked around, saw the transport was about to take flight, and ducked into the cover of his transport's ramp, motioning Tipson to follow.

Tipson fell behind for a moment but quickly caught up.

"Shouldn't we at least investigate? I mean—"

The lifting transport drowned out the rest of his words. Tipson closed his mouth and waited for the transport to leave.

Before he could continue, Chick-Chara asked, "What's the FO's ID?"

"He didn't give one."

Chick-Chara nodded knowingly as he stepped back onto the ramp. "And he contacted my most junior team leader."

"I was on the far perimeter," Tipson said. "With the local

comm system down, I might have been the only one in range of his comm."

"If he was able to reach you, he could've used our ad-hoc network to talk to Unit HQ."

"He didn't use our ad-hoc."

"Because it would've automatically sent his ID and location."

"Contact," came across his comm before he could expand his point. His eyes flicked to the map on his HUD as new icons populated it. The voice continued, "Seven civilians. Inbound. Front. Weapons and casualties."

Evacuees had been instructed to approach the RV without weapons, with the warning that being armed might result in them being turned away or engaged. So far, every evacuee had followed those instructions—most civilians understood that facing off with a squad of professional warfighters wasn't a good way to stay healthy.

Taking a moment to orient himself and identify the location of the sighting, Chick-Chara finally laid eyes on a group of five people rapidly moving down a set of patios cut into a community building in the center of the structures ahead of his transport. Further down, two more were in the process of climbing down the wall between the lowest patio and the plaza.

"Give me a close-up," he said into his helmet's comm.

A picture came to life in the upper right corner of his HUD. A marker identified it as the camera feed from the nose of his transport. Through eye movement, he brought it front and center to better see details. He had barely focused on the group moving down the patio when the camera feed suddenly widened to the full line of buildings in front of his transport. He was about to rebut his sensor tech, when his view lit up with enemy contacts. Not only the overlapping green dots highlighting the two groups moving down the patio, but also a slew of red dots highlighting every access point onto the plaza and even some aboveground windows and balconies.

"Contact, contact," came across the comm. "Traverse. Inbound. Small arms and shoulder launch."

At the same time, his visor lit up with alerts of possible hostile contact sightings in the other three building fronts.

"Shit."

Chick-Chara focused on the two people racing across the plaza. Males, mid to late teens, dressed in the style of local civilians. The other group was similarly dressed, but the AI behind the ship's sensors identified their age range as teens to mid-twenties—two females, three males, one of which seemed injured—carrying two long arms and one short gun. The two teens were halfway across the plaza when the shooting began.

SALAYLA REACHED the patio's railing first, leaned over, and promptly pulled back.

'Enemy sighted,' she signed. 'Below.'

The *whoosh* of a missile launching underscored her words. The missile left only the ghost of an afterimage as it made its way to its target, along with a half-dozen others. A second later, more *thuds* and *hisses* indicated the launch of more munitions. Fireballs erupted across the plaza, accompanied by a cacophony of small-arms fire.

A fireball blotted out Nitus and Leer just as they reached the RV's boundary. Kaydeen was sure it had fallen short. But had it been short enough?

Mica didn't think so. Taylor's hand clamping over the boy's mouth silenced his wail instantly, but not soon enough. Alarmed shouts sounded from the far side of the patio's border, only meters away.

The team scrambled back up the steps to the next landing and through the door to their right as a grenade landed on the lowest patio. The explosion shattered the glass behind them.

23

RETREAT

"One, this is Command. Give those kids some covering fire," Chick-Chara ordered.

"Working on it," came the reply.

"Command, this is Three. Sighted some heavier weapons."

"What type?" Chick-Chara replied.

"Shoulder-launched anti-armor."

"Activate APS," Chick-Chara ordered.

The comm network came alive as the section leaders called in contact reports.

"Command, this is Four. Contact. Engaging infantry."

"Command, Three. Engaging infantry."

"Command, Two. Contact rear. Infantry. Engaging."

Chick-Chara ducked back into the transport. He pushed the comm chatter into the background, minimized the camera feed, and pulled up the unit's tactical screen, entering its AR mode. The bulkheads around him became translucent, giving him an unobstructed view of the plaza, courtesy of an AI-generated collage that drew on the real-time data of the unit's cameras and sensors. Solid objects were still visible as outlines or shadows of different opacities, which adjusted to his viewing angle and level of zoom. At least as far as the sensors could reach. As it stood, the sensor techs had not been able to punch through more than three solid walls, so he wasn't able to see as far as he would've liked.

The AI voice cut across the comm net. "Rocket launch detected. APS launched."

Orange streaks initiated from eight of the red dots that had resolved themselves into human shapes. Moments later, eight turned into 40 as the incoming rounds divided into submunitions. The smaller size would do less damage to his ships but still be deadly to his troops. And the increase in numbers increased the chance that some would make it to their targets.

The *whir* and *thop* of the APS sounded in the background, indicating the transport's Active Protective System was tracking the incoming missiles and launching its munitions to eliminate the airborne threat mid-flight.

"Rocket launch detected. APS launched." The AI's warning cut across the comm again as six more orange lines grew from enemy positions.

Explosions thundered into the open hatch, some close enough to rumble through the decking he stood on, but so far, none had reached his hull.

Orange fireballs blossomed around him, punctuated by the *pling* and *sizzle* of small-arms fire impacts and the continuing chatter on the comms.

His unit's casualty markers flickered in shades of green and orange, but so far, no reds or blacks. The two runners, on the other hand, might not have been so lucky. One of the missiles had impacted a few meters behind them. Since the data of the casualty markers originated from the bioskins the troopers wore, he wouldn't get an exact status on the two boys until one of his medics triaged them. Not that he had time to worry about that right now.

The five people in the second group turned away from the

LZ and headed back for the buildings. Chick-Chara dismissed the AR view and pulled up the Tactical Overlay. The enemy icons showed an alarming number of soldiers gathering behind cover. *They're getting ready for a mass assault, and I don't have the weapons or manpower to hold this position.*

He highlighted the bigger concentrations of heavy weapons.

"All ships, concentrate fire on highlighted targets in your sectors. 1st Squad, secure the two wounded civilians. 3rd and 4th Squads, send a fire team to support 1st. 2nd Squad, pull back to your ramp. Do not load until my order."

The transport shuddered under the recoil of its weapons, but the sudden onslaught of heavy fire gave the escaping civilians the time they needed to make it to cover. He switched back to AR view. 1st Squad was picking up the two wounded civilians and making their way back to the transport.

"All squads, load the ships. Pilots, launch when loaded. Rally point, Tortiga Two."

Chick-Chara watched as the last of his troopers loaded onto the ship, bringing the two civilians with them.

"Get us out of here," he ordered the pilot.

As the ship took off, he ordered the landing lights to flash the 'Will return' code and wondered if he was leaving four of their missing SF troopers behind.

TONEE LED them down a short passage, through a few rooms, and back into the main hallway. From there, he aimed for a skywalk cutting across an inner courtyard but quickly backtracked when Traverse entered the courtyard below. The enemy squad stopped momentarily to look around, and then headed for a set of stairs, whose top landing was about 20 twenty meters behind the team. Tonee raced down the hall and into the first door presenting itself, right into a maze of shelves filled with books, games, and other leisure articles. Items rattled around them as an explosion shook the building, but the shelves stayed put. They raced on—into the next hallway, through a community bathroom, another passageway, and into what looked like a snack bar overlooking the plaza. Its windows were blown out, giving a clear view of the ongoing fight, and in turn, a clear view of them. Not the place they wanted to be right now, and Tonee was already crossing to the door on the far side. Kaydeen scanned the plaza as she followed. The Intergal troops were falling back to the transports under the ships' covering fire. Shortly after, the last transport closed its ramp and took off with its landing lights flashing.

Strange. Landing lights were steady, not blinking, and they weren't usually used during takeoff. This had purpose and a mind behind it. She slowed to watch the pattern for a moment.

Long, short, long, short; break; short, short, long; longer break. Repeat.

It was Ground Forces' code for 'LZ hot. Will return.'

She smiled and hurried to catch up with the others.

The next door led back into a main hallway that ran perpendicular to the plaza. They'd entered another building and were finally moving away from the plaza, but inside the block or on its edge? To put distance between them and the Traverse fighters, they needed the latter. A few minutes later, they came across another skywalk, this time crossing a street. They had finally found a way to exit the block. Now, they needed to do it without the Traverse swarming below noticing them. Luckily, the floor of this skywalk wasn't translucent like the one crossing the inner courtyard.

They hurried across, into the next block, and through three whole buildings before Tonee slowed his pace.

"We need to find a place to hole up," Kaydeen advised.

By now, Salayla and Mica were carrying most of Taylor's weight.

"Understood," Tonee replied. "But with the electronic locks on these doors, a break-in will announce our location."

"We could go up," Mica suggested. The teen was panting to catch his breath. "Away from the main traffic areas."

"That will work, as long as they don't want us too badly. But, if they put any kind of concerted effort into finding us, it won't take long to clear these hallways." Tonee shook his head. "These buildings are too clean-cut. Any alterations or breakage will be visible to the most cursory glance. We need something that's out of the way and less conspicuous."

"Battle damage," Taylor said, "or back alleys."

"Back alleys won't work." Tonee shook his head. "At least not this close to the plaza. Traverse are probably swarming through them, but damaged buildings will work." He nodded. "Where looters might have been and rubble blocking access points doesn't look out of place."

"You want to go back to the plaza?" Mica asked.

"No. But there's been fighting in other areas of the city. We saw it from the mountain trail and the fields." Tonee looked at him. "You remember?"

Mica nodded.

"Were any of them close to here?"

Mica considered for a moment.

"Yeah. There was one column of smoke that I thought came from Tortiga, but then realized it was further east. It shouldn't be too far."

"Okay. Let's head that way. Once we find a place to hole up, we'll re-evaluate and come up with a plan to make contact. The RV unit probably called for backup, or at minimum, reported the attack, so Command will be sending in units to clear the area. And hopefully, a QRF to find us."

"COMMAND, this is Evac One. LZ Tortiga was overrun. Fifteen casualties—six critical, four serious, five minor. Two civilian casualties loaded, but five others were cut off and escaped back to the city. Unconfirmed report that there are SF survivors among them. Request QRF and air support to return to the LZ. Standing by."

Dean perked up.

"Do we have IDs?" he asked the comm tech.

"Only for the first ten evacuees Evac One took on. Still waiting on the IDs of the two casualties to come through. Nothing on those last five."

"How about visuals?"

"Yes, sir, running through facial recognition now."

"Show me the visual."

The comm tech pushed a few keys. "Sir, on monitor five."

Dean moved over to get a better view. The video showed the group climbing down a series of balconies, but he couldn't get a clear look at their faces.

"Can you enhance the video?" he asked the tech.

"Sir, that is the enhanced video."

Dean squinted at the screen. Five people, with one much larger than the others, and another holding his ribs and being supported. But he couldn't readily tell if two of them were female.

"Sir," the comm tech said. "The IDs of the two civilian casualties just came through."

"And?"

"They're TRM evacuees that were no-shows for their scheduled pickup three days ago."

"Names?"

"Nitus Falk and Leer Vaktavian."

"What's their status?" Dean steeled himself for the answer.

Besides supplying the teens' names, Aksel had also given Dean their ages and some of their background.

"Falk was DOA," the tech supplied, "and Vaktavian is in critical condition."

DOA: Dead On Arrival.

The boy was fifteen years old. Dean closed his eyes and exhaled slowly. *And the only reason he was still groundside was to help four people he believed were our SF.*

Richards looked back at the comm tech. "Activate the QRF. Send them to Evac One's location." He then activated his comm. "Evac One, this is Command. QRF on the way to your location. Stand by."

DEBRIS FROM BUILDINGS and vehicles littered torn-up streets and run-down courtyards with smoke rising in columns or hanging in billowing, eye-burning masses. Collapsed buildings, or parts thereof, blocked thoroughfares and alleys, and the acrid stench of destruction permeated every corner. They'd found the area they'd been looking for.

It seemed deserted. Even the Traverse patrols the teammates had been forced to continually evade on their trek here had disappeared. Or maybe they'd finally outpaced them. It was time to find a place to hole up and catch their breath.

The team was hurrying across a wide, debris-littered street when Taylor suddenly shoved Salayla from him. She stumbled and fell. At the same time, Taylor moved in the opposite direction, pushing into Mica. An instant later, the *boom* and *whistle* of fired projectiles filled the air, and dirt sprayed from slug impacts a few meters past the spot the three had occupied. Tonee and Kaydeen bolted forward across the rest of the street and into the alley they'd been heading for.

Kaydeen skidded to a stop and scrambled back to the

corner to get her bearings. Tonee did the same on the opposite wall of the alley. Salayla was lying behind the burned-out hulk of a ground vehicle, clutching her left thigh, while Taylor and Mica lay in the open with only knee-high pieces of fallen wall for cover.

Kaydeen dropped to her knees and scanned the street to get a bead on the ambushers. From the impacts pelting the debris around her friends, she estimated there must be at least four or five shooters, but she had no angle on them. She scurried across the alley to Tonee, who was shooting steadily, and slid in front of his feet. Leading with her rifle, she scanned the buildings in the general direction of Tonee's aim. The impacts from his shots helped narrow her search, and she finally glimpsed muzzle flashes coming from a hole in the second story of a building half a block away. But she couldn't see the actual shooters.

Tonee's shots bounced all over the area.

"Slow down, big guy. You're not hitting anything."

"I know, but at least I keep forcing them to duck."

"Do you?"

"The rate of fire has slowed, hasn't it?"

That was true, but it was still heavy enough to keep their friends pinned. Especially since they now had two injured. Salayla had released her leg but was favoring it. Taylor had rolled onto his stomach and was talking to Mica, who was positioning himself to get to his feet.

"What's he doing?" Kaydeen wondered aloud, but then realized his intent. "Mica, no!" she called. "Stay down!"

The boy looked at her momentarily, then returned his gaze to Taylor and continued to push himself to his hands and knees. His back started to clear the debris.

A scream drew her attention to the ambushers.

"You got one?"

"Uh, no," Tonee replied. "Wasn't me."

"Then, who?"

Impact sparks flashed from the ambushers' hiding spot. Only metal bullets threw sparks like that, and none of the team's guns used those. Kaydeen scanned the street in the opposite direction.

"Stay down, Mica!"

Salayla's yell drew Kaydeen's attention back to the street as Mica pushed into a crouch. With his hands still touching the ground, the boy scrambled toward Taylor. Taylor waved him off, his eyes widening and his head shaking as he also told the teen to stay down. Mica didn't listen.

"Shit," Tonee mumbled above her and intensified his fire against the ambushers.

Kaydeen did the same, pulling the trigger of her carbine as fast as it let her. She walked her shots all over the dark maw, hoping it would be enough to protect Mica.

She spared a glance at the street. Mica, eyes frozen wide open, lay in a pool of blood barely out of reach of Taylor's outstretched arm. Salayla hovered at the edge of her cover and was talking to Taylor. The man ignored her and continued to inch his way toward Mica. Salayla threw herself forward behind a low pile of debris and reached an arm across the last bit of open space to grab Taylor by the shoulder. Still the man ignored her. She shook him, tried to drag him back, but he refused to budge.

Kaydeen returned her attention to the ambushers.

Something tapped her shoulder.

"Cover me," Tonee said above her.

What? They had just lost Mica. Salayla and Taylor were still out there, and now, he wanted to join them?

She paused to look up at him, but he was already stepping around her to sprint across the street.

"Shit." She immediately resumed her rapid-fire barrage.

The ambushers' firing rate dropped, then seemed to stop,

but she sure as hell didn't want to stop shooting to verify that impression. The third shooter had stopped, too. She hadn't seen any impact sparks for a while, now.

Salayla hobbled into her peripheral vision, using Tonee's rifle as crutch. A moment later, Tonee came in, dragging Taylor and Mica by their shirts.

He settled Mica on the ground a few meters past Kaydeen and sat Taylor against the wall a couple of meters past that.

"They've stopped shooting," Kaydeen reported as Salayla took her position. "Not sure if that means they're dead or repositioning."

She rushed to Mica.

Taylor struggled to join her, but Tonee held him in place.

"Let her do her job."

Blood had spread across the boy's chest and shoulder, staining his shirt a dark reddish brown. The entrance wound was at the base of his neck, right inside his collarbone. She couldn't tell if it had been a normal slug or one filled with plasma, but it didn't matter. He wasn't breathing or moving. She touched her fingertips to the opposite side of his neck in search of a pulse. Nothing. She considered pulling out the scanner to make sure but knew that wouldn't change the result and would only cost them time they didn't have right now.

She drew a heavy breath, slid the palm of her hand across his face to close the boy's empty, staring eyes, and shook her head.

"No." Taylor slumped against the wall.

Kaydeen moved back to Salayla and examined her leg wound.

"I should've stopped him," Taylor mumbled behind her.

"How?" Tonee replied. "You can't even walk."

"He was my responsibility." Taylor's voice had fallen to a whisper.

"Clean shot through the thigh," Kaydeen told Salayla. "It

will be painful and slow your movement, but it's not life-threatening."

Salayla nodded in acknowledgement. Kaydeen pulled a wound patch from her pack, enlarged the rip in Salayla's pants, and sealed the wound. "It still needs to be cleaned, but we can do that later. Right now, we need to move."

She offered a pain injection but wasn't surprised when Salayla waved her off. She closed and shouldered her pack and then helped Salayla stand.

"We can't—" Taylor's voice broke. He closed his eyes and took a wavering breath before continuing in a monotone voice. "We can't leave him."

"He's gone, Taylor," Tonee implored. "We'll come back to retrieve him. I promise. But right now, we've got to go."

He pulled Taylor onto his feet and settled him across his shoulders. Taylor groaned in pain but didn't resist the movement. He hung limp, the last of his energy drained. Kaydeen wanted to touch him, console him. She had never seen him in such emotional pain.

Instead, she kept her distance and waited for the others to move, so she could cover their retreat. Salayla took the lead, her limp still pronounced; but she soon grew used to the pain and found her stride.

Taylor groaned with each bouncing step. At least for the first few minutes, then he fell silent.

They made their way through alleys and buildings, taking as many turns as possible to lose their pursuers while avoiding other patrols swarming through the neighborhood.

24

LAST STAND

"There's an apartment in a partially collapsed building not too far away," Tonee said in between huffs as he removed the debris camouflaging Kaydeen's and Taylor's hiding spot.

After laboriously putting the debris in place not long ago, he now had to move each piece again to allow Kaydeen and Taylor to escape the little alcove they'd been waiting in.

"The building looks pretty bad," Tonee added, "but will work for our purposes."

"It borders a plaza," Salayla said from behind him, "which might bring more traffic past the building, but the apartment is hidden and defensible."

"Plus, the plaza will make it easy to bring the evac in," Tonee added as he removed the last pieces blocking his access. "How's he doing?" He nodded toward Taylor's still form.

"He keeps going in and out of consciousness, but his vitals are finally stable."

"You administered another dose?" Salayla was leaning against a wall, her skin tone chalkier than when she and Tonee had left for their scouting trip. It was high time she got off that leg.

"A few minutes ago." Kaydeen nodded. "The last one."

"Is he movable?" Tonee knelt and laid his hand on his friend's shoulder.

Taylor stirred at the touch. "Took you long enough to return," he mumbled.

"You don't even know how long we were gone." Tonee smiled.

"Long enough."

"If you say so," Tonee scoffed. "You ready to move on?"

"Sure. As long as you do the moving."

Tonee grinned. "Guess I can handle your skinny ass for a bit longer."

"Told you you'd be carrying me." Taylor grinned in reply, though it looked more forced than Tonee's.

Tonee handed his rifle to Kaydeen and then carefully lifted Taylor onto his shoulders.

"I'm not that fragile," Taylor mumbled.

"Could've fooled me." Tonee stood.

Salayla, whose limp was more pronounced than when she and Tonee had left, took the lead while Kaydeen fell back to bring up the rear. That was fine with her. It allowed her to keep an eye on her charges—the wounded and the drained. Even Tonee's stride had lost vigor and length.

It took only five minutes to reach the plaza and the building Salayla and Tonee had picked to hole up in. The structure had major damage on two of its four walls. Its southern wall had collapsed into a compact pile five stories tall that blocked all access from that end and left the upper floors exposed to the elements. The northern wall had a hole punched into it that had turned a third of the bottom three floors into a pile of rubble burying the bottom floor. Nobody in their right mind would pick this teetering-looking ruin as a hiding hole. Yet,

Salayla was heading straight for the makeshift ramp of debris to the second floor.

"You sure about this?" Kaydeen asked.

Tonee looked at her with a grin. "Exactly why we picked it."

"Won't do any good if it collapses on us."

"It's sturdy enough," he said.

"And he would know," Salayla said. "He climbed all over it."

"Okay. If you two say so." Maybe she should have been more worried about her friends' mental states than their bodies.

The rubble was tricky to navigate, but once on top, Kaydeen could see what had attracted her friends. Past the gaping hole of the collapsed center stairway, an intact wall and entrance into an apartment beckoned. All they had to do was navigate the eight-meter-long by one-meter-wide sliver that was left of the hallway. Support struts stuck out of the jagged floor edge, promising that at least part of their path would hold their weight. Kaydeen leaned forward to look underneath for further support beams connecting the struts.

"I tested it." Tonee grinned at her. "It'll hold."

"And how exactly did you do that?"

"I walked across and jumped really hard every other step." He looked at her innocently. "How else would I test it?"

"Did you at least have a line to secure you?" Mental images of having to recover Tonee from below came to Kaydeen's mind.

Tonee's grin broadened. "A safety line? Who has time for that?"

Of course, they did. Kaydeen looked at Salayla for confirmation. Her friend shrugged. *Or did they?*

Tonee slid Taylor off his shoulders, handed his pack to Kaydeen, and then slid his arms under Taylor's knees and shoulders to carry him against his chest. With his human load hanging over the edge, Tonee proceeded to sidestep to the intact part of the hallway in front of the apartment door.

Salayla followed him without hesitation. Kaydeen looked at Tonee's pack in her hand. Since she had Taylor's pack strapped to her chest and hers across her back, she would have to carry this one in her hands.

"Do I need to come back and hold your hand?" Tonee called.

"Oh, hell no," Kaydeen mumbled and started across.

She would've preferred to slide her back against the wall like Tonee had, but with all the supplies in her pack, she would've still been looking straight down into the hole. Better to do this head-on. She slid her arms through the straps of Tonee's pack, settled it on top of Taylor's, drew a breath, and then stepped onto what was left of the hallway. It took her about twice as long as Tonee, but she made it across without incident. And the big guy was smart enough not to comment.

They entered what seemed to be the apartment's back door into a short, dark section of an L-shaped hallway. The walls on each side of the door were lined with shelves, shoe cabinets, and coat racks. Ahead, in the far corner of the left-turning hallway, an open door allowed a view of the building's collapsed southern wall.

Cutting across the inside corner of the hall was a double glass door that led into an office. It was surprisingly intact. Two more smaller rooms were located across from each other at the far end of the hallway off the large landing in front of the more ornate eastern entrance to the apartment.

Outside the eastern door was a landing with what was left of a stairwell and lift. It looked like the reinforced lift tube was holding up a large chunk of the collapsed southern wall.

Kaydeen turned to look at Salayla, who stood in the corner of the hall.

"Where are the kitchen and bedrooms?"

"This way," Salayla replied and disappeared into the doorway beside her. Kaydeen, taking the double door by the eastern landing, followed her into what used to be an oversized living room but now was little more than a tunnel with an unmarred wall to her right and an overhanging arched wall of rubble to her left. She passed the door Salayla had come through, looked back at the apartment's northern entrance, and stepped through a partially blocked doorway into a smaller room. A dining chair stood against the wall ahead. She turned right, through the unmarred door into the kitchen. An island that took up the central floor space greeted her. Dust and small pieces of debris covered its surface, the surfaces of the countertops, cabinets, and appliances lining the walls, and the floor... *Maybe not quite unmarred.* To her left was another door leading into another hallway. This was where she found the bedrooms —a large one to the left, two smaller rooms to the right, and a bath at the end. The large bedroom was also filled with rubble from the collapsed southern wall.

A hole in the wall of the last small bedroom gave access to what was left of the neighboring apartment—two bedrooms and a bath. From the ruffled bedding and discarded sleepwear on the floor, it looked like the family of three had been asleep, or at least in their bedrooms, when the building was damaged. With the rest of their apartment buried under rubble, breaching the wall to their neighbors had been the only way to escape.

Had the residents of the first apartment also been home? If so, whoever had resided in the south-facing rooms was probably still there.

Kaydeen banished the thought and helped Tonee and Salayla settle Taylor on the bed. She pulled out the medscanner and checked his vitals. Still steady. Good.

She gave him some water, then proceeded to clean and rebandage Salayla's leg wound. Meanwhile, Tonee paced the room.

As she worked, they discussed defensive barricades and

how to best improve their chances of contacting Intergal while avoiding being found by the Traverse.

"You could leave me," Taylor said in a surprisingly strong voice. From the scanner reading and his rhythmic breathing, Kaydeen had assumed he was asleep. "Nobody in their right mind is going to enter this dump."

"That's not going to happen." Tonee stopped to look at him. "And you know it."

Taylor nodded minutely. "Going out to find them will have a better chance of success than waiting for Intergal to find us. They'll return to clear out this area, but as you just said, this building isn't very inviting from the outside or inside." He forced a grin. So, he'd been awake throughout their conversation.

"Not up for discussion," Tonee replied. He was pacing again. "We're not leaving you behind."

"You wouldn't be." Taylor tried one more time. "You'd be making contact and guiding in the evac."

"Nope." Tonee stayed firm. "Not happening."

While Taylor's reasons were valid, Kaydeen agreed that splitting the team was a bad idea. They were each pushing the edge of their limits. Kaydeen shook her head. They were running low on options.

"When's the last time any of you slept?"

Taylor waited a few moments for the answer. When they didn't speak, he said, "So, none of you slept last night or at the doctor's office, and only a few hours at the barn." He nodded to himself. "You really think your judgement is still good?"

"No," Salayla replied, "which is why we're not separating."

"I'm the only one who has slept in the last two days, and I'm the one who keeps going in and out of sleep." Taylor chuckled. "Kind of ironic, huh?" His face fell, allowing the color to drain a little more.

"You're not giving up," Tonee told him.

Taylor looked at him. Even that effort drained him. "I'm not."

"Good." Tonee nodded. "Then we each know our jobs." He looked at the others before looking back at Taylor. "Yours is to stay alive, so conserve your energy." He paused. "I want to see you on the other side."

Taylor nodded and closed his eyes. His features relaxed, but his concentration remained, focusing on exactly that: staying alive.

Kaydeen had no doubt he'd succeed.

Tonee laid his hand on Taylor's chest, as if verifying the truth of his intent one more time. He kept his gaze on Taylor's face while Kaydeen attached the med-scanner to Taylor's belt, then pushed off to stand.

"I love that asshole," Tonee mumbled as they approached the breach in the wall.

"Then let's get him home," Kaydeen replied and motioned him ahead.

Tonee nodded. "Let's." And he crossed into the other apartment.

KAYDEEN SURVEYED the ramp-like pile of debris leading up to the collapsed stairway. There wasn't much they could do with it. Most of the pile was in plain sight of the plaza and the lower levels of the buildings bordering it. Staying within the confines of the apartment would make it harder to monitor the outside, but it would keep as much solid matter as possible between them and any scanners the Traverse might be carrying. It wouldn't protect them from vehicle-borne scans, but it looked like the Traverse had been grounded, so any vehicles coming past should be Intergal.

She returned to the apartment's hallway, where Salayla was

putting the finishing touches on their defenses. Tonee, meanwhile, was busy on a last resort—their 'oh, shit' defense, as he called it. He'd rigged the debris forming the semi-tunnel to the kitchen door to collapse and seal the access to the kitchen and the back bedrooms. The trigger was a metal rod they could kick out as they entered the kitchen, which meant that at least one of them would be locked in with Taylor.

"Triggering that will trap us inside the apartment," Salayla commented when he explained its function.

"Yes." He nodded. "At least until we break through the kitchen wall into the hallway."

"And how are we going to accomplish that?"

"With brute force." He grinned. When Salayla raised her eyebrows at him, he elaborated. "The walk-in pantry has shelves we can easily pull down, and on the far side of those shelves is the low shoe cabinet with the seat cushion on top, which we can step over or push aside. So, the hardest part will be breaking through the wall, and that won't be all that hard since it's thinner than any of the others." He opened the pantry door and pointed out the lip of a door-sized alcove in the far wall. "Maybe it was a hall closet that was reconfigured, or a second entry into the kitchen that was closed off. I don't know." He shrugged. "But this wall is an add-on and only half as thick as the other walls, so it should be easy to break through."

"Should," Salayla said.

He considered her for a moment then grabbed the metal bar lying on the kitchen island and handed it to her.

"Steel beats plaster and paneling every time," he said. "Especially when it's not part of a weight-bearing wall." He nodded into the pantry. "Which that one isn't. I can't tell what the frame is made of, but again, it's not a weight-bearing wall, so a steel bar will still beat it. At least with some leverage."

"Okay," Salayla said. "You're the subject matter expert." She handed him the bar. "So, steel bar versus wall it is." She tilted her head at him. "Where are we going to store it?"

"In the hallway," he replied. "Because that will be the way we're headed when the 'oh, shit' comes down."

"You got a couple more of those?" Kaydeen asked, pointing at the bar.

"I do." Tonee nodded.

"Then, why don't we put this one in here, just in case."

He did, then pointed out the others in the hall.

Kaydeen grabbed two of them, placed one in the back bedroom and the other by Taylor's bed. She looked at the med-scanner's display. It showed Taylor's vitals steady, his breathing slow and even. She wondered if he was asleep this time. Either way, he was staying alive and conserving energy, and he didn't need her distracting his attention. She resisted the urge to touch him, turned, and went to join Salayla and Tonee in the front hallway.

Salayla stood by the back door, the butt of the L-Slugger pressed into the crook of her shoulder, its barrel pointing at Tonee racing toward her along the skinny ledge. No, not at Tonee but past him. Kaydeen pulled the carbine into ready position and went into a half-crouch. Her finger hovered over the safety switch, but she didn't flick it. She had no idea what set them off. Then she heard it—them. Traverse. Two, maybe three distinct voices approached the building. Tonee slid past Salayla and sidestepped the next obstacle—almost. His foot clunked against the low shoe cabinet with the seat cushion on top. They froze.

Maybe they didn't hear it, Kaydeen thought.

The voices fell silent. *Shit.*

Kaydeen slid behind one of the obstacles and steeled herself for the battle to come. And then she waited. And waited some more. *Where the hell are they?*

A shot echoed off the walls, then a scream, then a shitload

of shots. Kaydeen instinctively ducked. But nothing happened, other than the sound flowing into the apartment assaulting her ears. She looked around. *What the hell?* Tonee and Salayla looked equally confused. And then the shooting stopped, and their surroundings fell quiet again.

Could it be? Had Intergal finally found them?

The silence stretched on, and on, and on.

Come on, QRF. Say something, do something, give us a sign. Please.

Thunk, tuktuktuk, thud. The sound wasn't much, and not very loud, but in the expectant silence, it might as well have been an avalanche. Somebody was trying to be stealthy and had taken a wrong step...or maybe the debris was settling and had shifted on its own. Maybe an Intergal search party was making its way up the debris pile. Who else would get into a firefight with a Traverse patrol? But who said Intergal had won that fight? Maybe it was Traverse who were climbing that pile. Or maybe it was nobody. Maybe Intergal did win, but the troopers were unaware of the team's presence and bypassing the building. Maybe they should go out and make their presence known. But what if it wasn't an Intergal patrol? Or, what if she had misinterpreted the gunfire, and the Traverse patrol hadn't been taken out and had decided against entering the building?

If it was an Intergal patrol, and they allowed it to pass them, it would take that much longer to get Taylor the medical attention he needed. The longer it took, the worse his chances were going to be. But, if they drew the attention of an overwhelming Traverse force, then his chances would be zero.

Skittering snapped Kaydeen's attention back into focus. It had come from behind her.

She turned to look for the source of the sound. The corner of the L-shaped hallway was as bare as she'd left it when building her defensive position. She looked toward the other door into the apartment. It was open, its frame too warped to allow it to close. But access from that side was blocked…or was it?

They'd never climbed down the tube's shaft to make sure. But with the first floor buried under two huge piles of rubble, there was no way it could've been that easily found.

The skittering sounded again. This time, Kaydeen saw what caused it. A surveillance drone. Not the large, clunky kind the Tinareeans used, but the palm-sized autonomous kind the rest of the galaxy used, including Intergal and the Traverse.

Is it ours or theirs?

She couldn't tell, not without closer inspection. She leaned to the side for a better view of the telltale markings and angles—and then its pieces pelted her.

Shit. She ducked.

More fragments hit her. This time, from the barricade she ducked behind.

"Contact. East door," she called out at the same time as the shooting at the northern entrance started.

Salayla and Tonee had that side under control, so she could focus on the east side as they'd planned.

25

RICHARDS

The plaza Robert landed in was surrounded by multistory apartment buildings and large enough to easily accommodate his shuttle behind the boxy troop transport and the sleek Infiltrator already on the ground. Dean charged down the ramp before it was fully extended and jumped the last meter to the ground. He had unbuckled his safety harness and been out of his seat before the shuttle had fully settled and, ignoring Robert's calls to wait for him, had slapped the ramp's release on his way out of the cockpit.

Dean landed easily on the plaza's artfully inlaid stonework and slowed his pace to a fast march as he passed the whimsical fountain in its center. His body language and voice carried as much weight as the insignia on his chest. Nobody liked to listen to a frazzled, out-of-breath desk jockey, no matter how high his rank. And that was exactly how most frontline troopers would see him once they saw his rank's support designation—as a bumbling bureaucrat who didn't know his battle ground from his park. He chuckled. He'd done the same at the beginning of his career. And then he'd learned the fine art of using people's perceptions and biases to his advantage. Being perceived as a bumbling bureaucrat was quite useful in his current line of missions.

He pulled his gray sleeves down, rolled his shoulders back, and marched across the plaza.

As Dean passed between the two ships, the transport's squad leader, Andis, waved for his attention. Dean ignored him and continued to the partially destroyed building the shuttle's scanner had identified as his target. After a short sprint, Andis planted himself in Dean's path. He didn't salute since doing so in a combat zone could be unhealthy for the receiving officer.

His back stiffened as he scanned Richards' insignia. "Commander Richards, sir, we weren't aware you were coming."

"Is that a problem?" Dean walked past him.

Unable to stop him, the officer fell in beside him, "Yes, sir. I will need to recall one of my teams before I can supply you with a security detail." He paused. "You can wait in the transport until they arrive."

"Don't bother," Dean replied. "I'll find my own way."

Andis looked at him, dumbfounded, then said, "Sir, I can't let you do that."

Dean slowed his pace as he studied the young man's face. "Excuse me?" he paused. "And how exactly do you plan to stop me? With force?"

"No, sir, of course not." Andis pointed at the ten-story tall apartment building ahead of them. "But that's a hot zone. You can't go in without protection."

"It looks pretty cool to me," Dean replied. "There hasn't been a shot fired since Commander Mason's squad entered the building." He looked at his wrist comm. "Thirteen and a half minutes ago." He looked back at Andis. "So, I fully intend to enter that building now, with or without your security detail."

They had arrived at the indicated building. A huge hole

gave access to a pile of rubble that formed a ramp of sorts to the far side of the second floor. Dean stopped to study the eight bodies lined up on the ground to his left.

"They were DOA when we arrived," Andis supplied. "We recovered them from various locations in and outside the building. Haven't had a chance to bag them, yet."

Dead On Arrival, so they weren't killed by Mason's squad or the ground forces with them.

"Were you able to ID them?" Dean asked. When Andis shook his head, he added, "So, neither TRM nor Intergal. That's good."

Andis frowned. "Why would they be Intergal? They're wearing Traverse uniforms."

Dean ignored the question and stepped onto a metal beam sticking out of the bottom of the debris pile.

"Sir, I wouldn't climb that. This whole place could come down any minute."

Dean took another step, "It's safe enough for our people to be in there." Finding stable footing, he continued to climb the pile.

Andis exhaled in exasperation. "Hold up, sir. Let me get ahead of you."

Dean stopped and looked back at him. "Don't you have a better job to do?"

"Yes, sir." The squad leader looked at him with a wry smile. "Right now, it's to safeguard you."

Dean chuckled. "Son, I haven't been a CHiT in a long time, so I don't need a babysitter."

Andis' eyes narrowed at his use of the SF nickname. None of the other service branches used it, but they all knew what it meant.

"Go back and take care of your troopers, Squad Leader," Dean said. "That's an order."

Andis studied him a moment longer. "Yes, sir." He nodded and then pivoted to return to his transport and his squad.

Dean continued his climb. The rubble was compact enough for his footing to slip only once before he reached the partially destroyed inner hallway. He assumed the long, gaping hole, ripped into the hallway's floor and ceiling, used to be filled with stairs. He made his way across the jagged ledge running along the left wall and to the shattered door of the apartment on the far end.

The hallway past it was littered with large furniture pieces. A coffee table, a large settee, and a dresser, all placed to slow down whoever had broken down the door. Somebody had put quite a bit of thought into the layout of these defenses. The largest and heaviest pieces of furniture were spaced out along the two walls, forming a zigzagging trail that was wide enough to maneuver but too narrow to allow more than one person around each bend. Fragments of smaller furniture and other items were scattered all over. They must have been stacked to extend the barricades' height and allow for better fighting positions, which would explain their destruction, as they would have been the first targets of anyone trying to clear the hallway's obstructions. Scorch marks adorned the walls and furniture in a neat pattern of 'chase the rabbit into the hole,' and the ozone smell of gunfire still hung in the air.

Further down, the hallway made a left turn in front of a doorway that was blocked from the other side with rubble, indicating another, at least partial collapse of the building. From the scorch marks, it looked like that corner was where the defenders had made a major stand, which seemed odd and out of sync with the meticulous defensive plan. Why would somebody who put so much thought and effort into their defenses choose a hallway with two attack angles but no retreat routes to make their stand? If they had time to set up defenses, they had time to find a better location.

Before Dean got close enough to investigate the seeming dead end, he noticed a hole in the wall to his right that had been blocked from view by one of the barricades. It looked like the work of an APSCIT, an Adjustable Plas Shape Charge with Impact Trigger. Dean stepped through and into a small room that might have been a pantry. A few more steps brought him through a much more complete doorway into the kitchen. Scorch marks adorned the walls and cabinetry. The smell of ozone oozed from every surface. So, this was where they made their last stand. But how did they get here from the hallway corner? The door in the far wall, or what was left of the door and the wall, had clearly led to the one in the hall corner, but it was also blocked by rubble.

That puzzle would have to wait until Dean had resolved his issue with the two targeting lasers that had jumped to life on his chest.

The lasers were sourced from the carbines of two men who stood guard over three bodies on the far side of the kitchen's central island. Their uniforms, gray utilities with dark gray boots and belt, covered by black combat harness, identified them as Intergal troopers, even without seeing the identifying flag on their shoulders and back. Their high-tech gear and lack of visible name and rank insignia identified them as Special Forces. The shorter of the two mumbled something too low for Dean to make out, but otherwise both stayed silent.

"COMMANDER RICHARDS." A third trooper entered the kitchen through a doorway to the two troopers' left. "Squad Commander Vando Mason, 1st Squad, 615th SF, sir," he identified himself with a nod. "This area is hot." He spoke respectfully, but his tone clearly indicated what he thought of Dean entering an active combat zone. He signaled his squad members to lower their weapons but didn't bother introducing them. It was surprising that he'd introduced himself. With Special Forces, if you wanted to know who someone was, you usually had to ask.

"Not anymore," Dean replied.

Waiting until the two troopers had lowered their carbines, Dean stepped around the buckled center island. He didn't see any severe wounds on the man and two women lying by the far wall.

Mason followed his gaze. "They're stunned."

The three wore Tinareean-made civilian clothing consisting of casual pants and simple shirts. Their boots were more utilitarian—possibly military, but not Intergal. The man was unshaven, with stubble maybe a few days old. All three were dirty and had rips and tears in their clothing. They looked to be in their early twenties, with the male appearing slightly older than the females. They were a little haggard, but not undernourished—more slim and trim, although slim wasn't a good word to describe the man's bulk. Standing, he was probably taller than Dean and had at least one and a half times his shoulder span. Aksel might not be good with names, but he'd nailed their descriptions.

"We found them like this," Mason said. "But in the hallway." He nodded behind him.

"IDs?"

"Nope."

Dean looked at him. "You sure?"

Mason studied him as if weighing his answer. The taller of the guards beat him to it.

"We do know how to use a scanner." After a near immeasurable moment he added, "Sir."

Dean ran his gaze up and down the trooper, then turned back to Mason.

"So, why aren't they cuffed?"

"The scanner marked them as friendly," Mason explained. "But it gave no further information."

"Hmm." Dean looked back the way he'd come. "Did you make the hole?"

"No, sir." Mason shook his head. "Other than moving them out of the hallway, everything is as we found it."

"Traverse?"

"I don't think so." Mason shook his head. "Found two outside the building, three on the rubble, three in the big hallway, and four that are still buried under that." He nodded toward the blocked door behind his troopers. "But none in here."

"Then, how did they get knocked out?"

"I would guess some kind of a concussion charge or grenade that was lobbed before its owner got flattened."

"Who made the hole?"

"Still working on that."

"Where are the other two?"

"So, you believe these three are part of the five evacuees Chick-Chara reported?"

"They fit the description."

"Whose description?"

"The doctor who treated the injury of the fifth guy."

"Did this doctor contact Chick-Chara, pretending to be one of our FOs?"

"No, Doctor Mitalius had no way of contacting the Evac unit, which is why he contacted me."

"Ah." Mason studied him. "Did you contact the evac unit?"

"To inform them the QRF was on its way, yes." He chuckled and tapped the rank insignia on his chest. "This works pretty well to get people to do what I want them to. Trumps pretending to be an FO any day."

Mason smiled. "All right. Well, I think we found the fourth

person." Mason paused. "He was killed a few blocks away. It looks like they were caught in an ambush."

"Do you have an ID on him?"

"Yes." Mason nodded. "Mica Oilmen. A local teen—"

"Who was scheduled to go up with the first evac," Dean finished for Mason.

He released a slow breath. Another innocent casualty. Kids were the hardest.

Mason gave him a moment before continuing. "Now, here's the interesting part. Our sensors picked up the shootout, but by the time we arrived, it was over. About a block out, a casualty marker popped up that led us directly to the dead ki—to Mica," he corrected himself, "who was lying in a side alley. The marker had no signature, and the kid had nothing on him that could have triggered it. On top of that, the team I left behind to recover the body and investigate the scene just reported they found the ambushers. All of them were killed by a bullet commonly used in our high-powered sniper rifles, although the sniper seemed to have missed a few times."

"So, you're saying someone was helping them?"

"Not only that, but they again helped with the fight here." He paused to gauge Dean's reaction. "The two bodies outside and one on the rubble pile were killed the same way as the ambushers, with the same style weapon. Furthermore, three of the bodies we found in the hallway were shot from behind, from outside the apartment, which would suggest they didn't merely have support from afar, but that someone came in close and personal."

"Someone who had access to Intergal comm codes and our battle net."

"Well, when I first heard about the ghost FO, I suspected battle fog—partial and unclear messages and intel causing confusion and misunderstandings. But after the ambush scene and now this, I'm not so sure."

"Okay. Mica in the street, and these three...that still leaves one evacuee unaccounted for."

"Maybe that's our sniper."

"No." Dean shook his head. "The man was hit in the abdomen with a plasma slug and functional only through X-3." He looked at the three on the floor. "And since none of these three have that kind of wound, he's the one we're missing."

"So, that's why they took refuge here," Mason mused.

"Plasma?" the taller guard said. "Without armor? He must've had a good medic with him."

Dean searched the two females for the telltale bandaged fingers Aksel had told him about.

"That one." He nodded at the brown curly-haired female. "She dug it out with her fingers."

The short guard blew a low whistle. "Wonder if Medici would do that."

He suddenly cringed in pain and stuck a finger under his helmet to rub his ear. The other guard grinned and shook his head. "Don't mess with the medic who knows how to manipulate your comm."

"Do you believe they're ours?" Mason asked Dean.

The room fell silent with three sets of eyes scrutinizing Dean. He wouldn't be surprised if the rest of Mason's squad was listening in remotely.

"Do you?" he returned.

Mason shrugged. "We don't recognize them, but that doesn't mean they aren't transfers we hadn't met."

"Scanner says they belong," the taller guard said.

"It said friendly, not belong. And friendly doesn't make them ours," the shorter guard replied.

"Maybe Black Ops?"

"That would make them ours, but not necessarily friendly," Mason replied, but his gaze stayed on Dean.

Well played, Dean had to admit.

"THEY FOUND SOMETHING," Mason suddenly said and turned to disappear through the door behind him.

The two guards had perked up, too, so the comm call Mason was reacting to had come across the squad net.

Dean followed Mason along the short hallway into the last room on its right. It was a child's bedroom with the furniture scattered about, including a wardrobe that stood at an angle to the far wall. An SF was disappearing into a hole in the wall the moved wardrobe had uncovered.

"Got a body," he called back.

Mason slipped through the hole, Dean hot on his heels.

They entered another bedroom, an adult's this time, clearly belonging to the neighboring apartment. Clothing lay strewn across the floor. Otherwise, the room looked untouched by the damage the building had suffered. Two doors, one open and leading into a hallway and the other closed, were the only other exits. The SF who had preceded them into the room stood bent over the bed. A patch on his shoulder identified him as a medic. Once Dean stood straight again, he could see what he was working on. A young man with a blood-soaked wound patch across his abdomen lay on the bed. He wasn't moving. Were they too late?

"He's alive," the SF said and tucked his med-scanner back in its harness pouch.

Dean released a breath he hadn't realized he was holding. Mason gave him a curious sideways glance and then looked at the SF returning from the hallway.

"All clear," he reported. "It's a dead end this way."

Mason acknowledged him with a nod and a quick hand signal and then turned to his medic, who studied the display of a med-scanner he'd pulled from the injured man's belt.

"You got an ID?" Mason asked him.

"Nope," the medic replied, "but the data in this scanner matches his bio ID." He nodded to the man on the bed. "They used it to store his treatment history. Don't know why they didn't also add his personal data."

"They probably assumed he would pop up on an ID scan," the SF by the door said.

The medic snorted. "Shows you how well that worked. Two is one, one is none also holds for personal identification." Seeing Dean's raised eyebrow, he elaborated. "Having only one of any critical item means you have no back up. So, if it's important, you need to have at least two, because one of them will break. They always do. And if you carry only one, then you will end up with none. But if you carry two, then you will still have one."

"Anyway," he continued. "This med-scanner is registered to Doctor Aksel Mitalius." He paused. "Does that ring a bell?"

"Yes," Dean replied.

The medic looked at him expectantly.

"This is the fifth evacuee," Mason said.

"But he ain't ours," the SF at the door said.

"So, neither of you recognize him?" Mason asked. When his two squad members shook their heads, he exhaled in frustration.

Dean couldn't blame him. The last six months had been rough, especially on the SF troopers left with the Task Force. Three-quarters of their numbers had been wiped out in one strike. And there had been no time allowed to properly mourn them. With the Task Force still on mission and in comm silence, Commander Kilrian had refused to hold a memorial service or notify Command. At the same time, with the three SF Units' survival probability near zero, he'd refused to even consider mounting a rescue operation on the grounds that it might endanger the success of the main mission. And lack of manpower had forced him to deny any requests to build one into the new battle plans. Any rescue operation or investigation would have to wait until the main mission was complete. For all intents and purposes, the lost SF Units were considered dead and written off until then.

The QRF call had been a glimmer of hope that had lit a fire in Mason and his squad. If they found survivors, or proof that at least some of their brothers and sisters had survived, Kilrian might approve search and rescue operations, even if they had to do it on their own time, which Dean was sure some of them were already doing. But now, this chance had evaporated.

Dean understood their frustration. He had studied the reports and watched the footage those reports had been based on over and over, trying to understand what had gone wrong, what he could've done to avoid the massacre. The answer was, nothing. He and his team had done everything right. Someone he'd never met, who had never set foot on the *Cartage*, had betrayed the mission. A slip of the tongue, a pointed question, a stolen comm code, and 431 people had paid the price—but maybe only 427.

DEAN LOOKED AT THE MEDIC. "Can he talk?"

"He's awake, but critical," the medic replied. "He's at the tail end of his tenth X-3 shot, and from what I'm seeing on this scanner, I'm not giving him another one." He looked at his squad commander. "He needs to be evac'ed ASAP."

"I need to talk to him," Dean insisted.

"You can try, but I'm not sure how coherent he is."

The medic stepped away from the bed to make room and got on his comm. "We need a medevac."

Dean stepped beside the bed and knelt. The blood hadn't merely soaked the wound patch but had soaked his clothing from his chest to his knees. It was a surprise the young man hadn't died from sheer blood loss. His clothes were civilian, something a local teenager would wear, but the boots were military, mid-calf strap-ons, possibly Intergal issue. They looked old and worn, as would be expected if they'd been worn for six months straight. His black hair was a ragged, matted mess, his skin covered in blood and grime. His breath was shallow but steady, and his eyes partially open. He looked younger than the other three, easily by three or four years. Could he really be SF? But they'd already accounted for the three teens in the group. Dean shook off his doubt and forged on.

"Trooper." Dean turned the man's head to be within his field of vision. "Identify yourself." He paused and then repeated his order more forcefully. It took a moment, but the desired reaction finally came. The man's eyes fluttered open and slowly focused on Dean, first his face, then his uniform and the insignia on his chest. He moved his head to take in the room, pausing first on the medic and then on Mason, who watched him closely. Mason's hand suddenly flickered, giving the SF signal for 'all clear.' The young man visibly relaxed, and then focused back on Dean.

"SF4 Mark Taylor," he said slow and low, but clearly audible, "1st Squad, 315th SF Unit."

The words took a visible toll, but Dean couldn't let him rest. Not yet.

Beside him, Mason pulled out his datapad and started typing.

"Are you alone?" Dean asked.

Mason's eyes suddenly widened, and he turned his datapad for Dean to see. It showed a picture of the young man, much cleaner and less battered, in an SF utility uniform. In the background, the logo of the 315th could be seen on a bulkhead.

The medic immediately got back on his comm. "Where's my med-evac?" Listening to the reply through his earpiece, he answered, "That's a no-go. We have four of ours, and they need to go *now*." He paused again to listen. "I don't give a damn. Get your asses up here with stretchers."

Taylor drew a couple of unsteady breaths with closed eyes, then refocused with a last push of energy.

"No, sir," he rasped. "My teammates Patonee, K'Kaya, and A'Tourie should be in the vicinity." With each phrase, his breath became more ragged.

Mason continued typing on his handheld while Taylor spoke, nodding shortly after he input each of the names Taylor listed.

"They're the CHiTs Mitwa told us about, who arrived at his brother's unit halfway through train-up." Mason looked at the others. "That's why we didn't recognize them."

Dean looked at him. CHiTs were newly graduated Troopers with zero combat experience. They weren't assigned to units readying for deployment, especially not when the unit was already that deep into train-up.

The medic turned to Mason. "Boss, the pilot says he doesn't have authorization to take the wounded to the medical ship. He was told to take them to the ground medical site."

Mason looked at the medic, "Can they handle him?"

The medic shook his head.

"Take them to my ship. I'll take them up myself," Dean ordered.

"Sir, your shuttle isn't equipped for a medical transport, plus your mission—"

Leave it to SF to know details of my mission, Dean thought. Aloud, he said, "Squad Commander Mason, my mission is my concern. Load the casualties on my ship."

Mason hesitated only a moment. "Yes, sir." He then turned and started for the exit. He had barely made it to the hole when Dean's call spun him back around.

"Mason."

"Sir?" Mason's voice was clear, his gaze alert, yet Dean could sense a deep weariness and mistrust behind that mask.

"You're obeying *my* orders. The consequences will be on *my* shoulders. I don't allow others to pay for my decisions."

Dean signaled 'Comms off' in SF hand signal. Mason paused and then nodded at his teammates. He pulled off his helmet and deactivated the comm.

"An unknown person for unknown reasons rigged our systems so these people wouldn't be IDed by our normal scans. Until you manually entered their names, they were another set of civilians who were collateral damage in a war zone. I will find out who and why, but I can't do that if they're lost again." He paused. "They will not go to a general medical facility, but straight to the *Cartage*."

Mason considered his words, then nodded. "What do you need from us?"

"Be ready for my call."

Mason nodded again. "You heard the man." He put his helmet back on and got on his comm. "Where are those stretchers?"

Dean turned back to Taylor. The young man's half-closed eyes fluttered open to meet his gaze.

"My team," he whispered.

"We got them," Dean said as he crouched beside the bed again.

"Are they..." Taylor trailed off.

Dean smiled. "They'll be fine."

Taylor's eyes tightened. "They're my—" he broke off, drew a raspy breath and then started again. "Their status? Sir."

Dean studied him. He was dying and probably had had to depend on them to get this far. Yet, he considered their well-being his responsibility, although he had neither rank nor seniority over them and was spending possibly his last energy to verify they were okay.

"They were knocked unconscious defending your position but suffered no major injuries." Dean glanced at the medic for verification. Receiving a nod, he added, "It won't take long for them to be back on their feet."

Taylor nodded and allowed his eyes to lose focus, mumbling, "But they're not home yet."

Dean smiled and lightly patted Taylor's shoulder. "They will be shortly, son, thanks to you."

He turned to the medic, who had pulled a collapsible smart litter from his pack and unfolded it on the floor beside him. After verifying the litter's med vial storage slots were empty, he slid Aksel's med scanner into a side pouch and made the appropriate connections to sync the scanner's data with the litter.

Following the medic's instructions, Dean helped the three SF load and secure Taylor on the litter and then maneuver it through the hole in the wall. When they were on the far side, and his assistance was no longer needed, he keyed his comm.

"Robert," he said, "get the shuttle ready for takeoff. We're taking on wounded for direct transport to the *Cartage*."

"Roger, "his assistant replied. "Doing so as we speak."

Dean wondered how Robert knew, but he bit his tongue to keep from asking the question aloud. He looked at his comm's timestamp. It showed he'd authorized an open comm line with Robert shortly after he left the shuttle—but he hadn't. Although it would've been a good idea.

"You wanted to keep me in the loop, right?" Robert asked, seemingly reading Dean's mind.

Dean smiled and shook his head as he moved down the hallway. *I had to pick a psychoanalyst as my assistant.*

Ten minutes later, the four litters were loaded onto his shuttle and secured. Taylor was still conscious, but Dean couldn't tell if he was coherent enough to be aware of his surroundings.

"Do you want my medic to tag along?" Mason asked.

Dean looked at him, then the medic who stood behind him.

"Is the litter online?"

"Yes, sir," the medic said. "It's logged into your ship's comm and tracking his vitals. The MOs up top can access the data anytime to check his status."

"You left the med slots empty."

"Yes, sir." The medic nodded. "His system is flooded with X-3. Until you get him topside, and they purge the X-3, there is nothing else we can give him."

"So, what can you do for him if he crashes before we get there?"

"CPR."

Dean considered his words, then looked back at Mason.

"Thank you for the offer, Commander, but we are fine without him. I am qualified in CPR, as is my assistant. So, your medic's more advanced skills will better serve you than us."

Mason nodded and took his leave. He and his team would collect the last of the evidence at the apartment and then try to backtrack the path Taylor and his teammates had taken from Tortiga Plaza.

Robert closed the ramp and fired up the engine. They were in the air seconds later.

Dean commed Commander Liegus, the Medical Officer in Charge of *Cartage*'s Medical section, to verify that he'd received Taylor's status report and was tracking the shuttle's estimated arrival time. Then he turned to Taylor.

The young man's eyes were still half open. Dean climbed out of his crash seat and moved to the litter. Taylor's eyes fluttered but never fully opened or focused, but Dean was sure Taylor was awake. He glanced at Taylor's teammates, who were still out cold, and then back at Taylor. The young man's eyes fluttered again. And then again, a few moments later. Dean looked back at the other three and realized they were within

Taylor's field of vision. Dean smiled. Even barely conscious, the young SF was checking on his team.

Dean touched Taylor's shoulder as he leaned closer.

"They're fine, son." He spoke quietly. "We're in the air." He paused for a moment to consider his next words.

"You're bringing them home."

26

JUVAK

Juvak shifted the pack on his back as he took the stairs two at a time. He was glad he hadn't followed his impulse to dump the sniper system before he entered the firefight at the apartment, but he cursed its weight and bulkiness all the same.

His son's laugh echoed through his mind. "Come on, old man. Don't tell me you're gonna complain about a few kilos on your back straining you." Juvak banned the thoughts the moment they appeared. This wasn't the time to think about the boy or the explosion that had ripped through him. He was in good hands, and the best Juvak could do for him was to be there when the kid needed him most, when he woke up. That meant getting this part of his mission over with.

That was easier said than done. While seeing a full SF squad involved had not posed that big of a problem, having them advance as fast as they had had thrown a few bones in his plans. Nothing he couldn't handle, of course. More of an inconvenience than any kind of major obstacle, but it hadn't allowed him the time to evaluate the full extent of Taylor's injuries and medical needs. And without that, moving him in a hurry would have been too great of a risk. Again, not that big of a deal, even if they did find him. The new arrival, however, threw up a major question mark. Neither the BatNet nor the comm traffic had given any warning of the shuttle's arrival or given any hints as to who it might have brought onto the scene. Juvak had not been in position to see who exited the shuttle, and the comm traffic had been silent on that point, too. His best chance to evaluate the current situation was to get to an overwatch position that was not easily picked up by the transports' sensors or walked in on by the roaming GF teams.

He checked his datapad to verify his surveillance interference program was still up and running. With his SI program handling the local cameras, all he had to worry about were biological eyeballs. His blade-shaped eye-pro/HUD combo obscured his facial features from a distance, so that left people who came close enough to see through his eye-pro's tint. So far, that had not been a problem, but that might change once he entered the apartment he had picked for his overwatch position.

At least he didn't need to enter more than one apartment. Thanks to having spent the last ten years as a building engineer and manager, he had been able to access the local blueprints to identify the perfect location and the best route to reach it. If his systems could also tell him if the target apartment was occupied, this next part would be a cakewalk. However, while Tinareeans were adamant about their public domain being on display for all to see and access, they were as strongly opinionated about private spaces being just that, private. Most Tinareeans had zero cameras within their domiciles.

Maybe he'd be lucky, and the apartment's occupant was one of the many locals who had fled when the fighting had come to their neighborhood.

As he approached the designated door, he switched his carbine's fire control setting to stun, then held his wrist comm close to the door's access panel. An icon on his HUD blinked, indicating his system had accessed the panel and was overriding the door's security protocols. He checked the keypad access data for the last time the door had been opened. Three days ago. That could mean the apartment was indeed empty, or that the owner was holed up inside. He verified his carbine's fire control setting one last time, then opened the door. As it *shushed* aside, he scanned the adjacent entry hall and stepped inside. A touch to the interior keypad slid the door shut behind him. He stood still and listened. Silence. The floor was carpeted, so his steps would be muffled. Good.

He cleared the five-room apartment systematically as he worked his way to its far side, finding room after room empty. Maybe he had picked an abandoned apartment. He opened the door to the last room—an office with a large window overlooking the plaza. It also seemed empty, but a large, executive-style desk blocked his view of the room's far corner and the floor of the open closet behind it.

Movement in the plaza beyond the three transports caught his attention. It distracted him only an instant, but that was enough to take his focus off his sight picture and slow his reaction time when the brown and black mass of fur bolted from behind the desk. By the time he had refocused on his targeting sight, it was filled with spittle-dripping, white fangs and the dark throat beyond them. He pulled the trigger and tried to dodge, but the canine missile slammed him into the wall. Luckily, the effect of the stun bolt was instantaneous, and the maw muscles received no conscious signal to clamp onto his arm. The momentum of the attack and the weight of the dog didn't leave him unscathed, though. Sharp pain shot up his arm as the teeth ripped through his sleeve and across his forearm, and the impact with the wall expelled the air from his lungs. He shoved the body aside and pulled his carbine back in front of him just as the owner of the dog came at him, swinging a statue at his face. He blocked it with his carbine and slammed the side of the gun's buttstock into the woman's temple. She staggered and crumbled to the floor. He followed up with a stun bolt to her chest and stepped around the desk to clear the rest of the room. A small boy, about five or six years old, cowered in the back corner of the closet. Juvak dialed down his carbine's setting and stunned the kid, too. He had probably just committed the boy, and the woman, for months, if not years, of nightmares and need of counseling, but at least they were alive and able to fight off the demon he had become for them. He verified the three were breathing but otherwise left them where they lay. The less contact he had with them, the better. For them and him.

He studied the plaza and then pulled the desk into the middle of the room. A few minutes later, he was sitting cross-legged on its cleared surface with his assembled sniper system in front of him. The activity on the plaza had calmed, but the comm traffic had not. As Juvak monitored the chatter, it soon became clear they had found Taylor. The SF medic requested approval to evacuate him directly to the fleet's medical frigate. That would complicate things but not put Taylor outside of Juvak's reach. Command denied the request on grounds that neither the SILC nor the GF transport could be spared for the trip. That suited Juvak just fine. Taylor would be easier to retrieve from a ground-based or civilian facility, and being groundside would give Juvak more and easier options to make the kid disappear again. The comm chatter fell silent, to the point that Juvak became suspicious of the SF squad's activities and intentions. He verified his scope was synched to his datapad, which in turn was tapping into the fleet's BatNet, and then settled in to wait.

He didn't have to wait long before the procession of litters came down the debris pile. The first to be brought out was the big guy, Patonee. Then the two girls. And lastly, Taylor. Juvak scanned each person in sight so his system could retrieve whatever intel the BatNet had on them and store it and their identifying markers in his personal database. Most of the troopers were nothing special, at least as far as their history, background, and training went. No SF was to be taken lightly, but he knew their training and average capabilities well.

The last two to leave the building were a lone SF and a gray-haired officer—probably the owner of the shuttle. As was standard, the SF wasn't wearing insignia, but the BatNet readily identified him as SF7 Vando Mason, commander of 3rd Squad, 615th SF. The older man did wear insignia, which identified him as SII Richards. The BatNet identifier added that he was the fleet's TRM liaison. Juvak frowned. What reason would the TRM liaison have to come here?

His datapad *trilled*, signaling that it had found additional, pertinent personnel data, either from its own database or from a deeper search of the fleet's. Juvak keyed the information to his HUD.

Vando Mason. Special Operations. Satellite Team—

His datapad *trilled* again, this time with a higher pitch to signal this new data had a higher priority than Mason's. He keyed it to take the place of the previous intel. He read what appeared on his HUD, then refocused on the older man's face.

"Well now," he mumbled. "What have we here?"

The intel his system had dug up stated that the man had retired to regular branch service almost twenty years ago, so his branch identifier and official job title could be legit. But in their line of business, that didn't mean anything.

Things had just gotten exponentially more interesting and complicated.

His comm *chimed*, signaling that someone was trying to contact his TRM persona. His HUD identified the visual connection request as coming from Aksel Mitalius.

Juvak considered ignoring it, but if his guess about the

subject of the comm call was correct, Aksel wouldn't stop trying to reach him, and he would probably escalate his attempts to locate him.

Juvak exhaled slowly. He studied the scene in the plaza. All four casualties had been loaded into the shuttle, which was preparing to take off. There wasn't anything else he could do here. Richards had taken charge of Taylor and his teammates, so it shouldn't be that hard to track them down. Unless, of course, Richards wasn't here just as a liaison. But even then, there was nothing Juvak could do right now. Juvak took another slow breath. His comm was still chiming. He accepted the call, voice only.

"Yeah."

"Can you talk?" Aksel's voice was thick with concern.

"I wouldn't have answered if I couldn't."

"Good. I need you to come in."

"Why?" Juvak knew the answer, but Jupiter Vaktavian would not—should not.

The momentary silence as Aksel searched for the right words hung heavy between them.

"It's your son." Aksel finally breathed. "He's been injured."

to be continued...

DEAR READER

Thank you for coming along on this adventure and exploring the world Taylor, Tonee, Kaydeen, and Salayla live in. If you liked what you read please let others know. As a self-published author, I depend on my readers to help get the word out about my books.

Reviews also help in that endeavor. The number of reviews a book has impacts how many people see it, and therefore, how well it does, so I would appreciate it if you would leave a review. It does not have to be very long, just a few lines would be more than enough.

- Nic

About Nic Plume

Nic Plume is a Writer in Progress, Sufferer of Wanderlust, Human Sidekick, who learned English from Dragons and is always in search of the next "wheeee" moment.

Born and raised in Germany, Nic spent most of her adult life married into the US Army life. English is her second language, which she learned through school and refined through daily lessons with Dragons once she moved to the US (Ok, fine. She improved it through reading books, more specifically the Pern and Dragonlance series, but close enough!).

A question-asker and seeker of understanding, Nic explores the world and people around her. She currently lives full-time in an RV with her husband and German Shepherd and travels all across the US. Always looking for the next adventure, she prefers the roads less traveled - and loves to startle her copilot with a well-timed "wheee" right before the water hits the windshield.

Her stories tell the triumphs, tribulations, failures, and pains of the human experience through a lens formed by her association with the military.

If you would like to know more about her and her books, and keep up to date on when the next book comes out, you can sign up to her newsletter at https://sendfox.com/NicPlume, visit her website at www.nicplume.com, or find her on diverse social media.

Let's Stay Connected!

Loved this journey? There's more where that came from.

Be the first to hear about new releases, behind-the-scenes sneak peeks, and exclusive bonus content you won't find anywhere else.

Join the adventure online:

nicplume.com OR scan for Nic Plume's newsletter sign-up!

Your hub for news, events, freebies and all things **Nic Plume**.

Follow the story beyond the page:

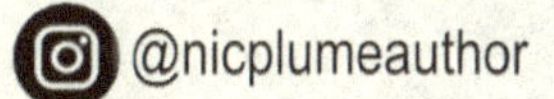

Subscribe to the newsletter

Get early access to cover reveals, giveaways and secret projects?

Sign up at nicplume.com/newsletter OR

scan for **Nic Plume** newsletter sign-up!

Let's talk!

Tag your favorite quotes, share your reviews, or send a DM—

I read every message.

#NicPlume | #TrialByInferno | #ShadowsOfPeaceSeries | #ReadersOfSci-Fi

Read on for a sneak peak at the next book in the *Shadows of Peace* Series...

EXCERPT

Tinaree - Forged by Crucible
Shadows of Peace, Book 2

Mason turned to join his team as a shot echoed through the tunnel. A slug impacted the wall next to him, passing through the space he had just vacated, followed by the sizzle of plasma boring vertical runnels.

He ducked and twisted to the side. The sole of his boot caught on the elevated walkway's grating, arresting his foot and transferring the turning motion from the ball of his foot to his knee. A sharp pain shot up his leg as his knee gave out, and he went down.

Ahead of him, the nearest crate began to smoke. Chat had taken cover between two of them when the shot rang out. Now he bolted against the opposite tunnel wall and opened fire past Mason. "Move, boss."

Ludo and Medici also started shooting.

Mason activated a painkiller injection from his armor's medical suite, gritted his teeth, and scrambled to his feet. Before he could take a full step, the smoking crate burst into flames. The container melted like an overheated piece of slag, turning the metal grating below it bright red.

A plasma round zinged past Mason's visor. He rolled to the side and brought his carbine to bear, but found nothing to target. He pulled the trigger anyway, laying down a steady stream of energy bolts in the general direction where his target should be.

"Boss," Chat called, "whatever's fueling this fire, it's playing havoc with our sensors. Can't even tell if the shots are penetrating the flames."

"Kind of busy." Mason rolled again, toward the burning wall of flame this time, and continued to fire. Sweat trickled down his face. While his armor and bioskins worked in tandem to regulate his body temperature, it could only do so much against the blistering inferno a few meters behind him.

Another slug went past above him. This time, he was facing where his sensors estimated the shot originated from and saw... nothing. *What the fuck?* That made absolutely no sense, but he didn't have time to puzzle through what his eyes were trying to tell him.

He aimed his carbine and pulled the trigger. Something crashed into the wall ahead of him. He continued to fire. It took five salvos before his target finally flickered into being. That was exactly what it looked like—as if he was watching through a camera that flashed in and out of connectivity or power. Electricity arced across the armor of a TST who appeared to only be in view every other instant.

Mason continued to shoot, sending one powerful bolt after another into the suit. At this close range, the kinetic punch of the carbine's energy bolts kept the TST effectively pinned, but the armor's energy shielding continued to absorb most of the damage. That was something else that shouldn't be happening. Not at this range, and not with his weapon set on full power.

The electricity arcing across the armor also didn't seem to affect the shielding negatively or the TST.

A warning flashed across Mason's HUD, informing him that his carbine's power was below 50 percent and rapidly declining. He'd have to change power packs soon, but that would allow the TST to get off the wall. At this proximity, that meant they'd be in a fistfight, with the fire still burning behind Mason. Not good odds when looking at the difference in size, power, and weight between them.

#####

Find out more at: https://www.nicplume.com

ALSO BY NIC PLUME

Shadows of Peace Universe

SoP Series Novels

Tinaree - Trial by Inferno

Tinaree - Forged by Crucible

Tinaree - Tempered by Blood

SoP Series Short Stories

CHiTs

Whatever it Takes

Prowler Series Novels

Prowler

Wilder

Last Brigade Universe

Rebels' Cause - A short story in the anthology 'Standing Fast on Foreign Shores'

Rebels' Choice - A short story in the anthology 'Standing Defiant on Foreign Shores'

www.ingramcontent.com/pod-product-compliance
Lightning Source LLC
LaVergne TN
LVHW050929080826
845145LV00001B/270

* 9 7 8 1 7 3 5 1 5 3 6 1 2 *